KINETIC STAR

JASON ANDREWS

For Lisa and Victoria, my superheroines.

And for Malenda, whose origin story ended too soon.

This is a work of fiction. Names, characters, businesses, places, events and incidents are either the products of the author's imagination or used in a fictitious manner. Any resemblance to actual persons, living or dead, or actual events is purely coincidental.

ISBN: 978-1-7321214-0-9

PART ONE

LIFE IS FOR LEARNING

SAMANTHA NEVER THOUGHT SHE WOULD DIE like this.

Sure, there was the time that Paul Harrowman had yanked her from the top of the jungle gym by her ponytail. It was an old playground, all hot blacktop and reinforced steel instead of padded rubber and beveled plastic. The crack of her skull on the asphalt was the sound of certain doom. She was done for, even though she could feel her eyes burning with tears. The school nurse sent Samantha home with an ice pack and a lollipop. It was lime flavored, but she survived anyway. Daddy named the knot on her head Natty Bumpo, and said that Mr. Bumpo would help her build character. Samantha had no idea what he meant by that. Natty Bumpo hurt like hell.

Her second date with Brannon Shultz had her gripping the armrest of his 1955 Ford T-Bird for dear life. It was a father-son project, a birthday present for Brannon's sweet sixteen as long as he handed his father the correct tools while pretending to show interest in the restorative process of decades-old automobiles. Classics, his father called them. Brannon never took care of it. The Colonial White spray job was more of an Ashy Soot, and he had dented the rear quarter panel within a week of his birthday. Samantha could smell the exhaust seeping into the cab even though the convertible top was down.

Brannon thought it would be hilarious to speed down State Route 40 with the headlights off. That was why they hadn't spotted the yearling until it became intimately familiar with the radiator grill. Natty Bumpo came back for a surprise visit that night and stayed for a week like the guest that never leaves. There was no third date with Brannon Shultz.

Then, of course, there was the accident—the *real* accident—that had happened years before Brannon Shultz and not long before Paul Harrowman. Samantha pushed that memory away. Shoved it back into the box where it belonged.

Time slows to a crawl when your capillaries are iced with adrenalin. It was taking forever to die. The starlight wasn't bright enough to see how far she was from the grassy field below, but it didn't matter. Samantha knew that black mass was rushing up to meet her, to smash her head into fragments and snap her spine like a pretzel stick.

Pretzel stick? Am I really hungry right now?

She wondered what it would feel like, if there would be any pain, and whether her end would come from an exploding brain or a severed spinal column. She recalled an episode of *Star Trek: The Next Generation* where these robot guys in black outfits had invaded the Enterprise. The robots went around the room, sharing with the crew the most efficient way to end their lives based on their species.

"Biological organism: Human. Sever spinal cord below third vertebrae. Death is immediate," said the robot. Samantha had never been into those shows, but Evan made her watch every single episode on DVD. The android was kind of cool.

The rushing wind coalesced into a chorus of taunts that pounded her ears. She was reminded of an 80's cassette tape commercial that Cole had shown her on YouTube.

"Maxell delivers...*higher* fidelity," says the narrator while Wagner's *Flight of the Valkyries* blasts from a stereo so loud that a man with blown-back hair has to catch his wine glass before it slides from an end table beside his chair. The music conjured the memory of another video that her brother had treated her to with great delight.

Kill the Wabbit, Kill the Wabbit—

"What were you thinking, Sammy?" the windy voices shouted, interrupting her manic train of thought. "Did you really think you could fly? Do you think you belong up here among us? Among the gods? What hubris!"

That pissed her off. Only her dad and her brother called her "Sammy". Only they were allowed. Now she would never see them again.

"Did you really think you could fly?" the roaring wind chided again.

Yes, actually I did.

Chapter One

THE ORANGE LINE WAS ALWAYS ON TIME, for the most part. The transit authority ran the trains closer together when the work day ended and the mass exodus from the bustling downtown into the quiet solace of the suburbs began. Samantha picked that time of the day to head in the opposite direction even though her shift didn't start until eight. She hated waiting for the train, and that was the time of day when more trains were available. The metro stations were hot this time of year, and the gargantuan fans did little to cool the throng of passengers standing shoulder to shoulder on the boarding platforms. The less time she spent on those platforms the better. A peppy, presentable bartender earned more tips than one with pit stains, frizzy hair and an attitude—depending on the type of bar one frequented, of course.

Sometimes she would stop off at a deli or food court to pick up a salad before heading uptown to start work. There was one place she preferred in particular when the thought of eating bar food again turned her stomach. Lettuce Dream had the best assortment of fresh greens, sprouts, olives, and dressings one was likely to find in a food court within a thirty-mile radius. Dinner in hand, she would make her way to the National Mall and visit one of the monuments while music blared through her earbuds.

Credence Clearwater Revival was great for the Vietnam War Memorial, Ella Fitzgerald for the World War II Memorial, and so on. Cole had made a playlist for her a couple of years ago for just that purpose. He knew music better than anyone, in her opinion, and had selected the appropriate soundtrack based on the era of each attraction. She particularly liked Nat King Cole while watching the ghostly soldiers march through the Korean War Memorial. The Lincoln Memorial was trickier, however. Songs such as *Dixie* or *Battle Hymn of the Republic* just didn't click with her. Samantha didn't visit Honest Abe very often. It wasn't about the music anyway. No, it was the voyeurism she enjoyed.

She'd watch tourists from all over the world wander around the National Mall, some chattering away in languages she couldn't understand as they took in one monument after another. She'd make up stories for them while picking at her bowl of romaine and vegetables (with just a splash of vinaigrette). The young British couple reading about Franklin Delano Roosevelt had grandparents that were children during the Blitz. The aging man bowing his head before the Martin Luther King, Jr. Memorial remembers being part of the march in Selma. Or maybe he stood by the Reflecting Pool during King's famous speech. Perhaps both. She loved being immersed in those crowds. Loved the cross looks when people would wander through a photo shoot. Loved the tiny American flags waving from ball caps and the cheesy "Capitol-ly Cute" or "Property of The White House" souvenir shirts purchased from street-corner kiosks.

The metro doors slid open and the boarding announcement rang out, reminding Samantha of the real reason she tried to catch the train from Clarendon to Federal Triangle every day at that specific time.

Samantha peered across the tracks at the train heading in the opposite direction. As usual, it was packed with people staring transfixed at their phones as boarders bumped and jostled them, trying to gain a handhold on a support bar before the doors closed and the metro car lurched forward. Then they, too, could pull out their phones and join the hive mind. Samantha's train car was less crowded so her favorite seat below the metro map was available. Samantha scanned the car from the corner of her eye, as she did every day. She was looking for that specific, particular shape.

There you are, Paperboy.

He was one of the few people left in the world that read the newspaper. Not the smaller, tabloid format full of snippets of local and world news (and maybe a sudoku or crossword puzzle) you'd find in dispensers near the entryways to the subway stations, but rather the full-sized newspaper that your father would skim through at the breakfast table then tuck under his arm as he left for work, always in a hurry. Paperboy was always in that train car when she stepped through the doors, and they always disembarked together at Federal Triangle where Samantha set off for the deli or food court and Paperboy to whatever mysterious and interesting job he had.

She had noticed him several months ago when she had come into the city early to run a few errands before work. He had looked up to see who was entering the car—as everyone does for the most part—and she remembered the way his gaze fell over the passengers entering ahead of her. He was sizing them up with a practiced eye. Measuring them in a sly, subtle manner that wouldn't draw attention to himself. Samantha didn't know why this was something she should take note of, but she had. When she boarded and saw him that first time, he had performed a flawless "double take" and his stoic countenance had softened.

Come on, Paperboy. You know I'm here.

His index finger curled down the corner of the newspaper, right on cue. Just enough to peek over the edge. The first three or four times that had happened, Samantha had used her peripheral vision to return his glance. Now it was common practice to look over at him and meet his eyes. He played his part as well, his eyes jerking up to the metro map above her as though wondering if his stop was coming up next. The same stop they used every day. There was no smile, no overt flirtation. Only that little lie they shared. Their little secret.

Samantha would stand at the doors when the recording announced their arrival at Federal Triangle and the train eased into the platform. That was her time to steal a glance back his way. It was part of the routine. By that time, he had the newspaper folded and tucked away in his messenger bag of distressed brown leather. There was nothing to hide behind. He would return the look by way of her reflection in the window glass. Samantha supposed she should be somewhat worried that he was a stalker, but that didn't seem to fit. Most stalkers don't wear nice suits, and she had counted at least seven, ranging from Armani to Prada. She looked down at her comfortable black slacks and the tight, white, button-down blouse that revealed just enough cleavage for a good tip but not enough for a catcall.

Oh. Maybe I'm the stalker.

The Bibbing Plot was deep into the dinner hour when Samantha tied the stark white waist apron around her slim hips and stepped behind the bar. "Bottomless Tankard" was scrawled in blue chalk across the Specials blackboard, which always meant a busy night. Throughout the month of May, you could pay the equivalent of two pitchers and drink to your heart's content as long as you had the stamp on the back of your hand. The tankards were almost as large as pitchers, not unlike those in Bavarian-themed brew houses where buxom servers in low-cut dirndls double-fisted thick mugs as big as their heads. The regulars loved the Bottomless Tankard.

June couldn't come soon enough.

The Plot offered the usual fare of Americana; burgers, ribs, wings, fried cheese, nachos, and pizza, as well as a smattering of authentic, original menu items such as Ben's Pickled Pickles or Scotch Cabbage salad—which was just a folksy name for kale. These were some of Benjamin Franklin's favorite foods according to the proprietor, although that assertion was suspect. The cleverness extended to the drink menu as well. Samantha had been trained in the creation of 18th-century mixological masterpieces such as the Printer's Punch (a rum and fruit concoction) and The Bite of a Mad Dog (made from garlic and rye). Both cocktails were quite popular with the tourists, for The Bibbing Plot was good, old-fashioned tourist bait. Samantha was asked to explain the name at least once a night.

"Benjamin Franklin wrote a book called 'The Drinker's Dictionary'," she would say. "In it, he created a list of phrases for being drunk. 'He has been in the Bibbing Plot' was one of them."

At that point she would wait for the inevitable follow up.

"What's a Bibbing Plot?"

"It's another name for being shit-faced. Ready for another round?"

Her toothy smile and ready-made reply would result in a refill more often than not. Only Evan had the useless knowledge—and bravado—to bring the historical inaccuracy to her attention. It was during her first week at the Plot.

"You're new here," he said, pushing his thin-rimmed glasses higher on his nose as he lowered the drink menu just enough to take her in. Samantha's back was to him as she fought with the register. Her training had only glossed over the bar service software, and she had been fighting with the program for three days straight.

"Yes, I am," she said over her shoulder, trying to cancel out an order she had placed incorrectly.

"Did you know that D.C. was just being developed around the time that Franklin died? This place should be in Boston or Philly."

She stopped hammering the touch screen and turned around. "Really?"

"Really." Evan's self-satisfied grin turned devious. "Tell you what, I'll give you the solution to your register problem if you give me your number. And a free Printer's Punch."

Samantha wiped her hands across her waist apron and pursed her lips. The orders were piling up, and so was her stress level. She didn't have time for nonsense. Still, she hadn't been in Washington D.C. for very long and it might be a good idea to know someone who could show her the ropes. It was a clumsy pickup line, and she wasn't even sure his "solution" would fix the problem. As it turned out, both of them had worked.

Her eyes were drawn to the stool at the end of the bar. Evan's favorite seat was now occupied by a stranger, as it had been every night since their romance had ended.

"Hey Sam! Did you get those beers for table fourteen? Buds, I think."

Claudio dodged past her and began thumping on the touch screen. "Sam" was okay. Especially for her boss.

"Just came on," she said, scanning the dining area for table fourteen. A couple sat across from one another. A flat-billed Nationals cap sat askew on the young man's head. He stared past the "Bibbing Plot" logo stenciled onto the large front window while his counterpart's attention was held captive by her smartphone.

"I'll get it," Samantha assured him, then turned to retrieve two large mugs from the freezer. Holding a mug at a practiced angle under the tap, she pulled the lever and let the lager flow. Her attention drifted to the bar-back mirror and caught the young man at table fourteen craning his neck to appraise petite, innocent Marcy as she passed. Blonde, shapely and sweet, Marcy was only a week into her server position and had been harassed twice in the past four days. The second time had involved actual physical contact. Marcy may be a little too cute for the Plot, but that was no excuse for grabby hands. Samantha had had a full mug cocked and ready to fire into the offender's head, but Claudio's quick intervention saved her from a lawsuit which she couldn't afford.

Samantha was leveling off the head of the second beer when Ball Cap's fingers snaked out to catch Marcy on her way to the bar. Marcy spun in surprise, upsetting the large tray of dirty dishes she carried. A napkin stained orange with wing sauce fluttered to the floor before she could regain control of the tray. She considered retrieving the fallen linen, but Ball Cap's suggestive leer made her think better of it. Phone Girl either didn't notice or didn't care. She was too interested in the device in her well-manicured fingertips to react. Marcy found her way back to the bar as fast as her legs would carry her. She plunked down the tray on the bar top instead of taking it to the kitchen where it belonged. Her glassy eyes were focused forward, seeing nothing. She chewed on her bottom lip.

Samantha looked past her to Ball Cap. "How many has he had?"

Marcy shot a glance at table fourteen then turned back to Samantha. Her face reddened not from anger, but from humiliation.

"Marcy? How many?" Samantha pressed, reaching out to squeeze Marcy's hand.

"Five."

"Five talls?"

Marcy nodded.

Samantha scooped up the fresh Buds and pushed past her friend. "I'll take these."

She circumnavigated the bar with mugs in hand. They were heavy. Thirty-ouncers. Ball Cap looked to be a large man, but even he had to be buzzed by now.

"I thought the other one was serving us." His lazy, Midwestern accent reminded Samantha of high school.

"Two Buds?"

She set them down before he could reply. Ball Cap peered around Samantha in search of his favorite server. Phone Girl tapped her phone screen. She was quite adept at it despite the overly-long fingernails. The way she had to twist her entire hand for skin to make contact with the screen could only have come from practice.

Samantha wasn't sure which of them annoyed her more.

Her gaze fell over the napkin on the floor, then switched to Ball Cap. This was the third time in less than a week. The customers of the Bibbing Plot needed to learn that this was not a brothel. She clasped her hands in front of her and addressed the couple. Her smile was painted on and her voice was filled with saccharin.

"Anything else I can get for you two this evening?"

She might as well have been talking to a wall. Ball Cap kept trying to find Marcy and Phone Girl continued tapping at her phone.

"Okay then. If you need something, you let *me* know."

She spun on her heel and bent at the waist. Her palm was clammy as she reached for the napkin.

Do it, asshole.

Her fingers closed on the stained cloth. She took her time in rising.

Come on, Ball Cap. I may not be Marcy, but—

The sharp slap on her left cheek startled her despite the fact that she had been expecting it, anticipating it. Samantha wheeled and extended a finger at his slightly-crooked nose.

"You're out of here! Get the fuck out! Now!"

Her voice seemed distant and detached even though she was screaming. She could lose her job for that, but wouldn't realize she had cursed until much later.

"What up, bitch? I didn't do nothing!" he said, arms wide and palms up. He kicked the chair away from the table and stood up. The man was easily six and a half feet tall.

Samantha was vaguely aware of Claudio bursting from the kitchen behind her. He would never get there in time. She felt the heat rising in her neck while the chill of fear coursed down her back. It was an odd sensation. She looked at Phone Girl, who acknowledged Samantha long enough to roll her eyes in disgust before returning to her entertainment. Ball Cap advanced. He was yelling something and flailing a meaty finger in her face. His other hand was clenched into a fist at his side. She was almost a foot shorter than him, and probably one third his weight. His fist reared back.

Samantha felt a pressure release in her brain, like someone opening the only valve to a massive dam. There was a rushing sound that grew louder and faster in the blink of an eye. A starburst formed in front of her, its brightness obscuring everything in her field of vision. It was a brilliant scarlet.

Time slowed.

Thinking back weeks later on the events that unfolded next, Samantha wondered why she had been so fixated on that smartphone. Phone Girl was either oblivious to or in denial of the fact that her boyfriend was a violent, lecherous prick. She was more interested in Snapchat or whatever app her umbilical cord was tied to that day than the guy she chose to spend time with. Why did this woman even leave the house? Was it to cart this drunken bully around from bar to bar to prey on women like Marcy who were too frightened to stand up for themselves? What could be so important?

Put the fucking phone down!

Samantha's face burned. Blood pounded through her ears in a deafening torrent. There was a flash of movement that she couldn't follow. Something hot and wet hit her in the face. It smelled like copper. Ball Cap stumbled away, tripping over a chair and landing hard on his rear end. He was holding his nose with both hands. Rivulets of blood ran between his fingers.

Samantha retreated a step as time resumed. There were gasps from the other patrons in the tavern. She looked down at her white shirt, now decorated with dozens of dark red dots and blotches. Something glinted up at her from the floor. Phone Girl's smartphone lay broken and dark on the rustic wooden planks, its glass touchscreen now shattered into thousands of tiny fragments. One corner was smudged with blood.

"Oh my god! Oh my god!"

It was Phone Girl. Her fingertips were bleeding as she desperately tried to pick up the remnants of designer fingernails that now decorated the tabletop instead of her fingers. Samantha felt a hand on her shoulder as Claudio stepped past her.

"You okay, man?" he asked with genuine concern.

"Bitch threw her phone at me!" cried Ball Cap as he let Claudio help him to his feet. "What's wrong with you, Tanya!"

Samantha felt the adrenalin drain away. Her legs grew weak but her mind searched for answers. Then Marcy was there.

"I saw it all. Thanks, Samantha."

Samantha nodded as Marcy took her arm and urged her away from the scene. Samantha turned back to Tanya, who stormed out of the Bibbing Plot clutching her ruined fingernails in one hand and her smashed phone in the other. An injured and irate Ball Cap followed close behind.

Claudio was shaking his head as he joined them at the bar. "Are you alright, Sam?"

"Yeah, yeah. I'm fine."

He handed her a bar towel and motioned toward the back room. "Go get cleaned up. We have a spare shirt for you. There'll be plenty of assholes here when you get back."

Samantha put the towel to her face, careful to hide her smile of satisfaction.

Chapter Two

THE PLOT'S LAST CALL was at two a.m. sharp, which put Samantha back in Clarendon around three to four a.m. after the registers were closed out and the tavern was cleaned and prepped for the next business day. The trains didn't run at that hour, so Claudio kept a wad of bills handy for cab fare. He didn't think Samantha knew he padded that fund from the tip jar, but she knew. The secretive pilfering was balanced out by his concern for the safety of his employees. They'd end up using their tips for cab fare anyway.

For Samantha, the pre-dawn hour was the ideal time to run off some steam. Tending bar was stressful, exhausting work—especially during drink specials—so she liked to put in several miles after her shift. The deserted streets provided a serene backdrop, and the gray, tonal light of the coming day was just bright enough to prevent a twisted ankle. She'd be back in her third-floor walkup and slipping between her bed sheets well before the morning commute began outside her window.

Running cleared her head. The constant beat of her pink and blue Asics thrumming on the pavement created a backing track for the film of the day that played out in her mind. Sometimes she'd run faster and stomp harder, speeding up the track as she expelled the stresses of the day, other times she'd slow her pace to savor the satisfying highlights. The latter involved Paperboy more often than not.

The Mystery of the iProjectile was the title of the film that morning. It had changed several times in the past week. *The Bibbing Plot Thickens* was another favorite. *The Bibbing Plot Thickens,* starring Samantha McAllister as The Heroic Barmaid. Samantha pored through the imaginary film reel frame by frame, as she had every morning since the incident. She studied the exact moment when Tanya's smartphone flew from those gaudy fingernails straight into Ball Cap's nose. Samantha rewound the frames and watched again and again, hoping, searching for something she may have missed. Something that would explain...*it.* But she always ended up with two undeniable conclusions.

Fact: I was hyper focused on the phone.

Fact: Tanya didn't throw it.

"Morning."

A fellow jogger passed Samantha with a nod. She realized that she hadn't been paying attention and could easily have smashed into him. She returned the acknowledgement with a friendly wave, but he was already past her. She pushed away the thought that he would consider her rude and returned to her examination of the film.

I was hyper focused on that phone. Tanya didn't throw it.

Samantha felt a blast of wind on her face. Her step faltered and she stumbled to one knee, smacking her hands on the street out of sheer reflex. She felt her face flush with embarrassment as she regained her balance and looked over her shoulder to see if the cordial jogger had heard her wipe out. He might enjoy that after her snub.

The man was four blocks away.

How...?

Confused, she looked up at the nearest street sign. North Edgewood Street.

But I passed him by the metro station.

She turned to search for the metro sign, and there it was four blocks away. Right where it shouldn't be. Spinning back around, she looked once more at the street sign. It still read North Edgewood Street.

Oh... Shit.

She spun in a circle, hoping to find someone that had seen something—anything, really—but the few people out at this hour had their noses in various handheld devices, overpriced espressos in hand.

It was a long walk back to her apartment.

The hot shower felt wonderful. Samantha stood beneath the steaming water for a long time before forcing herself to get out. She couldn't afford another outrageous water bill. The condensation disappeared from the medicine cabinet mirror with a wave of her hand. She leaned in, prying open her eyelids with two fingers. She opened her mouth and stuck out her tongue, angling her face toward the light to get a better look. She thumbed up her nose and peered into the darkness of her nostrils.

I don't even know what I'm looking for. This is stupid.

She toweled off and brushed her teeth before donning a pair of underwear and an old, threadbare T-shirt and slipping into bed. As expected, sleep would not come. Her thoughts projected a brand new feature film on the ceiling above her. *Four Block Boogie,* starring Samantha McAllister as Jill the Jogger. It played in an endless loop, interspersed with images of flying smartphones and blood-spattered work shirts, until sleep finally claimed her.

Cole was away at summer camp. Camp Hickory, to be precise. Not very original, but Cole loved it. He'd send them a letter every week, outlining with eager pride his adventures in wood carving and canoe paddling, and how tomorrow they were going to learn how to ride horses and fish. When his most recent letter arrived, Samantha tore it from the mailbox before hopping into the family's mid-sized sedan. Daddy was taking her to the library, then out to the dairy farm for milkshakes made with real ice cream. He told her they had special "ice cream cows," and that each udder produced a different flavor. Daddy's favorite was pistachio.

"Dear Daddy and Sammy," she began.

"Sammy, you know better," he scolded, going so far as to look down at her over the top of his horn-rimmed glasses. Grinning ear to ear, Samantha straightened the paper with her little hands and started again. Daddy always made her sing Cole's letters to the tune of Allan Sherman's *Hello Muddah, Hello Faddah*. They never rhymed, but neither of them cared.

"Hello Daddy,

Hello Sammy,"

Daddy's smile always faded just a bit after that first part. Samantha didn't figure out why until she was much older.

"Here I am at

Camp Hickory—"

The sound of steel twisting and ripping around Samantha was something she would never forget, nor the hush that fell over her world for scant milliseconds afterward, that span of time it takes for the human brain to register a negative perception.

Samantha's brain perceived she was falling.

She sat bolt upright. Her covers were gone and one of her pillows was smashed into the corner. Samantha blinked and took in the room, which had become a disaster area. Her dresser drawers hung open, her clothes strewn about as though caught in a windstorm. Most of her books were now on the floor instead of arranged alphabetically by author on the oak shelving. She leapt from her bed and heard a crunch under her foot.

Why is my lamp broken?

She ran to the door and yanked it open. Wide eyes squinted against the sunlight that streamed in from the windows as she scanned the living room and kitchen. Everything was in its place. Turning back to the bedroom, she brushed aside the room-darkening curtains and checked the window latches.

What am I doing? I'm three floors up.

Despite that fact, she checked rest of the windows in the small apartment. The front door was untouched and the bathroom was unoccupied. She found herself standing in her bedroom door looking at the mess, her mind jumping through endless hoops in search of an explanation. Her skin prickled and her hands grew hot. Samantha began to sway, then righted herself against the jamb. She shook her head to clear it. The dream came back to her.

Cole never went to Camp Hickory, whatever that is. He was born after the accident. Ice cream cows...what? None of this makes sense.

The opening notes from Scott McKenzie's *San Francisco* erupted from her phone as it charged on the nightstand. She barely heard it over her thundering heart. She forced herself to move, propelling herself across the bedroom on wobbly legs. The clock read 5:53 a.m. when she picked up the phone.

"Hey," she answered, bracing herself with one hand against the wall.

"*What's up? I didn't wake you, did I?*"

Cole's voice steadied her.

"No, no," she said, "I was up. Had a bad dream."

Samantha bent over to retrieve a fallen book. It was a self-help tutorial on money management. Useless when you're broke. She was tempted to let it lie. "Isn't it like three o'clock in the morning out there? What are you doing up, Cole?"

"*Big recital tomorrow night,*" said Cole, "*and there's only one way to get to Carnegie Hall.*"

"I hear you. I wish Dad and I could be there. I'm sure you'll do great."

"*Hope so. Anyway, thank you for the birthday stuff. How did you find gift cards to Bay Harbor?*"

"The internet is a wonderful thing, bro."

There was a brief pause from the other end of the phone. Samantha raked her hand through her hair then hooked a finger into the elastic of her underwear to remove it from her crack.

"*Sammy, you okay? You sound, I don't know, shaken.*"

"No, I'm fine. I think. Did we have an earthquake? Is there anything on the news?"

"*What? Not that I'm aware of,*" he replied. "*That stuff is supposed to happen out here, not on the east coast. Why?*"

"Nevermind. How's Jeremy?"

Cole chuckled at the clumsy subject change. "*Heh. Okay then. Jeremy's good. His parents are coming up from Arizona next week.*"

"Ooh...are you nervous?"

"*Nah. They're old hippies. It's Jeremy who should be nervous about meeting my goofball sister.*"

"Ouch. Now I can't wait to embarrass you."

"*They promised to give us a* real *tour of Haight-Ashbury. Which is funny, because they are too young to have been there during its heyday.*"

"Sounds like it's their Mecca," she said. "They want to show you the Hippie Holy Land. Hey listen, good luck on your recital."

Cole took the hint.

"*Alright, thanks. And thanks again for the gifts. Get some sleep. Talk to you soon.*"

Samantha held the phone in her hand long after their call had ended, deliberating on her next move, then finally dialed 9-1-1.

She had the presence of mind to put on a pair of sweatpants before opening the door. The police officers politely refused the tea or bottled water Samantha offered before sitting down on the couch across from her.

"Who else has a key?" said Officer Butler, a paunchy, older man with a dyed goatee of jet black and a face pock marked from some childhood ailment or bad adolescent acne.

"Only the landlord," Samantha said.

"And where does he live?"

"In Newport News."

"Then who do you call for emergencies?"

"You guys."

The officers exchanged expressions that were void of amusement. Samantha was pretty pleased with herself.

"He has a handyman for his properties here, but I have to be home to let him in," Samantha said. "Not the most efficient way to handle emergencies, but the rent is okay."

"And all of the doors and windows were locked?"

"Yes."

"Did you have any guests last night?"

"No."

Officer Butler wrote that down. His younger—and more fit—partner stood and walked into the kitchen area before returning to the living room and craning his neck to look into the bathroom. Samantha had already forgotten his name. Perhaps if he had a striking feature such as a beard that in no way matched his hair, she might have remembered.

"Ma'am, were you drinking last night? You sleep pretty late," said Butler's partner.

Samantha looked up at him. "I work nights."

"Where?"

"The Bibbing Plot. On E Street."

"Pickled Pickles," said Butler. He didn't write that down.

"Pickled Pickles," agreed Samantha.

Butler's partner walked to the front windows and parted the blinds. He took his time before continuing. "Are you on any medication?"

"No," Samantha said, "but after this I'm going to consider it."

They left shortly thereafter, promising to file a report and keep an eye on the building. Samantha felt better after their visit and considered going back to bed, but she doubted sleep would come. Instead, she returned to the bedroom to survey the wreckage. The room was small like the rest of her apartment, so it didn't take long to clean up. She noticed the broken bulb on the floor as she set the lamp back on her nightstand, and recalled the crunching sound while getting out of bed.

Damn. Must not have felt it through the adrenalin.

Hopping on one foot into the bathroom, she sat down on the edge of the tub and pulled her left ankle over her right knee. She leaned forward and twisted her foot around to get a good look at the cuts. The skin was untouched.

Wrong foot.

Reversing her ankle to knee position, she inspected the bottom of her right foot. Nothing.

Wait...

She brought the left foot back up and scrutinized it with narrowed eyes. Tiny bits of glass were stuck to her sole, reflecting like grains of sand in the bathroom lights. Samantha brushed them away and took another look.

Not even a scratch.

Samantha skipped her usual pre-shift salad and people watching the next day, and instead went straight from the metro station to the Staples on H Street. After nodding politely through the salesman's spiel about the pros and cons of every digital camcorder they sold, she picked a Canon HF model. Low end, but cheap—and good enough for her purposes. It wasn't as though she had much choice on a bartender's wage. She also purchased the largest memory card they carried. She'd need a lot of capacity for filming.

Wednesdays were usually slow at the Plot, and that particular Wednesday was no different. Claudio, Marcy and the others hadn't mentioned the phone-and-fingernail incident since the night it happened. Even their concerned, sidelong glances had disappeared after a few days. Everything was back to normal at the Bibbing Plot, just the way Samantha liked it.

Her attention never strayed far from the clock as her shift wore on. She had urgent business to take care of, and decided to skip her run when she finally got home early the next morning. Part of her chalked it up to the urgency of her agenda, but she had to admit to herself that she was afraid she might "jump" (she didn't know what else to call it) into a moving car or broadside some poor business owner's storefront if she kept to her usual post-work exercise routine.

The shrink-wrapped cellophane crinkled as she peeled it from the camera box and inspected the contents. It was apparent that the black cord with the square box was the power cord, so she attached it to the camera, flipped out the prongs, and plugged it into the wall outlet. Satisfied that the camera was charging—she wasn't sure, but hoped it was charging—she flung open her kitchen cupboards to forage for food. She found half a bag of semi-stale Chex mix. The contents of the refrigerator revealed her last bottle of unsweetened green tea, so she snatched it up with the Chex mix and plopped down on the couch.

Time to see what the world is up to.

Samantha folded over her tablet case and tapped it to life, throwing her head back to dump a handful of artificially-flavored wheat and rice snacks into her mouth while Facebook loaded.

Deidre Sullivan, a fellow Northwestern alum, had posted a video recipe for Buffalo Chicken Casserole.

Gross.

Cole's childhood friend Bob Anders wanted two thousand likes for a wounded warrior. He was up to four hundred seventy-three. Samantha hit the Like button. Holly Jaspers—the girl who had stolen Chad Haysbert away from her at the Homecoming dance their junior year—posted a video of cats peeking out from beneath a blanket. Their furry little paws rested on a laptop keyboard as though they were browsing the internet in bed together.

They keep looking at the camera. Kinda ruins it.

Evan Douglas shared an article about the dangers of climate change. The headline referred to weather patterns that had the potential to affect the D.C. area.

Why did I ever date that guy?

Further down the timeline page, Evan posted a meme about Game of Thrones. It was a photo of Ygritte the Wildling with the words:

6-8 inches of Snow tonight? Sounds good to me.

Oh. That's why.

Samantha hit the Like button.

She figured it was time to give her new camera a try when she had scrolled far enough down the page to recognize posts she'd seen before. Most of her fingertips were covered with snack dust (or were damp from licking away that delicious dust) so she closed out the app with her pinky knuckle before juggling the tablet on her forearms and dropping it to the sofa cushions.

The camera's power light was a solid amber. She wiped her fingers on her sweatpants before picking it up and opening the fly-out viewfinder. A small touch screen blinked to life. The display offered various cinematic recording modes and gave readouts of remaining battery life and recording time. The battery was nowhere near fully charged yet, so Samantha left it plugged in for now. A pleasant chime accompanied a notification message.

No external memory found

How polite.

She unwrapped the memory card and spent the next few minutes trying to figure out where to insert it into the camera. She refused to read the instruction booklet. Dad and Cole would be hurt if she had.

Ah, there it is.

The camera chirped as it recognized the card. The remaining recording time went from zero to six hours, 59 minutes. Satisfied, she slipped the camera over her hand and rotated it end over end and side to side until she found the Record button. It had been intuitively placed at the right thumb.

Duh.

She twisted the viewfinder upside-down and pointed the lens at herself. The LED display flipped to accommodate the new orientation and her face appeared on the screen. She hit record.

"This is Samantha McAllister and I'm going to take an overnight selfie," she said, giving the camera a snarling tongue poke before ending the recording.

It didn't take long to figure out how to watch a recorded video. Her voice replayed through the tiny speaker hidden somewhere on the device. Satisfied, she erased the test video and took the camera into her bedroom. She plugged the charger into the wall and placed the camera at eye level on the top book shelf, pushing it as far back as it would go. Double-checking the viewfinder to make sure the lens would capture as much of the room as possible, she quickly got ready for bed and pressed the record button.

She couldn't sleep at first. The knowledge that she was on camera made her self conscious. It didn't seem to matter that she was recording herself. She almost got up to turn the camera off several times, vowing to return it to Staples the following day, but laziness and fatigue kept her firmly in place. She decided to turn it off when she got up to pee.

Bubbles fell around Samantha.

She dipped the plastic stick back into the bright pink bottle and took her time withdrawing it, careful not to break the seal of soapy liquid in the O-shaped ring. She brought the stick to her mouth, ignoring the errant droplets that drummed against her best Sunday shoes. She pursed her lips and blew, knowing what was to come but nonetheless surprised when more bubbles exploded from the ring. She squealed in delight and danced through the cloud of glistening orbs. They popped and splashed onto the yellow floral dress that Aunt Lizzie had bought her for Easter, but she took no notice. Again the stick plunged into the bottle, and out came the bubbles. She was amazed at how many she could make, and couldn't wait until they popped so she could make more. In went the stick and out came the bubbles. Except this time, just as the first bubble touched the cracked concrete of the sidewalk, it stopped, frozen in time.

Samantha blinked. Her face dropped.

The bubbles reversed direction, flying upward past the stunned little girl with increasing speed. They multiplied in the blink of an eye and kept coming, growing into an armada of shiny, soapy pockets of air. She screamed spun around, looking for Daddy. He had just been on the porch with Aunt Lizzie, both of them grinning as Samantha danced across the sidewalk, but now he was gone. The sunlight faded, replaced by a murky, green darkness. She grew cold. More bubbles came. Beneath her, all around her, they were born and began their furious flight to whatever fate awaited them above.

"Da—!"

She tried to call out one last time, but her mouth filled with bitter, alkaline water. Darkness enveloped her like the wing of a giant, aquatic dragon, allowing just enough light for her to see that the bubbles were now getting smaller in size and number. She screamed again. The great water beast exhaled into her, filling her throat, her lungs, her stomach. Her diaphragm constricted. Her bowels let go. She lunged for the hole in the broken glass before her, but a wicked claw pinned her there, digging into her shoulder.

The plastic bubble stick floated past her with the last of the bubbles. They were nearly too small to see.

Samantha awoke drenched in perspiration. Several long seconds passed before she realized that she was safe in bed. She scrambled to the window and parted the curtains. The room was bathed in the warm sunlight of late spring.

Shit.

It was worse than before. The bookcase had toppled over this time, expelling her book collection all over the room. Two of them were in bed with her; Shel Silverstein's *Where the Sidewalk Ends* and *Modern Architecture: A Critical History*, a college textbook she'd never been able to part with. Her brand new camera lay in pieces, pinned to the carpet by the bookcase. Her dresser leaned to one side, its drawers once more spilling their contents. The clothes she had doffed early that morning hung from the ceiling fan. Everything that wasn't nailed down (and nothing was, of course) had been tossed, knocked, shifted, or overturned. It was as though a silent tornado had ripped through the room and disappeared without a trace.

Samantha rubbed her eyes against the sunlight. Only one item had been left unmolested. Although the alarm clock, lamp, and phone had been swept from the nightstand, the framed photo of her, Dad and Cole stood upright and defiant. It was her favorite picture. Their smiles were big and genuine. They had been so happy that day. Now that she thought about it, the frame hadn't moved the night before, either. She pushed that out of her mind as a chilling thought occurred to her.

What if whoever did this is still here?

Lurching from her bed, she rushed toward the door and reached for the knob. It swung inward before she could lay a hand on it.

Her sudden attempt to stop her forward motion failed miserably. She lost her balance and braced herself for the inevitable collision with the intruder. Instead, she tumbled through the door and sprawled into an empty living room.

Oh fuck. Oh my god.

Her knees were weak with terror as she scrambled to her feet. She tore open the front door and dashed into the hallway—or tried to. Both locks were still secured, the keyless deadbolt impossible to access from the outside.

That means...

She fought back panic and ran to the kitchen, seizing a skillet from the array of pans that hung on the wall. She also pulled a heavy chopping knife from the wooden block for good measure. She held her weapons high and listened. The only sound was the rush of blood pounding in her ears.

The rational part of her mind—currently crumpled into a tight ball in a corner of her brain in order to make room for the hysteria—whispered that she would have seen or heard someone by now. She didn't exactly live in a luxurious palace. There was nowhere to hide. But she wasn't convinced. Not yet. Shadows played just beyond her sofa, large enough to conceal a small person if he or she crouched tight enough. Samantha pounced onto the couch and raised the frying pan over her head. The clank as it hit the ceiling startled her. There was no one waiting in the shadows.

The bathroom wasn't hiding a bogeyman either. Samantha checked behind the shower curtain to be sure. By the time she had moved enough debris to investigate the bedroom closet, her terror had given way to giddiness. She felt drained but relieved. Her rationality resumed its natural proportions as she sheathed the knife and hung the pan in its proper place. Samantha paced around the kitchen trying to make sense of it all.

The phone in the Plot. The "jump" on the street. The bedroom last night. The bedroom tonight. The bedroom door just now.

And the dreams.

Explanations came and went, slipping through her fingers like water. She had to make sense of the strange events, to put them in a convenient box so she could pick them apart and analyze them. But each theory was shot down by logic and common sense.

The camera!

Pieces of it were strewn about in the aftermath of the fallen bookcase. The power cord had been torn from the outlet. She lifted the bookcase just enough to pry loose the ruined camera. She didn't need it anymore. She opened a small cover in the back of the device and pressed inward on the memory card. It clicked as the spring-loaded ejector popped the thin, square disk from the port. She held it between her fingers and managed a smile when she found it intact.

Gotcha.

She went to the closet and pulled her laptop from atop a plastic tub situated on the top shelf. She plopped it into her lap as she sat down on the couch, trying to remember where the power button was located. She spun the computer this way and that as it booted up, pressing the memory card into every port she could find. There was no opening to match it.

Dammit.

It was old. Evan had given it to her when he had upgraded to a newer version. He said he already had three towers, a server rack with four "bricks" (whatever that meant) and two laptops. He said he didn't need them both. She had made it up to him that night. It had seemed like a fair trade at the time, but not now.

Samantha tossed the useless device onto the cushion next to her and leaned back with her palms pressed to her eyes. She didn't dare take the memory card to a public store or to the library. She had no idea what was on it. What if it was a...

No. Don't be an idiot.

She could call Officer Butler and have him analyze it in the crime lab. Maybe they could get a facial match of her mysterious room wrecker.

No one was in here and you know it. Dammit.

She looked at the clock. 10:43 a.m. Marcy was most likely sleeping, and her other friends worked normal business hours.

All but one.

Dammit, again.

She glanced at the laptop on the couch next to her, then rose to get dressed.

Chapter Three

"TO GAIN INGRESS TO MY LAIR, you must first answer these riddles three."

Samantha turned away from the intercom and threw a smile to the passing couple, hoping they hadn't heard the obnoxious message that had crackled through. It was clear that they had, however, for her smile was returned by a pair of knowing smirks. She waited for them to pass before leaning in to press the talk button.

"Let me in," she said. Her voice was low and firm. She fingered the memory disk through the material of her blue jeans.

"Thirty white horses on a red hill, first they champ, then they—"

"Teeth," Samantha said softly, making sure that no more pedestrians were around to intercept the ridiculous exchange. "Evan, just open the door. This is embarrassing. For you, mostly."

A long silence followed.

"A box without hinges, key, or—"

"Egg." Samantha was growing impatient.

Another long silence.

"This thing all things devou—"

"Time, you prick. As in 'Time to stop this horseshit!'"

It was obvious that Evan had forgotten about her father reading The Hobbit to her as a kid. She was sure she had told him when he'd won the online auction for The Hobbit Adventure Play Set. Not a piece of merchandise from the recent movie trilogy, but a throwback to the Rankin-Bass cartoon. A rare item indeed.

"*Way to ruin it, Becks.*"

Dr. Samuel Beckett from the 80's sci-fi show *Quantum Leap*. The evolution of her nickname had gone like this: Samantha to Sam, Sam to Sam Beckett, and finally just Beckett. Becks was completely new, but she got the reference. It was a reach, but that was Evan. From there it would most likely morph into Becky, and Samantha wouldn't allow that. Becky Levy had ratted on her and Jane Stevenson for smoking weed behind the gymnasium back in high school. Marcus Schmidt had pulled out the joint unexpectedly, and Samantha had been the one to say "Fire it up!" She wanted to impress him, even though Jane said he was out of her league; honor student, varsity athlete, et cetera. But it was Becky who had made out with him under the bleachers the following week while Samantha and Jane served out their sentence in after-school detention. She'd refused Becky's Facebook friend request.

Bitch.

"Aren't you coming in?"

The door was buzzing away to the cadence of *Shave and a Haircut, Two Bits.* She timed her entry on the final note and mounted the steps leading up to Evan's "insidious lair," as he used to call it. His front door was covered in a large poster depicting a giant robot locked in mortal combat with monstrous reptile of some sort. The eye of the lizard had been cut out to reveal the peephole, which darkened as her hand reached for the doorknob.

Evan's muffled voice penetrated the door. "I ordered a brunette."

"Sorry to disappoint," Samantha said. Her arms crossed over her chest, a subconscious attempt to cover her breasts. She didn't like being ogled.

"Would you dye it and come back?"

"Would you stop being an asshole and let me in?"

The door swung open to reveal her ex-boyfriend. "Impossible!"

Evan's studio apartment was the lovechild of Chuck E. Cheese and Princess Leia if it had been conceived with Leia dressed in a Wonder Woman outfit while a bad fantasy movie from the 80's played in the background. The walls were exposed brick with wrought iron lighting fixtures that gave off a dungeon vibe. It was hot, mostly from the exhaust fans humming away behind a bank of computer stations that were connected to a wall of massive monitors. The dark, hardwood floors were stained in places from spilled energy drinks and caramel macchiatos, except where the Wookiee-skin rug lay in front of the fireplace. The mantel was decorated with plastic figurines and medieval weapons. Its centerpiece was a glass display case that housed replicas of superhero masks of varying shapes and sizes. His main piece of furniture was a futon with a pillow (complete with Voltron pillow case) and a Batman throw blanket balled into one corner. He never bothered to convert the futon into a bed. A pinball machine and two coin-operated arcade game cabinets were lined up near a corner. An overhead projector beamed *Carrie* onto a bare wall he had designated as his movie screen. The smell was a mixture of pepperoni, kitty litter, Drakkar Noir cologne, and unwashed socks.

Just like I remember it.

"You don't change much," Samantha said as she retrieved a Supergirl figurine from the floor.

Evan snatched it away from her as soon as he realized what she held. "Oh, that's um...dirty."

Samantha grimaced and tried to pretend she hadn't heard that. She wiped her fingers on his sleeve anyway.

"Where's Mal?"

"Around here somewhere. Come in."

Evan tossed Supergirl onto the kitchen bar and took two quick strides toward his gaming chair before jumping the last few feet. It was top of the line in gaming furniture. Speakers flanged out around the head and the armrests were dual control boards that collapsed over the lap in ergonomic harmony. The wheels skidded across the floor with his momentum, stopping with expert precision at a computer station where he swiveled around to face her. He performed a grand gesture toward the futon. A plump Siamese pounced into Samantha's lap as she accepted his invitation.

"There you are," Samantha cooed. "There's my good boy."

Mal liked scratches behind the ear. Satisfied purrs escaped with each breath.

"Has he been misbehavin'?" she asked. Mal always lifted her spirits. She looked at Evan with a crooked grin.

"Now, see..." Evan winked and pointed at her. "That's why we should be married."

"And Supergirl is why we shouldn't," she said without missing a beat.

"Aw c'mon. It wasn't all bad, was it? I mean, who else could make your toes curl while humming the theme from the original Battlestar Galactica? That's talent, Becks."

"No, that's just weird."

"You didn't seem to mind."

True.

She took advantage of the uncomfortable moment that followed to fish the memory card out of her pocket. "Can you play a video that's on this disk?"

Evan motioned toward his computer array with a cocked head.

"You're kidding, right?"

"I need to see what I recorded last night," she said, "but I need your word as a Jedi or a Vulcan, or whatever, that you won't tell anyone. Ever. Got it?"

Evan's expression brightened. "Sounds saucy."

"It's, well, I don't know what it is yet. But it's definitely not saucy. The camera I filmed it with is smashed all to hell, and this card won't fit in my laptop," Samantha explained.

"Why not take it to a camera shop? Hell, even Wal-mart or Giant could rip it for you."

She shook her head, her eyes flicking to the movie playing silently on the wall where Carrie's mother was forcing her into a closet replete with religious imagery. Samantha had never been able to make it past *Carrie's* opening scenes. Too disturbing.

Why is he playing this movie? He knew I was coming over. Is this a message? Passive-aggressive payback for breaking up with him?

He followed her gaze to the movie projection.

No. Evan wouldn't do that. He always says what's on his mind. Whether you want to hear it or not.

"Sorry. I can turn that off," he offered. He started to rise.

She waved a hand in the air. "No, it's cool."

He eased himself back into his chair and held out his hand. "So, are you going to give it to me or not?"

"I need your promise. On your honor, Evan Douglas. I'm serious." She knew she had him there.

His forehead wrinkled. "Well, I don't know what's on it. If it were a murder, let's say, I'd be obligated to—"

"It's a video of me in bed. I—"

Evan darted from his chair and snatched the memory card from her fingers. She'd never seen him move that fast.

"You have my word of honor," he mumbled, pressing the disk into a slot on one of his computer towers. He pulled it back out, realizing it was in backwards, then shoved it into the same slot with the correct orientation. Samantha rose and stood beside him.

"What's that?" She pointed to one of the monitors. A map of the world was displayed, the continents white outlines on a black background. Red dots flashed intermittently at various locations across the map. Several smaller windows were stacked along the left side of the screen. Lines of alphanumeric characters scrolled from top to bottom. The scrolling stopped from time to time with multiple lines highlighted in blue or red. She heard him tap a key. The monitor blinked and the map was replaced by a Halloween photo of Mal. He was not amused by his Yoda costume.

"It's nothing. Work," said Evan.

"Work," echoed Samantha. "You don't work, as far as I know."

"You rearranged your room," Evan noted as the video leapt onto his central monitor.

The onscreen Samantha was climbing into bed while the offscreen Samantha was wishing she'd put on pajama bottoms. The video showed her pulling the comforter up to her neck and looking at the camera one last time before rolling over and putting her back to it.

"What exactly are we looking at, Becks?" asked Evan. He sat back in his gaming chair and drummed out a broken staccato on the armrests.

Samantha leaned in and placed her hand over the mouse. She advanced the video at very short intervals, not wanting to miss anything. It was dim, but some of the morning sunlight bled through the darkening curtains. The display showed her tossing and turning when she couldn't get to sleep, once even rising to her elbows to look at the camera. She remembered doing that.

"Are we watching Paranormal Activity right now?" Evan whispered in mock suspense. Samantha shushed him, but had to admit that the lighting gave the video an eerie quality.

That's what I want you *to tell* me.

As she scrubbed through the video, the onscreen Samantha finally lay still on her back, breathing slowly. Samantha scanned further and faster this time. She knew what she was looking for, but was woefully unprepared when she found it.

"Oh my god!" she said.

Samantha's body rose from the bed, still prone like an assistant in a magician's trick. The comforter slipped from her to the floor, the magician revealing no wires. Her long hair tickled the pillow below.

She began to twitch as though she were entering the rapid eye movement phase of the sleep cycle. It was subtle at first, then grew more intense.

"Oh my god..." Samantha's whisper was tinged with dread.

Evan watched with a neutral expression.

The twitching stopped, but Samantha still hung suspended above her bed. Everything was eerily still for several long seconds. Then the camera began to shake.

"Da—!" Samantha's voice erupted from the computer speakers. She began to sputter and choke. Her body convulsed, arms and legs lashing out for purchase, for anything that would ground her. Books flew in and out of frame. The dresser shot into the air, slamming into the ceiling in a plume of drywall dust.

Samantha backed away from the monitor. Her hands tented over her mouth and her eyes welled up, clouding the visuals from which she could not look away. The camera shook with violent intensity. All objects in the room—save for a framed photo near the bed—levitated for the span of three seconds then slammed back down in perfect unison. Hard. Lighter objects tumbled into the air from the impact. The video went wild as the camera tumbled from the bookcase.

Evan's monitor darkened. Samantha's legs failed her. She stared at the blank screen from her knees, her mind reeling in horror and her mouth forming words that would not come.

"Good one, Sam!" Evan clapped. "That was pretty damn impressive. I didn't know you could conjure tears. Well done. Who put you up to this?"

Samantha forced herself to look at him, but she didn't comprehend.

"Was it Rory? He owes me one for hacking his Twitter account," Evan said. "No! No, it had to be James. Was it James? Oh man, I'm going to fuck him up. How did he get you to do this? I think you only met him like once. Was it that time we all went down to Virginia Beach? Sam?"

Samantha rose with supreme effort and gathered herself. She turned away from him, wiping an eye with the back of her hand.

Asshole. This was a mistake.

"Give me the memory card, Evan," she demanded with an outstretched hand.

Evan's jaw dropped. "You—you expect me to believe this?" He made no move to eject the disk.

"This was a mistake. Give it to me. I'm leaving," Samantha said. She wiped her other eye. Evan rummaged through the clutter on his desk and found a box of tissues. He held it out to her, but she ignored it.

"Samantha. Are you telling me this video is real?"

Her hand dropped to her side and she collapsed on the futon. Her head fell forward and she pulled at fistfuls of her hair.

Who else would believe you?

"It happened a few hours ago," she said. "It's real."

Evan stood up and stared at her hard. "If you're messing with me, Sam..."

She returned his gaze with matching severity. She watched him search her eyes, her mouth, her hands, scanning her for body language that would belie her assertion. They had been very close once and knew each other quite well. She had faith in his judgment.

Come on, Evan. You know I'm telling the truth.

"Holy shitballs!" Evan hopped up and down, then plunked himself into his chair and started the video again. Samantha waited in silence, listening but unable to watch it again. She pictured the events unfolding as the audio reverberated through the speakers once more.

"Da—!" came the cry, followed by the choking sounds, and finally the camera crashing to the floor. Then silence.

"Hm," Evan said. "Was it unnaturally cold in the room when you woke up?"

"What? No."

"Have you pissed off any creepy old gypsy women?"

Samantha cocked her head. Her face went glib.

"Kidding."

He got up and started pacing the room. "Is this the first time something strange like this has happened?"

Samantha suddenly found her fingernails very interesting. He stopped pacing.

"Becks, is it? Sam? Tell me, dammit."

What do I say? How much do I tell him?

He sat down beside her when it was clear she wouldn't answer.

"It's okay," he said. "You don't have to tell me anything you don't want to."

They sat in silence. His arm slipped around her shoulder and gave it a comforting squeeze. He leaned in close and put his lips to her ear. His voice was a whisper.

"As long as you tell me everything."

She couldn't suppress a laugh as she pushed him away.

"Jerk!"

They both sat forward and gazed at the floor for a long while.

Hell with it.

She told him everything. From the scuffle in the Plot to the video that morning, leaving out nothing in between. Evan was silent throughout the entire story. He had always been a good listener, even though an obnoxious joke usually followed. He didn't joke this time. He said nothing at all. Instead, he rose and walked into the kitchen, returning with a tall can of some sort of energy drink and a glass of water for Samantha. The can cracked open to emit a hiss of carbonation that broke the silence.

Evan was the first to speak. "What do you think it is?"

Samantha shook her head. "I don't know, Evan. I don't believe in ghosts."

He nodded in agreement "Me either. Besides, that wouldn't explain running four blocks in the blink of an eye. Or teleporting. Or...whatever you did. Do you believe in God?"

"We've talked about this. You know what I believe."

"Okay, then we can cross divine intervention off the list," he smirked. "But we'll use a pencil, just in case."

He began pacing again. Samantha curled up on the futon and folded an arm under her head for a pillow.

"Was your father a Dark Lord of the Sith?"

"No."

"Okay, we can cross that off the list too."

Evan returned to her line of sight and stood by the sprawling computer desk. He picked up a superhero figurine and twirled it through his fingers as he continued to ponder the situation. "Remember when you told me about the accident when you were a kid?"

He was moving the figurine's arm up and down. It was a red-haired woman wearing a green costume with a golden sash. An emblem of a stylized bird was emblazoned in gold across her chest.

"Mhmm," she said as a yawn overtook her.

"You said they declared you legally dead at the hospital. Then you came back."

"Mhmm."

Mal jumped onto her hip and began rubbing his neck against her jeans. She reached up to stroke his fur. Evan pressed on.

"Did they say how long you were dead?"

"I don't remember. Why?"

"Well, maybe you brought something back with you."

"Don't be ridiculous. This isn't a horror movie."

Yet.

"Okay. Let's approach this from another angle. Maybe we don't need to know the why just yet. Maybe we aren't supposed to. So let's consider the how. In the Plot, you were in a state of high emotion. You felt threatened."

Samantha sat up on one elbow and brushed a stray lock of hair from her face."The dude was six five."

"Right," Evan said. "And when you were running. What were you thinking about?"

"I suppose I was thinking about the incident at the Plot." She swung her legs from the futon and sat up. Mal wormed his way into the warm spot and curled into a ball.

"Okay, okay. And the dreams are a gimme. The impact of the crash, then the water. Damn! There's something we're missing here."

He tapped the figurine against his forehead, eyes closed in concentration.

"The common link is obviously stress, but I don't understand...how...how..."

Evan opened his eyes and held up the figurine.

"Evan?"

A tennis match ensued between Samantha and the figurine. His eyes flickered back and forth between them at least five times, growing larger with each volley. He moved to the computer desk and set the figurine down with a calm that unsettled her, then reached for the computer and ejected the memory card. Evan took a deep breath before facing Samantha.

"I'm keeping this. You need to leave now." He held the disk between thumb and forefinger and waved it before her eyes.

Samantha chuckled and reached for it. Evan pulled it away.

"No, I'm serious," he said. "Get out."

What the fuck? I don't think he's kidding.

"Evan, don't fuck with me. Really. Not right now."

She stood up. He backed away.

"You and Rory, or James—or whoever—tried to get one over on me, and now I'm going to send this video to every conspiracy website on the net. You'll be on those clickbait websites. 'You won't believe what this girl caught on video!' You'll become a joke. But this time I'll be the one laughing. Get. Out. *Now*."

His stern expression faltered. Samantha could sense his deceit, but couldn't figure out what he was up to.

He'd never do this. Not the Evan I know...or knew. Would he?

She took a step towards him and extended her hand. "Give it to me, Evan, then I'll leave and you'll never see me again. That I promise."

Evan swallowed hard. "You never really loved me, Samantha. I was just a boy toy for you. A distraction from your sad, lonely life."

Okay, that hurt.

"Why are you doing this, Evan?" she said. "Just give me the disk and I'll leave!"

Evan backed away as she advanced. They moved into the projection, casting large shadows across the brick wall. A violent scene from the film played out on Evan's face.

"You can't have it! Get the hell out of here!"

It occurred to Samantha that she had never heard him scream before. He had never even raised his voice to her. It startled her, wounded her.

"If you don't hand it over right now, I swear to—"

The disk was in her outstretched hand. Just like that, the tiny piece of plastic and silicon shot from Evan's fingers into her palm. Samantha stumbled back a step. Her mouth moved, but she wasn't saying anything. She was transfixed on the memory card now nestled in her open hand. She was afraid to close her fingers over it.

Evan stepped towards her, hands held high in a gesture of peace. When she finally looked up at him, she saw an eager grin spreading ear to ear.

"Samantha," he said. "You have telekinesis."

Chapter Four

"TELE-WHAT?"

"Telekinesis," Evan said. "The ability to move things with your mind. Oh man, this is so freaking awesome!"

The memory card still lay in the palm of Samantha's outstretched hand. She hadn't dared to move it. It doubled and tripled in her vision, moving within itself with translucent afterimages.

This is too much. I can't...can't...

Someone was shouting her name from far away. It was very faint. She decided to ignore it. She was too comfortable.

Then that someone slapped her in the face.

"Mother fucker!" Samantha jolted awake to find herself laying on Evan's futon.

"Sorry...sorry," Evan patted the air with his hands. "Don't put me through a wall, please. You passed out and, well, I didn't want you to have a bad dream and wreck my villainous lair."

She sat up and rubbed her forehead, then took a sip from the glass of lukewarm water that Evan had offered earlier. "I can't believe I fainted. Who faints?"

"Someone who just realized she has telekinetic powers, apparently."

"How long was I out?"

"Just a minute or two," Evan said. "Again, sorry for slapping you. I was calling your name but you were out of it. You feel okay?"

Samantha set the glass down and looked around to get her bearings, then smoothed back her hair and hung her hands on the back of her neck. "I'm fine. Aside from the anxiety, fear, and confusion, I'm fine. That was really messed up, Evan."

"Yes, it was a mean trick, but I had to know for sure. Had to see it with my own eyes."

Evan gave her some breathing room and opened his mouth to apologize further, but she stopped him with an upraised hand.

"Evan, I'm not sure telekinesis is the answer. It's...it's like something out of a comic book. It's not real."

Evan leaned against the edge of his computer desk and clapped his hands together in prayer formation. "Oh, but I beg to differ, ma'am."

He pointed at her with his fingertips and continued. "Research shows that humans use less than ten percent of the brain's potential. Some say the rest is filled with thousands of years of hard-wired instinct. Cro-magnon man's inherent fear of predators and all that. But others say that if we managed to unlock one hundred percent brain capacity we'd almost be superhuman."

Samantha waved it off. "'Research shows'? I'd like to see that research. Whenever someone wants to sound authoritative they always quote statistics or say 'research shows'."

"I'm sure I can find the research I'm talking about if you want to read it. Seriously though, maybe you can access parts of the brain that the rest of us can't."

"Like Bradley Cooper."

"Bradley Cooper?"

"That movie where he took those pills."

"Oh, right. But not exactly," Evan said. "That's more like the ability to instantly process every outcome of every decision. A form of precognition. The dude couldn't move stuff with his mind."

"It's all crap anyway. I read an article that said the unused part of the brain is just a myth. They've pretty much mapped out every part of it. Modern medical technology, you know."

"Where did you read that?"

"The internet."

"Oh, the internet," he said. "Well there you go. I once read on the internet that you can lose thirty pounds in three days by eating more ice cream."

Samantha dipped her fingers into the water glass at her feet and flicked droplets at him.

"If I'm using more of my brain, then why is this happening now? Why not when I was a child? Or, better yet, during puberty? That would make more sense, wouldn't it?"

"I don't know. There's a lot we don't know. Maybe it unlocked when you felt threatened by a giant douchebag," Evan said. "But let's say that the unused portion of the brain isn't the origin of your power. It could be anything. Maybe something happened when they shocked you back to life when you were a little girl. Maybe it's extradimensional or alien in nature. I'll do some digging so that I can properly use the phrase 'research shows'. In the meantime, you need to take a vacation from work and stay here with me and Mal."

"What?"

Like hell.

"For a couple of days at the very least. Maybe longer. Listen, Sam, you don't know what you're capable of. I need to monitor you. You might have other powers that—"

There was that word again. "Don't. Just...don't."

He's trying to crowbar me into one of his fantasies. This is insanity.

"Okay, you might have more *abilities,*" he said. "And the fact is, we don't know how strong they are. Someone could get hurt."

Samantha had heard enough. She rose from the futon.

"Don't leave, Sam." Evan followed her to the door. He reached for her arm but thought better of it. "Samantha!"

"I have to get ready for work. Thanks for letting me use your computer."

Where is my disk?

She patted the outside of her pockets and felt the outline of the memory card against her left thigh. Evan must have placed it there while she was out.

"Really, Becks? Just listen to me."

She threw him a warning look and closed the door behind her.

Evan paused for several seconds before pressing his ear against the door. He heard her Chuck Taylors on the steps, but waited until the building's entry door opened and closed before rushing to his computer desk. A few mouse clicks later he was watching the copy of her video he had made while she was unconscious. He put it on a loop and watched it over and over and over....

There was a chance that Evan was right, and it terrified her.

Just a chance.

The phantom film projector spun up during the train ride home. The feature was titled *The Adventures of Super-Becks,* starring Samantha McAllister as Herself. The frames of the reel flickered and slowed, showing the memory card inching through the air into her hand. She revisited that moment until she reached her stop at Clarendon station. When she disembarked and made her way to street level, she still didn't believe it was real. She turned her head and peered into the distance. There was North Edgewood Street four blocks away. Right where it should be.

I didn't "jump" either. People can't do that.

One thing was for certain, however; she didn't feel like going to work. She pulled out her phone as she started home.

"Hey Samantha."

"Hey Marce, listen. Could you do me a huge favor and pick up my shift tonight?"

Thursdays were usually Marcy's night off.

"*Of course,*" Marcy said, "*I'm glad you asked. I could use the extra cash for Vegas. There's still room for one more if you're interested. Jim and I and the rest of us would love to have you. He has cute friends...*"

Marcy sang that last part.

"You know I'd love to go, Marce, but like I said before I just can't swing it this month. Another time," Samantha said. "Plus, Claudio would be spinning in circles without one of us there to keep his head on straight."

Marcy laughed. "*I think he'd be okay. Let me know if anything changes.*"

"Will do, and thanks for tonight."

Samantha closed the door to her apartment and leaned heavily against it, taking a deep breath and closing her eyes. Going to Evan's had been a mistake. Now he knew about *it* and would never stop bothering her.

You're wrong, Evan. I don't have telekinesis.

She found the lighter in her junk drawer, buried beneath a potato peeler and an old box of plastic forks. She also pulled out a pair of salad tongs she had picked up on a whim at Crate & Barrel. She'd never had a use for them until now. She removed the memory card from her pocket and clamped the tongs over it. Up came the lighter, which snapped to life with a flick of her thumb. The hard plastic didn't burn very well at first, but she kept at it until she smelled an acrid odor. The disk began to bubble and smoke, the corners curling in upon themselves.

Beep! Beep! Beep!

"Shit!"

A few wild flaps of a dish towel quieted the smoke alarm. She looked at the ruined memory card on the counter. It was warped and misshapen. A last wisp of smoke drifted into the air and dissipated.

Good enough.

She ran it under cold water for good measure before tossing it into the garbage can and entering the ruins of her bedroom. The mess would have to wait. She stepped over her scattered array of belongings and climbed onto the bed, throwing an arm over her eyes.

You're wrong, Evan.

She listened to her breathing for a long time, warding away the thoughts that tried to flank their way back into her mind. She thought of her father instead. He was no doubt in a tense meeting or attending some sort of state function.

I wonder what he would have to say about all of this. Would I really even tell him?

She imagined that conversation with a smile.

"Hey Sammy, what's up?"

"Oh, not much. Work is good."

"Good, glad to hear it."

"Daddy, I found out I can move things with my mind."

"That's nice, Sammy."

"Daddy, do you think I'm a freak?"

"Go to sleep, Sammy."

She must have done exactly that, because she found herself lying on her side with a line of drool connecting her mouth to the pillowcase. Samantha lay still with her eyes at half mast, trying to decide whether to look at the clock or to doze off again.

I need to clean up this room.

She didn't move, however. The mess of her bedroom stared back at her, the toppled bookcase taunting her with its bulky girth.

Yeah, that's going to be heavy.

Closing her eyes, she pictured the bookcase lifting, righting itself. She opened her eyes. It still lay face down. She rolled to her back and looked up at the black underwear and cardigan sweater hanging from the ceiling fan.

Get in the basket.

They didn't move. Samantha drew her knees to her chest and wrapped an arm over them. She closed her eyes for a few minutes, thinking about how useful it might be if this nonsense was real.

She opened her eyes.

Underwear, get off the fan.

The underwear decided to stay where it was.

See, Evan? You're wrong.

Samantha stretched and yawned, then doubled up the pillow beneath her head. She should start with the bookcase and books, then refold her clothes, putting them in the drawers before replacing the drawers in the dresser. She wasn't sure what do about the broken dresser. Maybe putting matchbooks under the broken legs would level it out.

Yes, I'll start with the heavy, awkward bookcase. As soon as I get up.

Her attention returned to the dangling clothes like a scab she just had to pick. Her arm extended toward the ceiling. One eye squinted for better focus as she aimed her thumb and forefinger at the flimsy, cotton garment hanging a couple of yards away.

Underwear, get in the basket.

She flicked her wrist as though tossing the underwear into the basket. The underwear left the fan blade in a whirl of dust and dropped into the laundry basket which lay on its side halfway across the room.

"Fuck me!"

She didn't remember getting out of bed, but was now standing wide eyed and alert. Her stomach tightened into a knot and her heart pounded in her chest. She felt her face grow hot and her palms slicken. Her vision tunneled, blind to everything but the pair of underwear.

The underwear that lay unmoving in the laundry basket.

She tore her eyes away from the basket and fled the room, turned on a heel to re-enter, then retreated once again. She walked in tight circles in the middle of the living room. Her hands were shaking. A cold drop of perspiration slid down the back of her neck. She inched closer to her bedroom door and peered around the door frame. The black panties rested comfortably at the bottom of the basket.

Her eyes drifted up to the sweater. It was moving in a lazy circle on the fan blade, the motion of the underwear leaving the blades having nudged the fan on its axis. Her hand was still shaking as she brought it to chest level. She closed her fingers into a loose fist, her eyes never leaving the cardigan. Samantha swallowed hard. She raised her arm.

The sweater lifted from the fan blade.

"Okay...okay...."

She extended her arm toward the laundry basket. The sweater followed the motion, now suspended in midair an arm's length from the fan blade. Samantha jerked her hand toward the basket and relaxed her grip. The sweater missed the basket by a mile. Her breathing quickened as she walked through the door like an automaton. She wasn't in control anymore. Things were happening, and Samantha didn't fight them.

Don't think about it. Just do it.

Samantha faced the fallen bookcase. She bent at the knees and straightened her arms. She cupped her hands, palms up, and concentrated on the fallen piece of furniture.

I'm going to make you my bitch.

She pictured the bookcase tilting upwards and gradually extended her legs, letting them take the weight. But as it began to rise, she felt no weight whatsoever.

Oh man. Oh...oh shit...

She continued with the motion, curling her arms upward and flipping her hands around to push outward. The bookcase followed her commands, righting itself against the wall.

"Yes!" She pumped her fists in the air and let out a whooping yell.

The bookcase smashed into the ceiling. Drywall crumbled around it, sending a could of white dust billowing from the hole. It came to rest on the floor at an odd angle, then teetered for a split second before tipping over again.

She rubbed her hands together and prepared to lift it again, but something stopped her. It was a nagging in the back of her mind. A truth that she had denied since storming from Evan's apartment. Now it came upon her full bore, exploding like a racehorse from the gate. It was the crystallization of this madness summed up in one word.

Telekinesis.

Samantha sprinted to the bathroom and vomited. When she was finished, she sat with her back against the hard porcelain bathtub. The tips of her hair were wet with toilet water. The floor shifted beneath her. Her stomach was in knots and every muscle in her body was putty.

I have telekinesis.

She lunged for the toilet again, but there was nothing left to expel. Her stomach disagreed, and clenched like a vice until she could no longer draw breath. The bathroom went sideways. The tile was cool against her cheek.

It was pitch black when she awoke.

She didn't know where she was at first, but the memories flooded back to her when she smelled the vomit. She picked herself up and ambled into the kitchen, flipping on lights as she went. She wasn't nauseous anymore. As a matter of fact, she felt strangely calm.

She forced herself to eat a couple of fried eggs, and felt her strength returning with each swallow. She was out of tea, so washed them down with water. Her gaze was far away as she ate, and afterwards she stumbled to the couch and challenged a blank wall to a staring contest. Minutes ticked by. Distant car horns blared outside her window. Muffled music bled through her floors from somewhere below. The minutes turned into an hour, and Samantha remained in that deep, meditative state.

"Hey kids! It's the Pappy and Hoppy Happy Hour!"

She jumped out of her skin when the ring tone erupted. It was coming from inside her hand bag, which rested on the end table beside the front door. Evan had picked the theme song from a 50's-era children's television show as his ring tone. She kept forgetting to change the horrible jingle to something less obnoxious.

"Wellll Pappy jumped up on a hick'ry stump,"

She hesitated as she reached for the bag.

No, not that way.

"Ole Hoppy jumped up from his lily pad,"

She raised her arm and extended her hand toward the leather satchel. It was a Christmas gift from Cole, a purple-and-gold Marc Jacobs with a chain strap. Her brother knew how to shop. The gold clasp separated and the lid folded back.

"Pappy played his fiddle and Hoppy danced a little,"

She flexed her wrist with a come hither motion and coaxed forth the singing phone. It rose from the Marc Jacobs and floated toward her hand. When it was a few inches away, she pointed her fingers to the ceiling and thrust her palm out to face the phone. It obeyed, pausing in midair.

"Hey ho! What a time they—"

She let it go to voice mail.

As with the bookcase, concentrating on levitating the phone didn't take as much effort as she thought it would. She even twirled her index finger and the phone performed a 360 on its center mass. Samantha smiled. She brought up her other hand and slid her pinky left to right in the air. The phone screen unlocked.

Evan

Missed Call & Voice Mail

7 New Text Messages

She tapped the recent calls button with a phantom finger and found 16 missed calls from Evan and five voicemails. She willed the phone to the accent table on the other side of the living room. It took its position above the polished surface, then dropped to the table. Her palms rubbed across her denim-covered knees. She squared her shoulders and narrowed her eyes at the phone.

Come to me.

She didn't move her hand this time, but pictured herself with an impossibly long arm lifting the phone from where she sat on the couch. As before, it obeyed her command. Samantha retracted her "arm" and the phone drifted towards her. She felt the cold sweat returning. The fried eggs in her stomach began to shift. Bile rose in the back of her throat. Her mouth tasted metallic.

No. Not this time. This is really happening. Let it happen.

A long, slow breath placated the nausea. She endured the anxiety and let the phone come to her. She twirled it around, this time allowing an imaginary finger to do the work. The phone dropped into her hand.

This is getting easier.

She decided she needed to try something more challenging. The opportunity presented itself when she caught a whiff of her puke breath.

Samantha soon stood in front of the bathroom mirror. Invisible fingers opened the medicine cabinet door and the tube of Crest Complete jumped from the shelf. Holding it aloft mentally, she invited her orange toothbrush to leave its chrome holder and join the tube. It accepted her kind offer, and now Samantha had two objects suspended in front of her. She didn't have a third hand, but pictured one anyway and used it to open the hot water tap. The stream splashed into the basin.

Aw yeah. Now the hard part.

She lowered the brush into the hot water and held it tight, lest the water pressure knock it from her phantom grip. The toothbrush snapped in half. Both pieces fell into the sink.

Well that's not good.

Samantha steadied the toothpaste while using her hand—the one made of flesh and bone—to scoop up the ruined toothbrush and toss it into the wastebasket. She had her spare levitating under the running water in no time at all. The trick turned out to be canceling out the water pressure with an equal amount of force on the brush. It was guesswork, but her spare toothbrush would live to see another day. Leaving it there for the moment, she concentrated on the toothpaste. After a few tries, she was able to simulate the manual dexterity required to unscrew a plastic cap from a malleable tube—not as easy as one might think. Now she had the brush under the water, the toothpaste tube and the toothpaste cap all levitating separately. Samantha was very proud of herself.

She pictured the next maneuver in detail before executing it. In a single action, she closed the water tap, maneuvered the toothbrush to the tube, and set the cap on the edge of the sink.

Okay, that was pretty sweet. Multitasking.

Samantha was giddy now. It was probably a latent reaction from the recent stress but she didn't care. She had a task to complete. Her imaginary hand closed over the tube. The toothbrush wasn't as still as she would have liked, and fluttered in time with her heartbeat.

Interesting.

She squeezed the tube with careful tenderness. Toothpaste erupted in a rope of cavity-fighting, tartar-reducing goop, splattering onto the mirror and the adjacent linen cabinet.

"Damn it!" Her reflection was smiling despite her outburst.

She wasn't giving up just yet. She took her time in lifting the cap and replacing it on the tube before moving it back onto the cabinet shelf and closing the door. The toothbrush, meanwhile, floated to the mirror and scooped a minty-green glob from the glass. Peeling back her lips, she brought the toothbrush to her teeth and began an up and down motion.

I got this.

Her eyes flitted to the shower curtain behind her and she pictured the hot and cold dials just beyond it. She was careful to keep the toothbrush steady in her mouth as invisible hands snaked out behind her to activate the shower knobs. Water hissed from the showerhead into the bathtub. Not satisfied with a telekinetic teeth cleaning, she finished the job with her hand, making sure to scrub the tongue—she had just vomited, after all.

She reached for the top button of her blouse as she returned to the bedroom, but let her hands fall to her side. Samantha unbuttoned her blouse and shucked the piece of clothing into the laundry basket without touching it. The button on her jeans was much easier to manipulate. She kicked them off and into the air. They made a circuit around the room before descending into the laundry basket. The clasp on her bra was trickier, but she got it after a few tries.

So that's why men have such trouble...

She was experienced with underwear already. The bathroom was already filling with steam when she entered. She made a grand gesture of opening the shower curtain before she even reached it, and stepped under the shower head. Scalding water slammed into her.

"Fuckity fuckballs!"

Samantha's skin was bright pink by the time she finally got the water temperature under control. She relaxed and let the stress of the past few weeks spiral into the drain.

Let's see. I have a crazy ability that I need to learn to control. Probably shouldn't go out in public.

She massaged her scalp with lilac-scented shampoo.

On the other hand, I took the night off work and I'm young and single.

Shaving her legs was a job meant for real hands, not magic ones. She didn't want to bleed out because she got overconfident.

But Evan has a point. I almost put that bookcase into Mr. and Mrs. Vanderhoot's bedroom upstairs.

She shut off the water, opened the curtain and willed the plush, oversized towel into her grasp.

But it's been one hell of day.

She wrapped the towel around her wet hair and stepped in front of the mirror. She studied her refection for a long time as her id and superego fought a caged match in her psyche.

Sorry, Evan. Momma's going dancing.

Chapter Five

THE ADAMS MORGAN DISTRICT CAME INTO VIEW as the cab turned onto 18th Street. Samantha offered a folded bill to the cab driver and told him to keep the change as she stepped over the curb and into the myriad of restaurants, shops, clubs, and bars from which live music pealed into the street. The cool May breeze tousled her loose, off-the-shoulder tee and gauzy black skirt. She raised her face into the wind, letting the scents and sounds of the strip wash over her.

"Whoop! Whoop!"

"Strut 'dem boots, girl!"

A trio of young men passed her, craning their necks as they paid their playful compliments. Samantha smiled back and clicked her toes together. She much preferred leather, buckled boots to strappy heels, especially when dancing was on the agenda.

A pitchy rendition of Lorde's *Royals* reached her ears as she strolled past a basement karaoke bar on her way to The Lizard Queen. She considered stopping in for a shot and a song, but decided to wait until next time when she'd bring a group of friends to point and laugh at her from the audience. She was well aware of the fact that she wasn't much of a singer, and her song choices were sometimes questionable. No one wanted to hear the folksy stylings of Joni Mitchell. They wanted duets like *You're the One That I Want* from Grease or *Paradise by the Dashboard Light* by Meatloaf. Samantha had once been called an "old soul" as she left the stage after an off-key attempt at *Big Yellow Taxi*. She hadn't appreciated being labeled as such, especially since she had been the first one to have the guts to get onstage. No, no karaoke tonight. She had other diversions planned.

Samantha heard the thumping bass well before the neon sculpture of a crowned chameleon came into view. People lingered outside the club in small groups waiting for the doorman to beckon them forward. It was very crowded for a Thursday night, but this was the unofficial start to the weekend for most post-college, pre-responsibility-aged people like herself. A hulking bouncer noticed her and waved her in. She ignored the expected complaints from those waiting and pushed past them into the club. She flashed her I.D. to bouncer, who pressed a greasy stamp to the back of her hand before nodding to her.

"Have fun," he said. His eyes smiled but his mouth did not. Bouncers had reputations to uphold, after all.

I intend to.

A wall of humidity slammed into her as she entered, as if the doorway had been a magical portal to the equatorial tropics. The throbbing pulse of electronic dance music reverberated through her chunky boot soles straight up to her skull. The interior lighting was a laser show that weaved a multi-colored tapestry overhead and the rainbow of glow sticks, necklaces and bracelets that adorned the throng of people on the dance floor. High above, the DJ's body moved to the beat as her fingers danced over a tablet to prepare the next song. Two bars flanked the dance floor, both outlined in icy blue LED lighting that added to the surreal atmosphere of The Lizard Queen. The bars were packed with twenty-somethings draped in glowing plastic standing elbow to elbow. A claustrophobe would have been appalled at the scene, no doubt turning tail to flee to the safety of open air.

Samantha was energized.

She pushed her way to the closest bar and waited for an opening at the walk-up rails. Her head bobbed in time with the rhythm as she looked around for someone she knew. She thought she saw a familiar face, but it turned out to be someone who resembled a regular at the Plot. It wasn't. She turned back to the bar when she caught movement from the corner of her eye. The bartender was a heavily-tattooed young man not much older than she was. He looked at her expectantly while wiping his hands with a rag that was tucked into his waistband. This was his way of saying "What'll you have?" in an environment where thundering music won out over verbal communication.

"Whiskey sour. Double," she shouted over the din. She made sure to over-annunciate, and held up two fingers to accentuate the last part of her order. He nodded and went to work. She ended up with two whiskey sours, but shrugged it off and squeezed her way onto the dance floor.

Samantha blended into the mass of sweaty bodies, each interpreting the music in their own way. One song bled into another, never really beginning or ending and, if they happened to complement each other, even played at the same time to create a melodic fusion for the crowd. This DJ knew her craft. Samantha slid her full drink into the flimsy plastic cup she had just emptied and continued writhing about, now able to raise one arm to supplement her dance moves. Lasers arced overhead, creating new shapes with every pass. They became stroboscopic during breaks in the beat, solidifying once more when the music melded back into rhythm.

Uh oh, I think someone drank all my whiskey.

She shook the now-empty double cup, rattling the thin straws with the motion. She placed her empty cups among the dozens that littered a tall bar table at the edge of the floor and dodged her way back to the bar. This time she returned to the dance floor with a proper double whiskey sour and, to her surprise, a glowing orange necklace which she had no memory of receiving—or stealing.

Samantha was absorbed into the multi-headed, limb-flailing, hip-gyrating organism that undulated across the dance floor in time with the music that guided it like a snake charmer coaxing a serpent from a wicker basket. She was able to forget the stress of discovering her strange ability—and the ramifications of it—if only for a short while. She had escaped reality for the time being, and intended to make the most of it. She judged the passage time by the level of liquid in her cup. The beauty of this tactic was that the clock restarted with each new beverage. Samantha had never been a heavy drinker, but wasn't shy about cutting loose now and again. She soon lost count of how many whiskey sours she had consumed.

Young men sidled up to her from time to time, spotting a loner in the herd of clubbers that were beginning to hook up for the night. Her body language sent a clear message: *Not tonight, boys. I just need to breathe.* She received several free drinks and three more glowing necklaces despite refusing their advances. They eventually got the hint and left her alone.

Samantha kept dancing, her eyes always drawn to the spectacular lasers overhead. She was not in the least bit fatigued, despite the fact that she had not taken a break in the span of seven—or was it nine?—drinks she had consumed. She felt light on her feet, like she could dance forever. The beams of light joined her, spinning and crossing over themselves, widening and narrowing in flickering progression. They formed webs, pyramids, and other shapes of every hue as they flitted across the dance floor with blinding speed. Samantha was ensorcelled, and found herself wanting to be part of *that* dance. She grinned as they swept her up among them. She could no longer feel the bodies pressing against her or smell the mingled aroma of sweat and alcohol. Samantha couldn't even feel the floor beneath her boots.

This is it. This is where I want to be.

A shriek ruined the moment. Samantha's trance was broken. She searched for the source of the shriek and realized there was no one on the dance floor.

Where is everybody?

Another surprised outburst drew her attention downward. The faces of her fellow club patrons looked *up* at her. Some of them were pointing, others held up their smartphones.

How did they get down—?

The world righted itself like a gyroscope finding its equilibrium and the truth of the situation smashed into her. She plummeted to the dance floor, landing hard on one knee with an audible crack. Panic set in when the music stopped, giving way to the chatter of a multitude of voices. The people on the dance floor formed a circle around her and pressed in.

"Hey, you okay?"

"Does she work here? Was that a stunt?"

"Is she hurt?"

"I don't see any wires."

"What the fuck was that?"

The voices multiplied into a cacophony, enveloping and smothering her. Her chest tightened but she ignored it and forced herself to move, rising to her feet and batting away the hands that extended to her in offers of assistance. Something inside of her, perhaps instinctual self-preservation, gave her the clarity to remove the pin in her hair. Locks tumbled free, obscuring her face as she threaded into the crowd. People further away from the dance floor attempted to see what the commotion was about, making her egress difficult. They pressed in, the wave of bodies growing thicker as word spread.

"Move!" she shouted, trying to maneuver her way past them.

Have to get out. Have to get...

She wasn't making any progress. The crowd was too dense. That is, until the petite young woman in the gauzy black skirt and chunky black boots became desperate and panicked. Bodies fell away from her as she barreled forward, parting the unsuspecting crowd like a cutter through the waves. Drinks flew into the air. People cried out in alarm. Finally, the door came into view. She was going to make it. A subconscious twitch of her hand had the muscle-bound bouncer flattened against the narrow doorway like he was undergoing a police pat down.

Samantha burst into the freedom of the night and ran. She was three blocks away from The Lizard Queen before she slowed to a walk, blood churning through her veins and tendrils of hair plastered to her face and neck. She straightened her clothes and pulled the hair from her eyes, ignoring confused looks from those she passed. A quick over-the-shoulder glance was worth the risk. She had to see if anyone had followed. The bouncer and several employees stood in front of the club. They flagged down a police officer who was ticketing an illegally-parked Audi up the block.

Damn.

Samantha darted into a dark alleyway and pressed herself against a painted brick wall. She caught a glow in her peripheral vision and ripped off the plastic necklaces, then tossed them into an overflowing dumpster

"Hey, you okay?"

Samantha was startled to find a young woman standing on the sidewalk at the alley's entrance. Several others were close by, peering into the alley. She must have spotted Samantha and broke off from her group.

"Can you...would you flag down a cab for me?" Samantha said, gathering herself. As the young woman nodded and stepped out to the curb, one of her companions stepped closer. "Are you in trouble? There's a cop right down—"

He was pointing at The Lizard Queen. Samantha shook her head and took a backwards step deeper into the alley.

"I'm good. Just...just a little too much partying, I think. Thanks."

Indeed, her head was spinning and her lips were numb. She had to pee. Past the helpful young man, the young woman was leaning down to talk to a cab driver and pointing in Samantha's direction. Samantha darted to the cab with a few quick words of gratitude to the helpful strangers.

"Clarendon," she told the driver. She threw her head back against the seat and let out a relieved sigh as the taxi lurched into motion. She felt her panic ebbing away. The epinephrine in her system receded, letting the whiskey back in with a vengeance. Her stomach rumbled in defiance of the alcohol saturation.

"No, wait. I want pizza."

The apartment building entry door closed behind Samantha with a welcoming finality. She was home. She held an oversized slice of pepperoni in one hand and her keys in the other. The steep staircase shifted lazily in front of her. She contemplated the daunting steps, not looking forward to climbing three flights. She brought the pizza to her mouth, but missed horribly. Grease and sauce painted a trail on her cheek. She turned her head to bite at it instead of bringing it to her lips.

Miss McAllister, close your eyes, hold out your arms, and touch your nose with your finger.

But I wasn't driving tonight, officer, I was flying.

The building was quiet. She took another bite and considered the stairs again. There were so many of them.

Did I fly? No, that's stupid. Maybe I did. Let's see...

She closed her eyes and pictured herself floating up the steps. Her balance played a nasty trick on her, causing her to stumble to the left and forcing her eyes open in order to orient herself. She was still standing just inside the entry door.

She ate more pizza.

I didn't fly. I drank too much whiskey. That's what happened.

Then she remembered looking down at the crowd below her, a mass of neon colors and dimly lit expressions of horror. She had fallen hard on her right knee just before the panicked flight from the club. Samantha leaned over to inspect her knee. She didn't see a mark, but she did almost fall over again. Leaning back against the heavy door to brace herself, she lifted her leg and flexed it at the knee. There wasn't the least bit of pain, but the motion put pressure on her full bladder. She looked up at the imposing stairs.

In a minute.

She turned the slice of pie around, considering the best way to attack it for maximum satisfaction. She decided on the crust. As she chewed, her attention was again drawn to the staircase.

I was definitely flying.

She pushed away from the door with her rear end and swayed, taking a lumbering step to counteract the momentum. She figured she weighed about 110, maybe 115 soaking wet. This shouldn't be too difficult. The bookcase had been heavy too. She formed a mental picture of a second Samantha—a sober one—standing behind her and lifting her into the air.

Her boots left the floor. The slice of pizza splattered on the spot where her feet had been, and her keys splashed into the grease. She fought for balance, which would have been difficult even had she been straight. She bucked forward, arms flailing like plucked chicken wings, as her feet came up behind her. Samantha managed to steady herself there. She laughed out loud at the thought of someone coming through the entry door at that exact moment.

The next step was to propel herself toward the staircase. Invisible Sober Samantha carried Visible Drunk Samantha across the foyer. She reached toward the banister for support, but decided against it.

No, you can do this. This is no different than the phone or the toothbrush.

It was terribly difficult at first, but she concentrated and pushed herself upward. An unbidden image came to mind as she ascended the staircase. It was Luke Skywalker, his eyes wide in wonderment as little Yoda lifted his spaceship from the swamp.

Do or do not. There is no try.

Samantha burst out laughing and tumbled to the stairs. She lay there guffawing and rolled over, the edges of the steps digging into her back. She summoned the pizza slice from the floor and took a nibbling bite in between fits of giggles.

"There is no try!" she called out to no one in particular. "I can fly!"

Hey, that rhymes.

The quiet stairwell echoed with renewed laughter. She tried again when her amusement tapered off.

In her mind, strong arms lifted her from the steps and carried her to her front door. She had the hang of it halfway up the second flight. If anyone had been awake at that hour and were inclined to look through their peephole, they would have seen a young woman floating past, licking pizza sauce from her fingertips.

Visible Drunk Samantha dismissed Invisible Sober Samantha when she reached her apartment.

Thanks, buddy. My designated driver.

She was unable to get her legs under her in time and fell hard on her butt. Not bothering to rise, she searched the tiny pocket in her skirt for a full minute before realizing that her keys weren't there. It was a long time for such a small pocket.

Dropped them. Right.

She turned back toward the stairs and crossed her arms parallel to the floor in front of her chest, then twitched her head forward while picturing her greasy keys where she had dropped them next to the pizza slice. Samantha had no idea whether or not she could move something three floors down, but wanted to find out. She knew exactly where they were, after all.

"Did you drop a set of keys?"

A slender, middle-aged man in a blue work uniform rounded the corner from the staircase. He was holding up her key ring, but his arm lowered when he spotted Samantha sitting very unladylike on the floor. "You okay?"

She climbed unsteadily to her feet and tried to smooth out her skirt, but succeeded only in smearing it with pizza grease. The man walked toward her. She didn't recognize him. Maybe he lived on another floor.

"Are these yours?"

Samantha nodded. She looked him over as he handed her the keys. He was trim and had all of his hair. The embroidered oval below his left collar read "Rich."

"Rich, would you like to come in for a nightcap?" she tried to say. What she really said was, "Richoo wan comin fer nighcap?"

Rich smiled and held up his left hand. A gold band encircled the ring finger. "Sorry, young lady. Surely my wife wouldn't approve."

"Don callme Shirleee.."

What's your vector, Victor?

She burst out laughing. Rich shook his head and walked away.

It took her a full five minutes to find the correct key. She burst into her apartment and closed the door as images of watching *Airplane* with Evan came unbidden to the forefront of her mind. She started to giggle again.

Over, Under.

A sudden throbbing in her head quieted her. She pressed her back to the door and slid to the floor. Something tightened around her ribcage and she realized her shirt had caught on the doorknob and was riding up her torso. She gave up after several fumbling attempts to dislodge it, and instead stared into the darkness of her living room. The trapped shirt supported her weight as she nodded off, suspending her halfway to the floor like a discarded marionette. A final thought flitted through her mind before the whiskey got the better of her.

Wow. I think I can fly.

Chapter Six

WHAM! BAM! BAM!

The whiskey gnomes were forging a hangover inside her skull, their hammers striking the anvil of her brain with expert precision. Samantha groaned and sat up. It took her a minute to realize that the pounding wasn't just inside her head. Her fingertips flew to her temples and massaged them hard.

Wham! Bam! Bam!

"Samantha, open up!"

Evan.

"Hold on!" she yelled. The mere effort of raising her voice brought a fresh wave of pain. Her mouth felt like she had been grazing on the hot sands of the Sahara. She rose in fits and starts, bracing herself against the agonizing head rush that followed. Greasy pizza rolled around in her stomach, threatening to reverse its course from the night before through her esophagus. She took a moment to get her bearings. Her shirt was stretched into uselessness, having released itself from the doorknob sometime during the early morning hours. Her skirt smelled like stale sweat and pizza sauce. Her fingers were coated in a slimy film of a similar scent. Her boot heel slipped in a puddle of her drool that had collected on the linoleum entryway. Despite her bedraggled appearance, she opened the door which, in her stupor, she had forgotten to lock after making a fool of herself in front of Rich.

"Mornin' Sunshine." Evan stood in the doorway holding a coffee cup and a small, brown paper bag. His customary grin faded. "You look like shit."

Samantha turned and walked into the bathroom. She didn't bother to close the door as she flipped up her skirt and sat down. She heard Evan setting his gifts on the kitchen counter.

"Thanks for returning my calls and texts, Becks," Evan called. "You could have at least told me to get lost instead of freezing me out."

"When someone doesn't answer your texts and calls they're telling you to get lost, genius."

Samantha flushed the toilet, washed her hands, then retrieved two ibuprofen tablets from the medicine cabinet before returning to the living room. She summoned the cup of coffee from the counter. It leapt from its resting place and crossed the ten feet to nestle into her hand. Her lips creased into a smile as she tossed the pills into her mouth and flipped open the plastic tab on the cup lid. The coffee smelled glorious.

Evan's jaw hit the floor.

Take that.

She maintained her knowing smirk and brought the coffee cup to her lips. "Mmm, damn that is good. Thanks."

Evan shook his head as his grin returned. "Someone's been busy."

Samantha walked to the counter and rummaged through the paper bag. It was a blueberry muffin from Santangelo's. Her favorite. She wasn't sure if her queasy stomach could handle food, but she knew the pastry would soak up the alcohol. She took a bite and turned to face him.

"You have no idea," she said around the muffin.

"Actually, I do."

He retrieved his smartphone from the pocket of his worn and torn blue jeans. The phone case looked like a communicator from Star Trek. The original series, not the newer ones that Samantha liked. He slid a finger across the screen and tapped it a few times before extending the phone to her from the palm of his hand. Samantha took the hint. She levitated it towards her while taking another bite of the sweet muffin. She noticed that Evan was studying his palm instead of the floating phone. Plucking it from the air, Samantha saw that he had queued up a video. She tapped the triangular play icon in the center of the screen.

Orange and blue lights flashed across the screen in colorful tracers. A techno beat thumped from the phone's tiny speaker.

"This is fucking insane!" someone shouted offscreen. The footage was shaky, obviously recorded on a smartphone, but soon steadied as it focused on a female in an off-the-shoulder tee shirt and gauzy black skirt. She was floating above the crowd, her face obscured by the laser lights that danced around her.

The delicious muffin became dirt in Samantha's mouth. An icy spear lanced her spine.

No...

The music abruptly cut off, the deep bass rhythm replaced by excited voices. People pointed up at the young woman. There was a frightened shriek, and the woman appeared to be startled before she plummeted out of frame. The crowd surged forward and the videographer was jostled about. The video went crazy, lights flashing past the lens as people screamed. The image froze into streaks of orange, yellow and blue as the video ended. Samantha stared unblinking at the screen for a long time before meeting Evan's disapproving gaze.

"You can fly?" he said.

Samantha dropped the phone to the counter and braced herself on the sink. She didn't know whether she was going to puke or pass out. Evan darted to her and placed a supportive hand on her back. She leaned down and splashed cold water on her face, not bothering to dry it as she spun on him.

"That's not me," she said.

Evan met her denial with condescension.

"Hmm, let's see. Should I not believe you because A, you went as pale as a ghost while watching the video; B, you're still wearing the same clothes; or C, your name is Lying Liar McLiarstein? D? All of the above?"

Samantha looked down at her attire.

Well, shit.

Evan opened her fridge and helped himself to a bottle of water. He unscrewed the cap and took a long pull, his eyes never leaving Samantha.

"Where...where did you find it?" Her voice was defeated.

"You are damn lucky you chose to go to a dark, dank dance club, Becks," he said. "Your face isn't visible except in a few frames, and even then it is very difficult to make out. I could tell it was you only because I knew what I was looking for."

"How can you be sure?"

"That your face was in those frames? Because, I spent the last," Evan checked his watch, "four hours poring over this video with the best, pirated film editing software money can buy. As soon as it posted, I knew it had to be you. Samantha, this video is all over the web. Facebook, Twitter, Tumblr, Reddit, Instagram...you name it. You are *so* lucky no one can recognize you. Stupid and careless, but lucky. And by the way, you need to burn those clothes. No trash, no Goodwill. Burn that shit. Today. Do you know what would happen if someone found out it was—"

"—Alright! I get it! Fuck off!" Samantha threw up her hands and stormed from the kitchen. "I need time to think! I just...I just need time to think this through."

Evan crossed his arms over his chest and let her vent.

"I was a normal person before last week. Your typical girl trying to make ends meet by slinging beers in a tourist trap bar & grill. Now, I'm... I don't know what! This is all so sudden. I can't deal with it. I don't want this! I never asked for it! Jesus, Evan, I can move things with my frickin' mind! Last night I *flew,* for fuck's sake!"

Evan seized that moment to interject.

"Samantha, I know you don't want to hear this, and the last thing I want to do is to make things worse for you, but I'm pretty damn sure there's more to it than moving things—and yourself—with your mind."

Oh god. Here we go.

She collapsed on the couch and covered her face with her hands. "Tell me."

Evan cleared his throat and cupped his hand over his fist.

"First, promise me two things. You won't be this careless ever again, and you won't twist me into a pretzel when I tell you how I came to this theory about your pow—abilities."

Samantha rubbed her eyes and leaned forward to rest her elbows on her knees. As she did so, she remembered her knee crashing to the dance floor and inspected it for bruising. There was not a mark upon her. She turned to Evan and nodded.

"I'm not trying to be a complete bitch, Evan. Really I'm not," she said, "but you don't know what I'm going through. How could you? I have no life experience to deal with something like this. No way to put this into a neat little package that I can examine and fix. What is happening to me is something out of a...out of a..."

"Comic book." Evan finished for her.

"No, damn it! A nightmare! *This* isn't supposed to be real!"

To drive her point home, she leapt from the couch and sent an empty flower vase smashing into the opposite wall. It shattered upon impact, sending shards of glass everywhere.

Evan flinched and covered up, despite the fact that she had aimed the vase far away from him.

"How can I live a normal life knowing that I can do these things? What if I lose my temper? What if I hurt someone?"

Evan patted the air in a calming motion. "Okay, Becks," he said, "I get it. I really do. I'm here to help you make sure that doesn't happen. But first, you need more information. Information that I'm going to give to you. Knowledge is the key to controlling your abilities. And what we don't know, we'll find out together. But you have to trust me. And also not throw me through a wall. Promise?"

Samantha felt herself relaxing. Smashing things felt good. She sat back down. *He's always known how to talk me down from the ledge.*

"I promise," she said. "Lay it on me."

"Thank you. Now, after you left yesterday I studied the video you made, and—"

He held up his hands defensively as Samantha's face twisted into rage. "You promised!"

"You made copies?" She was standing again, this time with clenched fists.

"Samantha, wait. I made one copy, then deleted it when I was finished. My computers are more secure than the Pentagon's. You know this, Sam. And by the way, you're the one who made a video for the entire world last night, so chill!"

That seemed to appease her somewhat, but she remained standing.

"Go on."

Evan's expression was indignant. He took a dramatic pause before continuing.

"As I was saying, I studied your video over and over, frame by frame. I sharpened it and enlarged it, slowed it down and reversed it. I basically used every trick I know in an attempt to glean more information about the 'how' rather than the 'why'.

Now, physics tells us that something can't be lifted with a thought. Science fact. There is this little thing called 'gravity' that holds us all to the Earth. So something has to counteract that gravity, that is to say that an opposing force, stronger than gravity, has to be applied in order to counteract gravity's pull. I didn't feel it yesterday when you took the memory card from my hand because I was about to crap my pants, but I certainly felt it today when you lifted the phone."

"Felt what?" Samantha slowly sank back to the cushions.

"A force," Evan replied. "And I don't mean 'The Force' as in Star Wars, I mean an actual physical manifestation of force that you are somehow creating. I think that is what allows you to do what you do."

"You know," Samantha said, "That makes sense. When I tried to lift my underwear from the ceiling fan, it didn't move from my thoughts. I pictured my actual fingers lifting it up, then it moved."

Evan wore a bemused expression. "Your underwear?"

"Yeah, my underwear. Surely you saw them on the ceiling fan in the video you stole from me."

She arched an eyebrow to punctuate her dig at him.

"Well done, Becks," he said. "Anyway, that is just one small part of the puzzle. We're getting there, but we need to know your limits. You can do a drunken float on a dance floor, but can you really fly? You can lift coffee cups and smartphones—and underwear, I guess—but can you lift a car? A city bus? We need more data. Is there anything else that I don't know about?"

Samantha thought about it. Her hand absently rubbed her knee.

"Yeah, there is," she answered, "That first night, when I broke my lamp, I got out of bed and stepped on a light bulb with my bare foot. The broken glass didn't cut me at all."

Evan was intrigued. "Wow, okay."

"And last night when I fell to the dance floor I landed on my right knee, Evan. From... I don't know how high..."

"I figure you were at least fifteen feet in the air."

"Okay, fifteen feet then. I landed on my knee on a hard surface from fifteen feet in the air. That's like jumping from the roof of a house. And look. No bruising, no broken bones. Nothing."

Evan gazed at her perfect little knee.

"That's the only thing I can think of," she said. "Evan? Where did you go?"

She snapped at the air in front of her.

"Sorry, just thinking about the ramifications of that," he lied. "I'm going to have to think about all of this some more, but in the meantime we need to get more information. We have to find your limits, Becks, and we need to do so with extreme caution."

"So I don't end up hurting someone," she reasoned.

"Yes, but also so you don't end up in a top secret government lab getting poked and prodded and who knows what else. Samantha, you know that you can never, ever go public with this. Right?"

She nodded in agreement. "That would cramp my style."

Evan grinned.

"So what do you want to do first? Speeding bullet, locomotive, or tall buildings?"

"First, I want to finish breakfast. Then take a long shower and a longer nap."

"And after all of that?"

"Tall buildings, I guess," she said.

Wow, am I really going to do this?

"I'd hoped you would say that. I'm so jealous. And happy for you. Really, I am."

"Aw, that's sweet."

"Don't friend-zone me, Sam."

"Too late."

Evan's face wrinkled up in mock pain. "Sam?"

"Yes?"

He thrust his hands into his pockets and drew circles on the floor with the tip of his shoe.

"Can I be your sidekick?"

The 1985 Chevette sputtered several times before stalling out.

"This is a good spot," Evan decided as he pulled the key from the ignition.

Samantha opened the passenger door and stepped into the windy night, glad to be free of the cramped car after the long drive. Grassy fields stretched into darkness in every direction. The narrow, dirt access road disappeared when Evan shut off the headlights, making her feel even more isolated in the sweeping countryside.

"Wasn't a Civil War battle fought in Manassas?" she said.

"Are you referring to the First Battle of Manassas or the Second Battle of Manassas?"

"Smart ass."

"Dumb ass."

Evan withdrew a long mag light from his Transformers backpack and thumbed the button while slinging the pack over his shoulder. The ambient light from the strong beam enveloped them in a vast globe.

"Come on, let's get away from the road."

Samantha followed him into the fields and looked up into the clear night. "The stars are gorgeous. You can actually see them out here."

"Don't go near them. You'll burn up," Evan said, then added, "I think."

"Like I could ever reach the stars."

Evan halted and spun on her. He didn't say anything. He didn't have to.

Yeah, I know. We don't know what I'm capable of.

"Let's do this," she said, and pushed past him.

The tall grasses bent around their legs as they made their way deeper into the field.

"Right here," Evan said, unshouldering his backpack and shining the light in a full circuit around them to make sure no one was around.

Samantha spotted lights on the horizon, most likely from distant farmhouses. The moon was a white sliver in the distance. A twinge of anxiety crept over her. There would be no roof over her this time. The emptiness above was intimidating. Flying with liquor courage in an apartment stairwell was one thing, but this...

Evan was sticking something into her left ear. She reeled back and swatted at his hand.

"What the hell!"

"Two-ways," he said, tapping his left ear. "Here, put it in your ear."

"A little warning next time?"

But she took the small earbud and pushed it into her ear canal. Evan ignored her snark and fiddled with a black device that intermittently flashed red LEDs across its beveled top. He tucked it under his arm and pulled another, smaller device from his backpack. He reached for the bottom hem her sweatshirt.

She smacked his hand away. "What did I just say?"

"An altimeter," he said. "I'll be able to monitor your altitude to within a foot or two. Clip it to your waistband."

"So bossy," she said. "And grabby."

She did as she was told, however. The metal clip was cold against her skin. Evan turned and walked away until Samantha could only see the beam of light flashing about.

"*Can you hear me?*"

Evan's voice blasted into her head. Her fingers pressed into the earpiece. "Damn, Evan! Turn it down!"

"*Sorry,*" came the reply. "*There. Better?*"

"Much," she said.

"*Okay, good. I'm going to stick the mag light into the ground so you'll have a point of reference. I won't be able to see you, which is good because no one else will either. Oh, and you don't have to touch the earbud to talk to me. They only do that in the movies.*"

Samantha let her fingers drop from the ear piece. "How can you see me?"

"*I can't,*" came the reply. "*I'm sporting a self-satisfied grin right now, by the way.*"

"Of course you are." She rolled her eyes, then looked into the broad, starry sky. "Ready?"

Samantha pulled her hair into a ponytail and secured it with a rubber band. She inhaled deeply to steady herself, but her stomach erupted with butterflies.

"*One more thing,*" Evan said. "*Try not to go too high. Our satellites aren't pointed at us right now, but we can't be too careful. Maybe China's are.*"

"How do you know these things, Evan? And how do you have all of this equipment?"

"*You don't want to know,*" he said. "*And don't go too fast, either. Just take it slow. This is just a test run. Ready when you are.*"

Actually, I do want to know. But we're a little busy right now.

"Here goes," Samantha said, exhaling slowly.

"*Oh, one more thing. If you get into trouble, just concentrate. You're going to need to focus to maintain your—*"

"Shut up, Evan."

"*Roger that, Kinetic Star,*" came his reply. "*How is that for a superhero name? All of the good ones are taken, so I'm trying to figure out—oh, okay. You're flying now. Forty-seven feet and rising. Cool, okay. You got this.*"

Samantha let the ground fall away from her. She focused on a small star just outside a large cluster. It winked at her, inviting her closer.

I got this.

A cool breeze swept over her, and she tasted the clean country air with a grin. She willed herself higher, her anxiety all but forgotten.

"*Three hundred feet and rising, Becks,*" reported Evan, "*Three-seventy.*"

Samantha kept going. "Tell me when I get to a thousand."

"*Roger that, Crimson Marvel. Five hundred and twenty feet.*"

"Crimson Marvel? My hair is blonde. Nice try, ground control."

"*Sarcasm is beneath the likes of the dynamic Ginger Snap. Seven hundred and forty feet. And your hair is strawberry blonde.*"

The view was breathtaking. She could see the glow of D.C. on the horizon, thirty-odd miles to the east. Below her, a tiny dot of light on a sheet of blackness revealed Evan's location. The farmhouse lights didn't seem so far away in relation to Evan's light now that she was so high above them. Both would disappear from sight pretty soon. Raising her head once more, she could make out the star formations in crystal clarity as there was no other light to interfere with their majesty.

"*One thousand feet, Becks. You doing okay?*" Evan asked.

Samantha slowed her ascent to a crawl, then glided to a stop. It took some effort to maintain a hovering position, but she got the hang of it. She didn't feel as though she had expended much effort so far. Her heartbeat was elevated, but she chalked it up to exhilaration—and a touch of fear.

"Doing good, Houston," she said, "It's cold as hell up here. Listen, I'm going to try something."

Samantha thought back to her mysterious "jump" as she had jogged past Clarendon station and took another deep breath to center herself. She remembered how she had felt that day, the confusion and stress from the events of the Plot the night before. She held onto that memory and concentrated.

"Saaaam," Evan's voice warned in her ear, "*Don't do anything stupid. This is a test. That's all. We'll have more time to—*"

Samantha focused on her star and willed herself toward it with everything she had. The wind whipping around her was a thrill. It tore at her sweats and was so loud that she could no longer hear Evan's voice. She could feel her skin pushing away from her face, and thought of astronauts training in the "Vomit Comet." Elated, she went higher and faster.

Holy shit! This is unbelievable!

She could now see the curvature of the Earth, but the stars were still so far away.

Okay, I'd better cool it.

Samantha slowed down to get a better look. That's when everything went to hell.

An icy fist gripped her, counterpoint to the hot pain that erupted in her extremities. She inhaled sharply, and her lungs filled with fire. She gasped and faltered, her reflexes overriding any semblance of control. Shaking hands grasped at something to hold onto, something to orient herself, but clenched only frigid air. She couldn't breathe. Her joints exploded in agony. The furious wind resumed, but this time it came from below.

Samantha never thought she would die like this. The strangest thoughts came to her as she fought to maintain consciousness.

Biological organism: Human. Sever spinal cord below third vertebrae. Death is immediate.

She couldn't hear anything but the wind. Samantha knew the ground would meet her at any moment.

Can't focus. Did you really think you could fly, Sammy?

She wanted to scream out to Evan, to warn him somehow, but she couldn't even draw a breath.

Terminal velocity is around one hundred twenty miles per hour.

Why do I remember that?

I'm going to smash into the field at one hundred twenty miles per hour.

Fuck me...

Then it was over.

The impact was a thunderclap. Great chunks of earth flew into the air and scattered. Dust billowed into a monstrous cloud. The silence that followed was deafening.

Samantha sat up and gulped for air. A constant ringing filled her ears. She tried to stand but stumbled and fell back into the dirt.

Why am I craving pretzel sticks?

It took a long while to get her breathing under control. She tried to stand again. Her knees and elbows were stiff knots of pain—along with every other joint in her body—but she forced herself to stand. Her ponytail had come loose. She staggered about in a daze, pulling filthy hair from her mouth.

"Where the hell?" she said.

Better question: Why the hell? As in: why the hell are you still alive?

Samantha collapsed to her knees and gritted her teeth against the agony. It wasn't long before a beam of light flickered overhead. She forced herself to stand. She was freezing.

The beam centered itself and shined down on her.

"Oh my—"

She could barely make out Evan's voice above the ringing in her ears.

"Oh my *god*!"

Evan planted a hand on the ground and swung his legs over the edge of the small crater that Samantha had created upon impact. He slid into the hole and rushed to her, gathering her into his arms.

"I thought you were...I lost contact and..." Evan hugged her tighter, then held her at arm's length and shined the flashlight on her.

"Are you hurt? Well of course you are, but I don't see..." Evan said. "How are you even standing? What happened?"

Samantha coughed and disentangled herself from him.

"My joints hurt like a bitch and I'm having trouble breathing, but I don't think anything is broken," she said.

"Samantha, the altimeter clocked you at twenty-two thousand feet," he said. "That's over four fucking miles up! You went from a thousand feet to twenty-two thousand feet in...I don't know how long, but it was fucking fast! That is insane!"

"I need a cheeseburger," said Samantha.

Evan couldn't hold back his enthusiasm as he followed Samantha out of the crater. "This is so amazing! Just unbelievably incredible! You must have subconsciously generated a force dispersal to protect yourself like a...like a fucking inertial dampener! Yes! And it must be internal somehow too, or your organs would be liquid against your bones right now! What was left of your bones, that is. But that means your powers are part of a reflex arc! Has to be..."

Samantha tightened her jaw as she rotated her shoulder in its socket. The roaring pain in her joints was dissipating into a sharp ache. Beside her, Evan was droning on about invulnerability and friction reduction.

"Do you think any diners are open in Manassas?" she said.

He fell silent and stopped walking.

"Really, Sam? Food? Now?"

"Yeah. Now," she said.

He shined the light on her. "We should find a Wal-mart first."

She cocked her head at the odd remark, then looked down as Evan pointed the beam at her. Her hoodie and sweatpants hung from her in tatters and she was covered in grime.

"I see London, I see France," Evan sang, "I see The Crimson Cannonball's dirty underpants."

Samantha flipped the bird and kept walking.

PART TWO

LADY LUCK

Nineteen Years Ago

ROGER SMOOTHED OUT THE PLASTIC MAP and set up his painted soldiers one more time before dinner. It was a meticulous affair. Every regiment had to be positioned just so; the cannons spaced every couple of inches, the infantry in the center (arranged in straight rows as per the rules of gentlemen's warfare), and the cavalry on the flanks for support. It was a frontal assault this time, simple and direct. Two opposing forces clashing for control of land, culture and, most importantly, honor. He was well aware that his fellow eight year-old friends were also ignoring calls to come to the dinner table. But unlike Roger, they were exploring the cosmos in spaceships or managing their inventories to find out if a new set of chain armor provided more advantages than the armor from a previous quest. They were shouting insults at strangers who couldn't keep up with the fast-paced rhythm of digital warfare or loading a saved game because their avatar kept falling from a perilous cliff to avoid the onslaught of the big boss. No,

Roger preferred monochromatic blue and red figures of tin that had been carefully molded to play a particular role.

His peers couldn't do what he could do. If they could, they wouldn't have to rely on software algorithms and plastic-encased circuit boards for entertainment.

"Mister Harkins! Get down here this instant! I won't ask you again!"

Miss June's voice perforated his bedroom door for the third time. She only used his surname when she meant business. Roger sometimes wondered if she was jealous of his last name. The Harkins name was synonymous with respect and admiration. The name White was just...White. Father would sometimes remonstrate him, telling him to treat her with the respect he would show his own mother. But Roger didn't know how to do that. He had never known his mother.

"Just a few more minutes," he said, adjusting a metal cannon toward the enemy ranks.

"Your father will hear about this! Do you know what is involved in making duck a l'orange?"

Her footsteps were charged with attitude as they grew more faint. He decided to let her pout, knowing that Father wouldn't care if he chose not to eat dinner when Miss June said he should. Roger didn't like her cooking anyway. Garret Scanlon down the street ate macaroni and cheese with cut-up hot dogs for dinner. Joel Roland's mom made grilled cheese and tomato soup. Why couldn't he have that?

Roger was certain that Miss June would be fine tomorrow. His nocturnal bathroom visits would sometimes intercept her voice making strange noises from Father's bedroom. Her mood would always be brighter the next morning as she prepared his eggs benedict and buttery grits. Roger never asked why that was, but figured those were the nights that Miss June got paid. Maybe she would get paid tonight.

The long rifleman was out of alignment, so Roger pivoted him on his broad, flat base until he was flush with his comrades-in-arms and able to do his job. He wondered what his job would be when he was a grown up. Would he travel to Japan like Father? His attention drifted to the taketombo on his shelf. Roger had quickly tired of it. There were only so many times you could derive enjoyment from swiveling the wooden rod in your palms and watching the bamboo helicopter blades take flight. So he had tried to change it. For some reason, it had stayed the same. It wasn't like his army men. He hated it.

Roger crept to his door and listened for Miss June. Her melodic humming played counterpoint to the percussion of cookware as she cleared the kitchen of Roger's abandoned dinner. Satisfied, he turned back to the plastic map and its opposing armies. The multitude of red figurines loomed over the much smaller blue force. The banner men, artillery men, horsemen and gunmen wanted to take back the expanse of rubbery landscape from the blue patriots who were only trying to establish a homeland free from oppression.

Roger closed his eyes and let it come. A long, slow exhale escaped his nostrils as his eyelids parted. His lips creased into a thin smile.

The blue army was winning.

Chapter Seven

UNEVEN TRACKS JOSTLED THE PASSENGERS as the train rolled into the station. David lost his place on the sports page, but wasn't too upset about it. It was another opinionated editorial on how the Nationals made mistakes with their trades in the off season and were paying for it in the regular season. He'd never been into baseball, but sitting in the stands with a cold beer in one hand and a juicy brat in the other was always a good time. He'd made the mistake of taking Marissa once. She'd made an offhand remark about how her solid work was going unnoticed, so he treated her to a night game. It was the Nats against the Reds. Her baseball questions fired at him faster than Scherzer's forkballs, and he was relieved when they got drenched during the seventh-inning stretch.

"*Virginia Square. Doors open on the left. Next stop, Clarendon.*"

He watched the train car empty and fill up again, taking note of a young man who stood just inside the doors. The bottleneck forced others to maneuver around him, irritated glances writ plainly on their faces. The young man was strutting to a tune that only he could hear through the bright red Beats headphones clamped over his ears. David decided that the blocky bulge in the back of the blue-striped warm up pants, coupled with the way the pant legs sagged unevenly, could easily be a concealed weapon of some sort. David licked his thumb and turned to the financial section as the doors closed.

"*Clarendon. Doors open on the left. Next stop, Court House.*"

David shifted in his seat and lowered the newspaper just enough to peer over the top edge. She hadn't been on the train for the past couple of days, or at least not in the usual train car. He wondered if she was on vacation or had come down with something. Perhaps she had just grown tired of their unrequited flirtations and had decided to ride elsewhere. Then she slipped through the doors just before they closed.

He had never seen her in makeup. She had a natural, unassuming beauty that didn't require it. He liked that about her. This time, however, David detected a light layer of foundation and powder on her face, particularly under the eyes. He favored his sickness theory. Or maybe she'd just had a late night. She was attired in the same snug, white blouse and black slacks that she always wore—a work uniform, he had decided early on. Her long hair hung in a single braid that swayed like a cobra as she slid past the rude passenger who blocked the doors.

The young man now irked David, whereas before David had been indifferent about his inconsiderate body position.

She stopped in front of the seat just below the metro map, then turned to look at David. He lowered the paper further and gave her a friendly smile, nodding to the door blocker and rolling his eyes. She seemed to get his reference and glanced at the head-bopping young man before returning the eye roll. She didn't smile back, however, nor did she sit in her usual spot. Instead, she eased herself with delicate care into an empty seat under the window. His brow furrowed. Was she in pain?

"*Federal Triangle. Doors open on the left. Next stop, L'Enfant Plaza.*"

David's eyes had scanned the same paragraph for six stops as he tried to solve the mystery. When she used a support bar to get to her feet, he decided that she had indeed been ill and was now returning to work. That was it. He silently remonstrated himself for his insecurity. Still, she had not made eye contact with him after that first exchange. Her commute had been spent with her head resting against the window, eyes closed. Their game had been rained out.

They reached the door at the same time and David stepped aside to motion her through. She finally gave him that perfect smile he was waiting for as she disembarked. The smile seemed forced, but David appreciated the effort and mirrored it. He adjusted the messenger bag strap on his shoulder and prepared to mount the escalator behind her. She faltered at the expanding steps, her foot slipping out from under her, but David's hand snaked out to catch her by the armpit before she could go down.

"Whoa! You okay there?" he said.

A curse threatened to escape from her lips, but she stifled it and nodded instead.

"Thank you," she said. "These things eat people, I hear."

Her voice had a breathy timbre, deep but feminine. She blushed and looked away. He wondered if she thought that was a silly comment to make to a stranger.

David grinned. "At least they're working today."

The rest of the escalator journey was spent in silence.

"David Daniels," he said as they left the escalators and headed toward 12th street.

She took his extended hand. "Samantha McAllister."

"Pleasure to meet you, Samantha. Have great evening," he said.

"Back at you David."

They parted ways at Pennsylvania Avenue.

"Good evening, Mr. Daniels."

"Evening, Marissa," he said. "What's the word?"

He shrugged off his suit jacket and tucked it over a forearm as Marissa followed him into his spacious office, pointing at a stack of Post-it notes on his desk with a pen she produced from behind her ear. The motion caused her glasses to become askew. She righted them with a slender pinky and gave her report.

"ASAC Sullivan wants an update on the Missouri case, and there were two urgent messages from Director Sharp. Also, Cassidy's wife's birthday is Sunday so I've taken the liberty of sending her flowers. I like peonies, but thought that might be a little too feminine so I ordered carnations instead. I'm pretty sure she'll think that would be something you'd pick out. What else? Oh, I'll be out Monday for finals, so if you need anything, just—"

David slung his jacket over the high-backed desk chair and picked up the stack of notes. "I'll be okay, Marissa. And carnations are fine. Good luck on Monday, and thanks for coming in on the weekend."

Marissa had been a good choice. He preferred to work nights and weekends, and needed a dedicated assistant who was able to adjust his or her schedule to accommodate his. Marissa attended MBA classes at Georgetown during the day while working evenings for him. It worked out well for the both of them. He remembered the grueling interview process where a dozen young men and women had come through his door in hopes of landing a job that would allow them to rub elbows with government employees. It was a great way to get their foot in the door for a federal career. His first impression of Marissa Sanchez was that of an introverted college student with a sharp mind and respectable work ethic. She had put herself through undergrad, working first as a waitress, then third shift on the assembly line of a manufacturing plant. She wasn't afraid to get her hands dirty. Her interview had been in the middle of a July heat wave, yet she had chosen to wear a long-sleeved sweater. David didn't miss the purple tattoo that peeked out from beneath her cuff during repeated adjustments of her thin-rimmed glasses. Mousy, straight-laced Miss

Sanchez had a secret. Everyone had a secret. He had hired her the next day.

"No problem, boss. Oh, one more thing. It's probably nothing, but I noticed that the network is kind of glitchy today. I didn't see any notices about maintenance, so I'm not sure what's going on."

"Good to know," he said, shuffling through the notes without looking up. Marissa closed the door behind her. The phone rang as the door latch clicked into place.

"I got it, Marissa," he called, knowing that she was trying to go home. He cradled the receiver against his shoulder and reclined in the chair.

"Daniels."

"*Dave. I'd hoped you'd be in by now.*"

David plucked the receiver from his shoulder and leaned forward, dropping the Post-its onto his desk.

"Director, sir. I was just about to call you back. I'm going through your messages now."

David heard him cover the phone with his hand to speak to someone in his office. The voices were too muffled to make out any of the conversation.

"*I Emailed you some links,*" he said. "*Check them out and call me back.*"

Director Sharp ended the call before David could reply. David switched on his computer monitor and logged into the secure network. The log in took longer than usual. When his home screen finally came up, David summoned the Email application.

Inbox (219 unread)

He made a mental note to get Marissa a security clearance so she could weed out lower priority Email messages. For now, he hunted through the list of unread messages until he found what he was looking for.

From: Sharp, Henry (USDHS; Director's Office)

Subject: Eyes Only

Dave - Priority surveillance picked these up.

5/17: 2339 Hours
5/17: 2340Hours
5/17: 2345 Hours
- - - - -
https://www.youtube.com/watch?v=Hsg6y23a%g3w

David sat back in his chair and cupped his chin. A YouTube link? The other links were most likely satellite images, but a public video? His interest piqued, David clicked on the video first.

It was a rave of some sort being filmed from a smartphone. Multi-colored lights flashed past the camera. Dance music pulsated, over-modulated and grating.

"This is fucking insane!" someone said offscreen.

The camera angle shifted to capture the dance floor. A human silhouette—no, a woman—hovered above the crowd. The flickering light show surrounded the figure. Her arms were widespread and her head was tilted back. She had long hair of indeterminate color, and appeared to be wearing a loose T-shirt with a short skirt and thick boots.

The music fell silent, replaced by the excited shouts and murmurs of the club patrons. Someone shrieked and the hovering woman fell from sight.

The video shuddered and twisted as though the person holding the phone had been knocked off balance. Screams overwhelmed the audio just before the film ended. David looked at the video window just below the player.

1.2 million views

He left the YouTube window open and navigated back to his Email program. An image viewer sprang to life when he clicked the first link. The photo wasn't from a surveillance satellite after all. The status readouts embedded into the image showed it had been taken from a UAV. It was in the active infrared spectrum, depicting a wide expanse of grassy field in a bright, monochromatic green. David craned his neck forward and narrowed his eyes. An object was off center in the photo, but it could have been anything. A piece of farm equipment. A cow. The point of view was from overhead, so there was no perspective. He clicked on the second link.

"Now we're talking," he said.

This surveillance photo was taken just after the UAV had passed the subject, but now the drone's camera was in a better position to capture it. It was a person. A person over a thousand feet in the air with no discernable means of propulsion. The subject wore what appeared to be baggy clothes and sneakers. The monochromatic photo was too grainy to provide finer details.

Intrigued, David opened the third link to find a photo of a small crater in a grassy field. He was confused at first, then realized that Sharp had arranged these links in a particular order. He was creating a narrative.

But how was there a drone in that region, right at that time? Coincidence?

The phone rang.

"Daniels."

"*What do you think?*"

It was Director Sharp again. His call was perfectly timed. Another coincidence? David wondered if he had been monitoring his terminal, waiting for him to view all of the material. That might explain the glitchy network service.

"At first glance, I'd say we have a hoax," David surmised. "These were taken from one of our assets?"

"*Affirmative,*" said the Director.

"Okay. Providing that the drone wasn't malfunctioning or otherwise compromised, I'd say we have a human subject, age and ethnicity indeterminate. I might be able to discern physical attributes from the altitude, distance and trajectory of the asset, but it won't be concrete. It *looks* like a flying person, but these things have a way of turning into something else entirely."

"*That's what we pay you for, Daniels. Find out,*" Sharp said. "*And the video?*"

Daniels wanted to ask him about the happenstance of the drone being there—over American soil, no less—but instead clicked back to the video window and let it play with the sound muted.

"Creative cinematography," he said. "Any amateur can do something like this with a smartphone and a free app."

"*That's what we thought. We tapped into the SIM card of the phone that took the video. There was no doctoring. It was uploaded directly to the internet minutes after the incident. The location of the device was in the Adams Morgan district at the time of filming. The drone shots were taken over Prince William county. We'll be sending you further details pertinent to your investigation.*"

"Understood," said David.

He set down the receiver and interlocked his fingers behind his head, crossing his feet on the edge of the mahogany desk. Was Sharp trying to tell him that they had captured an *actual* flying human being on film? He clicked on the second image again and scrutinized it for a long time. Gender was impossible to discern, but he decided that it *could* be a woman. It would support Sharp's attempt to link the video to the surveillance images, but David hadn't earned his reputation by relying on conjecture. He needed facts, not theories.

The young man fidgeted with his glowing yellow bracelet. "You police?"

The body language alone told David that this guy was nervous and was probably holding, but that wasn't why the investigator was standing in front of a dance club on a Saturday night with a half-in-the-bag clubgoer.

"No," said David.

"You FBI?"

"No, not FBI."

"What then?" The man's tone became agitated. He scratched at his neck.

David held his hands out before him in a calming gesture.

"Listen, Mr. Garvey," he said. "I'm not here to bust you for anything. I just need to know about Thursday night. About the video you posted online."

Dallas Garvey's anxious countenance gave way to enthusiasm.

"Oh shit, man! That's what this is about?" He danced back and threw his hands into the air. "That was so dope!"

"Tell me."

"We was clubbing up in the Queen here." He motioned to the dance club beside them. "Shit was gettin' real when all of a sudden she was like flyin'!"

"Who was flying?"

"This shorty. We was all bangin' on the beats DJ Oasis was throwing down, then *POW*! There she was, all up in the lasers and shit. I had my phone out, so I was like 'Fuck it.' I got over a million hits on that shit."

"Can you describe her?"

"No, man. It's so dark up in there, you can't even see what bills you're givin' for your sauce. She had a black skirt on, I think. I could see some funky black boots, too."

"Was he working Thursday night?" Dallas followed David's nod to the big bouncer who watched them from the doorway.

"Yeah, yeah. That's my boy Duncan. He was here."

David pulled a twenty from his pocket and held it up with two fingers. "Thanks, Mr. Garvey. I got your cab fare. Be careful tonight."

Dallas took the bill and muttered some sort of thanks as he disappeared back into the club. David approached the towering bouncer who stood next to a small podium at the door. He took up a small stamp and pressed it to an inkpad as David drew near.

"Mr. Duncan?"

The bouncer jerked his head upward in dubious acknowledgement.

"I'm Daniels. Can you tell me what happened here on Thursday night?"

"I already gave you guys my statement."

"I know," David lied. "Tell us again. What did she look like? Any distinguishing marks? Skin color? Hair color? Height? Rough weight, maybe?"

"Nope. She looked the same as every other piece that comes in here, gets fucked up, then leaves with some pansy hipster. Only difference was, this one left alone and in a hurry."

"Surveillance cameras?"

"No, not here. We respect the privacy of our customers," said Duncan.

David seriously doubted that policy. He looked past Duncan into the darkness of the club.

"Did you try to stop her from leaving?"

"No, I was hauling in some kegs."

"Then who was watching the door?"

Duncan shrugged. "I go where I'm needed."

The bouncer scratched at his forehead, unintentionally drawing David's attention to the angry bruise there.

"Did she assault you, Mr. Duncan?"

The big man looked insulted. David took that as a "no."

"Mind if I have a look around inside? Ask the bartenders a few questions?"

Duncan raised the stamp. "You look old enough to drink."

David rubbed the ink from the top of his hand as he made his way into the Lizard Queen. It was still early enough for him to move around unimpeded by a throng of partiers cavorting about and spilling drinks everywhere. That wouldn't have been the case had he arrived later that night. Questioning the first bartender was more an exercise in lip reading than an actual interview. As with Duncan the bouncer, the man didn't offer any useful information. According to him, he served so many girls during the course of a single night that it was impossible to remember the details of a particular one. He had a good point. David didn't bother to speak to the other bartenders.

He drew bemused looks from the strutting, swaying dancers as he made his way onto the dance floor. Several young women flitted past him with drinks held high, measuring him up with sidelong glances, but David was interested in the weaving laser show overhead. He reached the center of the floor and withdrew a small flashlight from his jacket pocket. There was no sign of a wire rig on the ceiling, although it was difficult to see past the dizzying beams of light. The proprietors of the Lizard Queen would have had plenty of time to remove such apparatus anyway.

David redirected the flashlight beam to the floor. It was a marley floor, made from heavy duty, slip-resistant vinyl. He searched the area in a widening perimeter, pushing past the gyrating bodies in his way. A young man spun around to challenge him, but one look from David returned the dancer's attention to less dangerous pursuits. David's search ended abruptly when he spied a series of cracks spreading from a central point in the vinyl. He traced the lines with his fingers and discovered a shallow indentation, perhaps a foot in diameter. He tapped out a number on his phone as he exited the club.

"Yes, this is Inspector Daniels," he said when a friendly gentleman on other end picked up. He was always amazed at how many people just accepted an official-sounding title, even though it was completely made up. They rarely asked for details. "I'd like to know if any females have been admitted or treated and released for leg injuries since Thursday night. Sure, I'll hold."

The bouncer said she had left in a hurry, but mentioned nothing about limping. David wanted to be thorough, however. If she was drunk enough, or on something stronger, she might not have noticed an injury.

The hospital receptionist came back on the line. "Sir?"

"Yes, I'm here."

"I'm not showing any females coming to the emergency room with leg injuries during that time frame."

"Do you have access to records from nearby hospitals? Urgent care centers?"

"I can expand the search, sure." said the receptionist.

David heard the click clack of a keyboard.

"I see a treat and release for a bee sting, a tailpipe burn to the shin, and a lacerated foot. All three at MedStar."

"Thanks."

David hung up.

His next stop was the local precinct. He was given access to Thursday's incident reports after some artful persuasion as to who he was and who he worked for. Officer Little had been on patrol that night. He had responded to an audible distress call at The Lizard Queen dance club at 02:35 hours. After interviewing several patrons and the employee at the door, it was determined that no injuries had occurred. Only minor property damage to several of the patrons' personal devices. The officer concluded that it was a victimless disturbance on private property. A participant had fled the scene. The investigating officer had noticed a small contusion on an employee's forehead, but the employee declined to file a complaint.

David smirked. He returned to his office in the JFK building and spent the rest of the night finishing up the Missouri case report for ASAC Sullivan.

Missouri had turned out to be less complicated than he was led to believe. He hadn't even needed to travel. What was first thought to be multiple cult-related missing persons cases turned out to be five teenagers on a week-long hiatus from school—and their families—to play Dungeons & Dragons in a network of local cave formations. They hadn't bothered to tell anyone they were leaving for fear that they wouldn't be allowed to go. They would have been right. The "cult" rumor was started because several of the parents watched too much Nancy Grace instead of exploring their children's interests. David had played the role-playing game a little bit as a kid, and knew the rumors were false. It wasn't hard to predict where they had gone and what they were doing once he asked the right people the right questions.

He Emailed the report and looked at his watch. It was almost dawn when David requisitioned a sedan and headed southwest.

The morning sun had just cleared the flat horizon by the time he reached Manassas, promising another beautiful day. Sharp had provided the location of the drone at the time it had photographed the event. David thought it odd that Sharp would Email him directly when he had subordinates to perform these tasks. Until yesterday, communications from the director's office had always come through an agent or an assistant director. Sharp must have a vested interest in this case. Either that, or he was trying to keep a lid on it. Or both.

David had decided not to program the coordinates into the car's navigation system. It wasn't that he was a Luddite, he just liked maps. His office was decorated with them. Afghanistan, Kuwait, Iraq, and other maps of countries in which he had served. Unofficially, of course. Visitors to his office would sometimes inquire about the maps, to which he would reply, "Never been, but I hear it's nice." Superiors that were "in the know" probably saw them as a warning; David was reminding them that he could blow the whistle if they ever crossed him. That wasn't his intention, but he was fine with it. He just liked maps. On his birthday, Marissa had given him a framed print of an old map of D.C. before there were interstates or monuments. It was one of his favorites.

The sound of gravel giving way to dirt road told him he was getting close. He consulted the county map one last time, then considered using the GPS after all as there were no landmarks to be found. He slowed down and opened the windows to let the fresh country air wash over him. Tall grasses on either side of the road obscured what lay beyond.

"Well, damn." he said.

That was when he spotted the chunk of earth in the middle of the road. It was the size of a tractor tire. He slammed on the brakes, enveloping the misplaced chunk in a cloud of dust. He killed the engine and climbed onto the hood of the sedan to get a higher vantage point from where he could scan the countryside. The fields stretched into rolling hills in both directions. A farmhouse was nestled in a grove of young fir trees in the far distance. He picked a direction and dropped onto the road, deciding that a spiral search pattern would be the best strategy. David found the crater an hour later.

There was no doubt about it. This was the result of an impact. The debris pattern was uniform and directed away from the center. Striations in the bowl suggested a blast formation he had seen before. He approached the edge and dropped to a knee for a closer look.

After a careful inspection of the circumference of the rim, David counted three sets of footprints. But only five shoeprints? It didn't make sense. Then he spotted the bare footprint, possibly created from a socked foot. It appeared as though a male with a size eleven shoe had entered the crater, but two had people left. The person who had left the crater without entering it was missing a shoe. A much smaller shoe.

David stood up and estimated the trajectory of the footprints leading away. Unless they had changed direction after leaving the immediate vicinity of the crater, the footprints led back to the road. He made a mental note to search for tire tracks and pulled out his smartphone to snap a couple of photos of the prints, then took several steps back to capture the entire crater. Satisfied that he had what he needed, he descended into the pit.

A flash of white caught his eye as he rooted through the loose dirt with his spring-assisted knife. He pushed the earth aside with his hands until he saw it a white aglet protruding from the clumps. David produced a pair of latex gloves from his jacket and slipped them over his hands. He took the tip of the shoestring between thumb and forefinger and pulled a shoe from the dirt, brushing away loose debris for a better look. It was a women's size seven low-cut Chuck Taylor All-Stars, patterned in red and black plaid.

David stroked his chin as the clues came together.

One person had entered the crater, and two had left. Better yet, one person had entered the crater from the ground, the other from the air. The airborne subject had crashed into the field with enough force to knock her shoe—and he was now sure it was a "her"—completely off, creating an impact crater roughly twenty feet in diameter. Ignoring for a moment the fact that he should be standing ankle deep in a pile of gore and powdered bones, he pulled some quick statistics from memory to assist in his summations. The average height of an American woman is around five feet, five inches. Average weight is 145lbs. The asset captured her at around one thousand feet, but she could have gone higher after the UAV was out of range. He figured in terminal velocity and the depth and circumference of the hole.

David climbed out of the crater and took a few steps back. He looked up into the clear morning sky, then followed an imaginary line downward to the center of the hole. It didn't add up. There should be a shallow indentation in the earth at best. Not a crater over five yards wide. Whatever had impacted there had been much larger.

It just didn't make sense. Not yet.

Chapter Eight

THE NIGHTMARES FINALLY STOPPED. Samantha wasn't sure if it was because she was getting better at controlling her abilities or because she had almost flattened herself into a human pancake while trying to get better control of her abilities. Maybe they had stopped due to the shock to her system or the trauma of a near-death experience. She speared a hunk of radicchio and decided not to overanalyze the situation. She was just grateful that she was sleeping through the night—or morning, as it were—and waking up to an intact bedroom.

The pre-work dinner location she had chosen that day was the Washington Monument. It was her favorite monument, simple and majestic—and more than a little phallic, but that was just a coincidence. Parliament's *Chocolate City* filtered through her headphones as she sat on a well-worn bench picking at her salad. It was a gorgeous afternoon, and the usual throng of tourists surrounded the towering pillar taking selfies and commenting on its grandeur. Every time Samantha visited the monument, the tourists would invariably question the color difference in the stone that began about 150 feet up the obelisk. Evan once told her that production had halted for over twenty years due to funding issues and, when construction had resumed, the marble had been taken from a different source. She wasn't sure how accurate that was, but he seemed to be full of useless facts that tended to be correct more often than not. Samantha wondered what the city would look like from the very top of the structure, and decided she might one day sneak a trip up there. It was only 555 feet tall. She'd been much higher than that.

"That is disgusting! Where are their parents?"

A middle-aged woman wearing a fanny pack and pushing a twin stroller passed Samantha's bench. Her husband was busy taking snapshots of the monument, oblivious to her protests. Samantha followed the mother's gaze to the source of her disgust. A young couple was engaged in an intense, slobbery lip lock, their hands exploring places in ways better left to the bedroom.

That's just a bit too much PDA with children around. Or decent adults, for that matter.

Most of the tourists gave the couple a wide berth, but others held up their phones to film the public love scene with devious grins on their faces. Samantha rested her fork on the plastic food container and set it in her lap. She sipped at her vitamin-infused water and considered the couple's clothes. The young man wore black skinny jeans, while the girl was clad in short Daisy Dukes. Samantha felt the light bulb switch on above her head.

Depants commencing in T-minus 5...4...3...2...

She willed their pants around their ankles. They had no idea what had happened at first, but their fiery lust was quenched when people broke into fits of laughter. Samantha managed to hold in her own giggles until the couple became aware of their wardrobe malfunctions and tried to disengage. They fell flat on their rear ends like a pair of Vaudevillian comedians. This brought a fresh wave of ridicule from the surrounding tourists. Samantha resumed her dinner as the couple shuffled away red-faced, furiously trying to re-pants themselves.

That's definitely going to trend on Facebook.

Not satisfied with her hijinks, she popped a cherry tomato in her mouth and sought out her next victim. He was an overweight man with a toupee that didn't quite match the color of his seventies-era, mutton-chop sideburns. He held a small, silver control box in his hands and his eyes were upward, focused a toy drone that was swooping about overhead. Either he couldn't control it very well or he was trying to frighten people, because the drone buzzed the heads of the crowd several times like a raptor diving at its prey. Samantha scanned the crowd and counted at least seven toddlers, five strollers, and two mothers holding infants. She shoved the last bit of lettuce into her mouth and stood up to deposit the empty container into a nearby garbage can. Rubbing her palms together, she faced the drone pilot. Seizing a moving target was going to be trickier than a double depants, but she nailed it on the first try.

The drone was heading into a smooth dive when it suddenly shuddered, changed course, and shot back into the sky. The mutton-chopped pilot stood in stunned amazement as his toy became a tiny, black speck in the blue expanse above. His face blanched when that speck disappeared from sight, his eyes darting from the box in his hands to where he had lost sight of the drone, then back and forth again in quick repetition. Perplexed, he let the remote control drop to his side. His shoulders slumped like a pouting child. He looked around, curious as to whether anyone had seen him lose his toy.

Samantha pretended to look at her phone, oblivious to the despondent man. In reality, she was focused on controlling the toy at such a great distance. She brought the drone back into the lower atmosphere. It dove at its owner, who was unaware it had returned until it snatched the hairpiece from his head. She adhered the hairy accessory to the bottom of the drone and willed it to fly in narrow rings around the amazed and horrified man, who was alternating between clutching at his bald pate and trying to regain control of the aerial thief. It zipped by him, always out of reach, taunting him with his vanity before darting away again. He eventually gave up and dropped the useless remote, deciding instead to jump at the toy like King Kong swatting at biplanes. Samantha was guffawing now. Several others around her followed her stare and soon joined in her mirth.

Holy shit, this is great. I'm going to charge admission next time.

She let the dance continue a while longer, then smashed the drone onto the concrete a safe distance away from anyone. There was applause from the tourists. The man hustled to his busted toy and bent over to retrieve his toupee, but it skittered away from him like a bashful squirrel.

Tribble toupee? Yes, Evan would be proud of that one.

Again he tried to pick it up, and again it moved just out of reach. Exasperated, he stood up and searched for the source of his humiliation.

"Who's doing this? You owe me a drone!"

He was met with jibes from a few in the crowd, followed by warnings against flying "those dangerous things" around children. The man ignored them and tried to step on the elusive hairpiece to pin it down. Samantha moved it aside at the last possible moment, then sent it crawling up his leg with frightening speed. The drone pilot backed away and slapped at it, making high-pitched squawking sounds. The toupee took the beating, climbing his torso and coming to a rest in its rightful place across his scalp. Several tourists clapped in appreciation while others tossed money at his feet. Samantha pulled a dollar bill from her pocket and held it out to him as she walked by wearing a triumphant grin. His expression was still bewildered, but he took the money.

"Are those sticks up yet?"

The Nationals had won a big game that afternoon, which set the stage for the imbibing of celebratory beverages and the devouring of half-priced appetizers. This was the third time Samantha had checked on the order of fried mozzarella.

"Coming," Ernest said again, his voice raised above the sound of hissing oil and clinking plates. He was the best cook the Plot had ever had, but even he had his limits.

She returned to her station behind the bar and tried not to make eye contact with the patrons. They filled every available bar stool, and those that stood behind the seated customers looked for a way to squeeze in between them to shout their order at her. She placed two tankards under their respective beer taps and leaned over the touch screen to punch in new orders before the mugs spilled over. Marcy appeared at the gun as Samantha set the full tankards in front of a couple decked out in baseball paraphernalia and red face paint.

"Tip jar will be full tonight!"

Marcy's optimism was indomitable. She sprayed cola refills into a trio of empty glasses then replaced the gun in its bartop holster before disappearing into the crowd to deliver the fresh beverages.

Another glorious evening at the Plot.

It could have been worse. At least she and Marcy didn't have to do silly line dances or wear bosom-exposing shirts or short shorts. And aside from a few rare instances—Ball Cap, for example—the customers were respectful and often generous with their gratuities. Still, nights like this reminded Samantha why she didn't want to be here. Her college advisors had urged that she use her humanities degree to go into marketing or editing, but neither of those careers appealed to her restless nature. Part of her was jealous of friends that had chosen a profession early on in their education and were now firmly entrenched in their fields. It all seemed too predestined for Samantha. She just wasn't built that way.

"Hey Honey, another round over here!"

So instead, I endure folksy, sexist nicknames while slinging liver failure and serving diabetes.

She dipped a pair of tall pilsner glasses into soapy water and transferred them to the rinse basin before setting them upside down on a bar towel. The technique didn't really clean the glasses, but it gave the appearance that they were being washed to any patrons who might be watching.

"It's obvious bullshit. You can see the wires."

Samantha isolated the voice from the rest of the chatter at the crowded bar. She glanced over her shoulder and plunged two more glasses into the suds. A man was holding a tankard near his mouth and pointing at the small television above the bar. Customers to his left and right followed the pointing finger up to the screen. Samantha couldn't resist.

It was the same footage Evan had shown her of the historic first flight in the Lizard Queen. And it was being featured on Late News Now, the post-primetime comedy news show. The sound was muted, but closed captions appeared in blocky letters at the bottom of the screen as host Jake Mason read from the teleprompter with his customary smirk.

...and this is proof that young partiers will go to new heights to get pervy upskirt videos. Ladies and Gentlemen, I'm not saying this is a flying girl by any means, but Mary Poppins hasn't been spotted since she abandoned the Banks children in 1964. Just saying...

Fuck.

A slippery pilsner glass fell from nerveless fingers and plummeted to the floor. Samantha managed to catch it—but not with her hands. It had never happened before. She'd always had to focus, to direct her abilities on an object. This was pure reflex. She blinked at the hovering glass, then realized her mistake. Too many eyes were on her. She danced back in mock surprise as the glass exploded, shards scattering around her shoes. A round of applause followed, and Samantha performed a graceful curtsy with her waist apron before leaving the bar to retrieve a broom. Apparently none of the patrons had noticed that the glass had never actually hit the floor before shattering. Even better, Samantha had managed to distract them from her drunken misadventures that had now spread from the internet to nationwide television broadcasts.

In addition to the unexpected reflex action with the pilsner glass, another new development was that Samantha no longer tired from her post-work runs. Physical exertion was simply no longer part of the picture. She found it even more difficult to accept her abilities when they kept surprising her with new revelations, but decided to deal with it as best she could. Asking why or how only compounded the stress. There were no answers to those questions, but she hoped they would surface with time. For now, she just put one foot in front of the other. It was all she could do.

She changed into her workout clothes after her shift and jogged through the city to the Mount Vernon trail. There was barely enough light to see the cement path by the time she reached it, but she wasn't worried about skinning a knee or breaking an ankle. Not after Manassas.

She appeared to have the trail all to herself, which was exactly what she wanted. She set her stopwatch and began a light jog. It would be a while until she reached the edge of the Potomac if she ran at her normal pace, but Samantha had other ideas. When she rounded a bend and found a straight stretch ahead of her, she conjured the memory of her test flight. She remembered the sensation of soaring into the heavens at breakneck speeds. She increased the length of her strides, focusing on the vanishing point in the path ahead of her. She could feel the increasing force of the wind on her face, hear it rushing in her ears. She pushed herself and went faster.

The grass and trees closest to the path became blurs in her peripheral vision. The river appeared on her left, but she dare not take her eyes from the ever-changing direction of the trail to enjoy the broad waterway and the historic landmarks on the opposite shore. She ran faster. The lights of the Reagan airport were multi-colored tracers as she blew past. She heard the engines of an airliner overhead and wondered if Cole would be arriving in the same type of plane later that evening. She couldn't wait to see him.

Samantha tried to picture what she looked like running that fast. Her legs weren't moving at super speed—at least from her perspective. Her strides were very long, as though she were performing low, long-distance jumps that covered more ground as she accelerated. She decreased the distance of her strides and pumped her legs faster in an attempt to create the same velocity without the lateral jumps. It worked, and even helped her navigate the turns since her soles had more frequent contact with the ground. It didn't feel quite as natural as the previous tactic, but at least now she knew she could do it.

How is any of this natural?

She smiled at the thought. A bug flew into her teeth.

Samantha stopped in Alexandria, pausing her stopwatch as she got her bearings. She estimated that she was halfway to Mount Vernon, the end of the trail. Only three minutes had passed. Samantha did the math on her phone's calculator, her eyes widening at the result.

Roughly 180 miles per hour. I was running as fast as a Lamborghini and I haven't even broken a sweat. Holy shit! I'm the fastest mammal on Earth! I'm the Flash! Flashette?

Samantha reached Mount Vernon shortly thereafter, then turned around and ran the entire length of the trail twice more. She decided to call it quits when she spied a group of pre-dawn joggers stretching next to their cars in a parking lot next to the trail. She returned their friendly waves and walked toward a nearby thoroughfare to hail a taxi, consulting her stopwatch one more time as an attentive cab driver pulled up to the curb.

Fifty-four miles in eighteen minutes and eleven seconds. Okay, wow.

The cab let her out at the local deli where she picked up a breakfast burrito with extra bacon and a grapefruit juice before heading home to get cleaned up. She sat cross-legged on her sofa with the breakfast burrito balanced in her lap soon after.

The internal monologue from the Plot resurfaced as she shoved the lukewarm tortilla into her mouth. She certainly didn't intend to continue bartending for the rest of her life. Washington D.C. had a high cost of living and, as much as she loved Claudio and her co-workers, she needed to make more money. Samantha always paid her rent and other bills on time—her father had ingrained the importance of that on both of his children—but that usually meant eating mac and cheese for dinner with what was left over. She wasn't getting ahead, saving for her future. There had to be a way to boost her income without entering the rat race of a standard career.

Wait a minute...

She dropped the burrito onto the plate and rushed into the bedroom where she retrieved a notepad and a ballpoint pen from her nightstand drawer. She returned to the couch and swallowed a gulp of juice, then took up the pen and put it to paper.

Ways To Make Money

Her eyes drifted to the ceiling. The pen batted her lower lip.

1. Try out for WNBA, become champion, get endorsements

2. Rob a bank

No, forget that idea. Too risky.

She drew a line through the second idea and picked at the burrito as she considered how she could put her abilities to work for her.

3. Become courier, crush competition with speed

4. Become UFC fighter, beat the shit out of everyone, get endorsements

Now that could be fun. I'd even make them let me compete with the men.

As she pulled a cheesy piece of bacon from the tortilla, it struck her that fame would be an unwanted side effect. She'd be on the news. The Tonight Show. Saturday Night Live. Howard Stern. They would ask how she was undefeated while fighting men twice her weight. They'd ask about her technique, who she trained under. Stern would ask to see her boobs. She scratched out number four on her list, then paused before doing the same to number one.

Fame can't be part of this. It has to be under the radar.

She finished her burrito, enjoyed the last of her juice, then tapped the pen against her forehead and continued brainstorming. After a while, she crossed out number three as well.

Wouldn't pay enough, and might bring up too many questions. Damn it.

She crumpled up the paper and tossed it aside before starting again with a clean sheet.

1.

The pen hovered over the blank line, but every idea she came up with was shot down due to the risk of discovery. She went to the kitchen to clean her dishes, and soon found herself pacing about the apartment. The pen followed her, levitating and spinning in the air.

Astronaut? No. No fame.

Bodyguard? No. I need to make more money than that.

Rob an armored truck? No! Stop that!

Stuntwoman? Hm...

1. Stuntwoman

Wait, I'd have to move to Hollywood. Shit.

She drew a line through the idea.

2. Fly to Africa, take diamonds from mines

But where would I sell them? How would I get them cut? Can I even fly all the way to Africa?

Number two got crossed out.

3. Research old shipwrecks, hunt for treasure

Now you're just getting ridiculous, Sammy. I can't hold my breath for that long. Besides, no water...

She dredged her mind for any more ideas that might be waiting to be discovered, but her belly was full and it had been a long night. She climbed into bed, promising herself not to fall asleep before she could come up with one solid, prosperous idea.

Something woke her up. The natural light in her bedroom was all wrong. She fumbled for her phone. It was 7:22p.m.

"Crap!"

Samantha bolted from her covers and threw on a pair of dirty jeans and a fresh T-shirt. There was a heavy knocking at the front door—the most recent in the series of knocks that had awakened her. She emerged from the bedroom in a power-enhanced sprint, and barely managed to stop herself before barreling through the door. She smoothed back her mussed hair and reached for the door locks. A hint of yellow flashed in the corner of her eye. Her list still lay atop the sofa cushions. She whipped her hand and the top sheet of paper ripped from the binding. Her clenching fist crumpled it into a tiny ball, and a flick of the wrist sent it into the wastebasket. Cole's aggravation was tinged with levity when she finally opened the door.

"Dude, really?"

He was tall like their father, slim and handsome. Behind him stood a smiling young man with a cherubic face. He had gentle eyes and a bushy beard the color of autumn.

"Oh my god, I'm *so* sorry," Samantha said. "I was just heading to the metro, and I...wait, how did you find my place?"

Her brother held up his smartphone.

"The miracles of modern technology, sis," said Cole. "Are you going to let us in or what?"

"Pay the toll."

They embraced and kissed each other on the cheek.

"Oh, I missed you," she said.

"Me too, Sammy. Me too."

They disengaged with matching grins, then Cole waved his hand behind him.

"This is Jeremy," he said. "Jeremy, meet Samantha."

Jeremy also paid the toll and followed his partner into Samantha's home. After pleasantries were exchanged, along with several teasing jabs at Samantha's tardiness, she helped them take their bags into her bedroom, promising to change the bed linens later. She'd be taking the couch during their stay.

They had burgers and beer at Bleu's Beef & Brew—the best grill in D.C., according to Cole—then stopped off at several bars before returning to Samantha's apartment. She had refused to take her guests to the Bibbing Plot, explaining that her day off would remain her day off, and that she would inevitably be tapped to perform some task or another at the request of her employer if she showed her face there. It wasn't the best etiquette for a host, but Samantha was adamant. And she was the older sister, so she outranked them.

She learned much about Jeremy, and it wasn't just the alcohol that influenced her decision about him. She really liked the guy. He seemed to make Cole happy, and that was everything. Jeremy had endless stories about his "hippie parents", as he called them, including tales of living in a commune and how clothing was optional in their household. His first Phish concert had been at seven years old. Jeremy boasted that his foot bag skills were unparalleled, and Cole supported the tongue-in-cheek claim.

"Two jacks," said Jeremy. He dropped two cards facedown on the growing pile.

Cole and Samantha exchanged a look but remained silent.

"Two queens," said Cole.

He smiled at Jeremy and laid two cards on the stack.

"Real classy, Cole," said Samantha.

"Well, it's true."

The trio burst out laughing, then Samantha pointed at her brother.

"Bullshit!"

She reached out to flip the cards over. A six and a two were revealed.

"I knew it! This is all an act to get back at your parents for not hugging you enough as a child," Samantha said.

"Aw, someone's jealous," said Cole. "You can have him. He keeps winning this stupid game anyway."

"My turn? Three kings," said Samantha.

"Total and complete bullshit since I'm looking at two in my hand," Jeremy said.

He flipped Samantha's cards over to reveal two fives and a three. He slapped down his two kings and clapped his hands, holding them up like a blackjack dealer leaving his station. Jeremy had won again.

"Nice work, Mr. Jeremy," Samantha said. She rose to get another round of beers.

"Do you think they bet on Bullshit in Vegas?"

Cole's question hung in the air as he gathered the cards and began to shuffle. Samantha opened the first beer bottle and let the cap clatter to the countertop.

"I've never been, but I hear there's bullshit everywhere in Vegas," she said.

She chuckled with Jeremy and Cole, but her eyes traveled to the ball of yellow paper lying in the trash can.

Vegas...

Samantha set the beverages on the coffee table and tapped her iPad to cycle to the next song. Sia's *Chandelier* boomed from the Bluetooth speaker.

"One two three, one two three drink," she sang, lifting her bottle into the air.

"Throw 'em back til I lose count," Jeremy continued.

Cole stood with arms wide and belted out the chorus in perfect pitch. Samantha and Jeremy stared open mouthed at the incredible display.

"Sorry," he said, sitting back down. "I think I've had too many."

Jeremy and Samantha shared a glance. His face was beaming with pride.

"Did they teach you that one at school?"

Cole shook his head at his sister and began dealing new cards. His cheeks were a deep pink.

"Nope, just like the tune," he said.

Jeremy turned in after winning his fifth game of the night, citing a long flight and beer lethargy. The siblings said their goodnights to him then reclined on the sofa with fresh drinks as Jeremy closed the bedroom door.

"He's a good man, Cole," Samantha said. "He knew we'd want some time to catch up."

"He'll do for now," Cole said.

His eyes twinkled. She hit him with a throw pillow.

"Asshole."

"Floozy."

"'Floozy'? Are you from the roaring twenties?"

"Hell no," he said. "I never could have lived through Prohibition."

With that, he upended the beer bottle and smacked her playfully on the knee.

"So tell me what's going on," he said after a wet belch. "You never tell me if you have a man in your life. It's always about work. Tell me your deepest, darkest secrets, Sammy."

Samantha pulled her bare feet onto the sofa and tucked her hair behind her ear as she took a sip.

Oh, you're not ready for that.

"Well, let's see," she said.

I wonder what he would say. Would he think it was a joke like Evan had at first?

"There's this guy on the train that flirts with me. And I flirt back. He finally introduced himself, but that's as far as it has gone. I don't know. There's not much to tell."

What would he do if I floated from this couch right now? He's my brother. He loves me. I'm sure he could keep the secret.

"That's a start," Cole said. "What about guys that come into the bar? Isn't that where you met Aaron?"

"Evan."

"Oh yeah, Evan."

Cole had done that on purpose. Samantha let it slide.

No, I can't tell him. Not yet.

"I don't think Dad liked Evan very much," Cole said. "Thought he was too...too..."

"Weird?"

"No, although the guy was weird. I think Dad said there was something dishonest about the guy. Something in the way he treated you."

"Daddy only met him a couple of times. Evan treated me like a princess. Opened doors for me, bought me gifts, listened to my ramblings with genuine interest..."

"Then why did you dump him?"

"He was too weird."

She arched an eyebrow and took a swig just before laughter overtook them. Carbonation stung her sinuses. She leaned forward and performed a spit take into the air.

"I never knew that Daddy didn't like Evan," Samantha said when she had regained control.

"Dad would never tell you. You are his little girl. He'd never want to push you away by trying to make your decisions for you."

Samantha didn't miss the subtext of her brother's words. All Cole had ever wanted was to become a professionally-trained singer. Their father had railed against the idea, trying to get Cole an internship in the government right out of high school. The two never discussed their friction with Samantha, but she was well aware of the rift. Cole had defied their father's wishes and moved far away to follow his dream. She leaned over and rested her head on his shoulder. Cole's voice was soft as he changed the subject.

"Did you know Dad used to smoke?"

Samantha turned her face up to his.

"What? No he didn't."

"Yeah," said Cole. "When we were kids, I'd wake up to the smell of cigarette smoke coming through my window on warm summer nights. It was after mom died. I used to sneak downstairs to watch him. I knew some older kids at school had tried it, so I was curious. Dad would just stand there in the backyard, looking up at the stars and lighting one smoke from the other. Then he would start talking."

Samantha sat up and turned her body to face Cole. She wrapped her arms around her knees and drew them against her chest.

"What would he say?"

Cole cleared his throat and drained his beer bottle. He took a dramatic pause to set it on the coffee table before answering her question.

"He would talk about you. He would reassure himself that you were going to be alright. That he was doing everything he could to protect you."

"He was probably talking to mom."

"Maybe. But when did we ever go to church? I don't see it. Dad's way too pragmatic for that. I'm pretty sure he was talking to himself."

Samantha listened intently. Her bare toes clutched at the sofa cushion.

"Anyway, I remember a night when the sky was really clear and the stars were spectacular. It was a new moon and there wasn't a cloud to be found anywhere. I smelled the smoke and crept downstairs like a ninja. There he was, standing in the yard with a cigarette between his fingers talking to himself. There was a really bright star that night. Not the north star. It was different. And brighter. You know how stars like...twinkle, I guess?"

Samantha nodded.

"Well, he would say something and then the star would twinkle. It was like he was listening to it, talking to it. Then he'd say something else, and the star wouldn't flash until he was finished."

"Now you're just remembering strange childhood dreams."

"No, check this out," Cole said. "Here's the freaky part."

"Oh, that wasn't the freaky part?"

"No, actually. The freaky part is that you were standing with him that night, holding his hand as you both gazed up at that star. I remember him looking down at you..."

Samantha hung on his every word, enraptured by his tale.

"...and you were nodding to the star as it twinkled away."

Chapter Nine

I LOOK LIKE A TOTAL BADASS.

Samantha twisted around in the mirror to take in her full reflection. The shiny black leather and scarlet stripes racing down the sleeves of the jacket matched the leather pants she had already picked out. It was perfect. Her bright purple socks with their little yellow pineapples looked silly sticking out from the leather pant legs, but boots were next on the list.

"So these are lined with polar fleece?" she said.

Janie nodded and settled the jacket more squarely onto Samantha's narrow shoulders. Her hand ran down the back to smooth it out.

"Yes ma'am. And a Nomex weave, too. You'll be cold resistant and fire resistant, sweetie," said Janie. "We may not be the cheapest joint in town, but you won't find higher quality anywhere else."

The Stomping Choppers employee was white haired and weathered. Her arms were covered in a myriad of fading tattoos, but a newer one stood out in stark contrast to the wrinkled, pale skin of her neck. It was a purple racing wheel with snowy wings sprouted in flight. The ribbon below it read "Boys Ride Bitch" in flowing black script.

"Good. I don't expect any fires, but I'll be getting into some cold altitu— weather for sure," said Samantha.

Nice one, genius.

Janie ignored the word stumble and suggested a pair of black Harley-Davidson Fayette-style boots to go with the jacket and pants. They had three large buckles above the ankle and one that was offset across the instep. A long, square heel jutted from the bottom.

Samantha fell in love.

Their last stop was the helmet section. Janie kept trying to fit her into a half helmet-and-goggles combo because of the lighter weight which would put less stress on the neck, but Samantha was adamant about a full face with the darkest visor tint they had. She found a black one with thin, stylized lines that traced the contour of the helmet.

Perfect.

As an afterthought, Samantha perused the glove racks until she found a sleek, soft pair with Velcro straps.

"That comes to one thousand six hundred eighty-three dollars and seventy-five cents, " said Janie from behind the register.

Samantha swallowed hard, but pulled out a handful of hundreds from her wallet.

This is going to hurt more than getting the bends and plummeting thousands of feet to my supposed death.

Janie looked at the cash, then at Samantha.

"A pretty thing like you carrying around a wad of cash like that? Brave girl."

"I'm a bartender. I can take care of myself."

Janie was right, but Samantha had to cover her bases. She didn't want anyone to trace her back to this store if something went wrong, so no credit cards. Samantha had even covered her head in a bandana and donned large sunglasses in an attempt to conceal her features from the security cameras. It was a thin disguise, but it was the best she could come up with. Samantha could live with the mild suspicion that might arise from using cash. Credit cards meant personally identifiable information, and that was something she had to avoid at all costs. She slung the large shopping bag over her forearm and waved goodbye to Janie as she exited the store. The cab driver put down his crossword puzzle as he saw her approach.

"Back to Clarendon, please," she said, glancing at the clock on her phone. She'd have to hurry if she was going to make it to the Plot on time. She couldn't afford to be late.

Samantha waited until her regulars were contentedly sipping from fresh mugs before pulling Marcy into the back office.

"Is this about those days you missed? Claudio hasn't said anything to me, but I think he's—"

Samantha held up a hand to cut her off.

"No, no, no," she said, "I don't care about that. I decided to come to Vegas. Is that cool?"

Marcy's worried expression morphed into excitement.

"Really? Yes! Awesome, Samantha!"

They grabbed at each other's hands and forearms in awkward celebration, not quite committing to a full hug.

"Think Claudio will let you off?"

"Let me handle Claudio."

"Oh, this is so unexpected." Marcy's face screwed up with concern. "But our flight's already full. Can you get one on such short notice?"

"That won't be a problem."

McAllister Airlines has free business class.

"Perfect!" Marcy said. "We got a suite at Caesar's. Jim's dad knows some people who know some people. Plenty of room for you."

"Thanks so much, Marce, but I don't want to trouble you or Jim. I'll get my own place. This is going to be fun!"

"I know! I can't believe you're coming!"

"What's going to be fun?" Claudio poked his head through the door. They had no doubt he had overheard at least part of their discussion. "Will it be as fun as refilling drinks for table nine?"

The young women exchanged a look that said "We'll work out the details," and moved toward the door. Claudio stopped Samantha before she could escape.

"What's up?" she said.

"A holiday weekend without my best server *or* my best bartender? Really? And this after your mysterious disappearing act two days in a row? You wound me, young lady."

Manassas had taken more out of her than she had thought, and Samantha had been a no show while she recovered. She had risked being fired by not answering Claudio's calls. Not the smartest tactic, but her mind had been on more important things at the time.

"I just decided earlier today," she said, "and I wanted to make sure I was still invited. You were the next person I was going to talk to, so perfect timing."

Her boss sat on the edge of the small, particle-board desk that was covered with receipts and paperwork. He raised his eyebrows and drummed the desktop with his fingers.

Here it comes.

"Alan said he wanted to become a partner in the Plot when he introduced you to me," Claudio said. "I want a meeting with him."

Dad was trying to get me a semi-respectable evening job to get me on my feet after college. He was playing you. He's a diplomat, for Christ's sake.

"He's out of the country, Claudio, but I'll pass the message along when I talk to him."

"He's always out of the country!" Claudio threw up his hands. "You know I love you, Sam, and would do anything for you, but you're putting me in a really tight spot here."

You're right Claudio, but don't guilt me. I'm not your daughter.

"If you fire me, you'll never get that meeting," Samantha warned.

Claudio was taken aback. "Fire you? What are you—"

"But," Samantha interrupted, "if you give me time to work on him a little bit, I can not only get you a sit down, but I can—and will—tell him how well you treat your employees. Like when one needed some personal time to get her head straight and you did what you could for her even though she knew she was being an asshole for asking on such short notice."

That was unfair. What's wrong with you, Sammy?

Claudio's face reflected her thought. He stood and walked to the door, pausing for a long time as he perused his restaurant.

"Looks like Ken's bottomless tankard found its bottom, Sam," he said over his shoulder. "And have a good trip."

She slid behind the bar and smiled at Ken before taking his leather-bound mug and thrusting it under the tap.

"*You can't keep doing this, Becks. You need me. Call me back.*"

Samantha deleted the voicemail. She hadn't seen Evan since the test flight. Sure, she had replied to a handful of his text messages to let him know she was okay and hadn't done anything stupid without him, but that was just it.

We're not married, Evan. And we're not related. We're not even dating anymore. Back off.

But he was right and she knew it. Evan was the only one in her life who had some sort of understanding of what she was going through, although that understanding was still quite fragile. This was real, not a comic book or science fiction movie, yet his expertise in those areas was the closest thing she had to real answers. For example, his explanation of why she hadn't become field pizza was better than anything she could have conjured.

"If I'm right, and you reflexively redirected the force of the impact into a shockwave, then the possibilities are endless. The sheer size of the crater supports that theory," he had informed her over pancakes at a diner outside of Manassas. "Also, you must have stabilized your bones and organs in such a way that you saved your own life even while overcome with hypothermia and the gasses expanding in your lungs. And if *that* is the case, you're invulnerable to physical harm, both internally and externally. We won't know for sure until we do more tests. Every answer creates more questions. Damn it, I love chocolate chip flapjacks!"

Samantha slipped her phone into the inside pocket of her new motorcycle jacket. *Sorry, Evan, I'm putting your research on the back burner for now. Time for mamacita to earn some dinero.*

She peeked through the blinds of her apartment. The cab hadn't yet arrived, so she had time for one last check. Samantha unzipped her backpack and laid it open.

Toiletries: Check.

Three sets of comfortable-yet-socially-acceptable clothes: Check.

Slinky cocktail dress and heels: Check.

Unmentionables: Check.

While Samantha was glad she had been born in an era when people could say the word "underwear," she was still a fan of the term "unmentionables."

Makeup: Check.

Fitness Speedometer/Odometer Watch: Check

I.D., credit cards, and health insurance card: Check.

Stack of cash: Check. You poor, empty savings account.

Earbud headphones: Check.

iPad: Check.

That was all she could cram into the standard-sized backpack. Her eyes swept the apartment for anything she might have forgotten, and came to a rest on the bowl. It was the largest Samantha could find, an earthenware dish one might fill with heaping piles of food at a large family dinner. A white marble rested amid the markings inside, lines and numbers drawn in black and red Sharpie along the curved sides and flat bottom. She levitated the tiny orb from the bowl into her palm, blowing on it before depositing it into her pants pocket.

For luck.

A car horn called from outside. It was time.

"Hi," Samantha said as she climbed into the cab, "I'm meeting a friend up in Frederick. Do you have time to take me up there? I don't want to keep you from your family if your shift is ending."

"No, no problem," said the driver. "If you've got the money, I've got the time."

"I've got the money."

Benjamin, who Samantha came to know during their brief time together, smiled and accelerated toward the interstate. When he went home to his wife that night, he told her a story about a passenger whose eyes were glued to the sky all the way to her destination.

The sun had settled behind the horizon when Benjamin left Samantha at the interstate rest stop outside of Frederick, Maryland.

Perfect timing.

Samantha had paid cash for the fitness watch in a Georgetown running store. It used GPS to track speed and distance, and if someone tapped her GPS signal, so be it. There was only so much she could do to stay undetected, and she had to know how fast she was going. She put it out of her mind and strapped the watch over her wrist. When this idea had first occurred to her, she had Googled the average speed of a passenger jet, which turned out to be around five hundred seventy-five miles per hour. If she went too much faster she would break the sound barrier, which would be akin to shouting "Hey! Look at me!" in the form of a sonic boom. She'd rather not alert people on the ground to a woman dressed in a motorcycle outfit flying at mach one.

This is so insane.

Her stomach came alive with nerves. A short test flight was one thing, but a four-hour trip across the country...

Stay low and go slow. Don't try to kill yourself this time.

Samantha had included three stops in her flight plan. An hour to Indianapolis, where there should be plenty of open space for an incognito landing, then on to Kansas City. After that, she'd briefly visit the Rockies—there had to be a mountaintop or craggy outcropping with her name on it—and then on to Vegas, where she'd land in the desert and make her way toward the city in short, running bursts until she found a cab or someone willing to pick up a hitchhiker.

Landings, yeah.

She had been practicing those in her apartment, for what it was worth. Her eight-foot ceiling didn't much allow for experimentation, but she would nevertheless float up and press her back against the ceiling before lowering herself to the floor. The trick was to tilt her body to land on her feet. She had practiced the maneuver until she didn't have to think about it. Still, slowing her acceleration enough for a smooth landing while flying almost six hundred miles per hour would be quite different than a gentle drop in her living room. Then there was the problem of navigation.

She'd have to discern her position and heading in the darkness at a thousand feet. Samantha had thought long and hard on that problem. The compass on her backlit fitness watch would have to do. She could always use her phone's GPS mapping to put her back on track if she got lost, but she wanted to avoid that if possible. One trackable GPS device was more than enough. And her phone could be used identify her while the fitness watch could not—she had made sure not to register it. No, she planned to keep the phone turned off. Worst case scenario, she would get directions the old fashioned way: land behind a gas station, go in, and ask for directions. Not the most elegant solution, but it was tried and true.

Samantha paid a preemptive visit to the ladies room, then purchased two bottles of water from a machine in the vending area, taking a sip from one before stashing both in her backpack. She set the stopwatch on her fitness monitor and double checked the backlight one last time. It glowed an icy blue. She then shut down her phone before depositing it back into her jacket pocket. An aging couple ambled arm in arm up the long sidewalk toward the restroom building. Other than that, she was alone save for the MDOT worker who was probably in the back office or maintenance shed. Samantha stayed put, watching the couple through the vending outbuilding windows until they entered their designated restrooms.

It's time.

Samantha darted from the vending building and slipped on her helmet. She circled to the rear of the restrooms, passing picnic tables and rusted barbecue grills before disappearing into the thatch of undergrowth that marked the end of the rest stop property. She weaved through a stand of old oaks, wincing as twigs snapped under her thick soles. Turning around, she could barely make out the lights from the rest stop. There were no shouts of "Trespasser!" or any other signs of alarm. She heard only the serene chirps of nearby crickets and the gentle hum of engines on the distant interstate.

She took a deep breath before buckling the helmet strap across her chin and snapping the visor closed. Clammy fingers found the zipper the motorcycle jacket and pulled it as high as it would go. Her head tilted upward as she pulled the soft leather gloves over her hands. Her fists clenched and loosened several times.

Oh boy...

There was a *whoosh!* of displaced air as her boots left the earth. She concentrated on stabilizing herself and looked at the ground below with longing.

This isn't the stupidest idea you've ever had, it's the best idea you've ever had. Remember that.

She wasn't convinced but went higher anyway, slowing to a hover at what she estimated to be around seven hundred feet. The lights of the freeway stretched out below. The nation's capital shone on the far horizon in a soft glow. Samantha pushed back the sleeve of her jacket to consult her watch. She rotated in the air until a "W" appeared on the compass, then leveled her body parallel to the ground for minimum wind resistance and shot westward into the night.

Wind currents buffeted her as she got up to speed. Samantha brought up her wrist, trying to focus on the speedometer as it jittered and lurched from the wind.

Only a hundred seventeen miles per hour? What the hell?

She willed herself to go faster. The resistance became brutal. She tried extending her arms before her body, palms flat against each other. That seemed to help cut through the wind, but not by much. She became keenly aware of an obvious truth: the human body is not aerodynamic. She flew in that position for a while anyway, pushing herself to go faster before checking her speed again.

256 mph. 277 mph. 290 mph.

The wind tore at her. She pictured herself driving on the highway with her hand out of the window, snaking up and down through the air rushing past. Samantha tried that, lowering and raising her altitude in an attempt to slide through the currents. It didn't work. On the contrary, it became a battle to control her concentration, to keep herself aloft and on course. Every time she checked her compass she had veered to the north or south and had to correct her trajectory.

Like I could ever hit the sound barrier in this wind. This is going to take forever.

Another problem revealed itself as she accelerated further. Her breathing was becoming labored. She hadn't noticed it at first because she had been concentrating on her flight pattern. It wasn't until spots began to dance before her eyes that the truth became apparent. She hadn't thought of the fact that the normal rate of air entering and leaving her lungs would be interrupted if the air was rushing over her at more than three hundred miles per hour. She slowed to catch her breath and checked her watch yet again.

48 mph.

10:34 p.m.

Samantha had been fighting the wind shear for a little over an hour. She lowered her altitude and twisted around. Behind her, dark, rolling shapes were a dull contrast to the night sky. Below her lay a black mass of nothingness.

The Smokies, probably. I must be in West Virginia. Damn it.

She wanted to be in Indiana by this time.

Okay. Either I double my flight time or don't breathe. Tough choice.

Samantha reasoned that it wouldn't be daylight in Vegas until six or seven, and with a three-hour differential that gave her plenty of time. She'd just have to take it slower than "stay low and go slow".

Or I could stop somewhere and buy oxygen equipment.

But she knew that the chances of a medical supply store being open at this hour were slim. She decided to revisit the idea for the flight home and continued on her way.

The flock of birds hit soon after. She didn't see them rising from the black miasma below her, nor did she hear their warning squawks through the torrents of wind. The first one smashed into her outstretched hands a millisecond before her head was rocked backward by a second collision. The night sky and the dark horizon below it disappeared beneath a layer of gore and feathers. The bird might have smashed through her visor if she hadn't been looking down. Instead, it exploded against the top of her helmet. Samantha panicked and spiraled out of control, falling as though she were a cliff diver performing an insane stunt dive to entertain her friends. It was a horizontal plummet at a shallow angle that grew ever steeper. Her arms flailed and became tangled in the straps of her backpack. Darkness swallowed her, and she couldn't tell which way was up. She didn't have time to work out that equation, for something solid hit her with astounding force. A deafening crack vibrated through her helmet, ringing her head like a bell. She felt herself sliding to a halt. The world became deathly silent.

"Holy shit!"

Samantha flipped up the visor. Her eyes were the size of dinner plates. There was no crater this time, or at least none that she could detect. She ripped the helmet from her head and let the night air wash over her. Angry clucks sounded from far above, growing faint as the flock disappeared in the distance.

Fuck you, too.

She retrieved her phone and powered it on after peeling a glove from her hand using her teeth. The flashlight app revealed bloody feathers of gray and black smeared across the top and front of the helmet in a grotesque painting. She tasted blood, and saw that her gloves were also covered in bird remains. Samantha leapt to her feet and danced in a frantic circle, cursing and spitting the coppery taste from her mouth. She went for her backpack to get at a bottle of water that would wash the taste away.

It was gone.

"Come on, really?"

You were the one that decided to fly at night, Sherlock.

She held the phone light aloft to search for her belongings and found herself in another field. She came upon a skid mark of torn earth and followed it, retracing her crash course and piecing together the embarrassing sequence of events. It appeared that she had impacted at an angle and skipped across the meadow like a flat rock across a pond.

Girl, you are so lucky. What if this had happened over a populated area?

Something crunched underfoot. It was her iPad, the screen now shattered and smashed to hell. Soon after, she found one of her high-heeled shoes. She felt like a TSA official reconstructing a horrible plane crash. It was creepy.

The next discovery was the cocktail dress she had packed. The thin, hunter-green material was smudged with mud but otherwise unharmed. She'd have to postpone her plan for a day while it was at the dry cleaner—or she could just buy a new dress. She'd be able to afford it if her plan worked, a new dress and an entire wardrobe of expensive clothes.

A sinking feeling came over her as the search continued. She couldn't find her wallet. Samantha refused to leave her I.D., credit cards, and cash in the middle of a West Virginia pasture for a myriad of reasons. If she couldn't locate the wallet, there was no point in continuing. Panic rose anew. She had to find the wallet. She stumbled over the other shoe instead and, seeing that the stiletto heel had snapped off, dropped its mate next to it and continued on.

Looks like I'm buying shoes, too.

Her makeup kit was strewn wide across the field.

And makeup.

She came upon the backpack a short while later. Upon closer inspection, she surmised that the zipper had broken upon her first impact, spewing the pack's contents far and wide. She shined the light inside and breathed a sigh of relief. The wallet, her keys, and the rest of her belongings that she hadn't yet found were inside. Just to be sure, she opened the wallet. Everything was in its place.

Another bullet dodged.

She tucked the wallet down the back of her leather motorcycle pants—she wasn't going to risk losing it again—and pulled out a T-shirt before stuffing the rest of the contents back into the pack. She doused the T-shirt with water, using it as a rag to wipe as much of the bird blood from her helmet and motorcycle outfit as she could. She noted how both of them had held up nicely during her impact. She then tore the T-shirt into strips and tied them into a makeshift netting to hold the backpack closed. Samantha grew wistful at the loss of one of her favorite T-shirts, a Muse concert tee from the last time they had come through D.C.

Samantha was soon airborne again. The collision with the flock of birds had been a valuable lesson. She vowed be more alert to her surroundings and altered her flight plan, pushing six hundred miles per hour only in short bursts. When she began to struggle for breath, she slowed her acceleration to a leisurely pace and dropped closer to the ground to get her bearings. She stayed away from clusters of light that would occasionally appear in the distance. Cities meant airports. The geese had been unpleasant, but airliners would be a nightmare.

Instead, she focused on smaller batches of lights, which turned out to be small towns more often than not. She risked dropping down close enough to read a road sign several times during the remainder of her journey. The few motorists she saw were truckers, and she was careful not to expose herself to them.

The air eventually became warmer and dryer as the small towns grew fewer in number. After hours of flying over virtual nothingness, she came upon a majestic glow on the horizon.

Well hello there, Sin City.

As exhausted as she was, Samantha propelled herself toward Las Vegas with renewed vigor.

Chapter Ten

SAMANTHA SWIPED THE ACCESS CARD across the reader and waited for the green light to appear before opening the door. The room was spacious and welcoming, but she ignored the amenities and marched straight to the queen-sized bed, tossing her jury-rigged backpack into a chair and slipping off the heavy leather jacket before collapsing atop the flower-patterned comforter. It was her custom to strip off the coverlet before laying on a hotel bed, but custom could wait. She was exhausted. In addition to the strain of fighting wind shear for almost eight straight hours, she had walked in the cold desert for two more hours before getting close enough to civilization to find a taxi. The sun was a promising glow in the eastern sky when she had finally arrived at the Luxor. It had dipped well below the western horizon by the time she awoke in unfamiliar surroundings. Samantha rubbed her eyes and stared at the hotel room ceiling.

Oh, those poor birds.

She was still dressed in the stiff leather pants and boots that had shed desert dust and dried soil onto the comforter as she slept. She rose and brushed it off as best she could, discovering a grey feather in the process. She held it up between thumb and forefinger, then shook her head and let it drift into the wastebasket. The soiled leathers and boots deposited more sediment onto the carpet as she doffed them, but she decided to let the cleaning attendant worry about it. It was time to shower away the stressful flight and plan her next move. First order of business: food.

French toast. Definitely coffee and French toast. And bacon. Lots of bacon.

The diner she had spied on her way into town would do nicely.

What was it called? Die Cast Diner or something?

She wrapped a towel around her wet hair and donned the complimentary terrycloth robe, ignoring her growling stomach as she retrieved her phone from the jacket's inside pocket.

Marcy

3 Missed calls.

New text messages.

Damn. Sorry, Marce.

They had planned to meet up for lunch and she was probably worried. Samantha brought up her text messages and sure enough, Marcy was wondering where she was. She tapped out a reply and hit Send.

Hey Marcy. Sorry, I got delayed. Was exhausted when I got in. Flying is for the birds. Just woke up. Where are you guys?

Samantha was proud of her secretive repartee. She was almost dressed when her phone chimed with Marcy's reply.

Hey Sam! Glad you made it! We're drinking and gambling. Vegas, you know. Let me know when you want to meet up.

Samantha considered her answer, then sent:

I'm going to grab some food then do a little shopping. Will text you in a couple of hours. Don't get rich without me!

Her phone chimed again a few seconds later.

No promises!

Rinsing the carnage from her motorcycle leathers was a disgusting affair. The white, porcelain bathtub resembled a murder scene by the time she was finished. She hung the jacket, pants, and gloves over the shower curtain bar to dry, leaving the boots and helmet in the tub. Samantha wondered what the concierge had thought when she had stumbled into the lobby covered in filth and feathers. Then she remembered where she was and figured it probably wasn't the most outlandish thing they had seen. She had to clean up again when she was finished, but eventually gathered her things and placed the Do Not Disturb placard over the knob before letting the door close behind her.

Her first time in Vegas was complete sensory overload. In the haze of fatigue early that morning, Samantha had missed the Egyptian grandeur that is the entrance to the Luxor. She spent several minutes taking in the atrium alone, marveling at everything from the over-arching design and architecture to the hieroglyphic etchings that adorned freestanding obelisks, one of which reminded her of her favorite monument back home. She also discovered that the larger casinos were interconnected, and realized that one didn't need to go outside to get to the next place to lose your money. A plethora of shops lined the hallways between the casinos, and Samantha's arms were dripping with shopping bags by the time she made it back to her room. She had found the replacement items she needed—dress, shoes, makeup, and backpack; but the contents of most of the bags were pure impulse buys. She had been careful not to spend too much, however. She'd need the bulk of her cash to become independently wealthy.

Samantha met up with Marcy, Jim, and their friends later that evening. One of them was named Noah, a college friend of Jim's from the University of Maryland. He was one of those guys that had a story to tell about everything and, if you were agile enough to slip in a story of your own, he'd either correct you or regale you with another tale to top it. Noah's pedantic manner irritated Samantha.

Marcy would never admit it, but this was an obvious set up. Noah handed Samantha cocktails one after the other as the group weaved their way through the casinos, educating her on the history of each establishment. He went on to school her in the finer points of mixology, despite the fact that Marcy had informed him that Samantha was a bartender. It was obvious that he hadn't paid attention. Noah just stared blankly while waiting for his turn to talk again. Samantha eventually gave up and just nodded along with his monologues. He meant well, and was even funny in between his mini-lectures. Also, free drinks never hurt.

Noah offered her a peach-colored, slushy drink in a tall, curvy glass with cherries and pineapple skewered on a plastic pick that leaned against the sugary rim. The group had split up to seek their fortunes, but Noah was never far away from Samantha.

"Why aren't you gambling? Religious or something?" he said.

Saving my money for something else. Wait, did he ask me a question about myself? I'll be damned.

"No, not religious," she said. "Trying to get the lay of the land. I'll play a few slots eventually."

"You know, the Bible doesn't specifically prohibit gambling. It does warn, however, of the love of money and trying to get rich qui—"

"Come on, professor."

Samantha grabbed his forearm and hauled him across the floor to the gaming tables where Noah lost several hands of blackjack before giving up and moving on. He had her blow on his dice at a craps table where he also lost terribly, but decided to stay put in case his luck changed.

Samantha's attention wandered across the craps table to the next row of games. Three roulette wheels spun with a clacking racket as small, ivory balls found their homes in the numbered slots. She watched the wheels from afar as Noah continued cursing his luck beside her. She occasionally blessed his dice with puckered lips that were becoming numb from alcohol, but the majority of her attention was on roulette. She studied how and when players placed their bets and how the dealers behaved.

"Now that's what I'm talking about!"

Jim clapped Noah on the back as his friend raked in a stack of chips. Samantha had been too engrossed in roulette to notice Jim and Marcy's arrival. Noah slid a chip to the dealer as he turned away from the table, then held out a chip to Samantha. Marcy picked that moment to take a sip from her drink with raised eyebrows. Her eyes swiveled to Jim's with an amused glance. Samantha looked at the chip, then at Noah.

"How sweet of you Noah," she said, taking it from his fingers and stuffing it in his shirt pocket, "but I'm not your escort."

Jim shook his head and laughed. Samantha pivoted on her heel and left an embarrassed Noah staring after her.

She met Marcy and the gang for sushi the next evening, after spending half of the day at the hotel pool and the other half practicing in her room. Noah pulled her aside as they waited for a table and apologized for his misstep the previous night.

"It's cool," she said. "I just don't charge for that sort of thing."

She left it to him to decide what she was referring to.

You're a naughty girl, Sammy.

"We're going to see Cirque du Soleil tonight," said Marcy as their appetizer arrived. "You coming? We can still get tickets."

Samantha speared a spicy tuna from the large platter and popped it into her mouth.

"That would be awesome," she said around the fish, "but I want to do some sight seeing and maybe catch a band somewhere. Is it okay if I pass on this one? I'll meet up with you guys afterward."

I really do hate lying.

Jim's other friend Brody spoke up. "If you find a good blues place, let me know."

"Yeah, me too," Noah said.

Marcy leaned back in her seat and dropped her chopsticks to her plate. "Am I the only one who wants to see Cirque du Soleil?"

Jim leaned in a gave her a peck on the cheek. "You know there is nothing more I'd like to do, Snoopy Bear."

The table broke into laughter when Marcy's slice of ginger connected with his nose. They parted ways after dinner. Samantha returned to her room for a short nap before getting ready.

The new cocktail dress was the closest she could find to the one that had been ruined in the West Virginia Goose Incident. It was a slinky green affair with a plunging neckline meant to entice and distract. Samantha could live with the former, but was counting on the latter. The dress was silky and light, and wasn't designed to be worn with unmentionables, leaving her feeling quite naked as she sauntered into the off-the-strip casino. Her golden locks were carefully piled on top of her head and held in place with two silver pins that gave the hairdo an Asian flare. The centerpiece of the outfit was a small ruby pendant that nestled against her freckled sternum, intended to draw the eye to her bosom and away from her mischief.

Heads turned as she made her way across the floor to the cashiers cage, transforming her self-conscious discomfort into an empowerment she hadn't felt before.

My morning runs are paying off, I guess.

"Good evening, ma'am."

The metal speaker embedded in the bulletproof window distorted the cashier's voice.

"Hi," Samantha said, noticing that her hands were shaking as she pushed ten one hundred dollar bills through the domed opening in the glass. "Fifty-dollar chips, please."

She steadied herself and scooped up the plastic disks that slid toward her with an offer of good luck. A game was just ending as she approached one of the roulette tables. The dealer was a large, bald man with a close-trimmed goatee, and wore a maroon vest over a white shirt with a starched collar. He scooped up her black and white chips and exchanged them for larger, green chips.

"Pretty green chips for a pretty green dress," he said.

Samantha smiled at him and placed her trembling hands in her lap.

Okay, I can do this. That phrase is becoming my mantra.

She played it safe and placed a chip on red as the wheel started its rotation. The dealer sent the shiny white ball spinning in the opposite direction. Sitting next to her was an older man with bushy white eyebrows that furrowed beneath the wide brim of his cowboy hat. He moved his blue chips to different spots on the table as the ball began to slow.

The dealer waved his hands. "No more bets!"

The ball came to rest on thirty-one black. The dealer announced the result then swept the chips from the table. There were no winners.

Samantha waited for the command to place bets, and put a chip on the corner of twenty-two, twenty-three, twenty-five and twenty-six. She would win if any of those numbers hit, and she intended to make that happen. Her eyes followed the ivory sphere, waiting for it to tumble from the rim onto the spinning wheel.

Come on, you practiced this.

But she found that practicing with a white marble in a stationary serving bowl was quite different than a roulette ball in a full-sized, moving wheel. The ball skipped weirdly as she attempted to take control of it.

"Eighteen red," said the dealer.

Another fifty bucks down the drain. Focus, Sammy.

She wasn't successful until the fifth try, and even then she wasn't sure if her win had just been pure luck. That theory was disproved when she won twice in a row on the next two spins.

"Well done," said the dealer as he distributed her winnings.

The most difficult part was keeping track of her number while it revolved around the wheel's axis. It was akin to keeping track of a single blade on a ceiling fan. She also had to monitor the ball from the corner of her eye and take control of it at just the right time so as not to make it jerk or jump. Her mental manipulation of the ball had to be smooth and seamless with its natural course.

Samantha bet small and lost on purpose for the next three spins, but she was now becoming adept at placing the ball where she wanted it. She gave the man with the cowboy hat two wins in a row so her former stroke of luck wouldn't seem out of place. Plus, he reminded her of her uncle Robert.

And Sam Elliot. The Stranger.

Her strategy was to bet small and lose several times, then bet big and win. Samantha figured one success out of four attempts wouldn't raise any eyebrows. She continued in this vein for a while, then decided that overstaying her welcome might arouse suspicion. She placed two fifty-dollar chips on the table for the dealer and returned to the cashier before hailing a cab to hunt down her next target.

Three casinos later, it was one a.m. and her new valise was bulging with cash. Samantha had turned one thousand dollars into one hundred thousand since crossing the threshold of that first casino. But she wasn't finished yet. At the next casino, she was invited to the high stakes room where she quadrupled her total. A realization hit her like a slap in the face when the high stakes dealer pushed a rack of thousand-dollar chips toward her.

I might leave Las Vegas a millionaire!

The possibilities multiplied the more she thought about them. There were many more places where she could ply her trade: Reno, Atlantic City, Monte Carlo... If she was careful not to get greedy at each casino, she knew she could turn a million into fifty million. Even a hundred million over time. She fantasized about a house in Malibu. Another in the Hamptons. Dad and Cole would have anything they ever wanted. She'd never have to pull another tap handle, never have to listen to slobbering drunks badmouth their wives or children. She could start a charitable foundation for...for whatever. The world would be hers. She'd never have to use her abilities again.

Samantha couldn't wait to keep winning, but caution took hold and she returned to her hotel room to deposit the stacks of cash into the safe that was nestled into the wall just beyond the door. She set aside one hundred thousand dollars to play with at the next venue, then stopped into a store on the way out of the hotel to buy a handbag large enough to accommodate more cash. Now she was ready to reap her rewards.

The cab driver told her of an old casino that had escaped the corporate gentrification of Las Vegas. It had recently come under new management and was looking to build its reputation. It sounded perfect. She was straying into questionable areas of the city, but knew she had no choice unless she wanted to return to the well-known casinos and take advantage of their tables. That hadn't been part of the plan. She might run into Marcy or Jim—and Noah wouldn't leave her alone if he spotted her. Aside from that, she didn't want any undue attention from "helpful" management or photo-happy tourists if she started to draw a crowd. She had read online that the lesser-known establishments drew locals who had seen it all before. No, she had to stick to her plan.

Samantha tipped the cab driver handsomely and exited the car. The casino building stood on a street littered with garbage. A triple X gentlemen's club next to it flashed a neon sign in the shape of a topless dancer blowing a kiss, while the casino's neon simply read "Slots" and "ATM".

Just one more casino. Then I'll go back to my room and roll around in all of my filthy cash while blasting Ain't No Stopping Us Now.

She was met at the door by a tall man in a pristine suit. He eyed her roomy handbag as she passed him with a smile and a nod. Neither social grace was returned. She strode into the main casino area and plunged headlong into a cloud of cigarette and cigar smoke that hung in the air like a pestilence.

Do people still smoke? Really?

The cigarette that hung from the wrinkled cashier's thin bottom lip was more ash than tobacco. Samantha emptied the bag onto the counter and piled the stacks into manageable piles for her.

"Hold on, sweetie," she said, reaching for a nearby phone receiver, "you're gonna need an escort."

A giant man soon appeared in a tailored, pinstriped suit. He was closer to seven feet tall than six, and was built like a locomotive. An angry scar ran from the milky white cataract where his right eye had been to the tip of his chin. His nose was swollen and off center, having healed wrong many times.

"You come. You play," he said, reading the hesitant expression on her face. He seized the case of chips from the counter before Samantha could get at them and walked toward the gaming tables.

"You play blackjack? You play poker?" The accent was thick, from somewhere in eastern Europe.

"Roulette," she said, peering through the smoky haze.

The clientele of the casino was too engrossed in slot machines to notice the high-stakes VIP walking in their midst. Samantha was fine with that. Many of the slot players had roots growing from their behinds into stools that were ripped, rusted or in other states of disrepair. Luck charms decorated the slots and overfilled ashtrays protruded from each machine like cancerous growths. One man stood up and shook a machine, bashing his head against it while shouting obscenities that even Samantha had never heard—and she cursed like a sailor. Her scarred escort nodded to the doorman, who proceeded to seize the disgruntled gambler's ear and drag him to the door.

Fuck. This.

"You know what," Samantha said, reaching for her chips, "it's late. I'm going to call it a night."

The hulking man was wounded.

"No, no you play. For little while, you play. You big spender so we give drinks. Anything you need. You like vodka, yes? We have best vodka."

She gave up and nodded, intimidated by his presence.

The roulette table was manned by a thin fellow in a black shirt with a red bowtie. He had a hawkish nose and little round glasses over piercing eyes that missed nothing. He took her chips from Scar and pushed red ones toward Samantha. She made sure to count them. Scar took several steps away from the table, but remained in close proximity. She could feel his lone eye on her back. There were no other players at what was apparently the only roulette table in the casino.

"Have you played before, young lady?"

The dealer's accent seemed similar to Scar's, but she couldn't be sure.

"A time or two. But never on a single zero table."

"Yes, this European roulette. Better chances for you."

He grinned and spun up the wheel. Samantha decided to lose for a while. She was down two grand after several spins, and threw up her hands in exasperation.

And the Oscar goes to...

On the fourth spin she controlled the ball and won back her two thousand. Samantha adjusted her dress strap, using her peripheral vision to see if Scar was still behind her. He was, so she bet small and went back to losing in an effort to drive him away. She knew that there was no possible way they could tell what she was doing, but he was making her nervous nonetheless. He hadn't moved after a multitude of small losses, so she decided to try another tactic.

"That's it for me. I might have better luck at the slots," she said, moving her red roulette chips toward the dealer.

"Come back when you feel lucky," he said.

She tucked the casino chips into her bag and retrieved a twenty as she sat down in front of Alpine Landslide, a five-row slot game with stacked screens for winning streaks. After half an hour of more losing—she had no power over a digital slot machine, after all—she pulled a compact out of her purse and pretended to check her makeup. The reflection in the tiny round mirror showed no sign of the ever-present Scar. Samantha returned to the roulette wheel.

"You feel lucky already?" said the bespectacled dealer as he traded in her chips once again.

Samantha shrugged. "As lucky as I'm going to get tonight."

She won three grand on the first spin just to irritate him.

"Whoo!" She spun in a victorious circle, fist pumping the air. "You were right! European table! Better chances for me!"

The dealer was not amused. She kept going.

Two more small losses, then a moderate win. Then four small losses and a big win. She was now up ten thousand dollars. She celebrated by backing away from the table and doing a little dance number. Her back bumped into something solid. A vise-like hand gripped her upper arm.

"Come with me, please." The voice was low and menacing in her ear.

Samantha's head swiveled around to find a man she hadn't seen before. His hair was dyed jet black and slicked over his skull. He smelled of cigars and cheap cologne.

She jerked her arm from his grip, "What is this about?"

Surprise passed over his features, but he composed himself and spread his hands into the air.

"The owner would like a word with you." He stepped aside and motioned across the gaming table floor. "If you please, ma'am?"

Better not cause a scene unless I have to.

"What about my chips?" she said.

"They are safe with Emile," he said. "We'll have you back at your table momentarily."

Samantha looked at the dealer, who nodded in agreement. She thought she detected a slight smirk on his face as she was ushered away from the table and into a back room.

A cigarette burned in a chunky crystal ashtray that rested on a broad table in the center of the room. Stacks of money littered the table, along with a digital counting machine and an ornate decanter of clear liquid which was most likely vodka. Several smaller tables with more stacks and similar money counters were spaced evenly about the room. Metal shelves filled with boxes, empty money bags, repair tools, and other casino-related minutia hugged the walls. A camera was mounted in every corner of the room, missing nothing. Bright red LED lights indicated that they were active. A man in his late fifties or early sixties perched on the edge of the center table next to the ashtray. He was dressed in an expensive suit the color of stone with a black pocket square neatly tucked next to his left lapel. The thin beard that traced his square jaw line matched the stark hue of the snowy ponytail that swept over his right shoulder. He brought the cigarette to his thick lips and beckoned Samantha forward.

"Sit down, Miss..." he urged, motioning to a metal chair in front of him.

Samantha heard the door close behind her and peered over her shoulder. Scar was locking the door with one of many keys that adorned a silver ring. He slipped the key ring into his jacket pocket then stepped in front of the door with his hands clasped in front of him. The man who had led her to the room rested his elbow on a nearby shelf and pulled a cigar from his breast pocket, followed by a golden cigar cutter.

"What is this about?" she said, not taking the offered seat.

They know. Damn it all to hell, they know.

Her stomach grew queasy. The muscles in her legs weakened, but still she did not sit. The pony-tailed man took a long drag of his cigarette and narrowed his eyes at her from beneath frosty brows. His accent was not quite as heavy as the others.

"Vasyl Yaroslav," he said. "That is *my* name. I run a successful, honest casino that I am proud of. Years of hard work and smart decisions led me to become its owner. It is a place where people can come to have fun and relax. Please relax, young lady."

Again, he motioned to the chair. Samantha looked behind her at the towering Scar, then straightened her dress and sat down. She crossed her legs and pulled up the front of the low-cut garment as best she could.

"Good, good," Vasyl said. "See? You relax too."

"Why am I—?" she started, but was cut off.

"You like roulette, yes?" Vasyl said. "You're a big winner all over town tonight?"

That's right, asshole.

"I don't know what you're talking about," she said.

Vasyl took the last pull from his cigarette and inhaled. His eyes locked onto hers as he tilted his head and exhaled through his nose. Samantha couldn't escape an image of Smaug, the dragon from the Hobbit, as the tendrils of smoke left his nostrils. She could hear her father's voice impersonating the monster as he read from the leather-bound book once she had been tucked into bed.

Well thief! I smell you and I feel your air. I hear your breath. Come along! Help yourself again, there is plenty and to spare!

"My friend called me from his casino," Vasyl said. "He said 'Pretty girl in green dress broke the house tonight. You be careful, Vasyl,' he said."

He lit a second cigarette from the first one, then took a long time pushing the first cigarette into the crystal ashtray. A wisp of smoke trailed his hand as he gestured toward her and continued.

"Then another friend called, then another. They all said 'Watch out for young woman in the green dress. She will take all your money.' So, when Olav here told me that a pretty girl in a green dress is now at *our* roulette wheel, well..."

He let the sentence trail off. The third man snipped off the end of his cigar and lit it. He didn't put the cutter away. It opened and closed in his sausage fingers. *Snik snak! Snik snak!*

"Well I'm just a lucky girl, I guess," said Samantha. She started to stand, but a firm hand pushed her back into the chair. She had not expected that despite their scary intimidation tactics.

Okay, this just got real.

"You want to leave? We are having a good conversation, no?" Vasyl said.

He shared a look with Scar, who Samantha now knew to be Olav. The bruiser opened the door to a utility closet next to him and leaned into it. Samantha heard switches being flipped. The LED lights on the four cameras went dark. The spark of fear that she felt upon entering the room now reignited in her belly. It turned to ice and flared up her spine.

"Where is it, divchyna?" Vasyl said, standing up and exhaling a plume of smoke.

Where is what? Oh shit. Okay, calm down. Oh shit. Oh shit.

She felt her handbag leaving her arm with a violence that pulled her halfway from the chair. Olav tossed it to Cigar Man, who in turn upended its contents on a nearby table.

"Hey!" Samantha exploded. "You can't go through my shit!"

Again she started to rise, and again Olav forced her back down. Samantha felt the adrenalin now. It clouded her thoughts.

"What? You call police?" Vasyl said, his accent growing with the volume of his voice. "How did you do it? Give me device!"

He was in her face now, towering over her and screaming.

"I don't...I don't..." she said.

He looked over his shoulder at Cigar Man, who was going through her belongings. He tossed aside her compact and upended her valise before shaking his head. Vasyl turned back to Samantha.

"You have magnet, maybe? Something else?"

Magnet? But how would that work on a roulette ball unless...

Samantha fought through the rising panic and reasoned it out.

They tried to cheat me and it backfired. The game was rigged from the start.

Fear gave way to anger. "You dirty pig fuckers! What's wrong? Someone beat your fixed game?"

The backhand struck before Samantha knew it was coming. Her head snapped to the side. It didn't hurt in the least, but she was stunned. No one had ever hit her before. Vasyl grabbed his hand and turned his back to her. A wail escaped his lips. Cigar Man looked at his boss with a confusion that turned to concern.

"Газа шлюху! Найди это!"

Vasyl was screaming in his native language as he spun back around. His right arm cradled his left hand in the crook of his elbow. The fingers were misshapen and swelling.

Samantha felt Olav's massive hand encircle her slim neck from behind, pushing her forward. Hairy knuckles slid against her spine at the top of her dress. Silky fabric shredded and left her. Samantha's heart leapt into her throat. Her vision sharpened into a bloody red tunnel that saw everything in perfect detail. Her hands rose in slow motion as time slowed.

Olav's forearm was corded with muscle beneath the sleeve. She squeezed.

Feels like styrofoam.

Somewhere, far away, she heard the brute scream like a child. Samantha rose from the chair and wheeled on him. She took Olav by the lapels of his slick suit and thrust him against the metal security door. It bent from the impact. Ribs cracked like toothpicks.

A thick arm snaked over her left shoulder into her right armpit. Something hard punched her in the back. She took hold of the restrictive arm and simply folded it away from her. The cracking sounds were grotesque. She could feel the vibration of snapping bones through the surrounding muscle and sinew.

No, not styrofoam. More like peanut brittle.

Cigar Man fell away from her. She spun to find him kneeling with his teeth grinding together, whimpering against the pain of his ruined arm. A serrated knife fell from his other hand and clattered to the floor. It might have looked dangerous if it hadn't been missing half of the blade.

The notion to fling Cigar Man and Vasyl across the room and flee to safety crossed her mind, but she pushed it away.

They put their hands on me.

Vasyl stood agape as Samantha buried her hands in Cigar Man's hair and brought her knee into his chin. Blood flew in ropy tendrils from his mouth. Teeth skittered across the floor like dice on a craps table. He stopped whimpering after that. She let him collapse and stepped over him to face Vasyl. The casino owner held up his hands and backed away. His face was ashen.

"What?" Samantha said. "You call police?"

"Wh-what *are* you?" he said.

What am I? Good question. I don't really know.

"A friend called," said Samantha. "He said 'You go to casino by strip club, they rip you off' they said."

He lunged past her, trying for the locked door. She caught him by the pony-tail and flung him into the nearest table. Bills flew into the air and fluttered to the floor like wounded birds. Samantha loomed over him.

"You want to leave? We are having a good conversation, no?"

Vasyl grabbed at the money that was falling around him.

"Here! Here, you take! You take it all!"

Samantha pressed a hand to her chest in mock flattery.

"For me? You shouldn't have."

Her heel shattered his patella.

Definitely peanut brittle.

Vasyl screamed in agony. He clutched at his ruined knee, trying to put it back together. Samantha leaned in, her mouth an inch from his ear.

"You never saw me here, understand? If I hear that you mentioned a word of this to anyone, Vasyl Yaroslav, I will return. And not even an army of you slippery fucks will be able to stop me from ripping your spine out by your ears. Comprende?"

"Comprende?" What the fuck, Sammy? Real smooth.

Vasyl's eyes teared up nonetheless. He nodded emphatically.

"Good," she said, reaching into his pocket. She took out his driver's license and dropped his wallet. His eyes were watery as she held the card before them.

"I'll keep this," she said.

She stood and began to turn away, then wheeled on him. Her backhand snapped his jaw and sent him into oblivion. She took a few steps away from the prostrate Vasyl and surveyed the carnage.

Oh god. What have I done?

Three large men lay unconscious by her hand. One of them might be dead. Rational thought slipped from its hiding place to reassert itself as her adrenalin ebbed. Samantha wasn't sure who was to blame, as they had both tried to cheat each other, but she couldn't think about that right now. The fact remained that her situation had turned into a shit storm. At a loss for what to do next, she decided to stick to the original plan.

Get rich.

Samantha seized the empty money bags from the shelves and mentally commanded them to fill with cash. She concentrated on that while scooping her belongings back into her handbag. Satisfied that she had everything, she slung the handbag over her shoulder. That was when she noticed her state of undress. The expensive cocktail dress was ruined and hung from her in tatters. She covered her modesty as best she could and took up the bulging money bags, tying their strings together and slinging them over her other shoulder.

She projected Olav away from the dented security door with a flick of her wrist. He smashed lifelessly through the nearby utility closet door.

That's for shredding my new dress.

His keys levitated from his pocket into her outstretched hand. Finding the right key for the door lock was an exercise in madness. She just wanted out the accursed casino. Relief washed over her when the lock finally tumbled in its cylinder. Her hand paused over the door handle when Olav groaned.

Alive. Good.

That was when she discovered the bank of monitors inside the utility closet. It had been modified into a security office. Live recordings of the entire casino flashed on eight small LCD screens. Four more screens were dark from where Olav had switched off the cameras in this room. A multitude of wires connected a control panel that had been installed below the monitors to several computers that rested on the floor. Samantha ripped the computers from the closet, sending them smashing against each of the four walls in quick succession before letting them drop to the floor. Again, her hand reached for the door, and again she hesitated.

She sighed and sloughed off the bags before visiting each computer and dismantling it with a thought. She was pretty sure she knew what a hard drive looked like—she had dated Evan, after all—and deposited all of them into her handbag before returning to the door. She'd find a watery grave for them somewhere during the flight home.

What now?

She pressed her ear to the cool metal of the door and listened. Dead silence. Vasyl groaned behind her. She couldn't imagine that the cries or the commotion had made their way through the thick door and down the long hallway. Even if they had, the din of the slot machines would probably have muted the sounds. This room had been built for privacy and security, but Samantha couldn't be sure that the ruckus had gone unnoticed.

Have to do this fast.

She envisioned a path from the back room to the front door.

Hope I'm right.

Opening the door, she willed herself to the entrance of the casino as fast as she could. Samantha found herself in the middle of the street. An old woman was pushing a shopping cart across the opposite sidewalk, but the area was otherwise unoccupied.

So fucking lucky...

She found a taxi three blocks away, and shivered in the backseat all the way to the hotel. She didn't have the tools to process what had just happened. She was on autopilot now, yet feeling more alive than she ever had. For now, self-disgust took a back seat to elation.

It was close to six in the morning when she strolled bedraggled and weary through the atrium of the Luxor. Samantha opened the door to her room and tossed the bags inside. She thought about cleaning up and coming down from the excitement, but her blood was still burning. There would be no sleep in her foreseeable future. She wondered if this was how a boxer felt after winning a championship bout.

She heard her hotel room door shut and latch behind her as the elevator doors closed with a chime. She didn't remember leaving her room or entering the elevator. She didn't recall pressing the button for the twenty-seventh floor. Her body was moving and she was along for the ride. Alone in the elevator, she looked at her reflection in the stainless steel doors. An emotionless zombie stared back at her. She found room twenty-seven fourteen easily enough, and knocked on the door. There was no answer. She knocked again. After a long pause, Noah stood before her dressed in a pair of plaid boxer shorts. He squinted at her with sleepy eyes.

"Samantha? What are you—"

Her lips smashed into his. She pressed against him and backed him into the room. Her torn and bloody dress was pooled on the floor before the door had even closed.

Chapter Eleven

DAVID POURED HIS THIRD GLASS OF WATER and returned the glass pitcher to the polished conference table. He wasn't a fan of meetings, but disliked waiting for meetings even more. The ice had melted half an hour ago, and now the beads of condensation that clung to the outside of the pitcher were disappearing. He was considering leaving the conference room when he heard the elevator doors open.

"Sorry, Daniels," Director Sharp said as he entered the room. "I got pulled into another meeting."

David had investigated dozens of cases for the government, which meant he had interviewed hundreds of people. He was pretty good at spotting a liar, and the paunchy assistant director of Homeland Security was lying. David wasn't even sure that DHS was Sharp's home agency, but that was the game they played. Lying came with the territory.

David started to say "That's okay, Director," but the words died on his lips when another man followed Sharp through the doorway. He was tall and lean, his hair a flat plane of coal. Tattoos climbed his arms from the backs of his hands into the sleeves of the tight T-shirt he wore.

It wasn't the flat top haircut that gave away the man's military background, nor was it the urban fatigues and polished combat boots. David didn't need any clues at all—he knew the man.

"Lieutenant Daniels," the man said.

"Just Daniels now, Commander."

The man sat down at the urging of the director, who had taken a seat at the head of the large, ovular table.

"That's right, you served with Braithwaite," Sharp said as he reached for the lukewarm pitcher. "Any good stories?"

David stared hard at Braithwaite. "I'm sure the Commander has some. Braithwaite's great at telling stories."

The pitcher paused halfway to Sharp's glass as he detected the subtext of David's comment. The men's eyes were interlocked in unspoken communication until the uncomfortable silence was broken by Braithwaite's uneasy laugh.

"Maybe I'll tell you a few over a drink sometime, Director," he said, then turned back to David. "These DHS guys got you on a leash these days?"

David didn't miss a beat. "No more than you."

"Daniels works off-the-book extra-normal cases for us, Braithwaite," Sharp said. "Cults, UAPs, things that the Bureau doesn't want the public to know it spends resources on, but may be of interest to national security or, in some cases, military application."

Braithwaite whistled through his teeth.

"Wow, that's quite a step up from Coronado, Daniels." His eyes swiveled to Sharp. "So does a flying girl qualify as national security or military application?"

David's confused glance fell over Sharp. This was supposed to be eyes only and, as far as he knew, Braithwaite didn't hold that kind of clearance. But then again, he hadn't seen or heard from his former C.O. since David's honorable discharge.

"Now hold on David," Sharp said, placating him with a raised hand, "you're still point on this, but Commander Braithwaite is to be included on all sit reps."

David noted that this was the first time Sharp had used his first name. Ever. "So he's been briefed?"

Sharp nodded. "All the way up to the size seven shoe."

"Then welcome to the team. Glad you're here." said David without any attempt to hide his mendacity.

Braithwaite didn't respond.

"Great," Sharp said. "Can't wait to start the trust falls."

He grabbed a remote control from the table and pointed it at the lights even though the receiver was on the wall by the door. The lights dimmed anyway, and Sharp exchanged the remote for another. A sprawling, 4K monitor flared to life on the far wall, resolving into an image of an aerial view of a broad expanse of countryside. The active infrared hue indicated they were looking at a satellite photo.

"Sat Comm gave this to us," Sharp said, then clicked the remote in his hand twice more. "And this. And this."

Each slide zoomed closer on an object centered on the screen. It became apparent that they were looking at the subject of their investigation in crystal clear, high resolution.

"Better pics than the drones, huh?" Sharp said.

"Leather," said Braithwaite. "My kind of girl. I wonder if that's her super suit or something."

David scowled at him in the darkness, then rose to approach the monitor for a closer look. "This is the best photo yet."

"This is over the Ohio River," Sharp said, clicking through the satellite images, "and Kansas."

He brought up the final slide. "Then she landed in a desert outside of Las Vegas. Red Rock Canyon area."

David stepped back in astonishment. The photo showed her standing next to a desolate road, helmet in hand. It would have been a perfect view of her face if her head had been turned the right way. The facial recognition database could have targeted her identity within seconds.

Sharp turned the lights back on. "No positive ID," he said. "She's sloppy, but lucky. Very lucky. It's just a matter of time."

"She's also smart," David said. "She only flies at night."

Braithwaite smirked. "Or someone is coaching her."

Sharp sat back in his chair and tossed the remote control to the table.

"Did you deploy UAVs?" David asked.

The director shook his head. "Priority tasking. Sats only, this time."

"What could be higher priority than a fucking flying girl tear-assing around over American soil?" Braithwaite was shouting. "How do we know what else she can do?"

David opened his mouth to reply, but Sharp did it for him.

"That's why Daniels is here, Glenn. Until we know more, this is an unidentified aerial phenomena. UAPs are in David's wheelhouse. He's working this case with measured patience. No one needs this girl on the evening news. And if you raise your voice to me again, I'll see to it that your teeth are knocked so far down your throat that you'll have to brush with hemorrhoid cream."

David bit his lip to keep from laughing. Sharp turned to him.

"You know what to do, Daniels. And put two G's on the Penguins for me while you're out there. Game four. I'll give you a taste if Crosby pulls through."

"Not the Caps, sir?" David said.

"Not this season."

David and Braithwaite exchanged glares as they rose from their seats.

"Good luck, Daniels " Sharp said. " Glenn, a word please."

"I'll keep you posted, sir." David said.

David didn't acknowledge Braithwaite as he left the conference room. He looked over his shoulder as he turned the corner next to the bank of elevators. Sharp and Braithwaite were watching him through the conference room windows.

The dry heat evaporated beads of sweat from David's brow as soon as they formed. He closed the door to the rental car and cranked the air conditioning, then dug into his pocket for his phone.

"Marissa. I need you to call all of the big tourist hotels out here and get me a list of every female single-occupant that checked in last Friday between four and eight a.m. Also, call around to the taxi services and ask if anyone remembers accepting a fare from a young woman dressed in dark leather and carrying a motorcycle helmet."

"*You do realize that there are tons of prostitutes in Las Vegas, right? Many of whom are into the kinky leather thing,*" she said.

"I never said it was going to be a small list."

"*Okay, boss. I'll send it to your phone.*"

"Thanks, Marissa. And can you get me a number for local P.D.?"

He heard the *tik tak* of nails on a keyboard in the background.

"*Sending it now,*" she said, "*and don't work too hard. You're in Vegas, after all.*"

"I hear you."

He ended the call and brought up the phone number Marissa had sent.

"*Desk. Sergeant Watley.*"

David switched the phone to his other ear and reversed the car from its parking space.

"Good afternoon, Sergeant. This is Agent Daniels, Investigative Services."

"*Investigative Services?*"

"FBI," David lied. Sometimes people had the common sense to challenge him. Especially cops. "I'm on my way to you, and would like to take a look at incident reports dating from last Friday to present. Would that be okay?"

"*FBI, huh? I'll pull them.*"

"Thanks. You're next cup of joe is on me. Anything sexy happen over the weekend?"

There was a brief pause.

"*Until I see some ID, I can only tell you what the press has put out. Biggest news would be the robbery and multiple homicide at a rat trap casino off of Stoll night before last. Ukrainian outfit. Maybe mob related. Or maybe just a disgruntled gambler. The investigation is ongoing.*"

"Thanks again, Sergeant."

David knew where to find Stoll Street, and from there it wasn't difficult to find the murder scene. Yellow police tape and a trespassing notice sealed the facade of the dark building.

"You can't go in there."

A rail thin, elderly lady with leathery brown skin stood staring at him from behind a grocery cart filled with dozens of plastic bags of various sizes, shapes, and colors.

"That's sealed. You can't go in there," she said.

David's knife said otherwise.

Like most—if not all—casinos, there were no windows. The interior was pitch black save for the dull, red glow of several exit signs. The beam from David's small mag light swept through the main entryway and into the spacious area of the casino proper. Ranks of slot machines stood dark and silent in eerie contrast to their purpose. Personal tokens of luck still adorned many of the machines, indicating that the patrons had fled the scene at the sound of the first gunshots. His light reflected from the mirror behind a large bar that spanned the majority of the south wall. Drinks sat half empty. Flies buzzed around abandoned plates of appetizers. Decks of cards and stacks of casino chips lay scattered atop the gaming tables that dotted the room.

He found the first victim behind the cashier counter. An outline of white tape showed where the body had slumped to the floor with its back to the wall, legs sprawled apart in the throes of death. Blood decorated the velvety wallpaper in the head area of the outline. An evidence marker was tacked beside two forty-five caliber bullet holes in the middle of the bloodstains. He pivoted to shine the light on the thick, bulletproof glass and found it intact, then knelt to inspect the door frame through which he had entered the cashier cage. There were no signs of forced entry. Either the killer had stolen the key from an employee, or was an employee himself. Or *her*self.

David surmised that the next victim had been the roulette dealer. The large white outline on the floor behind the roulette table suggested a male when compared to the smaller outline in the cashier cage, which now indicated a female. Not a fact. Just a hunch. But his hunches were usually correct. Two triangular evidence markers near this outline implied that spent round casings had been collected as evidence during the initial investigation.

He swiveled the flashlight upward to scan the entire ceiling and counted five tinted camera domes protruding from the tiles. The police detectives had most likely confiscated the security videos but David wanted to see for himself. He found a narrow hallway in one corner of the room and followed it until the corridor ended in an open door. David stepped through to find three more white outlines. The floor and several broad tables were decorated with evidence markers, as were the shelving units that lined the walls. It was a lot to take in, but David took his time.

The blood patterns were very similar to those of the previous victims, all of them head shots. David scratched his chin and put the pieces together. These weren't happenstance murders, results of a botched robbery or a psychotic gambler. These were executions.

He stepped back and widened the beam of light. More blood was evident, but not from bullet wounds to the head. Large droplets and pools showed spillage, not spatter. Had the murderer—or murderers—beaten the victims before shooting them? No, that wasn't consistent with his knowledge of execution-style killings. Why waste time?

"The plot thickens," he said in a half whisper.

Another scan of the room revealed cash counting machines littered across the tables, but no cash. Either it had been taken into evidence or this had indeed been a botched robbery after all.

He found the security monitoring station inside a converted utility closet near the main entry door. Small monitors decorated a control console, their screens dark and lifeless. Frayed wires and broken cables stuck out from beneath the console in chaotic disarray, as though someone had ripped out the computers by hand. He turned away from the security closet and inspected the floor of the main room, his light held at a shallow angle beneath the tables. A smashed USB receiver was nestled against a table leg. Not far beyond it was what appeared to be a CPU fan. David stood up and shined the light over the security closet door. He tested a theory by flicking the beam to the nearest wall as though following an imaginary trajectory. Sure enough, a chunk of sheet rock was missing. There was no evidence marker beside the hole. Either CSI had missed the computer parts and the fact that someone had chucked a computer across the room, or hadn't deemed this evidence to be pertinent to their investigation. David knew sloppy detective work when he saw it and, if they had missed those items, there would be other gems to discover.

It took him close to an hour of intense searching to find the clue he had been waiting for: a piece of green fabric that lay in the corner of the room just below the hinge of the security closet door. It was perhaps ten inches long, thin with frayed silk at both ends. David brought it to his nose. Perspiration mingled with a faint lavender and vanilla scent. A fragrance a woman might select for a lotion or body wash. He tucked it into his pocket and turned to leave. That was when he spied the indentation in the entry door. The thick, metal entry door. Something had smashed into it from the *inside*.

The morgue was cold and sterile, but the county coroner's assistant was warm and vibrant. It was a strange dichotomy.

"What can I do for you, Agent Daniels?"

She had a pleasant disposition for someone whose bread and butter was death. Her eyes were blue as a summer sky and the pink in her cheeks wasn't enhanced by cosmetics. An orchid that matched her cheeks perched in her hair Hawaiian style and bobbed about when she spoke. She nodded her head a lot for some reason, and not always in an affirmative manner. He decided he would ask her a question that would garner a negative response just to see what would happen.

"Thanks for seeing me on such short notice," he said. "I'm investigating the murders at the casino off of Stoll Street. Sorry, I didn't catch the name of it."

"Oh yes," she nodded, "I don't think that casino ever had a name. Not a very nice place, from what I've heard. Sign in here and follow me."

She pushed a clipboard toward him and set off down the hall. David mimed his signature, then dropped the pen and followed her into an examination room. One entire wall was a bank of cold storage units.

"Which one do you need to see?" she said, donning a pair of latex gloves.

"All of them. Have they been autopsied yet?"

The flower bounced up and down as she handed him a stack of reports. "Yep. We'll start with Miss Lafayette."

A blast of cold air washed over David when she opened the stainless steel door. The tray slid toward them on squeaky rails. She unzipped the body bag and parted it to reveal an elderly woman with bushy white hair and painted eyebrows of ashy kohl. The stitches of the Y incision that spread down her chest pulled at her parchment skin, tearing it in several places. Her blue lips were parted just enough to illustrate the sharp inhale that had been her last breath. Twin holes decorated her wrinkled forehead.

David consulted the report.

Two .45 caliber slugs entered the frontal lobe at 15 degrees, piercing the parietal lobe before exiting through the skull to the rear of the cranium.

"Were there any other injuries? I don't see anything here," he said.

The assistant coroner shook her head. David's experiment was a success.

"No. Mr. Blatsky—the roulette dealer, I believe—sustained only gunshot wounds as well," she said. "The other three are a different story."

David arched an eyebrow. "Show me."

All of the cadavers revealed double taps to the head, which confirmed David's hypothesis. These were professional hits. In addition to the bullet wounds on the last three victims, there were broken jaws, missing teeth, and crushed bones. The gargantuan man with the scarred face was the worst. His sternum had been cracked, ribs shattered beyond repair, and his spine broken in the thoracic vertebra region. The radius and ulna in his right arm had been pulverized into powder. But the cause of death for all five of the victims was from small firearms discharge. That meant these three had indeed been beaten to a pulp before being executed.

But why? David ran a hand through his hair and frowned at the reports in his hand.

"I see that the times of death for all five of them are within three minutes of each other," he said. "But is there a way to tell how much time passed between the injuries for these three and when they were shot?"

She nodded. David's eyes were drawn to the dancing flower.

"The coagulation of blood in and around the wounds," she explained. "I think it's deeper in the reports."

She leaned close and flipped through the pages in his hand, pointing to a bordered table that illustrated a timeline for Olav Stokelski. "Here."

David skimmed the page for evidence to confirm his suspicions. He knew it was right there in front of him, he just needed to fit the pieces together. He flipped to the timelines for each of the men that had sustained bodily injuries. That was when he saw it. The answer was within his grasp, but one piece was missing.

"Thank you very much." He handed the autopsy reports back to the assistant coroner and left the room in a rush.

His phone pinged as soon as he closed the door to his rental car. Marissa had just Emailed him the list he had requested, but he didn't have time to go through it at the moment. He started the car and pulled into traffic, drawing shouts and angry honks from the motorists he had just cut off.

David's car screeched to a halt in front of the gentlemen's club next to the scene of the crime. He jumped out, not bothering to shut off the engine or even close the car door as he hustled up the sidewalk. His head swiveled about, eyes darting in every direction. She had to be here somewhere.

"Come on..."

He heard the screeching of metal wheels behind him, and pivoted to spot the leathery old lady who had warned him about entering the casino making her way around the corner. She parked her shopping cart and bent over a garbage can, her gangly arms disappearing inside.

"Ma'am!" He jogged toward the woman, startling her. She raised up out of the can with a quickness that belied her age.

"I lost my earring," she lied, taking the handle of her cart and aiming it at the crosswalk.

"No, no wait. I don't care about that," he said, slipping a twenty-dollar bill from his money clip. "You spoke to me earlier. In front of the casino."

If she had a recollection of their encounter, David was unable to tell. Her eyes were glued to the money in his hand.

"Were you here late Friday night, or early Saturday rather, just before dawn?"

He held the bill out to her. She snatched it away with knobby, claw-like fingers.

"Might be that I could've been," she said.

"Did you see someone run out of this casino?" He pointed to the dark, abandoned building. "A young woman?"

She nodded.

"She was a sweet thing, but looked scared. Those foreigners probably did something untoward."

David suppressed his excitement and thought it through. "What time was that? Do you remember?"

The woman made a show of trying to remember the details. She elicited a long, drawn out "Hmm..." as she tapped her chin and gazed into the sky.

Another twenty seemed to improve her memory.

"Well, Razzles was still open when she left," she said, "and they close at six. They open back up around eleven. That gives them plenty of time to clean the booths, you understand."

Missing teeth turned her S's and Z's into whistles. David found it quite distracting. "And did you hear gunshots before she left the casino?"

She shook her head. "No, by then I was doing my morning ablutions about a block away. I thought them kids was playing with firecrackers again, until I heard all of the sirens. No, that whole mess came later."

"Thank you."

He turned to leave, but a notion stopped him. "What can you tell me about her?"

She pondered for a moment, then looked at his pocket.

"You're a battle axe, you know that?" he said, offering a third twenty-dollar bill.

It joined the other bills inside her sweat-stained tube top, which she unceremoniously pulled higher on her emaciated chest.

"She was in a tight green number, but it was messy with blood and torn to hell. It didn't cover her very well, the poor thing. Her hair was all mussed too."

David leaned in, unwilling to miss a single word despite her odor.

"Did you see any distinguishing marks? Tattoos? Scars? Piercings?"

She shook her head. David considered for a moment.

"What color was her hair?"

The woman placed a finger over one nostril then turned to the side and shot mucous from her other nostril. David grimaced as he heard it hit the street.

"As golden as a Tallahassee sunrise," said the homeless woman.

Chapter Twelve

SAMANTHA HAD JUST FINISHED BRAIDING HER HAIR when another text message came in. It was Noah. Again.

Why do I have a habit of making messes?

She slid her thumb across the screen and summoned the messaging app.

Noah

10:14 a.m.

Did you know that sex burns 360 calories an hour? Have you worked out yet today?

Samantha scrolled down.

2:35 p.m.

Hey sorry. That was inappropriate.

Samantha scrolled down.

6:09 p.m.

I guess "What happens in Vegas...", huh?

Her thoughts went to Vasyl Yaroslav and the suitcase full of his money under her bed.

That's an understatement.

Samantha tapped her pinky into the reply field. The cursor flashed at her expectantly.

Got back into town late. Have been asleep all day.

She hit send. Her thumbs hovered over the keypad for a moment before she began typing again.

Let's leave that in Vegas, Noah. You're a good guy, but I have a lot going on right now.

She almost added "Sorry," but decided that she shouldn't have to apologize. There had been no commitment from either side. It was a one-time thing, an emotional outlet. A stress reliever and nothing more.

And I have other things to deal with.

She lugged the suitcase onto her bed and opened it for the fifth time that day. She liked looking at the money, but not the memories that came with it. Flecks of dried blood dotted several of the stacks. She made a mental note to wash the money when she was able to. When she was ready. The events of that night entered her mind uninvited, as they had the entire flight home.

Let it out. You'll feel better.

She felt no remorse over putting those three goons in the hospital. They had earned that themselves. No, she was experiencing the aftermath of fear and helplessness. She had been a prisoner for that brief span of time before...before she... A laugh slipped through her quiet sniffling.

Prisoner? Hardly.

But what if it had been someone else in that back room, forced into a chair and manhandled? Threatened? What if it had been a normal girl?

Normal. Right.

The film reel flickered into motion She closed her eyes and let the images come. Better to deal with it and move on, her father had always told her. The cigar cutter clacked in Cigar Man's fingers. She could see his mouth caving in against the bare skin of her knee, hear the teeth clattering to the vinyl floor. It was satisfying. Vasyl had fallen like a rag doll after her backhand. She had wanted his groveling to end. Samantha saw Olav's hand striking out, felt it squeezing her neck. She felt her dress tearing away as vividly as she felt his ribs cracking against her fists. She had buried what was left of that dress out in the desert. Vasyl's I.D. had gone up in flames in her hotel wastebasket with what she hoped would be the rest of that nightmare. But she was wrong.

The frames in her mind turned into surreal dreams as she drifted off. Now it was Noah threatening her, and she was powerless against him. Noah turned into Paperboy, who she now knew to be David Daniels. Except David wasn't threatening her. He was kissing her. No, that wasn't it—he was breathing air into her lungs as she lay helpless, cradled in his arms. She was drowning.

Samantha sat up and took a deep breath of sweet air. Her eyes burned and her cheeks were stiff from dried tears. She rose from the bed and stumbled into the bathroom to splash cold water on her face. The suitcase still lay open on the bed when she returned to the bedroom.

How the hell am I going to do this?

Her scheming had gone only so far. It was simple: use her talents to get money. But now what? She knew that she couldn't waltz into her bank—or any bank, for that matter—and deposit it into a checking account. The IRS would come down hard on her. She could report the income as gambling winnings, which was true for most of it, but giving half of her money to the government would be a hard pill to swallow considering all she had gone through to get it. She needed a legal explanation for it, and had to figure out what that would be sooner rather than later. She had cleared out her savings account to fund the venture, and now had no idea how she was going to pay next month's rent.

Samantha supposed she could launder the money somehow. She had loved Breaking Bad, after all. Walter and Skyler had purchased a car wash, gradually feeding the drug money into their earnings to make it look legitimate. She doubted she had the patience for such a scam.

You had better learn patience, Sammy, or you're going to get caught. And not just with the money.

Her stomach agreed, and said so with a hunger gurgle. Samantha placed a pin in the laundering idea and decided to go out for a gyro. She took a stroll around Clarendon after dinner and attempted to put money, casinos, one night stands, and supernatural abilities out of her mind. For now, she just wanted to people watch.

The sun was setting behind the buildings along Clarendon's main drag as she reclined on a bench and let the warm summer breeze tousle her braid. Samantha was glad she had taken the extra day off from the Plot. Jetlag was a bitch, especially when fighting six hundred mile-per-hour winds without a pressurized cabin. The oxygen tank and mask had been a nice touch; she had been able to breathe while sustaining high speeds on the flight home, which she completed in half the time of her troubled journey westward. The trick had been to set the tank's air pressure just right depending on her altitude. She thanked YouTube for that knowledge. Samantha decided she would try scuba diving one of these days.

A passerby dropped a folded commuter newspaper on the far side of her bench and kept walking.

Looks like a nice night for sudoku.

She reached for the paper before realizing she didn't have a pen, but unfolded the paper anyway. The front page headline screamed at her.

Massacre At Las Vegas Casino

Samantha's heart skipped a beat. Her palms went clammy. Despite her best efforts, she couldn't stop her eyes from moving below the headline. They were glued to every word as she scanned the article with exponential speed. Her stomach clenched tighter with every line. It didn't seem real at first, but then the names were right there in black print.

Vasyl Yaroslav

The paper began to shake.

Olav Stokelski

Oh god...

Emile Petrovich

The bench lurched beneath her.

The dealer? But I didn't...

Piotr Tchaikesky

Cigar Man. He broke his knife on my back.

Estelle Lafayette

Tzatziki sauce and spiced lamb roiled in her belly. Samantha dropped the periodical to the ground and leaned forward, fighting to keep the gyro down.

The cashier. Oh my god. Oh my god.

She felt a hand on her shoulder. A couple pushing a stroller had stopped and were looking down at her with concern.

"Are you okay?"

Samantha's mouth opened, but she just stared up at the concerned young man in mute horror.

"Sal, I think she needs help," said the woman at his side. "Call 9-1-1."

Samantha wrestled herself back to normalcy, or at least some semblance of it.

"No," she said, holding up her hand. "Thanks, but I'm okay. Bad gyro meat, I think."

Sal relaxed and smiled. His partner rummaged through her purse.

"Well I hope it's not food poisoning. Tums?"

Samantha took the round lozenge with gratitude and sat back on the bench as the couple continued on their way. She popped the Tums in her mouth, then reached for the newspaper again. A second time through the story provoked an emotional reaction instead of a physical one.

No! You're not responsible for this. You didn't kill anyone. They were breathing when you left. Weren't they?

The article indicated that they were killed by gunfire from armed robbers. She scanned the article for a third time, expecting the facts to somehow change and implicate her. They didn't.

Five people were found dead early Saturday morning...

...gunshots to the head...

...a regular customer interviewed at the scene referred to possible involvement in organized crime...

A mob hit on the same night? Did I get out just in time?

No, the chances of that happening were unrealistic. Still...

Would they be alive if you hadn't gone to that casino? Would they have been able to defend themselves if you hadn't flipped out on them? Did they deserve to die for assaulting you?

Samantha felt an overwhelming urge to rush home and get rid of the suitcase. She could go back to living a normal life as a bartender.

But you're not normal. Not anymore.

The nagging question that she had kept neatly tucked away in the back of her mind spilled forth through a mental breach created by pervasive, unrelenting guilt.

Now that you have these abilities, what are you going to do with them?

Samantha hadn't thought twice about going to Las Vegas and coming home wealthy. She'd had the means to do it, and she did it. Who wouldn't? But she had been selfish, and now people were dead.

The train of thought stayed with her on the walk home. Maybe it was a yin-yang thing. Maybe the universe had balanced out her avarice by punishing those poor people.

Poor people. Yeah, right. Well, the cashier lady was nice. The rest had tried to cheat me. Then they had tried to—

Estelle. *Her name was* Estelle. *And now she's dead.*

Samantha's throat tightened.

What are you going to do with them, Samantha?

She had no idea, but one thing was for sure. Her old life was long gone.

Things hadn't been the same at the Plot since she had talked Claudio into letting her have time off for Vegas. She had taken advantage of his good nature, and was now paying the price. It was the little things that bothered her. She was by no means lazy, but bussing tables and doing dishes had never been part of her job. And these new tasks were in addition to her usual assignment of tending bar. Samantha was convinced that Claudio knew she would never set up that meeting with her father—and he was probably right.

"Fourteen needs cleared, Sam," Claudio said as he uncapped two Heinekens and slid past her.

Table fourteen.

She looked across the tavern to the appetizer plates stacked with ravaged chicken bones and the empty glasses that littered the table. Apparitions filled the vacant seats, one wearing a red ball cap and the other with 1980's bangs and garish fingernails. The *tap tap* of those nails on the smartphone screen joined the soft conversation and the tinkling of flatware on melamine dishes that made up the soundtrack of the Plot. Samantha had worked many nights since the incident, and never before had table fourteen been a problem for her.

It all started right over there.

Claudio returned to the bar, breaking her line of sight to the table. He paused, first looking at the dirty table then back at Samantha.

"Table fourteen? Please?"

"No," said Samantha.

What are you doing?

Her fingers found the strings of the waist apron at her back.

"What are you doing?" Claudio's question echoed her own.

"I can't do this anymore Claudio," she said. "I'm a bartender, not a busboy."

His thick eyebrows tented over widening eyes. The tray he held lowered of its own accord. She whipped the apron from around her waist and dropped it on top of the bar.

What are you doing?

"Keep my last paycheck. Put it in the kitty for cab rides," she said.

Claudio followed her into the back and stared helplessly as she gathered her belongings from the employee cubbies.

"Sam, what's going on? Is this about bussing tables? I don't understand," he said. "You know we're looking for a busser and a dishwasher. We've all been pitching in until we fill the positions."

"I don't...it's just...." Samantha searched for the right words but they wouldn't come. "Please, Claudio, don't make this harder than it already is."

She slung her bag over her shoulder and moved for the door. She found it blocked.

"No, Samantha," he said. "You owe me an explanation. If you want to leave, fine. But I want to know if I've done something to cause this. I don't want to lose Marcy or Ernest or Carlos because I'm a horrible boss."

Her eyes drifted from Claudio to the door, then returned to Claudio. He moved aside.

"Good luck, Claudio," she said, pushing past him.

"Goodbye, Sam."

She exited the Bibbing Plot and leaned against the brick facade to calm herself. Benjamin Franklin stared down at her with disapproval from the old-fashioned shingle sign that hovered above the door.

Sammy, what the fuck did you just do?

This time, it was her father's voice.

Chapter Thirteen

THERE WAS NO POINT IN TRYING to go to ground. Her face was everywhere. Every news outlet in every civilized country around the world knew everything about her, and made sure to disseminate her likeness in an insatiable media frenzy. Religious cults sprang up, exalting Samantha as the second coming of whatever form of deity they happened to be waiting for.

That was where it had started.

The military became involved when she ignored the orders to turn herself in—and not just the United States military. The United Kingdom, France, Spain, Italy, China, Russia, Japan—all of the major world players were in an uproar that America had been hiding a "biological threat." International relations had quickly reached crisis mode.

Washington D.C. was under martial law until she could be found. The President and key government officials had been evacuated despite the fact that Samantha had fled the city at the first sign of trouble. She lived on the run, unable to show her face in populated areas without being recognized and either feared or worshipped, depending on the person. Daddy and Cole had been apprehended, having been labeled as "persons of interest." Their likenesses appeared on the television, their voices spouting coerced pleas for Samantha to give herself up. She knew they didn't mean it.

She had been spotted in the air several times by the phalanxes of fighter jets that now roared across the country on high alert. The pilots had orders to engage on sight. After all, one citizen was an acceptable loss when the stability of the planet was at risk. Their guns hurt, but not as much as Samantha thought they would. The missiles were easier to deal with. They were larger and slower than the bullets, so she was able to redirect them back at the aircraft. The Air Force pilots managed to eject most of the time, but sometimes they didn't have a chance. Samantha was mortified by that, but it wasn't like she had a choice anymore.

Her abilities got out of hand as the threat to her life became real. She no longer had control over the power that grew within her. All she could do was attempt to aim it in the hopes of minimizing human casualties. She was a starving, wild dog backed into a corner. Or, rather, a confused young woman with god-like powers that were far beyond her understanding. So she hung on for dear life.

She managed to find brief respites from the attacks on the tallest peaks of the Rockies, but it was lonely and freezing. She had to hunt for food, which usually involved raiding people's kitchens while they slept or stealing from isolated, roadside gas stations. It wasn't long before the military figured out the locations of her safe havens. Then the jets found her and good men died.

The force that found her in the middle of the Great Basin Desert was a multi-national effort. Tensions had eased enough for a global coalition to form with the sole purpose of eliminating the threat. Jet fighters circled in tight formations. Attack helicopters escorted a thundering herd of tanks and vehicles mounted with anti-aircraft artillery. Samantha first spied them by the massive cloud of dust they left in their wake, then the instruments of war revealed themselves. She rose into the air and braced herself for the onslaught.

Guided missiles and rockets arced toward her from above and below. She took control of them and sent them back to their source. The explosions were deafening, but she preferred that over the screams of dying men. Burning metal carcasses careened through the sky, leaving smoky trails that followed them to the ground. Black clouds rose from ruined anti-aircraft weapons scattered on the desert floor.

Samantha landed in front of the tanks and beckoned them forward. Their cannons twisted and curled in upon themselves like gnarled tree roots. Soldiers deployed from the armored troop carriers and advanced with assault rifles in a last ditch effort to eliminate the menace. Thousands of armor-piercing rounds were no more than gnats smashing into her body. Samantha only needed one bullet, however.

A white marble emerged from her pocket and began orbiting her head. She sent it into the ranks of the poor soldiers faster than the eye could follow, faster than a speeding bullet. Blood and cries of anguish erupted into the air as the projectile found its targets with deadly precision. It passed through flesh and bone like they were papier mache, leaving death in its wake. Those that escaped her wrath retreated with all haste. Samantha summoned the marble back to her, sparing their lives. She noticed red stains as it hovered before her. A single drop of blood fell from the orb only to be swallowed up by the thirsty dust at her feet.

A high-pitched whistle echoed from the rock formations in the distance. Samantha saw a massive warhead plummeting from the sky. She could never divert it in time. The armies had been both a diversion and a sacrifice.

She closed her eyes and waited for the fire to take her.

Samantha found herself staring at her living room ceiling. She lay on her sofa with a forearm draped over her forehead. The pins and needles started when she turned and rose to her elbow.

I thought the nightmares were over.

But this dream was more surreal, not as vivid as those that had come before. It was as though she were in a twilight state rather than fully asleep. She had been reclining on the couch, thinking about the events of the previous night at the Plot, when suddenly she found herself starting World War Three. She rubbed her eyes and looked around for her phone.

Her lucky marble floated mere inches from her face.

Samantha jumped out of her skin. She reached out and plucked the sphere from the air. Its cool touch brought back images of the ball tearing through flesh and bone. She rose to replace the marble on her nightstand where she had kept it after her trip to Las Vegas, then entered the bathroom. She splashed her face with cold water and stood facing the bathroom mirror.

What now, Sammy? Was it just another bad dream or can you suddenly see the future?

She dried her face and hung the hand towel on its rack, taking time to straighten it just so. She had errands to run and craved an iced coffee, but instead found herself staring into the mirror again.

What now? No job. A suitcase full of stolen money. Do you feel better about yourself?

Samantha returned to the living room and stood in indecision. Her bare toes gripped the plush carpet as she nibbled on her bottom lip. Someone on the floor above was blasting reggae. There was the sound of a broom handle thumping on the ceiling in the apartment next to her. She hadn't met those neighbors yet.

"Turn it off!" The command filtered through the thin walls dividing the apartment units.

I guess my new neighbors aren't fond of Burning Spear.

"Cut it out!" The protests came again, along with the rapping of wood on drywall.

Samantha wondered why they didn't simply go upstairs, knock on the door, and ask them to turn it down.

Turn it down. Turn it off.

Her fingers plowed through her hair, raking her scalp. It was her way of smacking herself on the forehead.

You haven't even tried that!

Samantha raced to her utility closet and retrieved an old cookie tin from the shelf. She had inherited her mother's old sewing kit when she moved out of the house. Not because she was a woman who must succumb to the female stereotype of cooking, cleaning and sewing, but because her father didn't know how to sew—and Cole refused to sew. Her brother was more apt to buy a new outfit than to repair the tiniest rip. She placed the tin on the kitchen counter and tore off the lid. Thimbles, straight pins and needles clattered amid spools of thread and stray buttons as she jostled the kit about. A tomato-themed pin cushion rolled onto the counter. Dozens of pins protruded from the fake fruit, their tips tiny rounded bulbs of varying colors. She pulled a yellow-tipped pin from the cushion and held it up.

Okay. I can control it. I can turn it off.

She pushed back the sleeve of her sweatshirt and plunged the straight pin into her forearm. It slipped from her fingers and rolled onto the floor.

Damn it.

She pulled a blue pin, tightening her grip this time as she pressed it against her skin. The pin's shaft began to bow.

Come on...

The next attempt was with a red-tipped pin. She pressed her fingers on the top and pushed as hard as she could. It snapped. Frustration now lurked behind her, waiting to pounce. A white pin, then a blue, then another red. Each one either bent or broke against her impenetrable flesh.

"Mother fucker!"

She swept the tin from the counter with an exasperated backhand. Sewing tools clattered against the wall.

I can't. I can't even suppress it.

She pulled a filleting knife from the wooden block next to the sink. The insanity of her sawing at her arm with sharpened steel was not lost on her, but Samantha wasn't willing to accept that she didn't have a say in all of this. Not after that half-waking nightmare of destroying the world's armies. She doubted she could ever make her abilities go away permanently, but wanted at least some control over when they were active. But as the blade dulled against her skin, she started to understand that she wasn't going to get what she wanted. She focused her will anyway, and pictured the steel piercing her skin. It didn't comply.

She slammed her palm against the countertop, fingers widespread, and brought the knifepoint down as hard as she could. Formica split and cracked as the knife struck the back of her hand. The blade warped into a U-shape before skittering from her skin to draw a deep scratch across the counter's surface. The knife clattered to the floor and Samantha slumped over, clutching handfuls of her hair and pressing her forehead to the marred counter top.

She found herself sitting on the floor sometime later, leaning against the refrigerator with her head in her hands. The kitchen was a mess, but that was easily remedied when you could move things with your mind.

She emerged from her apartment building the next morning, bleary-eyed and aching. Sleep had come in fits and starts, and she had awoken many times with jaw clenched and muscles knotted. She had no appetite and dark circles had formed beneath her eyes. Images from the nightmare had haunted her throughout the night, foreshadowing a future that could very well come to pass. It had all been fun and games until she had entered that last casino in Vegas. It had been innocent pranks on the National Mall and dreams of wealth. But now...

...now I don't know what to do.

Samantha hoped some fresh air would clear her mind. Besides, she needed a new filleting knife. She was just leaving the cutlery store when a familiar voice called out.

"Hey, aren't you the Ruby Revenger?" Samantha didn't see Evan until he was upon her. "Sorry, I was reaching on that one. I think Kinetic Star is way better."

Evan fell in beside her when she didn't stop. "You look like shit. Becks, what's wrong?"

"What are you doing here?"

"And a fine 'how do you do' back at you, Grumps. I was meeting a friend for breakfast and saw you shaking that thang down the street."

"Don't mess with me. I just bought a very sharp filleting knife," she said. "What friend?"

"You wouldn't know her."

She cocked her head and looked up at him. "Well good for you."

Maybe now you'll give me some breathing room.

Evan shook his head.

"No, it's not like that. I only have eyes for you. You know that." His grin was infectious. Samantha rolled her eyes, her worries forgotten for the moment.

"So how was your trip?" he said.

She stopped in her tracks, glancing left and right to see if anyone on the busy street had heard him, then grabbed the collar of his Incredible Hulk T-shirt and pulled him out of the path of foot traffic.

"What makes you think I went anywhere?" she said with a bit too much nonchalance.

Evan put on his best "are you kidding me" expression.

"You mean aside from you trying to ruin my late 70's era, limited edition, Lou Ferrigno-signed Hulk ring tee?"

She let go.

"A man signed your shirt? Hm..." she said. "Not that there's anything wrong with that."

"Seinfeld. Good one. Your decades-old reference disarms me," he said. "Listen, I'd be all over the place if I could fly. You must have flown somewhere, come on. You weren't answering your phone or your door. I almost called the cops to break it down when—"

"Stop this, Evan! Just stop! Fuck!"

She wanted neither his coddling nor his overly-concerned meddling. Not right now. Not ever. Samantha stormed away. Evan was close behind.

"Stop what?" he said, then changed tactics. "Okay. Okay! I'm sorry!"

She wheeled on him. "Sorry for what, Evan? Tell me."

For crowding me? For acting like you know what's best for me? Say it.

Evan held his hands out wide.

"For being the black private dick that's a sex machine to all the chicks?" he said, then raised his voice into falsetto and added, "Shaft!"

Samantha shook her head and turned away to hide a smile that she couldn't resist. Evan had a way of doing that to her.

"You're a dick, all right," she said over her shoulder as she continued walking. Again, she heard Evan's footsteps behind her.

"Paris? Rio? No, I got it. Barcelona! Acapulco?"

She ignored him.

"We need to talk, Becks."

He is a goddamned broken record.

"If you don't talk to me, I'll tell everyone on the street about your superpowers," he said. "I'll do it!"

She heard Evan's raised voice when she refused to stop.

"This girl can fly! Right here! This girl has superpowers!"

Holy shit!

She spun on him again, but this time she took the front of his T-shirt in her fists and pulled his face an inch from hers. Her voice was a low hiss.

"What are you thinking? I'm going to pluck out your fucking eyeballs and feed them to you on a spoon!"

Evan wasn't threatened in the least. "Sounds fun. Let's do it somewhere private so we can talk afterwards. I don't need my eyes to speak."

She knew what he wanted to talk about. Her abilities fascinated him. But there was so much he didn't know...

Stop feeling sorry for yourself, Sammy.

She released him, but kept her eyes locked onto his. Her pursed lips quivered with indecision.

You're suffering from this, both physically and emotionally.

No.

Just see what he has to say.

No!

Maybe he can help.

NO!

They were walking up the steps to her apartment shortly thereafter.

"Can I get a soda or something?" Evan said as he leapt onto her couch and threw an arm over the back. "Maybe a Yoo-hoo?"

Samantha leaned against the kitchen entryway with arms folded over her chest.

"Talk," she said.

Evan leaned forward and clasped his hands together. "Okay. The way I see it, I am your Alfred. You know I care about you, and—"

"Alfred?" Samantha cut in.

"Yeah." Evan looked wounded. "Batman's butler."

"Wait, wait. Batman?" Her nose scrunched up in mock confusion.

Too easy.

Evan blinked, then grinned. "Nice one. So yeah, I am here to watch your back and help you along the way. Alfred is much older and wiser than Batman, and keeps him grounded. He also saves Batman's ass from time to time. And please don't make a lame butler joke."

Her carefully prepared witticism died on her lips.

Damn.

She had to admit that Evan being there took her mind from her predicament. His sense of humor and caring disposition distracted her from the incessant pressure building on her shoulders—even if he was talking comic book nonsense.

"So *you're* going to save *my* ass?" she said, placing a hand on a cocked hip.

"Nice superhero pose," he observed. "But you never know. It could happen. Mostly, I'm going to train you. Teach you how to use your powers without hurting yourself or anyone else."

"That you don't want to hurt, I mean," he added.

Samantha drew her braid over her shoulder and searched the tip for split ends.

"Becks?"

Here goes...

"Evan," she said, "There are some things you aren't aware of. I can't elaborate, but people have already been hurt because of me. Hurt really fucking bad. So I'm not going to use my pow—abilities anymore. I want to get rid of them, turn them off somehow. I...I just...I just can't handle the pressure anymore."

He stood up and placed his hands on top of his head. His expression was incredulous.

"What?! That's impossible, Samantha," he blurted. "It's classic comic book plot. Hero sees or does something traumatizing. Hero fucks up. Hero feels guilty. Hero hangs up his cape. Then do you know what happens? Do you, Becks?"

She picked an imaginary piece of lint from her shirt and flicked it away. Evan didn't wait for a reply.

"Maniacal villain appears and threatens the world. Threatening the world means threatening everything that Hero holds dear. And then guess what? Hero puts cape back on and saves the fucking day!"

Evan danced across the living room with his hands held flat, fingers together as he made swooping sounds. "Don't worry, citizens, I was gone but now I'm back in the nick of time!"

Asshole.

"Can we just skip this part?" Evan said, "Wherever you went, whatever you did, deal with it and move on."

Samantha looked up sharply.

Deal with it and move on.

"Don't do this, Samantha. Let me guide you," he said, returning to the couch. "Let me be your Alfred."

She rubbed her eyes with the palms of her hands and let loose an exasperated sigh. Evan watched in anticipation of her next words.

What are my choices here? Am I just going to continue to deny what's happening to me? Swallow the crippling fear and guilt and hope they go away on their own? Try to go back to being "normal"? I don't even know what that is anymore. The more I use them, the stronger they get. I don't want to hurt anyone else. No one else should die because of me. And if there is the slightest chance that he knows what he's doing...

She stared at him hard. Evan didn't look away.

This is probably going to be a huge, huge mistake.

"Who's the black private dick that's a sex machine to all the chicks," she said resignedly and without a hint of enthusiasm.

Evan pumped his fists.

"Shaft!"

Chapter Fourteen

IT WAS STILL DARK when Evan's Chevette sputtered out of D.C. and merged onto Interstate 95. Samantha didn't know where they were going, only that Evan had told her he knew of the perfect place to begin her training, and that they should leave before dawn. A sullen soundscape played through the old, dashboard tape deck that Evan had modified to pull music from his smartphone. Strings swelled into percussive explosions that gave way to low, sweeping melodies in minor keys.

"This is depressing," Samantha said. "What is it?"

Evan adjusted the rear view mirror and changed lanes. "*The Dark Knight* soundtrack."

"Can we listen to something else? What about the theme to *The Avengers*?"

"God no!"

"How about the song from *The Incredible Hulk*?"

"Too depressing."

They pulled into J.C.'s Salvage just before dawn. The sky was a beautiful rosé glow on the eastern horizon and promised a clear, crisp morning. Evan jumped out and pushed a key into the heavy padlock that secured the wide double gates at the entrance. He pulled the thick chains from the steel posts and waved Samantha through as he slid the gates open. She took the hint and slid into the driver's seat. The car lurched into gear, and she eased it inside with jerky starts and stops. Evan slipped into the passenger seat and guided her past a converted shipping container that now served as the main office.

"A junkyard, huh?" Samantha said as she followed Evan's directions through stacks of beat up, rusted out vehicles. "Smart. Who owns it?"

"My uncle's friend's dad. It's the family business," he said, "and the perfect training ground for budding superheroes. Over there."

I'm not a superhero.

Samantha pulled the car next to a massive crane with an equally impressive magnet dangling from the arm. Evan opened the hatch and pulled out a gym bag. He looked Samantha up and down as she joined him at the rear of the Chevette.

"What?"

"Where is it?"

"Where is what?" She followed his eyes in confusion. She wore her usual exercise clothes; black yoga pants, a tank top, a light sweatshirt and sneakers.

"Where is your costume?" he said. His expression was sincere.

"No spandex, Evan. And no masks or capes. Ever."

Evan shrugged. "Well if you have a wardrobe malfunction, don't blame me."

He walked away from the car.

"And you may want to reconsider the mask part," he added over his shoulder.

Samantha looked down at her clothes and thought of the crater incident.

Is that all men think about? What an adolescent.

"Now remember what we talked about," he said as they entered a large clearing in the wreckage. Broken glass accompanied errant bolts and nuts that were strewn about the area amid oil spots and old, broken asphalt.

The entire ride from D.C. had been a monologue from Evan about the importance of what they were doing, and that she had to trust him implicitly. Samantha had stopped interrupting him early on with assurances that she wouldn't have agreed to this if she didn't think he knew what he was doing. But it was apparent that his speech had been prepared and rehearsed, so she let him get it off his chest.

"I remember," she said.

"Alright, good. You ready?"

"As much as I can be."

"See that yellow dump truck behind you?"

Samantha turned her head and nodded. "Yeah."

"I want you to go stand next to it," Evan said. "This will be your first test."

"Test? I thought we were training. Tests usually come after training. Not before."

"Just go stand next to it."

Samantha headed toward the truck. After three steps, something slammed into the back of her head an instant before a sharp report echoed from the stacks around them. Her head jerked forward and she had to perform a stutter step to keep her balance.

What the fuck? Was that a...

She pivoted on Evan in disbelief. He stood wide eyed, the look of horror on his face melting into a shit-eating grin. In his hands was a large, smoking revolver.

He fucking shot me!

"You fucking shot me!"

Evan opened his mouth to speak, but couldn't stop smiling.

"You fucking shot me in the head! You fucking asshole!" Her screams bounced around the wreckage in furious echoes.

She started towards him, her face twisted in anger as she tried to think of worse things to call him. And to do to him.

Men only need one testicle, right? I'm sure there's a hospital nearby...

"Sorry! Sorry!" Evan lowered the gun and held up a hand to stay her. "It worked! Oh man! Yes!"

Samantha stopped, speechless. Her hand went to the back of head where the bullet had struck her just below the ponytail. There was no lump and it wasn't a bit sore. Her fingers came away free of blood.

"I had to know," Evan said. "I mean, I was pretty sure it was involuntary, but I had to be sure. I wanted to see what a bullet did. Amazing. Truly amazing."

"I could have told you that it was involuntary, you prick!"

I had no idea that Cigar Man was trying to stab me in the back. Can't tell Evan though.

She forced herself to calm down. She had agreed to this insanity, after all.

"If it's any consolation, I was aiming for your right cheek. They say that the butt is the best place to get shot."

Samantha raised an eyebrow. "Your aim needs improvement."

"You're able to resist injury without even being aware of the danger," he said. "I bet the nerves in your spinal cord sent an alarm to your brain the instant the bullet touched your hair. Which means your reflex response blows ours out of the water."

"'Ours'? What do you mean by 'ours'?"

"I mean a woman with abilities far beyond the wildest dreams of the rest of the human race, a race that would be insane with envy if they knew what you could do. *Your* reflexive defenses versus *ours*. You win. Get over it."

Dick. Yeah, I'm pretty sure men only need one ball.

Evan walked in a small circle as he reasoned it out. He tapped the barrel of the pistol against his forehead, mumbling to himself. Samantha watched him pace, her fingers pressing against the back of her head for a second opinion. His face lit up.

"Got it! Let's try something else. Becks, if I'm right about this one too, you are going to be so fucking cool..."

Without warning, he shot her again. The ricochet put a bullet hole into the quarter panel of a smashed up Toyota.

"For fuck's sake, Evan!" she fingered a hole in her sweatshirt just above her navel. "A little warning before you shoot me?"

"Okay, I'm going to shoot you again," Evan said with growing excitement. "But this time, I want you to push your ability away from your body."

"Did you say 'push' it? How the hell am I supposed to do that?"

"I don't know, how did you figure out how to do any of this? Picture it, then do it." He pointed the gun at her.

"Wait, damn it! I'm not ready yet."

Samantha closed her eyes and recalled the memory of floating up her apartment building stairs. She had formed an image in her mind of a second Samantha lifting her body into the air, an ethereal double carrying her physical form.

"I already know you can fly, Sally Field." Evan said.

Samantha opened her eyes. She was hovering several feet from the ground.

"Shut up. I'm trying." She lowered herself to the ground and made another attempt.

I got this. I flew to Las Vegas and back. I overpowered three thugs without breaking a sweat. I manipulated a tiny ivory ball and got semi-wealthy.

She screwed her eyes tight and took a deep breath. Samantha pictured a second layer of skin over her own, made of the same ethereal mass as her double, then imagined it growing. It expanded like a shell, like a suit of armor extending away from her body.

"Whoa! Whoa! *Whoa*!"

Evan's voice broke her concentration. Samantha opened her eyes again, this time to find that her clothes were ballooning out from her body.

"As much as I'd like you to continue, I don't think it would be very productive. And you don't want everyone looking at your lady parts if you have to do this while foiling a bank robbery or something."

Samantha's face reddened. She was glad her workout clothes had some elasticity. She relaxed and let the shell dissipate.

"I think you're getting the idea. We'll revisit that later. Let's test your power levels instead. Cool?"

Samantha nodded and pulled at her yoga pants. They were no longer as tight as they used to be.

"Put that car on the crane magnet."

Evan pointed to a two-toned Mercury luxury sedan with busted out windows and a smashed front end. It was from the early eighties, back when cars were made from steel. She hadn't lifted anything so heavy as of yet, but was willing to try. Samantha shut out everything but the old Mercury, forcing her will upon it with increasing intensity. The car shimmied, the gravel around its ruined tires scattering as she took control. The body lifted from the wheels as though being jacked up to fix a flat, then it rose into the air wheels and all. She made a show of not using her hands to guide it. It was just like her phone, like the roulette ball. It was just mass that would bend to her will—albeit with a greater gravitational pull that forced her heels into the ground. Samantha's grin was triumphant when the Mercury slammed into the magnet and hung suspended above her.

"Very good," Evan said. "Now pick up the crane and put it over there."

Samantha's smile faded. Her eyes followed his pointing finger to a spot across the clearing. She approached the gargantuan crane and steadied herself.

This is crazy. That thing is huge.

For the first time since she had begun this journey, Samantha felt the true weight of her abilities. It started as a pressure in her head, not unlike the sensation of squeezing the eyes shut and bearing down hard. From there, it grew into a heaviness in her chest. Every muscle tightened, her ears popped. She ignored the deafening pulse in her ears and invited the crane into the air.

It resisted her command, but wobbled and teetered precariously. The Mercury swung like a pendulum, threatening to tear free of the magnet and crush her.

Do it, Sammy. There is no try.

Her head throbbed from the effort, her breath coming in raspy bursts of air. The crane screeched in protest as it left the ground. Samantha had to use her hands for this one, and guided the crane to the spot Evan had designated. It dropped to the ground with an earth-shaking tremor.

"Okay..." Evan said. He blinked several times to make sure he had really seen what he had just seen.

Across the clearing, Samantha was panting heavily. Her blood was pumping now. An unfamiliar feeling enveloped her. She knew there was a name for it, but she couldn't grasp it.

Elation?

"No sweat," she said.

"We need to think of this as a muscle," Evan said. "As we demand more from you, the more you'll stretch that muscle. So take a breather."

She shook her head. "I'm just getting warmed up."

Evan stared at her. "You sure?"

She nodded and shook her hands to loosen them as she hopped on the tips of her toes like a sprinter preparing for a race.

"Okay. Fly up to the Mercury and pull it from the magnet without moving the crane."

This was going to be trickier. She had to stabilize the crane while shaping her will to separate the car from the magnet. Samantha projected herself into the air and hovered beside the Mercury.

Evan's voice drifted up from below. "You're getting pretty good at the flying thing, aren't you?"

She ignored him and concentrated on the task at hand. The first attempt shredded the undercarriage. She flew a circuit around the car and considered another approach. Samantha pictured a giant hand pulling the car from the magnet. But the harder she pulled, the further she descended to the ground.

Well, shit. Leverage is a bitch.

"Hurry up!" Evan said. "The bad guys are closing in and the poor family in this car needs you to rescue them."

Samantha thought she had a good handle on multitasking with her abilities, but trying to fly while manipulating a half-ton Mercury dangling from a multi-ton crane was a far cry from manipulating a toothbrush and a tube of toothpaste at the same time. She forced herself to take a step back and reconsider. The magnet hung from a steel cable that was supported by a friction-controlled pulley at the top of the crane's arm. If she could create enough pressure to break the cable...

No, that's not it. There's something else you aren't thinking of. Don't make the solution harder than it needs to be.

Evan called up to her. "Here they come, guns a'blazin'! Little Suzi won't leave the car without her doll!"

Then it hit her.

So obvious. Stupidly obvious.

She peered through windows of the crane's control cab and started moving the levers. She got lucky and disengaged the magnet's polarity on the first try. Samantha darted beneath the falling car to carry it to safety.

The Mercury split around her and crashed to the ground in two pieces.

"Oh!" shouted Evan. "Physics, Becks! Physics!"

He ran up to her as she descended next to the ruined car.

"Poor little Suzi and her doll!" he said. "Think about it, Samantha. What happened?"

"I went through the damn car," she said. "That's what happened."

"Right!" He flicked his index finger into her face. "Picture it this way. The pressure required for a needle to pierce skin is very little because all of the force is being projected into the point of the needle. Now what if a plate made out of the same material as the needle were used with the same force? What then? It would just smack against the skin without breaking it."

Samantha nodded. "I get it. This goes back to the pushing thing."

"Sort of," Evan said, "Do you know how Green Lantern's powers work?"

"Of course," she said. "Four twenty rolls around, then he smokes a ton of weed and imagines that he's a superhero."

"Cute," said Evan, "but no. He has a ring that he uses to create constructs of unimaginable power. He makes shapes, Becks. I think you can do that, but without the ring."

"So I'm Green Lantern."

"Well, not exactly. If I'm right, you're Green Lantern, Marvel Girl, and the Invisible Woman all mixed together into a special sauce—with a dash of Supergirl and Wonder Woman thrown in for good measure—but we can't be sure of anything until we figure out where the hell your powers come from. In the meantime, just work with me here. If you truly use force to move things, fly, and protect yourself, then there is no reason to think that you can't use that same force to create constructs. Think about it. A steel needle versus a steel plate. Suzi would still be alive if you'd used the plate, a construct, instead of the needle, meaning your body."

He had her full attention now.

"Here's another example: flying. Let's say you wanted to fly at high speeds for a long period of time and be able to breathe while you're doing it."

Samantha shifted her weight and crossed her arms over her chest.

Does he know?

"You could create an aerodynamic construct around you in the shape of a bird or a plane that would reduce wind shear, provide loft, and maintain a pocket of breathable air for as long as you wanted—or at least until you had to slow down to capture more oxygen by reforming the construct. And air is also the best insulator. Higher altitudes means lower temperatures. If you were going fast enough, the friction heat moving across your construct would keep you warm. Of course we don't know how fast you can go yet. You wouldn't want to burn yourself up, but you get the idea."

"I'm with you. But it will take practice," she said.

Evan spread his arms. "That's what we're here for. Try pushing it out again. And this time form it outside of your clothes."

It took the better part of an hour, but eventually she was successful.

"Okay," she said. "I think I got it."

Evan fired a shot from the gun. This time there were no casualties to her outfit.

"Good, now hold it," he said as he lowered the gun and walked to her. "Shape it into a bubble around you. Levitate to create clearance below yourself if you need to."

She was sweating from the concentration required to maintain the shell around her, but pushed further. She pictured the construct changing into a sphere, then sensed it doing exactly that. Evan stumbled backwards as the invisible bubble pushed against him.

"Yes, that's it."

Evan knelt to gather a handful of dirt which he cast at Samantha in a wide arc. The curvature of her bubble became visible as the dirt dispersed across its surface.

He winked at her. "Just a tip in case you ever have to fight invisible enemies."

She nodded, her teeth gritted against the strain of concentration.

"Remember that you have a limited air supply inside that thing," he said. "How does it feel?"

"Weird." Her voice bounced back at her from inside the sphere. She wondered if he had heard her reply.

Samantha dismissed the construct and bent over, grabbing at her knees for support as she gasped. She hooked her sweatshirt hood with her thumb and used it to wipe the perspiration from her face.

"It's difficult to...keep that up," she said between breaths, "Moving objects...and flying is one thing, but I was....hardening the air around me. I guess...that's what I was doing."

"What you were doing was manipulating molecules, Becks. Decreasing the space between them to change matter. Gas, liquids, and solids are all built from the same blocks, it just depends how closely the atoms bond together. Your potential just increased a hundred fold."

She stood upright and straightened her sweatshirt. "Potential for what?"

"To be scary," he said. "Do you realize what you're capable of?"

She shook her head. "Well..."

"Good," said Evan. "It's probably better that you don't. At least not until you're ready. Let's take a break."

He reached into his duffel bag and brought out a can of Yoo-hoo and a bottle of unsweetened iced tea. He tossed the latter to Samantha before cracking open the former. She twisted off the cap and brought it to her lips, but paused there to consider Evan.

"How thoughtful," she said, smiling at him, "Maybe you aren't such a jerk after all."

"Even superbabes need hydration, right?"

She motioned to his beverage with her own. "Here's to lifting cars and cranes."

Evan's eyes followed the bottle of tea as he lifted the yellow can in his hand. "To your training."

They drank in silence. Samantha perused the stacks of wreckage that surrounded them, but her thoughts were on the progress she had made that morning. She had just performed feats that were light years ahead of what she thought she was possible. It excited her, intoxicated her. She had just tasted power and, for the first time since discovering her strange talents, wanted more.

"So what's next?" she said, taking another pull of the refreshing tea.

Evan was biting his lip. All color had drained from his face.

Are his eyes welling up?

"Evan? What's—"

Samantha's veins filled with ice. Her vision doubled, then tripled. Three Evans danced and intertwined together. Her extremities turned to lead. The bottle fell from nerveless fingers.

Oh god... no...

She propelled herself into the air in desperation, but there was no equilibrium. The world turned sideways and she heard, rather than felt, herself hit the ground. Her eyes were open but unseeing. There was a faint smell of cologne then Evan was there, stroking her face with the back of his hand. The last thing Samantha heard was his broken voice.

"I'm sorry, Samantha. I'm so, so sorry."

PART THREE

FREE FALL

Nine Years Ago

"YOU'RE REALLY NICE, but I don't think so."

It only took eight words to crush Roger Harkins. Prom was still three weeks away, and Roger had bet it all on Mercy. Had he waited too long to ask her?

Naomi had made overtures, but Roger's friend on the golf team said that she was a gold digger. He had heard from Melissa's cousin Willow that Celia was willing to reject Kirk's offer in order to go to prom with Roger, but Celia had a weird tick that always made him think he had something on his face. One of the Gerber twins was taken, but Olivia hadn't yet been asked. Roger considered asking her—she had developed early, after all—but the thought of doing the "twin thing" on prom night put him off. No, Mercy was the one. He had been attracted to her since their sophomore year when he had covered for her in the principal's office after she had been caught smoking on school grounds. Roger had claimed that he'd pressured her into it, and Mercy's surprised look of gratitude had made his punishment worthwhile. Not that it was much of a punishment after a stern call from Father had persuaded the principal to reduce Roger's sentence from a week-long suspension to a day of detention. It paid to have a parent who threw fund raisers for prominent city councilmen's re-election campaigns.

"You're really nice, but I don't think so."

The words burned in his brain. Who was she going to go with if not him? That peasant football hero Richie Hernandez? Jonathan Kolsevich, who used to shit his pants in elementary school but was now a frontrunner for valedictorian? It didn't make sense. Roger wanted to ask Miss June why this was happening. She always knew what to say.

"Roger, there is someone for everyone."

"Roger, there are many fish in the sea."

"Roger, the Tin Man wanted to feel, and he was better for it."

Her platitudes were endless, but they always brought Roger a sense of peace. He wondered if she was looking down on him as he stood crestfallen next to Mercy Werner's locker, his back pack hanging from drooping shoulders. He wondered if his mother was still alive, and if she was capable of conjuring words that would comfort him as well as Miss June's had.

The announcement came over the intercom three weeks later. Mercy Werner and Richie Hernandez were gone, fatally injured in a car accident on the way to prom. During lunch period later that week, Roger would come to learn that Olivia Gerber heard from her uncle Derek who worked on the fire department that they had never seen a car so mangled. It was as though two Mack trucks had crushed it at full speed from opposite directions, not at all indicative of losing control and colliding with a guard rail.

Roger scooped up a spoonful of baked beans and shoveled them into his mouth. He pictured Mercy lying in broken glass, looking up at the young paramedic who was trying to stem the flow from her severed arteries while pleading with her to stay with him. Roger could hear the words as clearly as if she were whispering them into his ear.

"You're really nice, but I don't think so."

Chapter Fifteen

DAVID STARED INTO SPACE for three stops in a row. He couldn't shake the memory of Sharp and Braithwaite watching him, waiting for him to leave their sight after the meeting. David had survived his time in the service by relying on his instincts, and those instincts now told him two things: Sharp and Braithwaite were up to something, and whatever it was had something to do with Sharp's sudden silence. The Director's office had cut off all communication with him. That really pissed him off, but David decided he would continue the investigation until he was told otherwise.

The trouble was that David had very little solid information to go on. He had suspicions, but no solid theories. Was it circumstance that the case had taken him to Las Vegas shortly after the multiple homicide in the casino?

"*Virginia Square. Doors open on the left. Next stop, Clarendon.*"

The announcement returned David's attention to his surroundings. He watched the doors as the train rolled into the next station.

"*Clarendon. Doors open on the left. Next stop, Court House.*"

Samantha McAllister didn't board. Again. David sighed and picked up the newspaper from the seat next to him. Today was the day he was going to ask her out for coffee.

He disembarked at Federal Triangle as usual, but instead of exiting onto 12th street he made his way to Pennsylvania Avenue by way of the plaza between the Benjamin Franklin Post Office and the Ronald Reagan Building. From there it was a short walk to 15th Street.

Old Ebbitt Grill hummed with conversation as people met for post-workday cocktails and appetizers. David clapped Tony on the back as he sidled up to the bar.

"Saved me a seat. Thanks," said David. "I appreciate you coming over."

They shook hands. He sat on the barstool and made eye contact with the bartender, pointing to Tony's Glenlivet then holding up an index finger to order one for himself. His other hand slipped into his jacket pocket.

"What kind of trouble have you been getting into lately?" Tony said after a sip of his Scotch.

"The usual."

David accepted his drink from the bartender with a nod and tossed a bill onto the bar. "For both," he said, indicating Tony's glass.

David turned to his old friend. "How's the Agency been treating you?"

"The usual." Tony grinned.

They sat in silence for a long while.

"Did you hear about that big storm forming off the coast?"

David nodded. "Yes, I did."

Tony took another sip.

"It's supposed to be the biggest one on record in this area."

"Hurricane level, maybe."

They finished their drinks and went their separate ways. David headed back to the metro and soon stepped off the train at Pentagon City. The sprawling, multi-story shopping mall above the train station bustled with activity. He could smell the Cinnabon and soft pretzels when he stepped off the escalator. After a brief consultation with the store directory, he made his way to the Microsoft store. The salesman caught David before he was even inside the door.

"Welcome, sir. What can I help you with?"

"What's the cheapest device you have that can read a USB drive?"

The young man fumbled for an answer, apparently caught off guard. "Well, if you're looking for something with the latest USB version, we have the—"

"Nope. Just something inexpensive that will read a USB drive."

Ten minutes later and three hundred dollars poorer, David sat in the back of a cab with his new micro laptop. He'd made sure it had been pre-loaded with all of the basic software he might need. He unwrapped the new earbuds he had purchased with the computer and plugged them into the headphone jack. David glanced up at the cab driver as he reached into his jacket pocket. The driver was paying no attention to him. The operator's license on the separator window told David that his name was Lonnie. Lonnie had a sense of humor about his religion, as indicated by the bobble head Jesus that danced on the dashboard with the car's motion. David watched the plastic martyr and prayed that he had been given something useful as he fingered the USB drive that Tony had slipped to him during their handshake. He plugged it into the proper port.

A window appeared with a folder named "D-Day." David smiled at the play on his initials. Tony had always been the witty one. He opened the folder to reveal an audio file, an image file, and a text file. He positioned the cursor over the audio file and tapped the touchpad twice. The media player opened and Tony's voice filtered through the earbuds.

"*I could get lost in a dark hole for this. You owe me,*" Tony said. "*Sharp is a ghost. Definitely not DHS. I don't have much more than that, but you'll find a dossier on a loaner he requested from us for a high-level project. Need to know only, and I wasn't on that list. Word is that you are part of Sharp's team, so this may be nothing new. The loaner was a former analyst who was trained and re-tasked as a field agent. Talented kid. Hope this helps.*"

The audio ended. David opened the image file next. It was a black and white headshot of a man in his late twenties with a goatee beard. He memorized the face, then opened the text file.

Douglas, Evan
Field Operative
Current Deployment: TDY

Skill Set: Satellite Communications, Information Technology, Global Mapping Technology, Espionage, Asset Management...

David skimmed past the irrelevant data until he found what he was looking for.

Known Associates:
Williamson, Gerard T.
Psychologist
Cleveland, OH

LaMonte, Anson J.
Graphic Designer
Lexington, KY

Page, Gregory C.
Studio Engineer
Philadelphia, PA

McAllister, Samantha A.
Bartender
Clarendon, VA

David froze.

He ripped the USB drive from the small laptop and slammed the computer shut before removing the ear buds from his ears. He shoved the tiny drive into his sock while looking up at Lonnie, who was beating his fingers on the steering wheel in time with the soft jazz oozing from the car speakers. David saw that they had just passed the sign for the 14th Street Bridge. He rolled down his window.

Lonnie was startled when his passenger threw a laptop computer from his cab into the Potomac River far below. "Sir! You can't do that!"

Bobble Head Jesus nodded in agreement. David shrugged.

"Bad information error," he said. "Next time I'm getting a Mac."

Samantha McAllister's address wasn't hard to find, especially when investigation was your bread and butter—or when your administrative assistant was an expert in Google searches. It was a third-floor walkup not too far from the Clarendon metro station. The apartment building was not the most affluent that David had visited, but it fit the income of a single, twenty-something bartender.

The knob lock would have been easy enough to pick, but the single cylinder deadbolt above it would have taken some time. With three different peepholes pointed at him from across the hall, David decided to go with the less elegant solution: two swift kicks and a shoulder thrust. He darted inside and closed the door behind him, then flipped on a lamp that rested on an end table just inside the door. A plush leather sofa the color of creamy coffee was situated against the wall next to the door. One cushion was more lived in than the others. A thin black lamp sat on another end table at the far end of the couch. There was no television, and the walls were adorned with stylistic watercolors of tropical flowers. A third small table against the far wall was unadorned. David spied a circular area free of dust in the center of it.

Moving into the kitchen, he found dishes neatly stacked in a drying rack by the sink. The contents of the cupboards were organized by food type—most of which was healthy—and her glassware and dinnerware were arranged by size and shape. Several black and red marks on the rim a large serving bowl stood out to him. David pulled the stack of bowls from the cupboard and removed the smaller bowls from inside the largest one. He found himself staring at a crude facsimile of a roulette wheel.

"Okay, Miss McAllister, so you're a gambler," he said.

An inspection of the bathroom revealed a dry shower curtain and loofah. Her toothbrush was also dry, and the small waste basket beneath the sink was empty. He pulled several bottles of lotion from the vanity, uncapping each one to sample its scent. The third lotion smelled of lavender and vanilla.

David moved into the bedroom and knelt beside a laundry basket full of clothes, pulling free a familiar white, button-down blouse. He fished through the pockets of the black slacks just beneath it but found nothing. He tossed the clothes back into the basket and stood up to continue his search. He didn't really know what he was looking for, but the roulette bowl had been a valuable find. The lotion less so. Despite the fact that he had smelled it on the piece of silk fabric found at the crime scene, lavender and vanilla was a common scent. Elyse had been fond of it. He wondered if she still was.

A framed photo next to the bed revealed Samantha standing between a man in his mid-to-late fifties and a younger man no older than twenty. The older man had salt and pepper hair and his face was creased with laugh lines. The younger man was dark haired and had the older man's features. David heard something roll onto the floor when he replaced the picture on the nightstand. It was a white marble.

He dropped to a knee to retrieve it, and decided that it wouldn't hurt to peek under the bed while he was down there. Several garment boxes were nestled together beneath the box springs, obscuring a larger object that loomed behind them. David pushed the boxes aside and stretched his arm past them. His fingers brushed over a leather handle. It wasn't unusual for people to store empty luggage beneath their beds, but as he pulled the suitcase free of the garment boxes he quickly discovered that this suitcase was far from empty. He grunted against its weight as he slung the piece of luggage on the bed with a heavy bounce that jostled the pillows. David drew back the zippers, his eyes widening as he opened the lid to reveal the source of the suitcase's considerable weight. At first glance, he estimated that he was staring at five hundred thousand dollars. Probably more. David pushed the suitcase back under the bed and replaced the garment boxes in front of it. He scooped up the marble and moved to the nightstand, but thought better of it and instead slipped the tiny sphere into his pocket. His fingers continued to play with it as he pieced together his findings.

Samantha had been at the casino that night. She somehow took the Ukrainians for a ride at roulette, then got pulled into that back room where they tried to sweat her. But how did she get away? And where are the facts to support that she truly is the subject of his investigation? Just because Samantha cheated a casino out of a lot of money didn't necessarily mean she was the flying woman. And if she beat the piss out of the casino owner and his employees, then executed them—both of which David highly doubted—that was a matter for Vegas P.D., not him. The blood evidence didn't support that theory anyway. What then? The task at hand was to find a flying woman.

A flying woman in a motorcycle suit.

David pulled the garment boxes from under the bed and rifled through them. Nothing. He went to the bedroom closet and flung open the door, rummaging through hanging clothes and plastic tubs. Again, nothing. He was about to give up when he spotted a bulky shopping bag that had been pushed into the corner behind a white wire shoe rack. He thought he could make out the word "Choppers" in the logo printed on the bag. He grinned in spite of himself.

"Gotcha."

A familiar feeling washed over him as he reached for the shopping bag. It was the feeling that had saved him and his squad many times over. They all had it, a sixth sense one doesn't learn through training but rather from being put in dangerous situations time and again. It was the feeling that woke him up in the middle of the night for years afterward, drenched in cold sweat and convinced that someone was standing over his bed trying to kill him.

This time, however, that someone was standing right behind him.

Instinct took over as David threw his weight to the side, planting a leg under him for support. Something struck his ear a microsecond after he heard a deafening report. He used his support leg to hurl himself backward, twisting at the waist and bringing his arm up in a defensive motion. David's forearm connected with flesh and bone, and he got his first look at his assailant.

Wally Pritchett stared back at him.

They blinked in surprised recognition, then David's forehead smashed into Wally's face. Wally managed to turn away just enough prevent a broken nose, but the thick skull bone connected painfully with his jaw. David's attack was a distraction, however, and he went for the revolver in Wally's hand. Wally had always preferred the revolver because it was more reliable than a slide-action pistol. The gun discharged again, sending a round into a pillow on Samantha's bed. Wally retreated to get a clear shot but David followed closely, not letting him bring his gun to bear. Fists and elbows flew as the two engaged in close-quarter combat. David managed to trap his arms, but a quick foot stomp gave Wally time to disentangle himself. David ignored the pain in his instep and pressed forward with a head feint followed by an all-out body tackle. It was a risky move, but David had to take control of the situation or he was going to get shot.

The pair slammed into the bookcase, showering them with Samantha's book collection. The revolver barked for the third time. David didn't know where the shot went, but was pretty sure he hadn't been it. His head was below Wally's as he bulldogged him into shelves. Setting his feet, he snapped his neck taut and caught Wally on the chin. Pain erupted on his scalp when he connected, but it was nowhere near the pain he had inflicted on his old squad brother. David seized Wally's wrist with one hand and pivoted, twisting Wally's arm until the palm faced the ceiling. David's other arm weaved beneath Wally's limb to grasp his own wrist. He flexed his arms and arched his back. The gun popped into the air. Wally screamed as his elbow erupted in agony. David's backhand chop to the neck turned the scream into a choked gurgle. He released Wally and shuffled back a step, bringing his foot up to slam into Wally's solar plexus. The man hurtled into the bookcase for a second time. David was on him again, sinking his hands in Wally's hair to fling him bodily across the room. Wally bounced off the window pane and fell to his knees.

David scooped up the revolver and flipped open the cylinder. The beaten man planted a foot under him, preparing to rise. He held up his hand to David.

"Wait," Wally said.

"Did Braithwaite send you to watch McAllister's place?"

David's fingers went to his stinging ear and came away bloody. It was just a graze.

"What? Braithwaite? No," Wally managed, wheezing from the plexus kick and throat strike.

David emptied six cartridges into his hand, three empty shells and three live rounds. He slipped a single cartridge back into the gun then spun the cylinder before closing it with a flick of his wrist. He deposited the rest of the cartridges into his pocket while bringing the weapon to bear on Wally.

"You used to be a good soldier, Wally. It was an honor to serve with you."

Wally stood up and patted the air with his hands. He spat a glob of blood onto Samantha's carpet.

"Okay...just wait a second, David."

Click!

The cylinder rotated to the next chamber.

Wally flinched but stood his ground. "You know better than anyone that I'm not afraid to die. Not after what we went through."

"How much is he paying you?" David sneered, "We're SEALs, Wally. How much did it take for Braithwaite to turn you into a spineless murderer like him?"

Click!

The cylinder rotated to the next chamber.

Wally ducked and threw his arms over his head, recoiling from the revolver. "It's just business!"

"You're running out of empty chambers, Wally," David said. "You'd better tell me something soon. Start with why you're here."

"The money," Wally said. "The girl took a shitload of money from the Ukrainians. I didn't know you'd be here. I thought we were on the same team, man."

David considered his words and lowered the gun just a bit. "We used to be."

Wally nodded. "I know Sharp hired an investigator for appearances. I didn't know it was you until Commander Braithwaite told me."

"What do you mean, 'for appearances'?"

"The commander only told me what I needed to know, but I put it together. Sharp knew that there was a chance there would be sightings of the girl; people reporting a flying woman, like at the dance club that night."

And there it was. Case closed. The pretty girl from the subway. How long had Sharp and Braithwaite known about McAllister? How long had Sharp been playing him?

Wally had David's full attention now. "Go on."

"Do I have to spell it out for you?"

Click!

The cylinder rotated to the next chamber. Wally flinched and covered up again.

"Don't be a smartass or I'll make you my bitch again, then shoot you! Talk!" David thundered.

Wally took a deep breath and wiped the blood from his chin. His eyes flicked from David's face to the gun.

"Sharp needed to initiate an official investigation while he conducted his own in secret. He needed a paper trail to show his superiors if this ever went public—proof that he had performed his due diligence. You were his insurance. Luckily for you, this never went public. It's over now, David. We got her. Come in now and I'll put in a word with the C.O. We could use you on the team."

David studied his face. Wally Pritchett used to be a talented soldier. Demolitions expert. He could spot an IED from a mile away.

What a shame.

"It's not over." David said. "Where are Sharp and Braithwaite holding her?"

Wally shook his head. "Sorry, old friend."

David's mind raced. He knew he was approaching the point where the revolver would no longer be a threat. Wally was a seasoned soldier just like him.

"Tell me where she is, then take the money and disappear. Braithwaite owes you at least that much for the shit he put us through." David said.

"Can't do it, David." Wally said, his hands spread wide. "So what now?"

"What are they doing to her? I swear to god, if Braithwaite lays one hand on her..."

Wally lowered his hands. "Come in and find out. I'll take you to her."

The barrel came in line with Wally's forehead.

"Tell me!"

"You know what, David?" Wally said, his posture relaxing, "I'm going to bet my life that you put an empty cartridge in my gun. The odds are fifty-fifty that I should have a bullet in my head by now. I can live with those odds."

He took a step forward. David retreated a step to keep the distance between them.

"See?" Wally smiled, then pulled a combat knife from his boot with practiced efficiency and lunged.

David darted aside and flipped the revolver in his hand to grasp the barrel. The butt of the gun lashed out to parry the slashing knife, but David received a nasty cut across the knuckles in the process.

"Come on, Wally," David said as they squared off, "you don't want me to embarrass you again."

Wally responded by feinting with the knife then connected with a left hook to David's jaw.

"We'll see, Lieutenant." He grinned through bloody teeth.

David shook off the blow and blocked the blade attack that he knew would come next. He wasn't disappointed. His right foot snapped out in a distracting low kick, striking Wally in the knee. The gun hand followed in an overhand blow that became a feint when Wally threw up his free hand to block it. That momentarily drew Wally's attention away from his knife hand. David seized the wrist and yanked downward with all of his might. His leg was already in motion from the first attack, so he wrapped it over the arm in his grasp, catching Wally's elbow in the crook of his knee. David dropped the gun and took hold of Wally's weapon arm with both hands. He dropped to the floor, snaking his other foot around to interlock with the leg holding Wally. Wally screamed in pain as David applied pressure, but he refused to relinquish the knife.

"Let it go, Wally. I'll break your fucking arm this time," David said as he wrenched the elbow.

Wally's groans filled the small room. David spotted Wally's hand reaching through the tangle of limbs towards his crotch. David expected the move—he had taught it to Wally in the first place—but hoped it wouldn't come to this. He flexed his back muscles and heard a sickening pop. The knife fell to the floor. David released the hold and scooped it up.

"Stay down, Wally."

His warning was futile. David knew in his heart that this fight would be to the death.

Sure enough, Wally threw himself at David. His right arm hung useless, but the left one flailed in a desperate attempt to defeat his opponent. The former SEAL was willing to die rather than give up on his mission. David's old friend, his comrade in arms, wanted to lay down his life over an order from their dishonored military commander. A man who had been disgraced and now ran a band of mercenaries that sold their elite training and tactics to the highest bidder. U.S. Navy Lieutenant Walter Pritchett was choosing to die for money. David reversed his grip on the knife and granted Wally's wish.

He slapped aside Wally's clumsy attacks and stabbed out. Slap and stab. Slap and stab. Blood spewed from the puncture wounds to cover both men. The defensive strikes weakened.

"It's over, Pritchett," David said. "You were a good man once."

Wally tried to get to his feet, but the loss of blood wouldn't allow it. His body was going into shock.

"Dav...David..." he gurgled as his lifeblood filled his lungs. "I...I'm sorry, David..."

David yanked Wally's head back. "Me too, Wally."

A final slice across the throat ended it. David let the body fall to the light blue carpet that turned a deep violet as it was bathed in Wally's lifeblood. David sat down next to his former ally and waited for the sickening choking sounds to stop. He couldn't remember if Wally had any family, but promised himself that he would find out and let them know he had passed. He was certain that Braithwaite wouldn't have the decency to do it.

He retrieved Wally's dog tags, then went through his pockets. One of the utility pouches near Wally's ankle revealed a burner phone. He flipped it open and searched through the recent text messages.

D at location. Advise.

The text was to a local number. A reply had been sent a few minutes later. Long enough for David to inspect most of Samantha's apartment.

Retire D. Confirm.

David squeezed Wally's bloody shoulder. A large part of him regretted it had come to this, but Wally's final text gave David some sense of justification.

Standby for confirmation.

He dragged the corpse into the bathroom and heaved it into the bathtub then washed up as best he could, taking great care to thoroughly clean his wounds. An athletic wrap was the closest thing Samantha had to a bandage. He winced as he wound it around his knuckles. He would need stitches, but couldn't worry about that at the moment.

David went through Samantha's drawers until he found the largest T-shirt she had. It was far too small for him, but he had no other choice. Stripping off his bloody button down, he donned the T-shirt and stepped in front of the bathroom mirror. A grown man wearing a skin-tight, sky blue Taylor Swift T-shirt stared back at him. It would have to do.

David slid the suitcase out from beneath the bed. He took a stack of hundreds and pushed the case back into place. Embry's Hardware was only a couple of blocks away. In addition to fixing Samantha's front door, he had a body to dispose of and tracks to cover.

It was going to be a long night.

Chapter Sixteen

DAVID DECIDED THAT THE MOST EFFICIENT use of time would be to visit the rest of the known associates of Evan Douglas in the order in which they were listed on the dossier Tony had given him. Finding their addresses hadn't been difficult for Miss Marissa Sanchez, Assistant Extraordinaire. David had told her to forget the addresses as soon as she had delivered them. He needed information fast if he was going to find McAllister, and didn't intend to play nice. Marissa was already involved in this case more than he would have liked. No need to implicate her further.

The suburban neighborhood was considered upper-middle class for Cleveland. David had seen dozens of these cookie-cutter houses clustered into identical communities all across the country. In larger, more affluent cities, upper-middle class meant larger versions of the same dwellings. Most of them had well-manicured yards with play equipment in the back and bicycles in the driveway next to minivans or SUVs with decals boasting children's first names and jersey numbers. He spotted quite a few sports signs in the landscape beds out front, mostly rooting for the Buckeyes or the Browns. David didn't hold the idea of a sheltered, predictable lifestyle against these people, he just hadn't grown up that way.

He parked a few doors down from his destination. It was difficult to determine which of the doppleganger houses matched the photo Marissa had found online but, luckily for him, the house numbers were stenciled on the curb in reflective spray paint. A dog barked from inside a home across the street, but David wasn't worried. It was 3 a.m. These suburbanites were deep into their sleep cycle, dreaming of soccer games and how to keep their illicit affairs hidden from their spouses.

A few jiggles of his knife had him past the privacy fence gate and into the backyard. He didn't see any children's toys or signs of a dog, but stepped lightly anyway. The sliding patio doors required his lock picks, so he tucked away his knife and went to work. He closed the glass door behind him several minutes later and found himself in a great room that expanded into a kitchen with a broad island in the center. To his left, a staircase ascended into darkness. David slipped his picks back into his pocket and padded into the kitchen. A plate of brownies rested on the island. He peeled back the cellophane with gloved fingers and helped himself to chocolaty square. He hadn't eaten anything since leaving Washington.

David searched through drawers and closets until he found a large metal mag light on a shelf next to the garage access door. Satisfied with his discovery, he moved toward the steps. The house was solid and recently built, so the stairs didn't creak under his weight as he ascended to the second level. He checked the spare bedrooms to make sure they were unoccupied before entering the master bedroom. The only sounds were the deep, rhythmic breaths of slumber. He confiscated a pair of smartphones from the nightstands before pulling a chair away from the dressing table and taking a seat. David retrieved Wally's revolver from his waistband and situated the flashlight on the dressing table so that it pointed at the bed and kept his features in darkness. The bright beam fell over Gerard T. Williamson and his wife

Fiona as they lay motionless beneath a flowery duvet. Drool darkened the powder blue pillowcase at Gerard's mouth.

"Jerry!"

The couple jolted awake and sat up, disoriented. Gerard shielded his eyes from the light and fumbled for his glasses.

"I have a gun trained on you," David said, moving the weapon into the light.

Gerard froze while Fiona scrambled for the phone that was no longer next to her. Dismayed, she wheeled about and squinted with her hand held flat above her eyes.

"Who are you! What do you want!" she demanded.

"I want you to follow three simple rules. Don't move. Don't scream. Don't lie. That last one is the most important. Understand?"

Gerard's hand stopped moving toward the edge of the covers as David laid out his expectations. He nodded.

"It's going to be okay, Fiona, just stay calm," he said. "Take what you want and get out of my house!"

"I intend to," David said. He reached for the phone he had taken from Gerard and removed his glove before sliding his thumb across the screen. It was locked.

"What's your phone code?"

Gerard was panicked. There was no answer. Fiona pressed against him, peering at David over her husband's shoulder. She was visibly shaking. David understood. They thought they were safe in this neighborhood.

They were sheep.

"What's your phone code? Don't make me ask again."

"Six three one four," said Gerard.

"Your wedding day," David mused as he punched in the numbers. "Here's a tip, Jerry. Don't let your wife program your phone's security code."

The code worked and Gerard's home screen appeared. He scrolled through the contacts but didn't see Evan Douglas listed among the names. Gerard slowly took his wife's hand in his as David perused the phone.

"First question," David said. "Where is McAllister?"

Gerard's expression didn't change. He didn't twitch or alter his demeanor in any way. Either Gerard was a great actor or he had no idea who the hell David was talking about. David felt the seeds of doubt begin to germinate.

"Who?"

"McAllister. Where is she?"

"I don't know. I don't know who that is," he said. "Please, I have several thousand dollars in cash. Just take it."

David didn't like to be bribed.

"Remember my rules, Jerry. Follow them and you and the missus here get to go back to sleep. Break them and I dial your mother and let her listen to me shoot you in the face."

"Who is she, Jerry? Just tell him if you know," Fiona said.

Gerard looked over his shoulder at his wife and shrugged while shaking his head. His eyes were frantic and reflected his helplessness. David was convinced. He switched tactics.

"What is Evan Douglas doing for the NSA?"

This time Gerard's expression went from fear to confusion.

"Ev—Evan? What are you...I don't..."

"I understand that the worst thing a parent can go through is outliving their child," David said as he thumbed through Gerard's contacts. "Imagine the nightmares of actually hearing the child beg for mercy before he—or she—dies."

He disliked threatening what seemed like a gentle, normal couple, but he didn't have time to be nice. He had to get answers fast.

"Evan? I haven't heard from him in years! Please! I haven't seen him since graduation!"

Gerard was starting to panic. David could see that he knew he didn't have the information that would keep him and his wife alive. Fiona knew it too and began to bawl.

"Fiona," David said. "Is this true? Do I have to call your mom too?"

"I've never met him. I don't know what you want from us," Fiona said between sobs.

David took his time pulling back the hammer, making sure they heard the mechanical clicks. They cried out and clutched at each other.

"One last time, Gerard. Where is McAllister and what is Evan doing for the NSA?"

David rose from the chair. The bright flashlight beam masked his exit from the room. Gerard's tense voice reiterated what David had already heard. David was out of the house before Gerard stopped bargaining for his life. The next-door neighbors found two smartphones in their mailbox the next day. Police found no fingerprints on the devices.

Interstate 71 switched from flat cornfields to rolling hills as David reached Cincinnati. More of the same greeted him as he connected with I-75 and crossed the river. Lexington was still over an hour away.

"Sorry to wake you, Marissa," David said when her sleepy voice greeted him through the speakerphone in his car.

"That's okay, boss," she said after a yawn. "It's why I make the big bucks. Twenty-four seven availability."

"What's the latest?"

"Your contact picked up the SIM card earlier, but I haven't heard back. He said he'd know something tomorrow."

Tony had agreed to look into Wally's burner phone on the condition that he be gifted a bottle of Pappy Van Winkle Family Reserve and four tickets to the Rolling Stones at the Verizon Center.

"I told him it was urgent," David said. "What else did he say?"

"He said to tell you he knew you were going to come back knocking on his door."

"Thanks, Marissa. Keep me posted."

The Lexington address for LaMonte was in Holiday Hills, a neighborhood in the northwestern part of the city. It was a storefront in a dilapidated strip mall that may once have been a thriving shopping center, but now For Lease signs had replaced store signs in most of the windows. As for the remaining stores, David spotted a flea market and a discount tobacco shop, as well as a shady-looking check cashing outfit. The sign that decorated LaMonte's address simply read "Taekwondo."

Anson J. LaMonte, the second on the list of known associates, came through the door as David was pulling into a parking spot at the far end of the lot. He watched the young man lock the door behind him and walk to a silver PT Cruiser with a large yin yang symbol that covered the rear window. It was just after eight-thirty in the morning, and David had a hunch that Mr. LaMonte was going out for coffee. He waited for the PT Cruiser to leave before moving his own vehicle closer, and took a quick look around before exiting his sedan and approaching the storefront door. There was no sign of a security system. He peered through the plate glass and didn't see any motion detectors in the corners. The bolt lock wasn't difficult to pick.

Plastic chairs lined the walls of the dojo, which was a wide open space with thin blue mats covering the floor. Protective headgear and gloves were arranged on wall-mounted racks, and an expansive Korean flag covered the opposite wall. David delivered a jab to one of the rubber practice dummies situated in the corner by the rear door as he opened it and walked through.

The back room had been converted into living quarters. A cot hugged the far wall next to a corner computer desk upon which sat a widescreen monitor. David pressed the power button on the front of the CPU and clicked on the monitor. A class photo appeared on the screen. Children and adults in white gis knelt in front of a standing LaMonte who wore a black gi and matching belt which was decorated with red stripes at the tips. David located the web browser and double clicked it. He was amazed at how many people set their Email screen as their homepage and left the account logged in. He opened the search tool and typed in **Evan Douglas**, which garnered eleven results.

The most recent Email was several months old. He read through all of them, but none referred to Douglas's CIA activities and only one exchange mentioned Samantha. It appeared as though she had dated Douglas for some time, but broke it off with him before it got too serious. The messages from LaMonte to Douglas were supportive, leading David to believe that Douglas had been quite fond of her and was devastated. One passage in particular raised David's eyebrows. LaMonte had told Douglas that there would be a time when Douglas would be able to get back at her. Perhaps he meant Douglas would find a mate more suited to him than Samantha had been. Perhaps he meant something else.

He feared that LaMonte was another dead end, but David wanted to be sure before he moved on. He didn't have to wait long.

The jingle of keys outside the front door filtered into the back room. David closed out the browser window and wiped down the keyboard with one of LaMonte's shirts that lay scattered about the living area. LaMonte was humming to himself as he locked the door behind him. David walked into the dojo and crossed his arms over his chest, waiting for LaMonte to notice him. He was carrying a small paper bag and a large Styrofoam cup, both of which hit the floor when he saw the intruder. Coffee splashed across the blue mats and pooled into the cracks.

"Who the fuck are you?"

David advanced on him. "What is Evan Douglas doing for the NSA?"

LaMonte risked a glance behind him, then shifted his weight to look past David.

"Just you here, huh? Alright then," LaMonte said, relaxing somewhat. "I have a right to defend myself. Get out before I hurt you."

"Where is McAllister?"

"Who is that? Didn't you hear me? Get the fuck out!"

LaMonte tried to circle around David to get to the back room. David moved to block him.

"Samantha McAllister."

Recognition filled LaMonte's dark eyes. "Oh, the bitch that dumped my friend? Evan told me about her. He also said she was doing half the guys that walked into that dive she works in. Charging by the hour. Evan said she's got a real sweet—"

He didn't see David's punch coming. LaMonte stumbled backwards, his hand covering his split lip. His surprise turned to anger when the threat became real.

David's voice was calm. "Where is McAllister? Why is Douglas working with the NSA?"

LaMonte moved in a tight circle around the intruder, throwing a series of kicks and punches at the air just out of range as if to warn his opponent that he knew what he was doing. David rolled his eyes.

LaMonte began his attack with a feint, a front snap kick that he didn't retract quickly enough. David sidestepped and scooped LaMonte's leg with the crook of his elbow. His right foot lashed out to connect with LaMonte's support leg, dropping the Taekwondo instructor to his back. David kept control of LaMonte's kicking leg, bracing it against his shoulder and twisting it at the knee. LaMonte screamed. David pressed a hard-soled shoe into his neck.

"This isn't a dance, Anson. Tell me what I want to know or I'll snap your knee."

Anson LaMonte squeaked out a curse. His eyes darted about in terror. David applied pressure to the knee. He let up on LaMonte's neck just enough for him to speak.

"I don't...know..." LaMonte managed through gritted teeth.

"I didn't hear you," David said. "They say knees never heal quite right. Don't make me ruin your teaching career. I'm sure you do good work for the kids."

He twisted the joint to accentuate his point. David could feel that it was at the breaking point. LaMonte screamed in agreement.

"Haven't...ngh!...talked to Evan in...months..."

"If I find out you're lying I'll come back here and embarrass your sorry ass in front of your entire class."

David released LaMonte and took a step back. "Stay down until I leave."

LaMonte cradled his knee and erupted into a violent fit of coughing. David went to the front door and unlocked it through the fabric of his jacket pocket.

"You blink before you attack, LaMonte. You need to work on that."

He let the door close behind him and made his way to his car. He wasn't worried about LaMonte calling the police. A Taekwondo instructor getting his ass handed to him on his home turf would be bad for business. Besides, David suspected that LaMonte's bruised ego would rather pretend it had never happened.

David was now zero for two, but hoped that the third known associate of Evan Douglas would provide the information he was looking for. He fired up the ignition and checked his watch. It was going to be a long trip to Philadelphia.

"I'm looking for Gregory Allen, please."

The receptionist didn't look up from his computer screen. "What time was your appointment?"

"I drove all day to get here. Any way you can squeeze me in?"

The receptionist's eyes swiveled to David without moving his head. "Mr. Allen doesn't do walk ins, sir," he said. "Let me see. I have a two-thirty open the day after tomorrow, or—"

"—tell him I have bad news about Evan Douglas."

"Evan Douglas? How am I supposed to know who that is?"

"You aren't," David said, "but Mr. Allen will know. Call him and tell him it's urgent. Help a brother out here."

The young man clicked his tongue and issued an exasperated sigh before picking up the telephone. Soon, a man wearing a Led Zeppelin T-shirt and khaki cargo shorts appeared through a side door. He had a curly pompadour and several large tattoos on his forearms.

"What's this about Evan?"

David shook his head. "Is there somewhere we can talk? Somewhere that's not here?"

Allen took David in from head to toe as he considered the request.

"Sure, sure. Where are my manners," he said, motioning to the door from which he had emerged. "This way."

David followed him down a corridor plastered with photos of musicians. The Sharpie autographs were all made out to Allen in messy script and punctuated with hearts or musical notes. The fusion music David had heard in the lobby was louder in the corridor, a mix of blues, hard rock, and funk. Allen bobbed his head to it as he showed David into his office. Two gold records hung on the wall behind his desk, just low enough to be in David's eye line as he sat down across the expansive desk from Allen. The studio engineer pressed his fingers together and reclined in his brown leather chair. It protested with a faint squeak.

"You have news about Evan?"

Allen's eyes tightened as he asked the question. David heard the heel of his moccasins tapping on the hard plastic floor mat beneath his chair. The intention was to press Allen as he had Gerard Williamson and Anson LaMonte, but he held back and instead sent an unflinching stare across the desk. Something wasn't right, and he wasn't ready to show his cards just yet. This unnerved Allen. He dropped his hands to the desk and began to drum the lacquered surface with his fingers.

"Well?"

A single drop of sweat slid down Allen's temple. David continued to stare. Then the game was up. Allen reached into a drawer and drew a pistol. He almost dropped it in his haste, but righted it and stood up.

"Yeah, that's right," Allen said. He wiped his brow with the back of his hand. "Jerry called me. Warned me you might be coming."

David slowly brought his hands up and placed them on the armrests to placate the nervous man. Allen held a Kel-Tec PF-9 semi-automatic, small and concealable. David was familiar with the older models of this weapon. The recoil impact was higher than other firearms in its class, which meant that it took longer to bring the barrel back in line with the target for a second shot. Allen would only get one shot before David could close the distance between them. The problem was that Allen wasn't likely to miss at this range.

"That's right. He said you threatened him and Fiona," Allen said. "Asking about Evan and some girl. How dare you! I introduced him to Fiona! And you threaten to kill them?"

David kept his focus on the trigger finger and let Allen vent.

"I'll make you a deal, Greg," David said. "May I call you Greg?"

Allen pushed his chair away and pressed his back to the wall. His free hand came up to support his gun hand. He didn't reply. He was too busy sucking in nervous breaths.

"Greg, here's my offer. If you put the gun down right now, I won't arrest you for threatening a federal officer. How does that sound?"

"What? No." Allen's lips pursed in confusion. He didn't lower the gun.

"Listen to me very carefully, Greg," David said. "You need to put the gun down so we can talk. I don't know what your friend told you, but I have never met Mr. or Mrs. Williamson. I'm here because of that incident. I'm on your side, Greg. Okay?"

Allen wasn't convinced, but at least he was talking instead of shooting. David considered that progress.

"How do I know you're not lying?"

"A statement from the first responder said that the suspect forced his way into the home and held them at gunpoint. That's a fact. I walked through your front door and asked for you. This is how we do investigations, Greg."

A shadow of doubt fell over Allen's face. The gun barrel dropped slightly.

"I don't...I..."

"Greg, look at me. Look at me," David said, relaxing his expression. "At least take your finger off the trigger. If you slip, you're looking at life without parole. Even if you don't hit me."

Allen took his finger from the trigger. He ran his hand through his hair. Anxiety pinched his face.

"Thank you," David said. "Now, have a seat and let's talk."

Allen considered his options, then lowered the gun and turned to pull his chair closer. David was across the desk in the blink of an eye. He intercepted Allen's arm as it rose and stripped the pistol away with a well-practiced disarm technique. Allen yelped in pain.

"Don't hit me!"

Allen tried to fall into his chair but missed horribly and landed on the carpeted floor behind his desk. David resisted the urge to do just that. He instead removed the magazine from the weapon and checked the chamber. Allen hadn't even loaded a round. David replaced the mag and did it for him.

"Man, it's been a hell of day," David said. He pointed the Kel-Tec at the studio engineer. "How does that feel, Greg? Not so good, does it?"

Allen covered up and issued a canine whining sound. David walked around the desk and locked the office door, then returned to his chair.

"Get up, Greg," David said. "Have a seat. Let's talk."

Allen's face peered over the top of the desk like a tortured puppet.

"Go on," David said, pointing at the chair with the gun. Allen obeyed, finding himself on the wrong end of his own weapon.

"I've been driving for almost twenty-four hours now to hunt down little pieces of shit like you. Sometimes my fingers twitch when I'm tired. So you'll forgive me if I accidentally shoot you. I won't mean it."

Allen's eyes widened into saucers. He held his hands up like a teller in an Old West bank robbery.

"Put your hands down, Greg. Now, you probably won't be able to help me either, but I have to follow the clues where they lead. And, unfortunately for you, they led me here. So I'm going to ask you some questions and you are going to answer them honestly. How do you know Evan Douglas?"

Allen's mouthed moved, but he could only stare at the gun. No words came out. David sighed and rested the gun in his lap.

"Go ahead," David said.

"College...we met at Carnegie Mellon," Allen said finally. "Fiona, too."

"Did you know he was in the CIA?"

"Yes. I'm not supposed to tell anyone, but you have a loaded gun. So, yes."

"And what did he tell you about his job in the CIA?"

"He said he was working with satellites and UAVs, monitoring classified operations."

"So he risked his job and his freedom to tell you that. Why?"

"We're buds. I mean, we're good friends. I don't know."

David's brows furrowed. He raised the gun.

"I swear! I swear!" Allen's voice quavered. David was surprised when he made the sign of the cross, considering that the Star of David was inked into his forearm.

"What else?"

"Last time I talked to him was several weeks ago. A month, maybe? He said he was scouted by some higher ups to do something else. Something outside of the CIA. He didn't say what, but he did say he wished he could tell me."

"And?"

Allen looked crestfallen. By his expression, he was convinced he had just spilled the beans in exchange for his life. David suppressed his anger and frustration as it became clear that his third and final chance at locating Samantha had just fizzled out. Allen must have seen the sudden change on David's face.

"That's all I know," Allen said. "You're not going to kill me now, right? I told you everything."

David stood up and tucked the gun into his belt, pulling his suit jacket over it.

"This is mine now," he said.

A thought struck him halfway to the door.

"One last question," he said to the visibly relieved Allen. "Did he say anything about Samantha McAllister?"

"Samantha? No, that ended a while back."

It was as David thought. He nodded and turned to leave.

"Wait," Allen said suddenly. "Evan did say something that was out of left field. It's probably nothing important though."

"Tell me," David said. "Whatever it is, tell me."

"Well, he was going on and on about his new orders, trying to sound cool without actually saying anything that would give away his mission. I think he was drunk, but he sounded really excited at the same time. More so than when I got him laid for the first time. Anyway, he said 'She's fucking unbelievable!' or something to that effect. That made zero sense to me considering he was talking super-secret government stuff. Was he talking about Samantha?"

David rubbed his eyes and pulled out of the rest area. Sleeping in his requisitioned sedan wasn't the most comfortable way to spend the night, but he had slept in worse places in his life. He powered on his phone and saw a missed call and a new voicemail from Marissa. He ignored the message and called her back. Marissa's voice was apologetic as she filled him in on the results of the phone trace.

"The SIM card came up empty, Mr. Daniels. The Digital Forensics team couldn't find anything."

David wasn't surprised. Wally's phone would be very hard to crack if Douglas had encrypted it. "Who looked at it?"

"Tanaka," said Marissa.

"Isn't he sweet on you?"

"I agreed to have dinner with him if he kept this on the down low."

"I think you need a raise, Marissa."

"He's not that bad," she said. "Are you headed back to the city?"

"Not yet. I have one last stop to make."

He reached Baltimore less than an hour later and made his way to the row of townhouses that perched near the bank of the Patapsco river in Cherry Hill. David tucked Allen's Kel-Tec into the small of his back and grabbed the paper sack from the passenger side floor before exiting the car. A group of young men with burning cigarillos hanging from their lips shot David suspicious looks as he passed them. David didn't acknowledge them as he scanned the house numbers on the front of the townhomes. He found the one he was looking for and ascended the stoop.

A woman dressed in a stained, yellow housecoat greeted him from behind a screen door outfitted with thin iron bars. Her kind eyes were magnified by thick lenses set into thicker frames. Frizzy white hair stuck out in all directions as though he had interrupted her game of sticking forks into wall outlets. Her big eyes narrowed in recognition.

"I know that face," she said.

David had heard stories about her, but they had never actually met. He assumed she was mistaking him for someone else.

"Come in, come in." She unlocked the door and swung it open for him. "I'll pour you some coffee."

"Thank you."

David had once been in a hoarder's home while working a case in Appalachia. This one was no different. Every surface was overflowing with bottles, boxes, papers, jars, knick-knacks and tchotchkes. Stacks of yellowing newsprint littered the floor. The living room furniture was also covered except for a small space on the sofa where she could sit and work on her knitting, as evidenced by the dozens of balls of yarn scattered nearby. A photo cluster on the wall caught David's attention, and he stepped over a pile of empty Ritz boxes to take a closer look. One picture stood out from the rest. They were all there. It was their graduation from Coronado, and the six of them stood sharp in their dress blues. David stood next to Gonzales, then came Lange, Acevedo, Capelli, and finally Wally. Only he and Wally had served under Braithwaite. David had long since lost touch with the others.

"I put a little bit of milk in there for you."

The frame glass showed the reflection of Wally's mother emerging from the kitchen. David turned and accepted the small cup and saucer, ignoring the white hair that floated on the mocha surface.

"Thank you," he said. "I don't think we've ever met, Mrs. Pritchett. I'm David Daniels."

"Oh, I know who you are David," she said over her shoulder as she cleared coffee cans and plastic grocery bags from one of the chairs. "I see your face every day."

David took the offered seat as Wally's mother reclined on the sofa. He looked back up at the photo and forced away the images of sawing Wally's limbs from his torso.

"How is my boy? I don't hear much from him these days," she said.

David mimicked sipping from the coffee cup. "Well, ma'am, that's why I'm here."

He cleared his throat, unsure as to how he should proceed. His mouth had gone dry. He had practiced this speech dozens of times since killing her son, but now, looking into the woman's eyes, his carefully prepared words fled like quail bursting from cover.

"Walter—Wally got mixed up with some bad people after we came home," he said. "How do I put this, Mrs. Pritchett, your son...he ran into some trouble. He's gone."

Mrs. Pritchett's cup and saucer joined the refuse on the floor. Her face became a mask of grief and she bowed her head. Her hands clutched at the sleeves of her housecoat and her shoulders began to shake.

David set his saucer on a pile of carry out menus and reached into his pocket before moving to comfort Wally's mother. The irony didn't escape him. He and Wally had played a dangerous game, and her son had lost. It wasn't self defense. It wasn't a mercy killing. Their missions had collided, and David had been left standing. He took no satisfaction in that fact as he patted Mrs. Pritchett's shoulder and murmured soothing words.

"These are for you." He pressed Wally's dog tags into her trembling hand.

A fresh wave of grief washed over her as her eyes fell over them. David retrieved the sack he had brought and set it on the floor at her feet.

"This is to help you through this painful time," he said. "I'm sorry for your loss, ma'am. Wally was a good man."

Mrs. Pritchett didn't acknowledge the sack. She rocked back and forth with her hands clasped in prayer formation against her forehead, the dog tags jingling solemnly below them. David's fingers found his own dog tags beneath his dress shirt. His jaw clenched as Braithwaite's smirking visage flashed through his thoughts. He took one last look at the group photo before leaving Mrs. Pritchett to her mourning and making his way to his sedan. The young men from the corner met him halfway there, perhaps seeing him as an easy target, but gave him a wide berth when they spied the dangerous look in his eyes.

Mrs. Pritchett's devastation haunted David the entire drive back to D.C. He hoped she would find some peace inside that paper sack once the initial pain had receded. Fifty thousand dollars was small consolation for the loss of a son, but he was sure she could use it. Besides, Samantha McAllister, wherever she was, wouldn't even know it was gone.

Chapter Seventeen

"*WAKE UP, Miss McAllister*."

Samantha was freezing.

"*Wake up, Samantha*."

A disembodied voice filtered through the black where before there was only darkness. She was pretty sure that she was awake, but it was hard to tell. It was like that moment before you open your eyes in the morning, still cozy and warm in bed; you know that you should open them and start the day but you just don't feel like it. In this case, however, Samantha's eyes were wide open. There was simply nothing to see. No light, no colors, no shapes—nothing.

"*Good*."

The voice in her ear could somehow discern that she was awake. She became aware that she was sitting in a chair. She could feel the cold hardness against her legs and back. Her forearms pressed into the armrests and she could feel the chill of its metal legs against her bare heels. She jerked upward and felt something strong holding her in place at the wrists and ankles. There was something in her right ear. The vibrations itched her when the voice spoke.

"Before you move, Miss McAllister, before you use your power to rip the restraints to shreds in an attempt to escape, know that you are in a sealed room with walls of reinforced titanium several feet thick."

Samantha ripped the restraints to shreds.

A light in the ceiling flared to life, bathing the room in a red glow. Samantha got her first look at her prison—a ten by ten by ten room with metal, riveted walls. No doors or windows were to be found. She bent over to free her ankles and realized she was wearing only a dark, sleeveless smock. The garment reminded her of those enemy combatant interrogation scenes from the movies. The rough material chafed her skin.

Have to get out of here.

There was a hissing noise from above and an acrid odor pierced her nostrils. The room turned sideways. She felt the chair tipping, but never heard it hit the floor.

"Wake up, Miss McAllister."

Fuck me.

Her head was clamped in a vise, her temples throbbing against it. Her mouth was filled with sand.

"Fuck you!"

She swooned from the effort of her outburst, and had to fight back a sudden nausea. It was pitch black again, but she determined that she was still in the reinforced room from the sound of her voice bouncing around the confined space. She could smell remnants of the strange odor. Her wrists had been restrained to the chair once more.

"Please control yourself, Miss McAllister. I don't want to have to do that again."

Samantha needed time to think, but the pounding in her head made it difficult.

Evan. What did you do?

She lowered her head and clenched her fists. Her toes curled against the agony in her heart that now competed with the pain in her head.

They had been in the salvage yard. Evan was coaching her, helping her to control her powers and discover their limits. She remembered being out of breath, thirsty. The bottle of tea...

Oh my god, Evan. Why?

"*Very good.*"

The voice had mistaken her silent reflection for submission.

"*McAllister, Samantha Anne. Age twenty-three. Born to Alan and Madelyn McAllister in Centerville, Ohio. Graduated summa cum laude from Northwestern University with a degree in Humanities and a minor in Sociology. Marital status: Single. Employment status: Full-time. Bartender. Not exactly ambitious, are you Miss McAllister?*"

Samantha raised her head and spoke into the darkness. "I see you've been to my Facebook page. Congratulations. I need to update my employment status, actually."

Have to stay strong. Can't let them know I'm about to piss myself.

"*Did you know that the Scottish surname McAllister draws its roots from an earlier form of a word that means 'defender of mankind'?*"

"That's interesting, Mr. Douchebag," she said. "Did you know that the surname Douchebag means 'coward who restrains women in locked cells because his mommy took his temperature anally until he was twenty-five'?"

She couldn't be sure, but Samantha thought she heard a faint snickering through the earpiece.

He isn't alone. Of course he's not.

There was a long silence.

What did I just do? No, keep it together. If they wanted you dead you wouldn't be having this sad excuse for a conversation. So what do they want?

"Isn't this where you tell me your villainous plans and then put me in an easily-escapable trap while you go tend to other, more important matters? Sharks with frickin' laser beams or whatever?"

There was no answer. Only silence.

Have to appear confident even though I'm not feeling it. Is Evan listening to this?

"Hello?" she said. "Mr. D-bag? Come in here and talk to me like a man. Bring Evan too, that piece of shit."

Samantha hoped her eyes would have adjusted to the darkness by now, but that required even the smallest mote of light. There were no seams in the titanium walls, no imperfections that would allow light to enter the cell. She thought about breaking the restraints again, hoping that the red warning light would come on again. At least then she would be able to look for some sort of weakness that she could exploit. She had lifted an industrial crane! Surely she could figure out a way to break through these walls. But she decided against it. The gas would knock her out before she could do anything, and she wasn't ready to risk that. Yet.

"*Are you quite finished, Miss McAllister?*"

"Can I get a bottled water or something? Maybe a hoagie?" Her tone was flippant. They were called "submarine sandwiches," typically abbreviated to "subs," where she was from, but she liked the word "hoagie." It sounded old-timey.

"*What is the origin of your powers, Miss McAllister?*"

There's that goddamned word again.

"Didn't your lackey tell you before he drugged and kidnapped me?"

There was a pause.

"*How did you get your powers, Miss McAllister?*"

Apparently Evan hadn't told this man everything about her. Not that Evan knew the answer to the question any more than she did.

Maybe that's why I'm still alive. Have to deflect as long as possible.

"The Force runs strong in my family," she said. "My father had it. I have it. My...*sister* has it."

Thank you for that one, Evan. But I'm still going to kill you when I get out of this.

More silence, then, "*You don't have a sister, Miss McAllister. Do not lie again.*"

"Wow, you're a sharp one. Okay," she paused to conjure another lie. "I found a lamp and rubbed it, and a big blue genie popped out. He granted me three wishes then launched into a song about the rules. He sounded a lot like Mrs. Doubtfire. There was a magic carpet and a—"

The light came on. Samantha held her breath and burst from the restraints as though they had been fashioned from cardboard instead of steel. The gas burned her eyes as it engulfed her. She leapt from the chair with the intent to throw herself against the far wall with all of the strength she could muster. The escape didn't quite go as planned. Her legs were rubber beneath her. She stumbled to her knees. Pins and needles thrust into her lower extremities.

I can't believe this. My legs are asleep. How long have I been sitting there?

The pressure built in her lungs. She wanted to take a breath so bad, but refused. Tears filled her eyes from the toxic fumes pouring into the small room. Samantha forced herself to her feet and lunged for the wall again. Her numbed legs weakened the attempt, but the impact still created a shock wave that resounded throughout the cell. Her ears rang from the clash. She took a step back and tried to focus her energy for another charge, but the pressure in her chest was too much. Samantha took one last look around the cell and committed the image to memory. The red light was recessed into the ceiling. A tiny vent was next to it, the opening covered in a latticed grate.

That's probably where the camera is hidden. I see you.

She dropped to the floor and succumbed to her captors.

Samantha awoke of her own volition this time. It was the urgent need to vomit that brought her out of the unfeeling nothingness. She retched violently, but her empty stomach produced only bile. The voice in her ear waited until she was finished.

"You need to cooperate, Miss McAllister. Your body can't sustain repeated countermeasures."

Samantha dry heaved again, then spat the caustic taste from her mouth in frustration. She brought her forearm up to wipe her mouth and found that she was no longer restrained.

"You'll find a bottle of water at your feet. I'd advise you to drink it slowly."

She fumbled around in the darkness and found the plastic bottle. It crinkled as she unscrewed the cap and brought it to her lips. Samantha hesitated, sniffing it.

"I assure you that what you hold in your hands is pure, untainted water. No need for overkill."

She sipped the water. It tasted better than anything she had ever drunk in her life. She took a longer drink, then screwed the cap back on and set the bottle on the floor. She wanted to say something sarcastic, but was no longer in the mood for games. The headache had tripled in size and the nausea threatened to overwhelm her.

"How about a little light?" Her voice sounded weak in her ears.

"*No,*" came the reply. "*You give me something, I give you something. That is how this works. I gave you freedom to move about the room. I gave you water. Your turn. How did you get your powers, Miss McAllister?*"

"You 'gave me'? You '*gave me*'?" she said. "You took my freedom, now it's something to be traded back to me? Are you fucking insane? Let me out of here!"

"Your rights as a citizen of this country were revoked the moment you became a threat to national security, Miss McAllister. The moment you decided to use your abilities around innocent civilians, your freedom became forfeit. Or are you going to tell me that the young woman flying in the dance club in the Adams Morgan district was not you? The same woman who used her powers to cheat at roulette in crowded Las Vegas casinos?"

Samantha had the wherewithal not to look up at the hidden camera that was no doubt using night vision or some other means to watch her.

So he's from the government. I should have known. I hate to admit it, but he has a point. I was careless.

"How much did you pay Evan to betray me?" she asked without thinking. "Is he some sort of secret agent?"

"How did you get your powers, Miss McAllister?"

She took her time reaching for the bottle of water.

Think, Sammy. Think!

Maybe she should give up, tell this man everything she knew and hope they go easy on her. She still had the money to return to its rightful owners. She hadn't killed anyone at Vasyl's casino, though she couldn't prove it. A good lawyer could, though. Maybe Evan had been right in bringing her here. Maybe she *was* a threat to national—

No! Stop!

The voice in her ear was silent as she moved about the cell. She took another sip of water and girded her resolve.

I won't be a victim. I refuse.

She fought through the cobwebs in her head and began to work out the problem. An image of the tiny vent beside the recessed light kept flashing in her mind.

"I'm waiting for an answer."

What the hell am I going to say? I don't know the answer.

She opened her mouth to speak and hoped for the best.

"It was when I was at Northwestern. My third year."

That's it. Use something he can confirm. The best lies have some truth to them.

"My friend Jayna was dating a guy who was getting his doctorate at MIT. Real brilliant type. Geeky, but with social skills. We took a road trip out east so that Jayna could see him. Her parents were overprotective and didn't want her to make the drive by herself, so off we went."

She paused in her fabrication to concentrate on the events that took place at the salvage yard with Evan. Her mental film projector sputtered to life, creaking under the weight of the lingering effects of the gas. She searched through the grainy, flickering memories for something to hold on to, something she could use.

"*Go on.*"

"Hank—that was Jayna's boyfriend—was performing some sort of experiment in a very controlled environment. He wouldn't let us into the lab, but said that he'd meet us afterward. Well, Jayna is Jayna, and no one ever says no to her, so she said she was going to surprise him. I thought it was a bad idea, but we did it anyway."

Static erupted in her ear. Another male voice spoke in the background. It was deeper than the voice that had been talking to her, and Samantha thought she detected anger.

If Evan is listening to this, he knows I'm bullshitting. It's a risk I have to take.

She continued her memory search, flipping through the events as fast as she could. She saw an old Mercury splitting apart around her. She was having trouble concentrating, focusing her talent on something specific.

Evan shot me, then...what?

The memory was close now, just out of reach like a word that was on the tip of the tongue but just wouldn't come. It had been a major breakthrough. Something that had amazed her and Evan alike.

"Hank worked in the physics lab, which was down in the basement," she continued. "There were strange sounds coming through the laboratory door. Sort of like a humming that would get louder and then quieter. Like a pulsating sound, I suppose. Again, I told Jayna that we shouldn't surprise him while he was working, but it was no use. When she got something in her head, she wouldn't let anyone talk her out if it. We called her 'Jayna No-way-na'."

There was commotion coming through the earpiece now. It sounded like someone's hand was covering the microphone. The two voices bled through in dribs and drabs. She was able to pick out certain words.

"*...girl... ...interrogate...*"

It was the new voice. And it wasn't Evan's. Then the man who had been talking to her came through very faintly.

"*No! She... ...send... ...I'm in command...*"

She advanced the film reel while they argued. The memory she was looking for finally crystallized in her mind.

"*...relocate... ...Russian... ...helo...*" said the second voice through the muffled microphone.

Alright, it's now or never. Oscar time. It's Escape From Psychotraz starring Samantha McAllister as The Enemy Combatant. You can do this!

She took a drink from the water bottle then dropped it. Gathering herself, she lowered her shoulder and took a run at the wall with everything she had. Reinforced titanium squealed and warped from the impact.

Whoa. I just dented solid titanium.

As expected, the red light came on. When Samantha heard the familiar hiss, she hammered her fists on the wall. The strikes reverberated in her ears, deafening her. She slipped to her knees. "No! NOOO!"

She slumped over and lay still. It was difficult not to pant. Creating the force bubble had taken a lot out of her.

Come on...

Samantha parted her eyelids into a sliver. The red light went out and the hissing stopped. She concentrated on keeping her sphere over the vent.

Come on...

She heard the sound of machinery activating. Pneumatic presses roared to life and a stark, fluorescent glow appeared in a thin line at the juncture of the wall and the ceiling. The light grew as the wall lowered like a drawbridge and created a ramp into her prison.

"Douglas! Stop!"

The voice belonged to the man who had been interrogating her. He sounded out of breath. A dark silhouette came into Samantha's field of vision. The light hurt her eyes, but she dare not let her eyelids flutter.

"She can't keep getting dosed like this!" said the second voice.

Evan.

He was very close to her. It took everything she had not to crush his skull like an egg.

I wouldn't even have to move.

"Then she needs to cooperate. This is going to be a very long process, Douglas. Get out of my way and let me do my job."

Samantha turned her head a fraction of an inch to get a better look. Her eyes were still adjusting to the light, but she could make out a plump figure walking up the ramp to join Evan. The first voice was huffing and puffing as it drew closer to them.

"Damn it, Douglas! Confirm that the subject is subdued before approaching! This is the last time I'm going to tell you!"

"She's not a fucking lab rat, Director," Evan's voice was tinted with genuine concern. "Can't we at least clean her up?"

She saw Evan's velcro-strapped Pony high tops. They were so close that Samantha could smell the leather. Unwanted emotions welled up within her. Sadness and anger at Evan's betrayal shouldered past the fear and anxiety of her immediate situation.

Why, Evan? I just want to know why.

Playing opossum in that moment was excruciating. Freedom was right in front of her.

Wait, Sammy. Wait until you can see what you're doing.

Evan grasped her arm and pulled her into a sitting position. She suppressed the urge to recoil at his touch and instead concentrated on the globe of gas hovering above them. Her timing had to be perfect or she'd end up back in that chair. Or worse.

The Director—as Evan had called him—entered the cell and knelt next to her. Samantha smelled cigar smoke and stale sweat.

"Get her up," the Director said. "And where the hell is Braith—"

Samantha shot out of the cell like a bullet. She still couldn't see very well, but managed to stop her flight at the bottom of the ramp. She spun on the stunned pair.

"Night night," she said.

She released the force bubble while at the same time raising her hands to lift the ramp. The effort of moving the ramp against the pneumatic press that tried to keep it in place threatened to drop her where she stood, but her strength redoubled at the sight of Evan's traitorous face.

"Samantha!" Evan's plea was drowned out as machinery ripped apart with an awful screech.

The ramp became a wall once again, sealing itself in place. Samantha held the wall for a long moment, savoring the percussion of fists on metal. It didn't take long for them to quiet. She let the ramp fall back to the floor with a resounding thud. Evan and the Director rolled onto the ramp, the toxic fumes having taken their toll.

How does it feel?

Samantha found herself in a massive room with catwalks along the walls and caged light fixtures hanging from long rods in the ceiling. It appeared as though her cell had been built in the center of a cavernous, underground chamber. The exterior of the cell looked like something out of a sci-fi horror flick. It was a perfect cube, each titanium side reinforced by thick, steel arms connected to heavy machinery that served to further strengthen the walls. It occurred to Samantha that this prison had been built for her in anticipation of her capture. This had been planned for a long time.

Samantha spotted an exit door at the top of a metal staircase in the corner of the chamber. She gathered her will in preparation to fly to the exit door, but stopped when she caught the odor of the filthy black smock that barely covered her. Evan's grey T-shirt and stonewashed blue jeans looked inviting. They wouldn't fit her, but still...

Better than a vomity potato sack.

She mounted the ramp and stood over Evan. His T-shirt came off with a wave of her finger and floated into her waiting hand. She held it up. The screen print depicted one of the Decepticons from the Transformers movies that he liked so much.

That's apropos. Asshole.

Slinging the shirt over her shoulder, she twisted her hand in the air to flip her former friend to his back. She removed his shoes and jeans, noticing a tattoo on his calf that looked exactly like his cat Mal piloting a spaceship.

That's new.

She dropped Evan's clothes to the ramp and took hold of the smock at the collar, preparing to strip off the foul garment, but froze when she heard a deep groan. The Director was already coming to. Samantha considered the best way to put him back under. She couldn't have a government agent calling in the military on her. She'd seen the end of that tale.

Maybe I'll make him crap his pants in terror before I—

Her internal monologue turned into a scream of agony. Her body seized up, all muscle control lost as tendrils of white hot electricity coursed through the metal of the ramp. She toppled to the titanium like a mannequin, limbs rigid and fingers curled into claws. The current ceased after what seemed like an eternity. Samantha heard heavy footfalls on the metal staircase far across the room.

I'm going to die.

A dozen polished boots entered her field of vision, blurring and clearing through her miasma of pain.

"Stopgap measure."

The voice was deep, vaguely familiar. A heavily-tattooed man knelt in front of her. He was lean and muscular in a corded, sinewy manner, and dressed in combat fatigue pants and a tight, black T-shirt. His hair was dark, close cropped into a flat top. His eyes were the color of dead leaves clinging to a frozen branch just before the first snow. They were dark and dangerous.

The other voice in the earpiece.

"Electricity, sweetie," he said, holding up a tiny fob. "Did you know that titanium is a shitty conductor? If this thing had been made of copper, you'd be dead. Instead, I just turned this entire deal into a giant taser. Old Sharpie didn't think we'd need it to contain you."

His gazed roamed over her from twitching toes to matted hair. Scarred fingers reached out to pull down the hem of her smock that had ridden a touch too high for decency.

"I thought otherwise." he said.

He seized her wrist and dragged her bodily to the top of the ramp. She caught a glimpse of five men in similar fatigues. Each one had a sub-machine gun trained on her. She didn't have time to investigate further as he dumped her onto the cold metal.

"Wait here a sec," he said. "I need a quick word with the Director."

Samantha had no choice but to comply with his request. Although the intense pain was subsiding, her muscles were useless and her brain felt like it had been blended with a whisk. She couldn't focus, couldn't use her abilities.

I'm a fucking meatbag. I'm going to die.

The tattooed man stood over the Director. Disappointment fluttered across his features as he dropped to a knee and went through the Director's pockets. A plastic card appeared from the inside pocket of the Director's suit jacket. The tattooed man smiled at his prize.

"Well, Sharp, we tried it your way, didn't we? And now look at you."

The Director was groaning and trying to sit up. A bullet to the forehead ended his attempts. Samantha jumped in surprise even though her body didn't move. The balding, pudgy man that smelled of cigars fell back to the ramp. Samantha hadn't even seen the tattooed man draw his sidearm. The pistol was in his shoulder holster one second and smoking in his hand the next, like an Old West gunfighter.

The man turned to Samantha. "I just did you a favor. He wanted to—how did he put it—'study you'. Yeah, that was it."

He shot the Director again, but his eyes were still trained on her. The Director's body lurched once, then was still.

The muzzle rotated to the unconscious Evan.

NO!

The slide retracted and snapped forward in slow motion. Evan's brain matter decorated the ramp. It was an image that would never leave her.

"Make that two favors," he said. "He's the one that gave you up. You owe me, young lady, and I intend to collect."

Samantha's scream of horror came out as an unintelligible whine. She was unable to turn her head away from the gruesome display. Her face was stone, but inside she was a slobbering mess. Never had she felt so helpless.

Evan...

Then the murderer was kneeling in front of her. She hadn't seen him approach, unable to tear her eyes from Evan. His voice was low and threatening.

"This is where I tell you my villainous plans for you."

He gathered a handful of her hair into his fist and jerked her face upwards. His breath smelled of mint and tobacco. "You're going to be broken, reduced to a sniveling wretch. Stripped of your humanity and beaten into a shapeless block of clay. And once you're nothing but a shadow of your former self, I'm going to mold you into the greatest weapon of mass destruction this planet has ever seen."

His lips pressed against her ear, his voice barely a whisper.

"And my finger will be on the button."

Samantha's skin crawled. Her tongue was thick in her mouth, muting her cries of defiance. She fought against the aftereffects of the electrocution, tried to bring her will to bear.

Have get out of here... Evan!.

But Evan was right there in front of her, the contents of his skull leaking onto the titanium. The image was frozen in negative exposure as the hood slipped over her head.

Chapter Eighteen

SOMEONE WAS SCREAMING.

Samantha couldn't tell who the scream belonged to or where it came from, but its echoes surrounded her. A second scream joined the first one, then a third howl piped in with the first two to create a symphony of agony.

The floor was cold against her knees and the tops of her feet as she was dragged by strong hands clamped tightly over her wrists, pulling her like baggage. The soles of heavy boots clacked on either side of her. There was a grating squeal, possibly from the hinges of a heavy door, then the odor of mold and mildew penetrated the hood. Freezing air gripped her. Samantha could hear the rattle of ductwork overhead, and the accompanying chill made her wonder if a cooling system was working overtime to force this environment into the ice age. She was lifted from the floor and set down again.

"Stand up straight." The voice was gruff and thick with a Russian accent.

A strong hand seized her upper arm, hefting her into the air.

Gotta focus. I'm going to make them pay when this hood comes off.

Voices spoke in low tones nearby. One of them was familiar—the tattooed man, the one who had killed Evan and Sharp. Something hard and cold clamped around her wrists. She heard chains rattle.

Chains? They think chains can hold me?

Her arms were raised above her head as steel links jangled through pulleys high above her. They didn't stop until she was on the balls of her bare feet.

I can feel my legs now. I'm getting my balance back. It won't be long.

The smock tightened on her back and she was jerked forward in the chains. The scent of tobacco mixed with the mildew. The voice was low and intimate.

"There are certain things in this life that we'd die for, McAllister." It was the tattooed man. "They are the same things that we live for. These things are different from person to person. For some, it's their property. For others, it's their money. Those people are weak."

He released her, but the voice stayed close.

Not yet, not yet.

"Now me, I'd die for my country. I don't think you would. So what is it that you hold most dear, girl? I think I know, but I'm going to find out for sure. In the meantime, meet Galina."

The sound of heels clicked close to her. Samantha could smell expensive perfume.

"She's a sculptor," said the tattooed man. A hand patted her cheek through the hood. "Play nice."

Samantha heard him moving away from her. Old hinges yowled as the door slammed shut with finality. The cries she had heard in the corridor pierced the door, reverberating throughout the room.

"The screams you hear belong to a family from Louisiana who wanted to see the capital of this glorious nation."

Galina's voice was soft, her accent very faint. Samantha froze, and so did her thoughts of escape.

No. Please, no.

"Tourists never quite know the lay of the land, and are receptive to misinformation. They were taken without a fuss, with no one the wiser," said Galina. "They are here because of you, my darling."

Samantha's mind raced.

Oh my god. Can I get free and find them before something happens to them? Is she lying? Maybe I can use her as a hostage, trade her for them.

"Now before you get it in your head to do something heroic, know that there are sensors on both the chains and your manacles. If they are disturbed or, say, snapped like threads—which I'm sure you are quite capable of—a signal will alert my associates that you are trying to escape. They have been ordered to end the family's sightseeing expedition if that happens. Nod if you understand."

Samantha's stomach twisted into knots. Fear gripped at her, tightening around her heart.

That poor family...

Tattooed man's words came rushing back to her like water through a sieve. *You're going to be broken, reduced to a sniveling wretch. Stripped of your humanity and beaten into a shapeless block of clay. Meet Galina. She's a sculptor.*

"Do you understand?" Galina's voice was sharp.

Samantha nodded.

"Good."

Galina's heels tapped away from her. An eerie silence followed. Samantha's breath quickened inside the hood. There was a faint squeal somewhere in the room.

Samantha didn't know it was water at first. It hit her like a cannonball, driving her back with brute force. She heard herself cry out in a surprised yelp. The force of the water didn't hurt in the least, but it was ice cold. The heavy stream shifted from her torso to her face. Samantha held her ground as best she could, but the water bled through the material of the hood. It rocked her head back, filling her nose and mouth. She couldn't breathe. Panic set in, shattering any chance of using her ability to protect herself. Her chest tightened and her legs grew weak. She bucked in the chains against the frigid onslaught, turning her head every which way in futile attempts to escape the torment. Samantha didn't have time to feel relief when it finally stopped. That's when the electricity switched on.

It came up through her toes, traveling through her body in an agonizing torrent. Muscles seized and twisted into taut cords. Her jaw locked up, teeth clamped like a vise. An eternity passed before it was over, leaving Samantha hanging from the manacles, a shivering mass of wet misery. She didn't hear the woman approach. The hood left her head with a quick tug.

Galina was a thick woman in a spotless, white business suit. Her blonde hair was pulled back so severely that it stretched the pale skin of her face like a drum head. Beady eyes were set deep under a bony brow decorated with uneven, painted eyebrows, and her lips were thin over a strong chin. She appeared to be in her late forties. A satisfied smile creased those narrow lips. Samantha coughed and choked out a mixture of water and blood from where she had bitten her tongue. Manicured fingertips cleared the saturated ropes of hair from Samantha's face. The woman cupped her chin and raised it, appraising her features.

"Such a pretty girl," she said. "I could get a handsome price for you back home."

Samantha found the strength to spit at her.

Galina moved with surprising dexterity, sidestepping the bloody glob of water. Rage flickered over her face, but disappeared as she composed herself. She straightened her white jacket and replaced her smile.

Score, bitch.

Samantha's satisfied grin transformed into a grimace as her rigid muscles resumed their normal blood flow.

This hurts so fucking much.

"Do you think you're strong, girl?" said Galina. "Better than me? Such is the lie of your people. The 'ugly American' is what you are called in my country. Entitled and spoiled. You spit at my observation, but strength is what saved me from the brothel and brought me to power. Strength that you do not possess. You are weak."

Samantha blinked and looked down, trying to focus her swimming vision. She stood in a clear, plexiglass enclosure that rose just above her knees. A few inches of water had collected at the bottom, and through it she could see that her feet were touching a wide plate of rusting iron. She surmised that the electricity had come from a power source beneath it. The water would carry the current to her even if she raised her feet from the plate.

"Now," Galina continued, "normally I would pull out your fingernails or pluck out your hair lock by lock until you told me what I wanted to know, but this is not an interrogation and you are far from normal."

I know.

Samantha raised her head and looked past the woman as she monologued. The room was spacious with cracked and rotting plaster walls covered in yellow streaks. A large utility hose, similar in size to those used for fire emergencies in office buildings, hung on the wall next to a thick, rusted water pipe. Water still dripped from the hose nozzle. A broad, flat-screen television resting on a wheeled cart hugged a nearby wall. Black cables extended into the base of the wall below it. A stainless steel table nestled against the opposite wall. It's spotless surface reflected the single, pale light bulb that hung from the ceiling in a caged dome. A security camera was situated next to it, trained directly on Samantha. Galina ended Samantha's tour of the room by stepping in front of her.

"You are very special," she said, "and require a special touch. I'm told that your abilities protect you from harm, and that you are capable of fantastic things. Things that weren't thought possible before you appeared. Your friend was quite thorough in his evaluation of you. Unfortunate, what happened to that one."

Why, Evan?

"It is these talents that the Commander wishes to harness. All you have to do is agree to aid him in his cause and the family will be released. You will be free to make the world a better place."

Galina paused, watching for a response. Samantha hung before her in silence, her chin fell against her chest.

I'm going to kill this woman.

Again, Galina forced Samantha to look at her.

"You're going to hate me even more in the coming days, my dear," she said. "But eventually everything I say will make sense to you. My values will become your values. My beliefs your beliefs. And when that happens you will come to understand that, with the Commander's guidance, you can save this world from true evil."

It required supreme effort, but Samantha forced her tongue to work, her lips to move. What came out was a cracked whisper. "When...when I get...free...I'm coming for...for you...first."

Galina took two steps back and turned to look up at the camera. When she nodded, a dull hum began at Samantha's feet. A dead calm fell over Galina's features as the electricity came. It was the last thing Samantha saw before consciousness fled.

"What's wrong, Becks?"

Evan caressed her face with a gloved hand. He was in his superhero costume, probably getting ready to fly off and save the world again.

"I'm so cold," Samantha said through chattering teeth. "I can't get warm."

She held out her wrists to him. They were encased in ice. Sharp edges dug into her skin, bathing her hands in rivulets of blood that dripped from her fingertips. There was a red spot on his forehead. It grew larger and darker, soaking through the material of his mask.

"Your head," she said, reaching up to lift the mask from his face.

The face that was revealed was not Evan's gentle countenance. It was a pale, gaunt demon with burning eyes and a slathering, forked tongue that snaked out from between gruesome fangs. A hole in its forehead dripped corrosive, green liquid that hissed as it blistered and burned the demon's skin.

"What's wrong, Becks?"

The voice was not his either. It was not of this world, harsh and terrifying. She opened her mouth to reply, but gushing water silenced her.

Samantha's cry was a gurgling, drowned wail as the freezing water crashed into her face. She turned her head away from it, but the stream always found another spot on her body until her head came back around to receive the thrashing once more.

Galina waited until Samantha's sputtering died down before approaching her prisoner. Her hair was in the same tight bun, but she was now clad in a grey business suit with subtle white pinstripes. Samantha raised her eyes. Her entire body palpitated. They stared at each other in silence. Then the screams perforated the metal door.

What am I going to do? What can *I do?*

"Please," Samantha said, her voice stronger now. "Please let them go."

Galina raised her hand just above her shoulder and extended two fingers. The water, which was now up to Samantha's ankles, erupted as current coursed through it. It was only a short burst, but enough to sting Samantha.

"You are not to speak until told to do so."

Galina's hand shot out to wrap around Samantha's neck. Samantha could feel the pressure, but there was no pain or obstruction to her breathing. She could see the Russian woman's arm shaking from exertion as she tried to choke Samantha. Galina finally let go with a puzzled expression.

"Your skin and flesh are pliable, yet there is something there. Just beneath," she mused. "Your friend told us you are impervious to bullets. How is this so?"

Samantha sagged in her chains. Her head lolled onto her shoulder. Somewhere beyond the cell, the screaming had stopped. Galina's hand slipped inside her suit jacket and emerged with a semi-automatic pistol clenched loosely in her fist. She drew the slide back and pointed the barrel at Samantha's chest.

Crack!

The ricochet buried itself into the moldy plaster wall nearby. The empty shell casing hit the floor and rolled to a stop behind Galina. Samantha barely moved from the bullet's contact.

Fuck you, bitch.

"How is this so?" Galina said. "You may speak."

Samantha stared ahead through half-lidded eyes. Her throat was raw and her joints ached.

I just want to go home. I want to go to sleep forever in my nice, warm bed.

Galina's painted eyebrow curled upward. She returned the firearm to her suit jacket and marched back to the hose, releasing another powerful stream of glacial water at Samantha. It went on for a long time before she closed the spigot.

Samantha retched, trying to expel the water from her lungs. She couldn't draw a breath. Agonizing paroxysms seized her. She undulated in the chains, writhing in wide-eyed panic. As she fought for oxygen, she was vaguely aware of Galina moving the television in front of her. She switched it on and left Samantha to her misery. The screen was a solid blue.

It was a while before Samantha's breathing returned to normal. The freezing water was now above her ankles. Her toes were numb. Some of the hose water had found its way down her esophagus, relieving her thirst somewhat. Now hunger set in, gnawing at her belly from the inside out.

I can't remember the last time I ate. I'd give my right arm for one of Ben's Pickled Pickles right now.

She tried not to think about it.

Thick, juicy burgers dripping with melted cheese and bursting with fresh veggies. Aunt Lizzie's old-country lasagna hot out of the oven with a chunk of buttery garlic bread. Charcoal-grilled filet mignon with just a touch of pink in the middle melting in my mouth... Stop!.

She looked up at the camera and contemplated shouting something profane at it.

No, I don't feel like becoming a lightning rod again. I need to remain calm and figure this out. Let's see. Cold. Electricity. Gas. Oh, and drugged iced tea. Now I know I'm not invulnerable. That makes me feel a little bit less like a freak. But they also know my vulnerabilities. How could I have been so stupid as to trust anybody? Evan, why did you do it? How did you get mixed up with these monsters? Why do I miss you?

She cocked her head closer to the door as someone walked past.

I have to at least try to save those poor people. But how? If I break these chains and blow the door from the hinges, then what? How can I possibly find them before—

The television flickered to life, the blue screen switching to an image of a middle-aged man with perfectly coifed hair. He looked familiar, but Samantha couldn't remember his name. His rich baritone radiated from the television speakers.

"*Our New York affiliates are receiving eyewitness reports that an aircraft has crashed into the north tower of the World Trade Center. Not much is known at this time, but we'll stay with this story and bring you details as they emerge.*"

Images taken from helicopter footage filled the screen. Black smoke billowed from the majestic skyscraper.

What is this?

Samantha had been a child when this tragedy struck. Her father had explained it to her and Cole as best he could, but they had been too young to understand. New York city had seemed so far away from southwestern Ohio. Father had said they were safe there, but he didn't seem convinced.

"*We have received information that the aircraft may have been a passenger jet out of Logan International Airport in Boston. The Federal Aviation Administration has not confirmed this as of yet, but we are awaiting official word.*"

Samantha eyes were glued to the images on the plasma screen. Anchors' voices floated through the room, bouncing from decrepit plaster walls into Samantha's ears. And through those voices the horrible sequence of events continued to unfold. The south tower. The Pentagon. Shanksville, Pennsylvania. Time slipped by, and Samantha was transfixed. She had never revisited this horrific chapter in American history as an adult. Why would she? Samantha, like many Americans, had gone on with her life. Now she was being forced to relive it. Someone was falling from one of the towers. The news anchor reported that people were jumping from the burning buildings. The south tower fell, followed by the north.

Samantha's cheeks were wet even though she had long since dried from the dousing.

Hours passed as the frantic news cycle covered every aspect of the immediate aftermath of the attacks. The screen switched to photo of a benign-looking man in a white head dress. The caption read:

al-Qaeda Leader Takes Responsibility for 9/11 Attacks

A translation of the man's voice played in concert with the photo.

"*...we are free ... and want to regain freedom for our nation. As you undermine our security we undermine yours.*"

The footage changed to news coverage of large gatherings of people in foreign countries supporting the attacks.

I never knew. I never knew we were hated so much.

The television then depicted American military operations in Iraq and Afghanistan. The President had proclaimed a war on terror, and this was Samantha's very own private screening. A front row seat to the evil of terrorism. The screen went dark when the presentation was finished.

Samantha had no sense of how much time had passed. Her eyes were full of sand. Hunger pulled at her, weakening her. She realized she had been leaning forward in the chains, watching the television open-mouthed. She licked her dry lips and heard the water swish as she adjusted her stance for the thousandth time. The light bulb pulsated, pounding audibly in her head in its pervasive silence. She swayed, and would have fallen if her bonds had not caught her weight.

"What's the matter, Sammy?"

"I'm so tired, Daddy."

He was dressed in his superhero costume. Green had always been his favorite color. It suited him well.

"It's okay. Go to sleep," he said.

His hand rustled her hair. It was a familiar sensation. One of her oldest memories.

"I can't, Daddy," she said. "Not yet."

Samantha's eyes shot open as the voltage coursed through her. Then the current was gone, replaced by the familiar pain of her contracted muscles.

I want to go home. Just let me go home.

The screams returned, and Samantha could do nothing but stand shivering in the icy water and listen to them. She wondered what was being done to the family, what tortures Galina was inflicting that wouldn't work on Samantha. Was she pulling out fingernails, ripping hair from their scalps?

The television switched on.

"*Three bombs were detonated in the London Underground this morning...*"

Samantha remembered this news story a little better than that of the 9/11 tragedy. As minutes stretched into hours, she became very familiar with the details of the 2007 attacks. She closed her eyes and tried her best to block it out. An idea came to her, a game she used to play with Cole.

Brad Pitt. He was in Sleepers with Kevin Bacon. That's one degree of Kevin Bacon.

Chris Pratt. He was in Guardians of the Galaxy with...what's that guy's name? The blue guy?

"A fourth bomb was detonated on a double decker bus, bringing the total casualties to fifty-two people dead and more than seven hundred injured."

Samantha shook her head and concentrated.

Dammit. He's been in a bunch of stuff. Matthew? Michael? Michael Rooker! Chris Pratt was in Guardians of the Galaxy with Michael Rooker who was in JFK with Kevin Bacon. That's two degrees.

Ambulance sirens issued from the television, filling her prison. The anchor's voice permeated the room as he continued his depressing report. Samantha glanced up at her manacled wrists.

I could snap them like twigs. I could fly out of here. It's not my fault that the family got caught. Maybe I can live with that if I—

No, Samantha.

This time it wasn't her internal monologue. She turned her head with frantic twitches, searching for the source of the voice. The room was empty.

Now I'm hearing voices? I'm going crazy. No, wait. People who are going crazy don't think *they are going crazy. They just go crazy.*

She buckled down and picked another hunky actor to relate back to Kevin Bacon.

Channing Tatum. Channing Tatum was in—what was the name of that movie? He was in...

The television screen flipped to news footage of the beheadings of American citizens. It was too much for her. Samantha's wail was primal, drowning out the sounds of the television, the rattling chains above her, and the sloshing water below her.

"Stop it! Just stop it!"

The television darkened and went silent as if she'd spoken the magic words. Her labored breathing was all she heard. Then came the *tick tack* of heels as Galina entered the cell. This time her business suit was black.

How long have I been here?

The woman went to the hose and opened the valve. Samantha flinched when the nozzle was pointed at her, preparing herself for another frigid onslaught.

It never came.

Samantha gave Galina a cautious look. The blonde woman was staring back her with an unreadable expression.

What's happening?

Drops of water fell from the nozzle to the floor, breaking the eerie silence with sporadic plips and plops.

She's waiting for something. Waiting for me to agree to her terms.

Samantha's dry, reddened eyes got the better of her and she lost the visual standoff. She rubbed them against her shoulders in an attempt to soothe the aching, then looked back at Galina.

She was gone.

The hose was coiled on its large hook, exactly as it had been for hours. Or had it been days? Samantha blinked several times then searched the room. No one was there. Her fear intensified tenfold.

No no no... I'm losing it. I'm losing my mind.

Tormented cries echoed from the hall. Samantha could only listen, staring at the black television screen in a state somewhere between waking and sleep. The reflections in the screen twisted into faces that were clear only if she didn't look right at them. Their features were a mystery, but she could see mouths agape in silent screams.

Galina was there, standing right in front of her. This time Samantha hadn't heard the door open or the sound of her heels on the hard floor. The hallway had fallen silent.

"Do you want a hot bath? Something to eat, my dear?" Galina said.

Samantha's smile was weary. "You're not real."

Galina narrowed her eyes. She reached up to pat Samantha's cheek like a grandmother after presenting her granddaughter with a piece of stale candy. The hand was warm against Samantha's chilled skin.

Is she really here?

"I'm here, girl." Galina said. "The Commander will return soon, and has authorized me to feed you and clothe you in something warm and comfortable. And to let you rest."

I don't...I can't...

"What about the family?"

Galina glanced at the door, then back at Samantha with concern writ plainly on her face. "I'm afraid they will remain our guests until the terms of our agreement are finalized."

But...but I never agreed. Did I?

Galina licked her thumb and rubbed dried spittle from the corner of Samantha's mouth, then motioned to the television.

"You saw what those monsters are capable of, Miss McAllister. Surely you see that the Commander only wants your help in bringing them to justice. Surely you understand now that he is not the enemy. They are. All of them."

Samantha's exhausted mind couldn't push away the images she had been subjected to. She knew that she had the power to do something about it. She could crush all of them.

Is this what I was meant to do?

She pictured a giant, stuffed burrito, spiced chicken and cool guacamole, all wrapped in a warm, chewy tortilla. The flavors exploded in her mouth as she took the first bite. She imagined slipping into her bed after a long, steamy shower, her soft comforter tucked under her chin. Samantha mouthed the words that wouldn't come.

I'll do it.

Evan's brains spilled onto cold metal. The Commander's breath was hot. Mint and tobacco. *And my finger will be on the button.*

"What is that, my dear?" Galina leaned in with her ear toward Samantha's mouth.

Deal with it and move on, Samantha.

Her voice was a murmur as she leaned toward Galina. "I...said..."

Galina leaned closer. Samantha tried to moisten the desert of her mouth.

"Go...go...*fuck* yourself!"

Galina's back hand lashed out, but Samantha didn't care. It smashed into her cheek with a sharp slap that echoed from every surface of the stark room. Galina's howl of pain drowned out those echoes. It wasn't unlike those of the poor, imprisoned family. She danced in a circle, cradling her broken hand.

Samantha's maniacal laughter was cut short by arcs of white hot electricity.

Chapter Nineteen

"WHAT'S THE MATTER, SAMANTHA?"

A woman stood before her decked out in black and red leathers and matching boots with heavy chrome buckles. Her face was concealed by the dark visor of a motorcycle helmet. Samantha stared at her with reddened, burning eyes.

I want to go home.

"You can't give them what they want, Samantha."

But I want to. So much.

The woman removed the motorcycle helmet. Fiery red hair spilled out, framing a freckled face with green, feline eyes. Samantha expected to be staring at herself—after all, the woman was wearing Samantha's motorcycle outfit—but it wasn't her. The woman seemed very familiar though, especially the sound of her voice.

"What does your dad always tell you?"

Deal with it and move on.

"That's right."

The woman tapped Samantha on the forehead and a brilliant white light flared before Samantha's eyes. Her vision withdrew into a majestic star field that moved away from her with exponential acceleration as though she were traveling backwards through the cosmos. She heard tinty musical notes playing in a tempo so slow it was excruciating, as though a wind-up key had almost reached its final position on a faraway music box. The stars extended into bars of light as they shot by with mind-numbing speed. They changed colors, twisting and weaving in among themselves before coalescing into a psychedelic tunnel.

Everything stopped.

Samantha felt an impact across her entire body, as if someone had slammed on the brakes doing one hundred miles per hour in reverse. Her surprised exclamation echoed through her ears in an infinite delay feed. She hovered in empty space. The star patterns were strange. Far away, a nebula sparkled in a mesmerizing array of colors. At its center was a brilliant red dwarf star.

So beautiful...

What was that? And why is she smiling?

Samantha was back in her cell. The water was above her knees from repeated quenching, and slopped over the edges of the container whenever she moved. The content of the terrorism videos had some time ago moved to current activities, mostly ISIS. She didn't know how long it had been playing. Samantha no longer had any sense of time.

A constant, high-pitched tone played in her ears. If felt like when she removed her earbuds after blasting music through them. It was the latest irritation in her miserable life.

Good. She's back with us. Time to give it another go.

The monotone note in her head vibrated with the words as though someone had plucked a guitar string. The last syllable sounded like it was falling down a deep well. The voice was familiar.

Galina?

Galina clacked into the cell as if on cue. Her business suit was dark red today. Samantha watched her stand beside the television with her hand resting on its top. The other hand was wrapped in bandages and hung from her shoulder in a sling.

"This is a modern threat, young lady," she said, tapping the television, "a problem that is not going to be solved by your weak government."

Samantha hung limp from her bound wrists. Her cracked lips were parted, her swollen tongue was thick in her mouth.

Is she too far gone to understand me?

"You've seen what their predecessors did to your country. Now these people have taken up the mantle. They want every American dead. You're not going to let that happen, are you?"

"No," Samantha croaked, too exhausted to question why Galina was speaking both in her head and with her physical voice.

Galina's face lit up.

Yes. This is good.

"No," Samantha said. "I...understand you."

Galina's head tilted in confusion.

What does she mean by that?

Galina approached Samantha and pushed the young woman's hair back from her face. Her voice was low and earnest.

"You could crush the terrorists with a thought. No soldiers would have to die defending their country. No innocents would be blown up in subways or in office buildings or in their very homes. Think of it! And in return, the Commander has told me that you will want for nothing. As his second, you will have anything and everything you desire. And many things you didn't even know you wanted."

She's almost there. Just a little more.

Am I hearing her thoughts? Or am I so far gone that I'm just hearing echoes of conversations from a long time ago? How many people have died in this room?

"He'll teach you to fight," Galina continued. "He'll hone your gifts, make them sharp. He'll outfit you with technology to compensate for your weaknesses. You'll be unstoppable, Samantha."

Samantha twitched. The chains rattled. It was the first time Galina had spoken her name. Her head lolled to the side, eyes far away. Galina watched for a long time, then switched off the television and stalked to the exit.

Stubborn little cunt. Time for more screaming.

The door slammed behind her, but it didn't suppress the family's tortured wails that followed in short order. They had become a song now. A song about pain and abject terror that played for hours on end. Samantha suspected she would hear the song as she lay down to sleep for years to come.

That's if they decide not to kill me. Maybe death would be better. Much better. She wondered if she could use her abilities to accomplish the task.

Samantha sensed motion across the room. It was nothing new. Her eyes constantly played tricks on her now. The entirety of her peripheral vision had become a playground for phantoms. Samantha looked toward the movement anyway.

He was leaning against the far wall, clad in a sharp, grey Armani. The newspaper was unfolded in front of his face. Pages rustled as he straightened out the creases.

Paperboy.

She knew his name, but it didn't come to her.

Why isn't he helping me? He's just standing there reading.

The headline on the front page was crystal clear, even though it was too distant to read:

MCALLISTER KILLS THOUSANDS IN YEMEN

Samantha's legs slipped away. An immediate, overwhelming sorrow smothered her. The wail came all the way from her toes, its melody a chilling counterpoint to the familiar song that played through the door. Across the room, an index finger curled down the corner of the paper.

But it wasn't Paperboy's handsome face that greeted her. It was the man Galina had called the Commander. The man who wanted to tame her, turn her into a tool for his ambitions.

Never.

Her gut-wrenching cry morphed into laughter. It was a cackling, terrible sound, borne of starvation, thirst and sleep deprivation. The mirage broke into millions of tiny shards that crashed to the floor with a crack of thunder. The water at her knees rippled from the vibration. The laughter died on her lips.

Was that real?

She stood still as a statue, not wanting to splash water on the floor as she strained her ears.

Boom!

There it was. She could feel the vibrations through her feet this time. Samantha wondered if it was raining too. Samantha couldn't remember what rain felt like, but she wanted to run through it more than anything at that moment. Let it wash everything away.

The light in her cell flickered. Samantha squinted as it came back on.

Kra-Boom!

This one was the biggest yet. She knew it wasn't a trick, and it wasn't a hallucination. Deep down, she just knew. It was real thunder. Something primal she could hold on to. She looked up at the wires running through the chains above her. The screams grew louder, as if they were competing with the storm.

KA-RAAACK!

Samantha was cast into complete blackness. The keening cut off as though someone had skipped the needle across a record. It just stopped mid-scream. She didn't move. Her heart threatened to pound out of her chest.

Are they dead? Oh no...

"Omega! Omega!" The frenzied shout came from outside her cell.

KRA-KOOM!

"Get the generators up! This is a Code Omega! Move!"

The voice belonged to Galina. She was frightened.

Samantha fought through her fatigue, tried to make sense of everything, anything. When the door to her cell opened, what little rational thought she had left was pushed into the back of her mind and locked up tight. Adrenalin replaced reason. She became the mother's arm lashing out to protect her child in the passenger seat. She became pure instinct because it was all she had left.

The chains shattered with a twitch of her arms. Men rushed into the room, red emergency lighting filtering through the door behind them. They continued moving, but not through any control of their own. Bodies smashed into the far wall, the left wall, and finally the right wall with such speed that they crumpled to the floor like discarded puppets when the pummeling was over. The plexiglass container shattered. Water flew in all directions, bathing the walls. The television screen fractured, then the entire device tumbled from its stand to explode against the steel table. Samantha floated from the metal plate and placed her feet firmly on the floor for the first time in what seemed like years.

Two more men ran into the cell. They wore gas masks and held short rifles with tubes that connected to metal tanks on their backs. The considerable lengths of chain still connected to Samantha's wrist manacles reared up like dancing cobras. They whipped at the men faster than their eyes could follow, knocking the guns from their grips and rending clothing and flesh. Their yells were muffled by the gas masks as the chains slipped around their ankles and pulled them from their feet.

Samantha exited the room with her thrashing prisoners in tow, and stopped just outside her cell. There was a closed door halfway down the hall, and another at the very end of the corridor. The first man was sent smashing through the nearest door as the chain holding him coiled, snapped and released.

"Нет! Подождите!"

The second man pleaded for his life just before he splintered the far door with his back.

The first door revealed a control room filled with audio visual equipment, including a large monitor and control panel. The tortured family was not inside. She ejected the unconscious mercenary from the room with a thought. Bones snapped as he connected with the corridor wall.

Peanut brittle.

The monitor was dark, as were the indicator lights that decorated the control board. She spied a dial with voltage and amperage levels defined around its perimeter. Beside that was a sound mixer, and next to the sound mixer were what appeared to be camera controls. P.A. speakers faced the walls nearest to her cell.

No...

She rushed from the room and turned to the door at the end of the hall, which led to a staircase. Stiletto heels tapped on the metal steps high above. Galina was running for her life. Samantha floated after her like an apparition. Her face was free of emotion and her arms hung limp at her sides, the chains rattling on the steps below her. Golden hair trailed behind her in tangled, ghostly tendrils. She caught Galina three flights up. Samantha's tormentor was on her knees, attempting to prime a generator with her good hand. The semi-automatic handgun with which she had shot Samantha lay beside her.

The firearm lifted from the floor of its own volition. The barrel pressed against the unsuspecting Galina's temple. She stiffened. The slide pulled back and released. A whimper escaped Galina's lips. Then the gun simply came apart. It disassembled itself into its component parts and clattered to the floor in pieces. Galina spun on Samantha with eyes wide. Her mouth opened to say something to the specter of death floating before her, but her blonde bun unraveled and she was jerked to her back by her hair.

Samantha flew back down the staircase, towing a bellowing Galina behind her. Each metal step was a new abrasion or bruise for

Samantha's former torturer as she was dragged unceremoniously down each flight by unseen hands. When they reached the cell, Galina found herself on her belly, head pressed against the metal plate. Samantha pictured the generator controls high above and started it with a thought. The room was bathed in the familiar, pale light, the only light Samantha had known for what seemed like an eternity. Nearby, a mercenary groaned in agony. There was a rumble of thunder high above.

"No! You don't want to do this, Samantha!"

Samantha could feel Galina trying to lift her head from the iron. The resistance was very weak as it pushed against her will, barely perceptible. She was a newborn kitten wrestling with a lioness. Samantha recalled the voltage meter dial. She summoned an image of the mixer and the P.A. speakers.

"I didn't piss myself until the third time," Samantha said. Her own voice was that of a stranger, low and dangerous in her ears. "Let's see how long you last."

Galina shrieked. Her skirt darkened with urine. Samantha hadn't even switched on the current yet.

Then she did.

Samantha activated the audio controls as her former captor writhed in agony on the wet floor. She had to be sure. As expected, three screams echoed down the hallway and filtered into the torture room. She shut it down in disgust.

You did the right thing. You didn't know.

Samantha ended Galina's torment with a turn of the voltage dial. The woman lay in convulsions as her muscles attempted to reassert control. Samantha knew the feeling well. She left the cell and returned to the control room. A small refrigerator in the corner revealed a feast fit for a queen. A half-eaten egg salad sandwich, a Snickers bar and two bottles of water. Samantha shoved every last bit into her mouth with ravenous abandon. She gave the dial a final twist while licking her fingers clean. Galina twitched on the monitor screen, and didn't stop moving until Samantha gathered her will and imploded the entire control panel in on itself. Sparks flew and acrid smoke wafted from the ruined electronics.

Samantha steadied herself against the doorframe as her adrenalin started to ebb. She felt better after the small meal, but it was far from adequate to replenish her strength. Her world was still distant and surreal. Her muscles were jelly. Another peal of thunder shook the floor, reminding Samantha that she needed to get out of this hellish place.

She made way her way to the staircase at the end of the corridor, ignoring the pleas of mercy from the mercenary-turned-battering-ram. She alternated between walking and floating as she ascended the steps floor after floor. Both forms of movement took great effort. She shut down the generator as she passed it and continued upward.

Let them learn what it's like to be terrified in the darkness.

Samantha pushed through a door and found sweet, natural air, but didn't have a chance to savor it. She found herself on hands and knees as powerful winds buffeted her. Torrential sheets of rain pounded against her body.

Rain. I missed you.

She harnessed her will and rose into the air, smiling as warm, pelting drops soaked her skin. The effort was taxing, but worth it. She was free.

Looking down, she found that she had exited an abandoned power station. A utility tower swayed below her in the mighty gale. Her eyes wandered to the horizon and found the familiar skyline of Washington D.C. An expansive patch of darkness was devouring the capital as power was lost. A flash of lightning revealed movement on the skyline. Samantha's gaze locked onto it. For a moment, she thought she was still hallucinating. If only that were the case.

The Washington Monument was falling.

The wind whispered in her ear. "Go to sleep."

I can't, Daddy. Not yet.

She propelled herself toward the city as fast as her gifts would allow.

Chapter Twenty

THE MAINE COON JUMPED INTO DAVID'S LAP for the third time. He leaned forward, trying to see the road through the deluge that the old Saturn's wipers couldn't compete with—not that any windshield wipers could compete with the Storm of the Century, as the news broadcasts were calling it.

"Marissa, please."

"Sorry, Mr. Daniels." Marissa scooped up the gigantic cat and placed it in her lap.

Lightning lit the sky twice in quick succession, disrupting the radio broadcast that struggled through the speakers. "*...please seek shelter. The greater—KSH!—area is under a hurricane warn—KSH!*"

"Damn it!"

David tried to adjust the tuning for a better signal, but it was hopeless. His grim expression wasn't lost on his administrative assistant who sat next to him, cradling her cat with terror in her eyes. He hadn't told her the entire story of why he had shown up at her door and ordered her to pack a bag, only that he had to get her to safety. The hurricane had hit with sudden and tremendous furor before they had even reached the end of her street in Alexandria. It was unnatural.

The safe house was out in Potomac, which meant either taking his chances on the beltway or driving through the city. Both options promised unfavorable outcomes. David figured that most of the people had already evacuated the metropolitan area, but that probably meant the freeways were stacked with cars. No, it was better avoid that mess if at all possible. He just hoped that the high wind speeds and dangerous flooding would allow them some sort of path through the city. So far it had been an exercise in futility just to keep the car on the road.

He had purchased the safe house several years ago, when he had first started his consulting company. Experience with black ops missions in the military had taught him to always have a backup plan in case things got FUBAR'd. This was one of those times. Debunking the paranormal and solving cult-related crimes for the FBI was one thing, but this was entirely different. He was deep into off-the-books NSA stuff, dealing with people that could—and would—erase you from society without thinking twice. And now he had killed one of his own, a SEAL-turned-mercenary working for Braithwaite, who in turn worked for an assistant director in the NSA. They didn't need David anymore, and now Marissa was mixed up in this by association.

It wasn't that Marissa had been complicit in any wrongdoing, nor had she been a partner in his investigation. She was simply doing what she was asked as an employee; making calls, doing research, and feeding him information. But Sharp and Braithwaite didn't know how much she knew, and they wouldn't take any chances. Sharp knew that Marissa worked for David. That was enough. This was FUBAR. Time to disappear for a while.

"Look out!"

David's smash cut back to the present revealed a car careening off the guardrail right in front of them. He wrenched the steering wheel and tapped the brakes to prevent an uncontrolled slide, which sent

Marissa's Saturn skidding around the out-of-control vehicle, missing it by inches. David brought the Saturn to a halt and looked in the rear-view mirror to see the careening car come down on it roof. It rocked several times, then was still.

"Stay here," he said as he unbuckled his safety belt and opened the car door.

David was pelted by needles of rain that flew sideways in the powerful wind torrent. He leaned against it and made his way to the wrecked automobile as best he could, using its headlights to guide him in the blinding downpour. The metal roof grated against the wet concrete as a sudden gust pushed it into the middle of the road. David wheeled around to see the Saturn sliding as well. He dropped to a knee to lower his center of gravity, but the gale bowled him over.

He cursed and rolled to his feet, deciding to approach the vehicle in a crouch. It was slow going, but he reached it at last. David wiped the rain from the cracked driver's side window and found a young woman suspended upside down by her seat belt. Her head was bleeding from contact with the tempered window glass. A toddler wailed in the backseat, his voice competing with the howling winds. The child's safety seat had saved his life. David tried the driver's door. It wouldn't budge.

"Son of a bitch!"

He gave up on the door and struggled to the other side of the sedan. A new pair of headlights swallowed him as he rounded the rear of the overturned car. He knew that they would never see the car in time to stop. David retrieved the small flashlight from inside his jacket and ran into the middle of the road, waving it about in wide arcs over his head.

"Come on!" David yelled. "See me!"

Red and blue lights flickered to life as a police cruiser materialized from the gloom.

"Small child in the back!" David shouted as two police officers outfitted in reflective ponchos emerged from the cruiser.

"Mother in the driver's seat with a head injury! Door's jammed!"

The first officer rushed to the car while his partner ran back to the police cruiser and popped the trunk. He returned with a crowbar just as David and the first policeman pulled the traumatized toddler from the wreckage. The mother was unresponsive when they laid her out in the river of rushing water that flooded the street.

"We got this!" said the first officer. "Get to safety!"

David was drenched to the bone when he returned to Marissa's car. She had watched the drama unfold through the rear window.

"Is she going to be okay?"

David nodded in false reassurance. He decided that Marissa didn't need anything else weighing on her mind at the moment. Their mission was to reach the safe house. He shifted the car into drive and pressed on the accelerator with a waterlogged shoe.

"See if you can get a radio signal now," he said, trying to take her mind off of the welfare of the accident victims.

The sky lit up, followed by a peal of thunder that was far too close for David's liking. Marissa punched the tuner buttons and the radio received the same warning signal they had been listening to for the past hour.

"*KSH!...shelter...KSH!...D.C. is under...KSH!...in your homes...BREEEEP!*"

They passed signs for the airport which indicated that the bridges were close, and soon the Potomac came into view as they rounded a bend in the road. It was swollen and angry. Trash cans and park benches had been swept from its bank, tossed about like miniatures in a child's play set. They now belonged to the mighty river.

"Mr. Daniels!"

David risked taking his eyes from the road to follow Marissa's pointing finger. A minivan drifted by, bobbing in the grip of the waterway like toddler's bath toy. Small hands appeared from within, flattened against the back window.

"No." David's voice was subdued. "Please, no."

He slammed on the brakes. The sports coupe spun in a complete circle on the flooded road before coming to an abrupt stop.

"Give me your phone," he said.

"What? No, there's nothing you can—"

"Now!"

Rattled from his outburst, Marissa pulled her phone from her purse with shaking fingers. He snatched it up and punched an address into a map application as fast as he could before thrusting it back at her.

"Follow the GPS. The key is in the drain pipe by the back door. Probably flushed into the yard by now. I'll be there as soon as I can."

He opened the door, then hesitated. David leaned in and delivered a quick peck to her cheek. "You're a good woman, Marissa."

David entered the maelstrom, leaving a stunned and blushing Marissa behind. The storm was now worse than when he had helped the poor mother and her toddler. He forced himself toward the river one step at a time. The wind had shifted and was at his back now, threatening to sweep him from his feet. Something struck him on the back of his thigh, ripping through his pants leg. A heavy branch whistled overhead, splashing into the water only to be swept away by the current. He knew he'd never make it to the minivan before the family inside it drowned, but he had to try—or die in the process. He had taken an oath to give his life to protect American lives. This was no different.

The Saturn sped off with a reassuring honk as he reached the newly-formed bank of the river. He trudged downstream as best he could, paralleling its course. The water crept higher with every step. The minivan was twenty yards from shore, kept afloat from the air still trapped inside. But that wouldn't last much longer. It caught on something below the surface and careened to the side, now taking the full brunt of the current that battered into it with relentless fury. The vehicle was now held fast, giving David a chance to reach it before it was carried away again. He could see several people beating against the windows from inside.

David threw off his jacket and loosened his tie. He regretted that he had never started a family, never healed the rift between him and his aging mother, never had closure with Elyse. There would be no one to throw a funeral for him when they found his bloated body washed up on the shore miles away from here. Maybe the Navy would hold some sort of memorial for him. He tensed his legs in preparation for the dive, gulping as much air as he could into his lungs.

The minivan rose from the water.

It was as though an invisible hand had plucked it from certain doom. The vehicle dipped nose down, spilling water like a huge metal strainer. David stood in stunned amazement when the rear doors ripped from the vehicle to splash into the river below. There was another flash of lightning. Outlined in that brief instant was the silhouette of a human female hovering above the minivan. No features were visible, only the momentary image of a goddess granting life to a family that had been deemed worthy to live.

David was vaguely aware of rainwater pouring into his open mouth.

The vehicle floated over David and landed on the road behind him with gentle care. He tore his eyes from the sky and craned his neck to see the family exiting the van. Doors swung open and people poured out with the remaining water. He knew he should go to them, make sure they were okay, but his eyes swiveled back up into the storm, hungry for another glimpse of her. The gray, swirling clouds revealed only water and roiling darkness. He made his way back to the road as fast as he could.

"Are you okay?" David shouted to the father, who was cradling his family as they huddled against the side of the minivan.

They weren't paying any attention to him. All eyes were looking up. David wiped his eyes with the back of his sleeve and followed their stares. A flash in the sky revealed the flying figure moving towards downtown. He ran toward the city as fast as he could.

He had to pause under a stanchion to catch his breath by the time he reached other side of the George Mason Memorial Bridge. He leaned against the concrete support and gathered his wits. He had to get to her. The case may be solved, but David wasn't finished. Not yet. His sense of duty hadn't diminished since his days in the service. He had a mission, and he was going to complete it. Samantha McAllister could lead him to Braithwaite. She needed his help as much as he needed hers. The young woman was in over her head. Superpowers or not.

David emerged from the protection of the bridge and plunged back into the hurricane. He had taken two steps when he saw the glint of chrome in the tall grass by the roadside. A Harley-Davidson Fatboy lay on its side, abandoned by its rider under the bridge but now forced into the elements by the powerful winds. It took many tries to get it started before David heard the satisfying rumble of the engine idling. He grabbed the ape hangers and pumped the throttle. The pipes backfired like twin gunshots. He couldn't help but grin as his toe tapped the shifter into gear. He hadn't ridden a bike in years.

His smile faded as the downpour transformed from stinging needles to piercing bullets that fired against his face, neck and hands. He ignored the pain and raced up 14th Street toward the National Mall. The city looked like a war zone—something David knew quite well. Cars were flipped on their sides or smashed against buildings with blown-out windows and crumbling stone work. Light posts and street benches were strewn across the roadway, ripped from their moorings and tossed about by the fury of the storm. Shingles flew from rooftops like shuriken, embedding themselves in tree trunks and utility poles. The Fatboy's wide front tire wouldn't do well in standing water, so he had to avoid the many pools that covered treacherous dips in the streets. The downpour had conjured the grease and oil from the well-traveled asphalt, slickening the road into a precarious stretch of ice. The hum of the engine dropped into a low growl as he shifted into higher gear for better traction. His torturous journey came to an end at Independence Avenue.

News vans and police vehicles had blocked off the street. Portable spotlights created beams of light that crossed over each other in the sky. He was surprised by the number of bystanders who stood in the hellish downpour. Most of them were pointing to the Washington Monument.

What was left of it.

David's eyes followed the spotlights and pointing fingers to the rubble that had once been the majestic obelisk. It had been decimated by Mother Nature's rage, snapped apart like a twig halfway down its length. David had endured Hurricane Irene not so long ago. Water had been found inside the cracked monument after she had passed, and Irene had only been a Category Three. This hurricane was otherwordly. The marble pyramid that had capped the towering structure now lay on its side in the muddy trench it had created upon impact with the Mall. The crest of the remaining structure looked like the ancient ruins of a European castle. Massive blocks of stone were scattered about the base, laying in the scarred earth like the playthings of a giant child.

"What is that?" The shout pierced through the gales of wind.

"It's an angel sent by Jesus!"

The spotlights came together, locking onto a central point high above. There she was, hovering over the remains of the monument with arms outstretched like a sorceress casting a spell.

Chunks of rubble lifted from the inside of the ruined monolith and smashed to the grass below. David felt the tremors through the seat of the Harley. A man floated into view, suspended by nothing whatsoever as he left the interior of the ruins. He was bloodied and unconscious. Another man followed, this one in a hardhat and reflective overalls. A rescue worker, David presumed. The pair were deposited near the police cordon with the tenderness of a mother laying her infants into their cribs. David snapped his attention back to the hovering figure. She faltered and dropped from the air, landing on her hands and knees atop a wide stone on the broken rim. Her head drooped. Howling winds whipped her long, drenched hair about her face and shoulders.

A woman close to David clasped her hands to her mouth. "Oh my god! Is she okay?"

She forced herself to stand, steadying herself against the monsoon that ripped at the loose smock she wore. She looked down into the chasm and levitated a third person from the depths of the collapsed structure. It was a woman this time, dressed in the same hardhat and overalls as the previous rescue worker. The worker descended into the waiting arms of the police. David looked back to top of the structure, but the figure was gone. He held his breath.

People held their phones aloft, not caring that the devices were getting drenched in the hurricane. They wanted a recording of this miraculous event. Police officers ordered the crowd to disperse and get to safety, but their commands were ignored.

Large stones suddenly ejected from the ruins like a volcano spewing ash, and she followed them out with a fourth rescue worker in her arms. Once he was safely on the ground, she hovered above the monument and shielded her eyes against the spotlights to survey the people below. Lightning smashed into one of the nearby stones, followed by a peal of thunder. When David's eyes adjusted from the flash, she was gone. Another strike followed, and David spotted her heading for the tree line to the south. David revved the motor and spun the bike into a U-turn. She was heading for the Tidal Basin.

The streets would take too long. He ramped over curbs, weaving through trees and around hedge lines in a perilous race to the body of water. The sky lit up twice in quick succession as he emerged from the cherry trees. A nearby tree was split in half in a brilliant display of destruction. In those brief flashes of light, David spied her nearing the Basin.

Her flight had become erratic as though she were disoriented. She slowed and lost altitude. One hand went to her head while the other searched in vain for something to steady herself. Then she plummeted from the sky into the choppy waters below. Her body caromed across the surface like a skipping stone; once, twice, and then a third and final time. Water splashed into the air in a mighty arc at her point of impact, then the surface settled until the only traces of her entry were widening, concentric ripples that were soon erased by the barrage of raindrops.

David dropped the motorcycle and sprinted for the edge of the Basin, tearing off his jacket as he went. He dove into the cold water and began a furious overhand stroke. He was blinded by the thrashing waves as he paused to get his bearings. One could easily drown in the swollen, angry Tidal Basin despite its shallow depth. He knew time was running out. She had saved that family from the Potomac. She had saved those people from the monument. He wasn't going to let her die. He treaded water, turning his body in every direction to find a landmark with which he could orient himself. The dome of the Jefferson Memorial rose over the surface of the water, serene and unharmed by the storm. He dove and swam toward it, but a horrible realization dawned on him as his chest and arms began to fatigue; he would never find her in these violent waters. He might never make it back to shore himself.

David pushed away the thought and dove again, and once more came up with nothing. He changed direction and dove deeper this time, staying submerged longer as his hands grasped for purchase in the darkness. His left index finger brushed against something lingering near the bottom of the Basin. He took hold of it and surfaced with a mighty exhale. It was a garment made of dark, rough fabric. David didn't take time to inspect it further. He kicked his legs out and disappeared into the murky water. His eyes were open but they were useless. The sky flashed as thunder cracked overhead. In that brief instant, he thought he saw a shape in the nebulous maw below him. He kicked deeper and clutched at the shape, ignoring the pressure in his chest. At first he thought he was feeling algae growing from the bed of the Tidal Basin, but it was too fine.

David seized the handful of hair and pulled it toward him. His lungs burned for air, but he wasn't letting go. His other hand came around to take hold of something solid. Slippery skin over soft flesh. His arm curled around her waist and he pulled her to him, then swam harder than he ever had in his life. He doubted he would have made it this far without his B.U.D.S. training in the Navy, but even that intense instruction couldn't prepare him for this. It was sheer determination that drove him, mind over matter. In the end, he pushed the lifeless body over the edge of the Basin and climbed from the churning waters with shaking arms. His heart threatened to burst from his chest. He couldn't catch his breath. But he wasn't finished yet.

He mustered the last of his strength and forced himself into action. Samantha wasn't breathing. He rolled her to her back and pushed the knotted ropes of hair from her face. His fingers pinched her nose as he sealed her mouth with his. Three quick breaths inflated her lungs, then he leaned back and stacked his palms just below her ribcage to deliver several sharp pumps. He repeated the resuscitation techniques, pausing to study her face for signs of life after each round. Maybe it was the exhaustion or the terror of losing her, but David's consciousness splintered into a surreal, second self that stood as a bystander watching the desperate attempts to save the young woman's life.

He was looking down at Samantha McAllister.

His investigation, everything he had pieced together for Sharp, had led to this moment. Deep down he had known the truth, but there was a part of him that didn't want it to be real. When his eyes had fallen over her name on the dossier Tony had given him, a part of him hoped his investigation would take him elsewhere, that it had just been a strange coincidence that she would be involved with Evan Douglas. But the facts didn't care about hope or coincidence. Facts deal with what is, not what should be. And now her identity was revealed, pale and lifeless before him. There would be no more denial. What came next was anyone's guess.

Her eyes flared open. She spat water into his mouth. David rolled Samantha to her side and thumped her back to assist. Her body shook as her chest contracted in violent, wracking coughs, expelling the water from her lungs. He pulled her into a sitting position and tapped on her back a few more times for good measure. It was a miracle she was alive. For many reasons. David had the presence of mind to retrieve his jacket and drape it around her shoulders. It was soaked through, but it was better than nothing. She looked up at him but her eyes were far away. Her voice was little more than series of whispered murmurs. One word was clear, however.

"Paperboy."

A sudden coughing fit dissolved into giggles. She wrapped her arms around his waist and pulled herself close. David felt her body shivering against him.

Paperboy? The poor girl was delirious.

Chapter Twenty-One

THE VOICES WERE THERE AGAIN. The man and the woman.

Galina and...who?

Samantha was the coldest she had ever been. Galina had somehow managed to make the room even more frigid than before. There was something in her right hand, hard and cylindrical. She knew that if she used it, people would die.

"Easy," Galina said. "Easy."

The man was looking at Samantha, standing close with concern on his face.

Is he here to rescue me? Why isn't he doing anything?

His features became clear. It was the Commander.

That's why. He's enjoying this.

Galina pulled a gun from her belt. It was an old-fashioned six shooter with detailed scrollwork along the cylinder and brass inlays decorating the grip.

"Your friend told us you are impervious to bullets."

What? No!

The pistol recoiled in Galina's hand. Samantha heard the shot at the same time she saw her blood paint Galina's pristine, white business suit.

"...fever...break soon..."

Something wet pressed against her forehead. A trickle of cool water slid into her ear.

"She's not... ...her lungs..."

Evan would have called it a nebula. He knew about such things. To Samantha, it was just a bunch of dust. It was fluorescent red, its hue borrowed from the massive star at its core. She slowed her approach. Her nose itched, but there was nothing she could do about it. The helmet prevented her from reaching her face. She doubted the bulky suit would allow her arms to go that high anyway. She had never been claustrophobic, but was considering it.

A song was stuck in her head. Something long forgotten, yet ever present. She was reminded of the sound of a fork tine being plucked. It made little sense, much like this entire mission. Her gloved thumb hovered over the trigger that would activate the camera in her visor. She'd snap a few photos from here, then move in to get close-up shots of the nebula.

Explosions rocked the crimson expanse when her digit depressed the trigger. Dust swirled into dozens of massive spirals that grew larger with each revolution. There was no fire, no sound. Not in space. There was, however, anger. A dark pupil and fiery iris swiveled into the center of the red star, transforming it into a hellish eye. It focused on Samantha with furious hatred, the pupil contracting into a black speck as it took her in. She found herself propelled toward that speck. It was the absence of all light in the universe and it wanted to consume her as well. It's pull was undeniable, relentless despite her desperate attempts to push her will against it.

I'm dreaming. This has to be a dream.

It was her last thought before being swallowed into oblivion.

There was a small crack in the stippled ceiling. Morning rays fell over a fly caught in a spider web that nestled in a corner of the window pane. She smelled cedar. It reminded her of the hope chest she had kept at the foot of her bed. Her pink prom dress was among the treasures inside. You couldn't tell that Andrea Thomas had spilled champagne on it.

Commuters pushed past Samantha with annoyed expressions as she stood on the platform waiting for the Orange Line train. Samantha was shivering despite the stifling heat. The crowd surged forward as the roar of the approaching train echoed from the tunnel. She estimated at least three hundred people waiting to board with her.

"Love that vest," said a young woman about her age.

"Thank you."

It was Samantha's going away present. Galina had made it for her. Each grayish-pink block had been arranged on the backing material in meticulous fashion, every wire plug inserted in just the right place. It was heavy and bulky, but Samantha didn't feel the weight. The best part was the handheld switch. The very tip of it was the color of a cherry lollipop.

The cars slowed as the train eased into the station. She recognized some of the people standing in the windows. There was Marcy, and next to her was Ball Cap. His nose still oozed blood. In the next car, Evan was trying to put his head back together. The gray matter kept squishing through his fingers like overcooked spaghetti. The last window revealed Paperboy. As always, he was sitting by the access door at the back of the car. Galina sat next to him. Their lips moved in silent conversation. Then, as one, their gazes fell on Samantha.

"Now?"

They nodded in tandem.

Sorry, everybody.

She flipped the switch.

Samantha was in someone else's bed. And not in the good way. She was also in someone else's pajamas. Definitely not in the good way. Bars of light fell over her as the afternoon sun tried its best to penetrate the vertical blinds that blocked the window. A wave of her hand slid them aside to admit the daylight. She sat up and took in her surroundings. The room was sparsely furnished, just the twin bed she sat in and a desk next to the entry door. A slatted door across the room was opened to reveal a tiny closet. None of the clothes that hung inside were familiar to her.

Where the hell...?

She pushed down the covers and climbed out of the bed. Her legs wouldn't cooperate, however, and she collapsed to the wooden floor. Every muscle in her body ached. There was a two-ton weight on her chest. Her lungs burned with each breath. She didn't bother to get up, and instead rolled to her back and lay there groaning.

"Oh! You're up!"

A slight young woman with bobbed brown hair and thin-rimmed glasses stood in the doorway. She held a tall glass in her hand.

"Well, I'm out of bed anyway," Samantha said from the floor.

"Here, you need to hydrate."

The young woman started toward her, but Samantha erected a barrier between them as she struggled to her feet. The woman's face turned comically sideways as she walked into it. Water splashed from the glass onto the invisible wall.

"I've had plenty of water," said Samantha. "Who are you?"

"Wow. Okay," said the young woman as she watched water droplets slide to the floor in midair. She straightened her glasses and retreated back to the door frame.

"I'm Marissa. I'm with Mr. Dan—David," she said.

David. David Daniels. That's his name.

Samantha clutched at the bedpost to steady herself as the memories returned. David introducing himself. The torture. The escape. The monument. The Tidal Basin. David rescuing her.

Paperboy.

"Well, wait," Marissa said, "I'm not *with* him. I work for him. He brought you here."

"How long have I been asleep? And where is 'here'?"

"Two days, Samantha."

Two days...

"This is a safe house. We'll be, um, safe here. Oh god, I'm sorry," Marissa said. "I'm just really nervous. I've never met...I mean, you..."

"Me what?" Samantha said. "You've never met a freak?"

Marissa was taken aback. "No! I mean you...you saved all of those people! You're a hero! You're all over the news! Trending on social media! Hashtag Hurricangel! Hashtag Monumazing!"

Wonderful.

It was too late to go back to obscurity now. Not that obscurity had worked any better for her.

"Lucky for you, no one can see your face in the videos and pics. As far as the world is concerned, you're this mysterious...I don't know what. And they don't either."

"Marissa?"

"I'm sorry. Damn it. Mr. Daniels told me not to tell you about that yet."

Samantha removed the barrier between them and took short, shuffling steps toward the door. "Marissa? Where's the bathroom? I really gotta pee."

Marissa chattered away just outside of the bathroom as Samantha relieved herself.

This girl isn't a bit shy about boundaries.

"You're really dehydrated," Marissa reiterated through the door. "You had a horrible fever when David brought you here, but that broke yesterday afternoon. I put you in an ice bath and that helped."

Nope, doesn't know the meaning of the word "boundaries".

"I'll be okay," Samantha said, pulling up the flannel pajama bottoms and flushing the toilet. She washed her hands and splashed water on her face. Her reflection in the vanity mirror was alarming. Her cheeks were hollow and pale. Dark rings encircled her eyes, giving them a sunken, recessed appearance. Her captivity had taken a toll.

"Thank you for all of your help, Marissa," she said, opening the door. "And I'll want to thank David too. Where is he?"

"He went to get dinner."

"Good. I'm starving. Literally."

"Make yourself at home," Marissa said. "If you want to shower, everything you need is in there. And the clothes in the closet are yours. I went shopping yesterday, after I convinced David to let me leave the house. I'm pretty sure everything will fit."

"What do you mean you had to convince him to let you leave the house?"

"It's just that...well, they're looking for us. David will explain when he gets back. He really wanted to be here when you woke up."

"I'm not going anywhere until I talk to him anyway," said Samantha. "I think I'll take you up on that shower. I can't remember what warm water feels like."

"Towels are in the cabinet." Marissa smiled and left Samantha to it.

Samantha had a good feeling about Marissa. She seemed like the honest type, unless the wide-eyed, "aw shucks" personality was all an act. No, Samantha decided that she liked her, and not only because Marissa had decent taste in shoes. A short time later Samantha emerged from the bedroom wearing hip-hugger blue jeans, a grey V-neck T-shirt and low cut, black Chuck Taylor All Stars.

Comfort clothes. Thank you, Marissa.

She was binding her damp hair into a loose ponytail when a delicious scent wafted in from the other room. Her stomach rumbled.

"Hello, Samantha."

David stood on the other side of the table, steely-eyed and square-jawed just as she remembered him.

An uncomfortable silence followed.

Say something, you asshole.

"Hey listen, David," she said, "I just wanted to thank you for—"

"Hope you like Kimchi," he said, opening food containers and laying out silverware.

What the fuck?

Then Samantha caught the quick flick of his eyes to Marissa, who was oblivious to the signal.

"It's Marissa's favorite," he said.

Okay. Not here. Not now.

"I'm so sick of deli food," said Marissa, spearing a piece of cabbage with her chopsticks.

"I hear you," Samantha said as she sat down at the table while delivering a quick nod in David's direction.

I understand.

David filled them in on the aftermath of the hurricane as they ate. It had been off the charts, but designated a Category Five since that was the highest classification. Gales had been clocked at almost two hundred miles per hour. He told them that the damage sustained in the greater metropolitan area alone was in the millions. Scientists had attributed the storm to global climate change. He never once mentioned any casualties or loss of human life, nor did he refer to the Washington Monument. That last omission lingered in the room like an elephant.

"And guess what they named it?" he said, taking a drink from a plastic water bottle.

"Hurricane Marissa?" said Marissa.

"Nope," he said.

His look invited Samantha to take a guess. She just raised her eyebrows and shrugged.

"Clarice," he said.

Marissa and Samantha wore blank expressions.

"Clarice. 'A census taker once tried to test me. I ate his liver with some—' really? Nothing?"

Samantha and Marissa exchanged confused glances.

"Silence of the Lambs. We used to watch that all the time in the service."

The young women nodded politely and filled their mouths with Kimchi.

The trio went for a walk after dinner when David's suggestion that Samantha return to bed was refused with stubborn vigor. She got her first look at the exterior of the safe house, which turned out to be a two-bedroom cottage on a twenty-acre piece of land out in Montgomery county. David told them that he had kept the property in his back pocket to use in retirement or as a place to disappear. He joked that there was little difference between the two. Samantha didn't miss the fact that David's eyes darted about as they walked, searching the tree lines and bluffs and always returning to the cottage.

Maybe he forgot that he walks beside the mighty Hurricangel, the invincible superhero that he had to rescue. Hashtag Embarrassing.

She vowed to return the favor someday. For now, she enjoyed the fresh country air.

Marissa retired early, coaxing her cat into a bedroom across the hall from where they had put Samantha. David waited until Marissa's door had closed before retrieving two Heineken bottles from the refrigerator and motioning to the long wooden porch that stretched the entire length of the cottage. Samantha took the hint and followed him outside. He uncapped the bottles and handed one to Samantha before taking a long pull from his own. The sun had descended below the horizon a while ago, but its light still painted the darkening sky in fading pinks and purples.

"I know you need rest," he said, "but we need to discuss some things. Important things."

Samantha crossed her arms over her chest and leaned against a wooden support post. He was looking at her differently now that they were alone. It wasn't unexpected, considering what they had been through, but she wasn't sure how she felt about it. Her eyes wandered into the trees beyond the porch.

Maybe I'm imagining things.

"I've been asleep for two days, according to Marissa. I'm not at all tired. Sore as hell, but not tired," she said. "So let's talk."

David sat down in a large, wooden rocker and nodded. "I hadn't seen you on the train for five days or so before the storm hit."

Five days? I was in that hellhole for five fucking days?

The look on her face must have given away her thoughts. David leaned forward with concern. "You probably had no sense of time wherever they kept you. It's a tactic."

"That means I've been missing for a week now," she said, moving to the door. "Holy shit! I need to go. I have call my dad. My brother...they must be going out of their minds."

"Now hold on. There are some things you need to know first. And things I need to know as well."

Samantha hesitated. She had enjoyed their flirtatious game on the subway, but she didn't know much about this man. Still, he had a point. She knew who had taken her and why, but David might be able to fill in the gaps. There was still much she didn't know.

"Yes or no questions," she said. "At least to start with. We'll take turns. You go."

David stroked his chin and considered his first question. His eyes never left hers.

"Were you stalking me on the train?" he said.

Samantha was speechless.

He knows it was me flying around and moving things with my mind, and that is what he opens with?

David waited for his answer.

"No," she said.

Maybe a little bit.

Then it was her turn. "Are you in the government?"

"No."

She studied his face for any sign of deception and found none.

"My turn," he said. "Are you okay?"

What the hell kind of question is that?

But she replied before she could stop herself. "No. Not even close."

The admission was a punch in the gut. She felt her eyes welling up. They were quiet for a long time before Samantha cleared her throat and asked her next question.

"Are you and Marissa going to be safe?"

"That depends." His answer came very quickly, followed by his next question. "Are Sharp, Braithwaite and Evan Douglas alive?"

Braithwaite? The Commander, yes. It makes sense. It's the only name I don't know, so it has to be. But how would David know who...?

She stared hard at him and set her beer on the porch railing. "How do you know those names?"

Evan betrayed me, too. It won't happen again.

David sat back and crossed an ankle over his opposite knee. "This is your game, Samantha. Did I win?"

She turned and stalked to the edge of the porch.

"We need to finish our talk before you fly away. The same two men to whom Douglas handed you over are the same two men who no longer have any use for me. I know too much. They aren't sure how much Marissa knows, but they don't give a shit. We're liabilities."

Damn it. Fucking damn it all to hell on a popsicle stick.

She turned around and picked up her beer, taking a long drink before wiping her mouth with her forearm.

"No, yes, and no," she said. "In that order."

David blinked. Samantha helped him to understand.

"Braithwaite, or 'the Commander' as Galina called him, murdered Sharp and Evan right in front of me. In cold blood, he shot...he..."

Evan...

She smoothed her hair and hung her hands on the back of her neck, fighting the emotions as she revisited the images for the hundredth time.

"Sharp's dead?"

He rose from the chair and paced the entire length of the porch when Samantha's nod confirmed it.

"Sharp didn't want to kill me. Neither did Braithwaite. Both of those horrible men wanted to use me, each in his own selfish way. For the good of the country, for the good of the world, like I'm some sort of weapon. Well I'm not a weapon, David. I'm not."

David kept pacing. "I know you're not. Okay, let's see..."

She took another drink from the bottle as she watched him. The carbonation tickled her throat. The alcohol went straight to her head.

There's more to David Daniels than a good Samaritan who happens to be a strong swimmer. And hot.

"So that means only Braithwaite and his men know about you. Aside from Marissa and I, that is" he said. "Who is this Galina?"

"He had people with him that spoke Russian," Samantha said. "Mercenaries, I'm pretty sure. I didn't see any official military patches on their uniforms. Galina was his torturer."

David stopped pacing and spun on her. Rage passed over his features. He closed his eyes and took a deep breath.

"Samantha, I—"

"She hurt me, David. On the inside."

His eyes filled with compassion. "You're safe now."

Again, Samantha turned to the darkness of the trees.

"What happened to Galina?" David said. "How did you escape? Better yet, how did they even keep you prisoner?"

"This is why I wanted to ask one question at a time," Samantha said, trying to sort out the answers. "She's probably alive and, if so, will be eating through a straw and shitting into a bag the rest of her life. I don't care either way."

"Yes you do, Samantha." David said.

He's going to fucking lecture me now?

"What?" Her tone was hot.

"I know killers. And you're not a killer."

Samantha wheeled on him. "You don't know me!"

"Not yet," he grinned, "but I want to."

That took the wind out of her sails.

Good one, Paperboy. Smooth.

"What I mean is that you spent five days being tortured, then risked your life to save people you didn't even know. You help people, Samantha. You don't hurt them."

David believes it too. Like Evan did.

"Unless you have to, of course," he added with a smirk. "I believe it's your turn now."

"My turn?"

"I asked the last question," he said. "About three of them, I think."

She nodded her head and cleared her throat. "How long have you known about me?"

"Ever since you started taking the Orange Line."

Samantha took a seat and crossed her arms. She raised an eyebrow and waited.

"Okay, okay," David said. "I'm an investigator that works cases for certain federal intelligence and security agencies."

Samantha unfolded her arms and gripped the armrests.

"But I'm *not* government," he said before she could protest. "Not technically. I'm former military. Navy. I'm a civilian independent contractor, if you want the official designation. Government agencies hire me to perform investigations they either can't or don't want to allocate internal resources for."

"Like flying girls?"

"Like flying girls. That one fell into the 'can't' category, though they definitely wanted to."

He leaned against the railing. His voice lowered even though they were in the middle of nowhere.

"Sharp is a bigwig in the NSA—was, rather. It all started with a video of a woman levitating in an Adams Morgan dance club. That's all it takes to get the attention of a government that monitors personal devices and sends UAVs over its own soil."

I can't believe I'm hearing this.

"UAVs?"

"Unmanned Aerial Vehicles. Drones," he said. "Surveillance drones, to be precise. Some time after that fun little dance club video, a farmer found a crater on his land out in Manassas. A drone caught you on film. Not such a fun little video, that one. I'm guessing it was Evan Douglas's idea to take you out there? The location of that UAV wasn't a coincidence."

Oh my god. He planned the whole thing.

"I'll take that look as a yes. Douglas was CIA, and you fell into his lap. I assume you two were friendly and you confided in him. Am I close? Anyway, Evan Douglas was pulled from the CIA into the NSA under Sharp to monitor you and, if I'm correct, evaluate your capabilities. I found your plaid Chuck Taylor in the crater, by the way."

"I miss those shoes." Samantha said.

"Next was the satellite that took photos of you over the Midwest, then an image of you landing in Vegas. I almost had you there. They got a shot of you taking off your helmet, but it was too grainy. I tracked you to the casino and investigated that clusterfuck."

She crossed her legs and covered her mouth with her fist. Her eyes drifted.

"That wasn't your doing. I know that, Samantha. It was Braithwaite's assassins covering your tracks," he said. "No one could know about you if their plan was going to work. They had to keep you off the radar. Remember, you're their *secret* weapon. I suppose they wanted to bring you in after that incident. Keep casualties to a minimum and all that."

David drained his beer before continuing.

"I was their backup plan. If you ever decided to go public or got outed by someone who knew your secret, I would be the official lead investigator in play. Sharp was covering his ass. The fact that I'm a civilian investigator would help him sell it to Congress if they made him testify. He would be able to assure them that he had an independent investigator on the case, and that the U.S. government was in no way to blame for the shit storm that would erupt in the press if the people of this country—of this world—learned about you. It would have been me that dropped the ball, not him and not the government. It was all very top secret."

I never thought of that. This is so much bigger than me.

David continued. "I'm not trying to alarm you, Samantha, but there are some things you might not have considered."

He sat down in the chair next to her and leaned forward. She let him take her trembling hand in his. It was big and warm.

"Imagine if an EBE—an alien—suddenly landed on the National Mall. The ramifications of that would be enormous. Religions all over the world would find themselves in crisis, their belief systems challenged as never before. World governments would try to capture or kill it in the interest of national security—starting with our own. Cults would grow around it. The media conglomerates would spin it into whatever stories served the interests of the corporations or political parties that run them, ultimately feeding disinformation to the people in the hopes of selling another widget or garnering another vote. Paranoia would run rampant. What is it capable of? How did it get here? Are there more coming? What will they do to us?"

Samantha squeezed his hand and smiled. "But I was born in Ohio."

"People fear what they don't understand, Samantha."

"You're not afraid of me."

"No," David said, "but I already know what true fear is. I've never met anyone like you, but I've been places and seen things that would give you nightmares. It took me a long time to get over them. Most of them."

"Tell me."

He let go of her hand. "Another time, maybe."

They sat in silent reflection after that. Samantha took in the warmth of the early summer air. Crickets chirped in the darkness around them, calling out to their mates.

"David?"

"Yes?"

"Were you ever going to ask me out?"

David chuckled. "Yes, I was. But you stopped showing up on the train. I guess I have Sharp to blame for that."

Another silence.

"Samantha?"

"Yes?"

"You know that Braithwaite won't stop coming for you, right?"

Way to ruin the moment, genius.

"I haven't had time to think about it."

"We're going to stop him, but it's not going to be easy," he said. "I need to know everything you are capable of and, more importantly, how they kept you prisoner for as long as they did."

Do I trust him? Can I really afford to take that risk?

He saved your life, Sammy.

She looked over at him. He sat staring straight ahead.

He's not pushing. Letting me work this out on my own. He knows I'm debating his trustworthiness. Damn it.

Samantha told him the entire story. He listened to every word with rapt attention, nodding for her to continue when she paused to remember certain aspects. She started with the discovery of her abilities in the Bibbing Plot, then filled in the details of the test flight over Manassas. She told him about Evan coaching her in the salvage yard and how she had learned to push her abilities further.

"Amazing," he breathed. "That's when Douglas took you, I assume."

"Yes."

Evan...

Samantha continued her story, relaying memories of how they had used gas to subdue her multiple times in the dark cell. He nodded in approval at the tale of her cunning escape, but the smile faded when she told him of her recapture. And the murders. Galina's torture methods were the hardest parts to relate. She skipped over the part where she questioned her own sanity and went right to the storm that had cut power to the building.

"I finally got outside right in the middle of the hurricane. I saw that it had hit the city," she said. "I couldn't believe that the Monument was just...gone. I knew people would need help, so I went to them. I didn't think about it. I just...went."

"And that's when I saw you rescuing all of those people. That was a sight to behold, Samantha. They'll never get to thank you, so I will."

Samantha grinned. "And my thanks to you. Apparently water and I don't get along so well."

David leaned back and stroked his chin.

I like it when he does that.

His hand curled into a fist. "Braithwaite's good, but he only has so much capital to fund his efforts now that Sharp is out of the picture. You took out five of his hired guns, right?"

"Six, if you count the one with the heels and the electrocuted face."

"Okay, six. They'll be stretched thin, but still dangerous. There is a strong chance that Braithwaite has other contacts within our government. Some might even owe him a favor. He'll be licking his wounds while at the same time formulating a plan to get you back. I have no doubt he'll be monitoring the skies around D.C. as best he can. I think you should stay here with Marissa while I find him on my own. I have contacts, too."

"You're not Batman."

"Says Supergirl."

They burst into laughter.

It felt good to share her story with someone, to put into words the insanity that had been her life since these abilities had unveiled themselves. She felt a sense of relief from the unrelenting burden she had been carrying. It had been different with Evan. He had tried push her into his agenda, and now she knew why. David, on the other hand, wanted to protect her—a bulletproof woman who can move solid chunks of stone the size of Volkswagens with a flick of her wrist.

They sat listening to the leaves rustle in the breeze. Somewhere, a bird whistled its last call before settling in until morning. She looked over at him. He was already watching her. The butterflies in her stomach this time weren't born from fear.

Do it.

No. This is too crazy.

Just shut up and do it.

Samantha levitated from her chair. Her body swiveled around to hover over him before lowering herself ever so gently, her legs straddling his. She pulled a stray lock of hair from her face and locked onto his eyes. Strong hands fell over her hips. Her heart leapt in her chest like a trapped hummingbird. His face rose to meet hers as Samantha leaned down, closing her eyes and parting her lips.

Finally...

"Is this the right charger, or do I need an adapter for—Oh!"

Marissa was leaning out of the front door with a tablet in one hand and two tangled cables in the other. "Oh my god! Sorry! Damn. I'll just, um..."

"It's okay," they said in unison.

Samantha stood up and straightened her T-shirt. David followed suit and took the device from Marissa.

"Let me take a look," he said.

His eyes followed Samantha as she slipped past Marissa and made her way to the bedroom.

What was I thinking? Too much, Sammy. Too soon.

She heard David explaining the ins and outs of different charger cables as she closed the bedroom door and reclined onto the twin bed. She heard Marissa returning to her own bedroom soon afterward.

David's footsteps paced around the living room, then the cottage fell silent.

Sleep wouldn't come for her. Her gaze fell over the bedroom door many times as the night wore on. She wondered if he was sleeping. Marissa wouldn't hear them if they were quiet...

No. Too soon.

She left the cottage before dawn.

Chapter Twenty-Two

EVAN'S IDEA FOR THE AERODYNAMIC SHELL had been pure genius. The air currents moving over the shape provided lift and allowed her to concentrate less on keeping herself in the air and more on keeping herself out of sight. It was the first time she'd tried to fly with a construct of her will, and she marveled at its usefulness.

Samantha took great care to make sure her flight into Clarendon went unnoticed. It wasn't difficult. The city was still shut down from the devastating hurricane. Cars and busses lay wounded and broken on the streets below. Windowless buildings leaned against each other as though huddling for support against the torturous winds that had long since dissipated. The once vibrant lightscape was gone. Now, only pockets of the city with emergency power were visible in the grayness before the sunrise. Samantha knew there would still be people in need of rescue, but she couldn't stop. She needed to center herself after what she had been through. Get her head straight.

I just want to go home.

She regretted leaving David and Marissa without saying anything or leaving a note. They were in danger because of her. Just like the people in the casino had died because of her. Just like Evan had died.

Because of her.

I was careless. I wanted to get rich. I was selfish and they found me. Now people have suffered. I won't let that happen to David and Marissa. But first things first.

Her apartment building loomed dark and silent as she dropped from the sky. The entire block was without power. Samantha pulled her hoodie tight as she hovered outside of her bedroom window. The lock unlatched itself with a simple command. She slipped into her bedroom and closed the window behind her, making sure to draw the curtains as well. She knew right away that something was amiss.

Why does it smell like bleach in here?

She pictured her junk drawer opening in the kitchen, and a cigarette lighter floated through the bedroom door into her grasp. Samantha kept a bag of tea lights under the kitchen sink for occasions like this, and they soon joined her in the bedroom. She lit all of the tiny candles, then sent them floating through the apartment like an armada of will-o'-the-wisps.

A wide swath of blue carpet in front of her bookcase looked like it had been scrubbed. She smelled fresh paint. A quick scan of the walls revealed repainted spots on two walls. She ran her fingers over them and detected slight irregularities, as though they had been patched prior to being covered with a color that didn't quite match the rest of the wall. A pillow was missing from her bed. The comforter was brand new, its material an ugly green the color of peas.

What in the hell?

The bathroom was spotless. Samantha had never been this tidy. The bleach odor was most pungent near the bathtub. She pulled the shower curtain back and smelled new plastic. It was similar to her old one, but not quite a match. She brought the tea lights closer to the tub and inspected the porcelain. A short, black hair lay atop the drain.

Samantha entered the kitchen and found her practice roulette wheel sitting on the counter top next to the stack of bowls in which she had placed it before leaving for Vegas.

Is this some sort of message?

After an examination of the kitchen and the living room, Samantha decided that the rest of the apartment appeared to be untouched. She returned to her bedroom and reclined onto the ugly comforter. Her bed felt better than she could have possibly imagined during those endless hours in chains.

Oh, how I missed you.

She rolled over and planted her face in the remaining pillow, inhaling the familiar smell of fabric softener and shampoo. Samantha savored the solace of her bed for a long while before a thought struck her. She rolled out of bed and dropped to her knees, flipping up the comforter. The garment boxes slid from beneath the bed like giant, cardboard rodents scurrying from cover.

Please, please, please be here.

The suitcase was still nestled against the far wall. Samantha coaxed it from its hiding place and the familiar scent of freshly minted bills wafted over her when she lifted the lid. Samantha leapt up and performed a victory dance. She returned to the suitcase to make sure it hadn't disappeared during her little jig and took a quick count. About fifty grand was missing. She stepped away from it, looking over her shoulder as though someone was still in the apartment she had just walked through.

None of this makes any sense, but I can live with five hundred and fifty thousand dollars.

So what now? This amount of money would last quite a long time if she was smart about it, but there was still the question of how to launder it. She'd never be able to justify this much money to the IRS.

Jesus Christ. I'm becoming a super villain.

The term brought his name to mind, unbidden and unwanted.

Braithwaite. He probably has someone watching my apartment right now. David was right. This guy isn't going to stop coming for me. Ever. He'll kill anyone who gets in his way, including David and Marissa. I've seen it with my own eyes. I shouldn't have left them alone. Another careless act, Sammy.

Samantha looked at her bed with longing. Her self-pity party would have to wait. She retrieved her backpack and the Stomping Choppers shopping bag from the closet and tossed them to the comforter. The suitcase was halfway under the bed when she thought better of it.

Don't know when I'll be back. Better find somewhere to stash it. It shouldn't be difficult to find a good hiding place when you can fly.

She pulled clothes from her dresser drawers and tossed them to the bed. Her favorite toy slid into view when she removed a stack of folded underwear from the top drawer, but she left it where it was.

With any luck I won't need Mister Rabbit when this is all over. And where is my Tay-Tay shirt?

The nightstand was her next stop, and her fingers trembled when they closed over her favorite photo.

Daddy and Cole...

So much had happened so fast. Samantha sat down hard on the floor. Her father was on assignment in Europe so wouldn't have been in the area during the storm, but Samantha knew he'd be looking for her, wondering if she was alright. Her phone was long gone, taken by Sharp or Braithwaite. There was no way for her family to get in touch with her. For all she knew, her father was already in the States trying to find her. Cole could have flown in from California days ago.

Samantha vowed to get a burner phone on her way back to the cottage, but had a bad feeling that it would be impossible to find one in the blackout. She rose from the floor and wrapped the frame in an old T-shirt before placing it in the pack. She searched the tabletop but didn't see her white marble anywhere.

Damn it. My good luck charm.

Samantha shrugged off the hoodie and slipped out of her jeans and shoes, then tied her hair into a loose bun. Her body left the floor, arms outstretched. The motorcycle leathers fluttered from the shopping bag like large, misshapen bats. The pants shimmied up her legs while the jacket slid over her arms. Heavy, black boots enveloped her feet and buckled tightly at her command. She dropped to the floor feeling whole again, stronger. The straps of the backpack slid over her shoulders, its bulk nestling against her spine. She grasped the handle of the suitcase and beckoned her helmet into her free hand. Samantha climbed onto the window sill where she paused to search the street for any passers by. When she was satisfied that the coast was clear, she took one long, last look at her apartment and slipped through the window. It closed and locked behind her.

Evan's apartment window was much more difficult to open. She wasn't sure if he had nailed it shut or had painted it shut. When the frame began to splinter and crack under her will, she realized he had placed a piece of wood in the pane to act as a brace. Simple but effective. She pushed the plank to the floor with a wave of her hand and slid the window open. Her voice called out as her boots met the floor.

"Mal! Where are you, boy?"

She lit her will-o'-the-wisps and sent them on their way. What they revealed was not at all what she expected to see. The place had been tossed.

Evan's Wookiee-skin rug had been thrown into the fireplace. The video games had been smashed into oblivion, screens shattered and access doors dangling from their hinges. All decorations had been ripped from the walls, and the futon was now a pile of kindling and polystyrene fluff. The CPU towers were gone, and the server bank was now nothing more than ripped wires that protruded from the racks like fiber optic tentacles.

Samantha steeled herself against a sudden and overpowering sense of loss. They'd had some good times in this apartment. Bringing Mal home for the first time. Performing shadow puppet commentary tracks over stupid movies projected onto the wall. Watching Evan throw tantrums when she beat him at Galaga. Fooling around on the futon. Fooling around on the kitchen counter. And on the Wookiee-skin rug. And on the—

That's enough of that, Sammy.

She directed the candles toward the kitchen. Mal's litter box was filthy. She levitated his empty water bowl into a sink full of broken dishes and opened the tap while retrieving a can of Fancy Feast from the cupboard. She set the bowls on the floor and scattered the tea lights into the main living area.

"Mal..." She coaxed the cat forth with sing-song tones. "Malcom Reynolds..."

The hiss made her jump. Mal emerged from the destroyed futon cushion with back arched and ears flat. His tail was as straight as a pole. The Siamese had never responded to her like this.

He's just hungry. And scared.

She knelt on one knee. "It's Sam. Come on, Mally Mal."

The cat sniffed the air and stalked toward her in a wide circle. She didn't blame him when he bypassed her completely and darted to his food bowl. He had lost some weight but otherwise looked unharmed. She removed her glove and stroked his back.

"Good boy."

She packed several cans of cat food while he ate, then continued her inspection of the studio apartment. Her booted toe kicked something on the floor by the fireplace. The display case had been knocked from the mantle. Its glass was broken and several pieces of material lay strewn about the flat wooden box. She levitated a piece of blue spandex into her hands. It was shaped into a double diamond pattern with two small eye holes in the center of each diamond.

Like this would fool anyone.

Another piece was made of golden leather with two sharp points reinforced with stiffer leather just above the eyeholes. She tossed the masks back onto the busted display case and checked on Mal, who was still scarfing the foul-smelling cat food. She summoned a second can from the cupboard and ripped off the top with a sharp thrust of her will. Mal committed himself to the second helping with no hesitation.

On a whim, she pulled the hairy brown rug from the hearth and brought it to her nose.

Pepperoni, kitty litter, Drakkar, and unwashed socks. And now ash.

There would be no room for Mal in her pack, so she went to work fashioning a sling from the ruined rug. She manipulated the lights around her project as she worked, tearing out threads and repurposing them into stitches which she then guided through the material with extreme concentration. It wasn't easy to make a needle out of sheer willpower. A reflective glint caught her eye when she moved a tealight closer to get a better angle with the invisible sewing needle. There was something else in the fireplace.

Samantha put her seamstress work on hold and crept closer to the hearth, bringing her lights with her. Something protruded from the pile of ashes. She swept aside the debris to reveal a thin garment box of shiny, white cardboard, perhaps large enough for a tie or a pair of gloves. Ashes exploded into a gray and white cloud when she pulled the box free and blew on it. A single word was revealed, written in black marker across the lid.

Becks

Samantha's vision clouded as she opened the box and pushed aside the tissue paper. Inside was a piece of black and red leather. She pulled it from the box and wiped at her eyes to get a better look. It was a cowl, much like Batman's but without the pointed ears. The eyeholes had been fitted with tinted lenses and were bordered in red leather that flared to stylized points.

Damn you.

She found an opening in the back of the cowl, several inches from the bottom. It was larger than the eyeholes, perhaps intended for a braid or maybe a topknot. A tiny zipper began below it and ended at the neck, allowing for easy donning and doffing. Samantha pulled it over her fist and spun it around. Instead of leather, the ear areas were covered in a thin, black material for better hearing. More red leather formed a racing stripe that ran down the middle of the skull onto the bridge of the nose, with two matching stripes coming to a point halfway down the jaw line. It was a perfect match for her motorcycle outfit.

Damn you.

She lowered the cowl and dropped the box to the floor. A folded note fluttered from the tissue paper. Samantha stared at it for a long time. Mal appeared and slid against her legs, belly full and whiskers wet. He tested the note with his paw, then looked up at her expectantly.

Samantha coaxed it into her fingers and unfolded it.

Don't be afraid.
—Evan

Damn you, Evan.

PART FOUR

TWINKLE TWINKLE LITTLE STAR

Now

HARKINS' TREASURES WAS THE CROWN JEWEL of the revitalized Warehouse District, now known as the Arts District. No longer were the French Quarter, Garden District, and Faubourg Marigny the most popular tourist destinations in New Orleans. Travelers came from around the world to see the exquisitely-designed building facade made from stained glass set into a framework of silver inlays.

Vandals had a heyday with the new gallery front at first, but their nefarious work was always undone the next morning. It had become a game to them; wait for the cover of night and hurl stones at the beautiful glass structure, then drive by the next day to find everything restored in pristine condition. Rinse and repeat. They eventually tired of it and left Harkins' Treasures alone.

"I love this piece," said a squat man with a Boston accent and a feathered fedora. "But I'd like to commission something similar. Can you remake it with the likeness of my wife?"

Roger wasn't the least bit offended as he ran his hands over the smooth curves of his life-sized sculpture. Female nudes were always the most popular, and this one was no exception. He had used clear glass as his medium, but had injected hundreds of multi-colored beads the size of birdshot throughout the piece. It lit up like a prism in the correct light. He had made a similar sculpture for Lorelei, but she had shattered it during their last fight. Roger had kicked her out after that. The divorce papers had arrived at her mother's house two days later.

"Absolutely," Roger said. "I'll need a photo and measurements, but should be able to have it ready for you in about three weeks. You'll pay for shipping, of course."

The fedora bobbed in excitement. "Yes, yes! Of course! Only three weeks? You do work fast, Mr. Harkins."

Roger's lips tightened into a grin. He could do it in three seconds, but this Yankee didn't need to know that.

"Dad! Look at this!"

A teenage boy and his parents stood between matching pieces Roger had created several days ago. Thousands of thin strands of copper and iron intertwined to form studies of male and female musculature. The copper represented muscle fibers and the iron formed ligaments and connective tissue.

"Look! She's flying!"

The boy's voice was on the precipice of adulthood, a mix of nasal squawk and throaty baritone. It was nails on a chalkboard. Roger resisted the urge to order his skinless statues to seize the boy and fling him through the ornate front door of the gallery. Besides, he was intrigued by the sounds that emanated from the boy's smartphone that was being pushed into the father's face.

The father was bored for the first few seconds, then his eyebrows drew together before arching high on his forehead over widening eyes. "Is that real?"

"Yes," said the boy. "All over the news."

Roger approached the family. "May I take a look?"

The boy nodded, very proud that a stranger would be interested in his discovery, and flipped his phone around. He tapped the play icon on the touch screen and a video began.

The camera shook from winds that howled into the newscaster's microphone, turning her excited words into gibberish. Roger realized he was looking at Washington, D.C. during last night's devastating hurricane. Moreover, he was looking at an upward shot of the Washington Monument. The top was missing. Spotlights roamed the ruined pinnacle, revealing shattered stone. A figure entered the frame from above. A spotlight passed over his—no, *her*—body as she dropped into the belly of the monument. The microphone picked up screams of fear and awe as the woman emerged with someone in tow. There were no wires or rigging. This was no trick. One of the roving lights centered on her as she lowered the victim to the ground. Roger caught a flash of reddish-blonde hair. He thought of Mercy Werner. Fingers curled into fists as the video ended. No way was he going to let this woman get the attention that he deserved. No one could do what he could do.

He boarded his private jet several days later. It was time to reveal himself to the world, and the Monument seemed like the perfect place to make his grand entrance.

Chapter Twenty-Three

MARISSA SAT ON THE PORCH ROCKER watching David pace back and forth in the yard. He had been scanning the skies all morning, and was now wearing away an anxious path in the grassy turf.

"She'll be back," Marissa said.

"She was careless. Again." He took a sip of tepid coffee. His face screwed up at the taste and he dumped the dark liquid into the grass. The mug followed soon after.

"Damn her," he said. "If she went home, she'll lead them right back to us."

"I don't mean to overstep my bounds, Mr. Daniels, but you need to calm down. She's been through a lot. She probably needed to clear her head, and I'm sure she is trying to find a way to contact her family."

David shook his head. "That's what I'm afraid of."

A tiny speck emerged from a puffy cloud bank to the east of the cottage. It grew ever larger, eventually taking on the shape of a person.

"Be nice," Marissa warned.

Samantha descended from the heavens decked out in a black and red motorcycle outfit and matching helmet. A knapsack was slung over her back. The Maine Coon perked up as a Siamese poked its head from a makeshift sling that crossed over her torso. She removed the helmet and shook out her hair.

"Morning," she said. "I'd love some coffee."

"Damn it, Samantha!" said David.

Samantha's face fell. "Glad to see you, too."

David looked up at the sky. "Satellites, Samantha. Think, for fuck's sake!"

Samantha lowered the animal to the ground and let him sniff around. Marissa's cat leapt from his comfortable spot in her lap to investigate the newcomer.

"I'm sorry, but what the fuck?" Her tone was venomous. The helmet fell to her feet, along with the knapsack.

"I don't work for you," she said, then looked past him to Marissa. "I feel for you, sister."

"Oh look, they're getting along," Marissa said, choosing to evade the comment. Indeed, the two cats were rubbing their necks together. The Maine Coon rolled to his back, submissive to the older Siamese even though he was twice his size.

"Braithwaite probably has surveillance access at the highest levels. I told you the guy is connected," David said. "It was foolish to rush off like that."

"Maybe, but let him come. I'll pop his head like a grape. And by the way, I took the long way around and had to be going at least three hundred miles per hour. The satellites would have picked up a blur."

David ignored that and turned toward the cottage. "Come on. I'll make a fresh pot."

He pushed a steaming mug toward Samantha as she draped her heavy jacket over the back of the kitchen chair and sat down. Her hands wrapped around the cup. "Thanks. It's cold up there."

"Didn't mean to snap," David said. "It's just that Braithwaite is no joke."

Samantha took a sip. "Really? I hadn't noticed."

David ignored that too.

"Did you get a hold of your family?"

"It took a while, but I found a place outside of the city that was open for business." Samantha reached behind her and produced a cheap cell phone from her jacket pocket. She powered it on and perused the screen. "Still no answer. I've been trying all morning."

David didn't like the sound of that. He changed the subject.

"Last night, when you were telling me about your captivity, I didn't hear you mention Braithwaite other than what Galina told you about him. Is that right?"

Samantha nodded.

"Did you see him after he murdered Sharp and Douglas?"

Her eyes sank into the mug of coffee. As first, David thought she was trying to recall the details, but then realized she was reliving a painful memory.

"Very briefly. He spoke as they put the chains on me. There was hood over my head, but I'm pretty sure it was him. I can't remember what he said. It's all very hazy. I didn't see him again after that. Sort of."

David's eyes squinted in confusion. Her eyes never left the contents of her cup as she explained.

"Towards the very end, I was...I started to hallucinate. The Comm—Braithwaite—was wearing one of your business suits, reading the newspaper. I thought he was there, but it was all in my head."

David reached across the table and took her hand in his, giving it a comforting squeeze. "I need you to remember what he said to you."

She turned her head to the side and let her hair fall between them. Her hand pulled away. "I can't."

"Try, Samantha."

She took a deep breath and craned her head back. "It was something about...dying, maybe? No. About what he'd die for. That was it."

David nodded and began rotating his coffee cup in circles as he processed the information. "What else?"

"He said he'd die for his country, then asked me what was most important to me. All I could think about was escaping so I didn't answer him. Then he said he knows what is most important to me. That's all I remember."

David's cup stopped moving. Coffee splashed over the rim. Braithwaite would have overseen Samantha's reconditioning himself unless he had something more important to do. There was no way he would have let her out of his sight if he didn't have to. David wouldn't have. He raised the mug to his lips and drained it.

"Okay," he said. "We have to assume he left you with this Galina for a particular reason. He'd want to watch her work on you, especially if she is truly an expert at what she does."

"Did."

"Did," he agreed. "Braithwaite is a shrewd and calculated son of a bitch. If I were a betting man, I'd wager he was looking for a backup plan in case Galina couldn't break you. If he couldn't convince you to join him one way, he'd find another."

Samantha furrowed her eyebrows. "It's too late now, isn't it? I got the hell out of there."

David rose and went to the sink, opening the spigot and placing his mug beneath the hot stream. He wanted to come out and say that Braithwaite was a megalomaniac, that he felt he was meant for more than life had given him. That he was going to take and take until he had what he wanted—everyone else be damned. And worse, Braithwaite was ruthless. Anyone who wasn't with him was against him. There was no in between. David wanted to tell her how he knew that Braithwaite would never stop coming after her. That everyone between Braithwaite and her were just pawns. Cardboard cutouts of real people to be disposed of when their usefulness ended. But when he turned to look at the young woman who was experiencing something no one else in the entire world could understand—including David—he decided to keep these things himself. He wanted to protect her from the true horrors that human beings were capable of, even though she had brushed the surface at the hands of Braithwaite's torturer. Even though she had seen Braithwaite murder two people in front of her. All of that paled in comparison to what David had seen Braithwaite do.

What Braithwaite had ordered David to do.

"Samantha," he said, "we need to take the initiative. Bring the fight to him."

The Siamese Samantha had brought bolted past Marissa as she entered the cottage and leapt onto the kitchen table. David was more of a dog person. He watched Samantha scratch behind the cat's ears. It closed its eyes and lifted its snout into the air.

"This is Mal," she said.

Marissa's face lit up. "Cool name! My guy's called Brownie. Short for Mr. Brownstone."

"Like the song?" Samantha said.

Marissa nodded. "Exactly like the song. My mom was a groupie for Guns and Roses, followed them everywhere. I'm pretty sure I was conceived on a tour bus. She had a thing for bass players, though I can't imagine why."

Samantha laughed, then they launched into a rendition of Brownie's namesake.

"Okay," David said when they were finished. "I guess I'll make breakfast while you two bond over...whatever that was. Omelets?"

They nodded in unison.

David pulled a carton of eggs from the refrigerator while the two discussed late-twentieth century hard rock. He wanted to finish his discussion with Samantha, but not with Marissa present. There was no need to subject someone so innocent to the horrors of this world. Samantha was a different story. While he hadn't known her before his investigation started, he was beginning to get an idea of who she was. He could tell that she was made of tougher stuff than his assistant. She had to be. Otherwise, she'd still be in that torture chamber. Worse, she'd be Braithwaite's heavy artillery in a spare-no-civilian offensive somewhere overseas.

"And he made her go into the crowd and pick out three more for the drummer!"

Marissa was recounting one of her mother's adventures on the road. Samantha was grinning.

"Now that's a serious appetite," Samantha said.

It was nice to see them share a moment of levity. If he was correct, there wouldn't be much to laugh about in the coming days. His prognostication became all too accurate when he placed the skillet on the stovetop. A faint pulse vibrated through the handle into his palm. At first he thought it was the coiled metal of the burner expanding under the heat, but then he felt the floor come to life with the same steady vibrations. He froze and cocked his head. Now he could hear it plain as day. And it was growing louder.

Marissa stood up. "What's that sou—"

Plink!

A nickel-sized hole appeared in the front window. The glass shattered into an awful mosaic. David's world slowed.

Samantha's expression shifted from joviality to horror as she sank to the floor holding Marissa. David threw himself across the heavy oak table, catching the edges with his hands and holding fast as his weight overturned it. Wood exploded next to his head. Splinters flew past his eyes with agonizing lethargy.

David was supporting the weight of the table with his back as time resumed its normal flow. He risked a glance at the two women crouched next to him.

"Samantha! Choppers approaching! Go to work! I'll try to—"

Samantha wasn't listening. Her eyes were locked on Marissa. A macabre pattern of blood was growing on her shirt just below the right collarbone. That bullet had been meant for him. If Marissa hadn't stood when she did...

David seized Samantha's shoulder and shook her roughly. "Samantha! Go!"

She blinked and nodded, taking one last look at Marissa before leaving the cover of the upended table and snatching up her jacket. David had never seen a human being—or anything, for that matter—move so fast. Samantha was just gone, the only evidence of her passing was the front door swinging on its hinges. David heard a third shot, but knew Samantha would be okay. He peeled Marissa's shirt away from her shoulder and inspected the wound. The shot may have pierced her lung, but he couldn't be sure. He pulled her close to look at her back. The exit wound was gruesome, but at least it was a through and through.

"Did I just get shot?" she said. "Where is Brownie? You have a message from the pharmacy. I forgot to give it to you, boss."

She was going into shock. David cursed under his breath. The helicopters were close now. He pressed her left hand against the gunshot wound. "I have to go, Marissa. Hold pressure here. I'll be back."

David scrambled from behind the table and leaned it against the counter to maintain cover for Marissa, then belly-crawled toward his duffel bag near the couch. Marissa's voice weakened behind him.

"We've been dancin' with...Mister Brownstone..."

"Keep pressure on that wound, Sanchez!"

The wound itself wasn't fatal, but loss of blood would be the end of her. He didn't have much time, and he wasn't trained to let a superhero rescue him. He had to do something fast. David fished inside his bag until he found it. A Kimber Raptor II .45 ACP. Flat black with a scaled grip. It was a good gun. The magazine revealed eight rounds. His hand dove back into the bag and searched for the backup magazine. Behind him, Marissa's singing grew more faint.

"...so the little got moah and moah-oo-woah..."

There it was. David shoved the spare mag into his back pocket and made a mad dash for the back door, flinging it open and darting to the side. Sure enough, he heard a sharp report from outside just after a bullet hummed through the open door to smash into the opposite wall.

He couldn't get a location on the sniper, but now he knew there were two of them—one covering each exit.

"Hang in there, Marissa!"

David took three short breaths and bolted through the back door. He squeezed off three quick shots from the Kimber to provide covering fire, then pivoted into a zigzag pattern and ran for his life. His left shoulder exploded in pain. David didn't stop running until he reached the tree line. Crouching in a grove of ash saplings, he swapped the pistol to his left hand and reached up with his right to explore the wound. His fingers came away sticky with blood, but it was just a graze.

"Amateur," he said under his breath. "Now I've got you."

He was able to estimate the sniper's position from the second shot, but had to move before the gunman could get to a new location. David rose into a ducking position and picked his way through the underbrush in a wide flanking pattern. Rotor blades beat the air overhead, drawing ever closer. David sank against an old elm and closed his eyes to concentrate. He held his breath and paused. The gunman had to be close. Birds sang in the distance, but nowhere near him. Something large shifted its weight in a thicket at David's six o'clock.

He kept his center of gravity low as he moved from the cover of the tree. Each footstep settled in to take his weight before he committed to the next one. Tall grasses rustled ahead. He focused on them through the sights of his Kimber. They parted to reveal a man in black combat fatigues rising into a kneeling position. He held a two-way radio to his mouth. David's finger covered the trigger.

A gut-wrenching scream sounded from back at the cottage, startling both David and the sniper. It was a female voice. Samantha's voice.

David didn't pause to consider the implications. His first bullet took the sniper in the chest. The second painted a deadly dot on his forehead. The man's head snapped back and he fell from sight into the thicket. David darted into the tall grasses and knelt down beside the sniper, whose eyes were open but unseeing. A trickle of blood ran sideways across his forehead from the perfectly-shaped .45 caliber hole. David gathered up the sniper rifle. This man had no further use for it.

It was a Steyr SSG 69 bolt-action sniper rifle with iron sights and a telescopic scope. It had been modified for quick break down and reassembly, and accommodated a silencer. David also appropriated the man's sidearm, a Glock 37 with a ten-round capacity. The sniper liked his Austrian weapons. David approved. He stripped the sniper of his armored vest and pulled it over his head, noting the indentation from David's first slug. He was glad he had taken the second shot.

David hustled through the woods until he had a clear view of the cottage, then brought the Steyr to his shoulder and pressed his eye to the scope.

"Mother fucker."

Two attack helicopters circled Samantha perhaps two hundred feet above the cottage. They were Apache Guardians, fast and mean. David knew them well. These were outfitted with AIM-92 Stinger missiles and Hellfire-2 anti-tank missiles. And that was just part of their charm. 30-millimeter cannons unleashed a barrage on the hovering woman, battering her with violent force despite the fact that she had manifested some sort of transparent shield. The ricochets ripped into the trees and earth below, perforating the cottage as well. This was bad. Very bad.

Then it got worse.

David knelt and adjusted the scope for a closer look. A person was bound to the bottom of each helicopter. Heavy-duty ratchet straps had been wound around their bodies and attached to the landing gear, suspending them between the struts. Any attempt to bring the Apaches down by force would kill the prisoners.

David's racing pulse shifted into overdrive. A familiar feeling crept over him, that moment of dread when the backs of your hands prickled and your bowels clenched into knots. He zoomed in closer and recognized Samantha's father from the picture next to her bed. He didn't have to inspect the other helicopter to know that her brother was the second hostage, but he did anyway. Everything fell into place when her brother's anguished expression filtered through the scope. That's where Braithwaite had gone. That's why he had left his prized possession, his single chance of dominating the Middle East and, if David's theory was correct, anyone else that opposed him. Always have a backup plan. It was one of the first things Braithwaite had taught him when David had been assigned to his command. And now Braithwaite was pulling the ace from his sleeve. He was hitting Samantha where it hurt most, threatening what she held most dear. David had no doubt she would surrender to save her family. It was just a matter of time. She didn't know that they were already dead, their sentence handed down the moment Braithwaite had abducted them.

David started to rise, but found himself on his back several feet away from his last position. His chest erupted in agony. He heard himself wheezing for breath. It occurred to him as he lay like an overturned turtle that he had forgotten about the other sniper. The inside of his skull would be decorating the dirt if he hadn't risen to his feet at that precise moment. He felt ribs grinding together as he forced himself to move. Pain washed over him in a torrent, but he gritted his teeth and snatched up the sniper rifle. David forced his limbs to obey and broke into a full run back to the cottage. Explosions rang out above him. Now they were firing rockets at Samantha. David knew she was powerful, but what else did Braithwaite have waiting in the wings?

"Be smart, Samantha," he said as he reached the cottage, "draw them away."

David burst through the back door and found himself staring through the house at the remaining sniper. The front door still hung open from Samantha's hurried egress, and the marksman stood in the front yard just beyond the porch, having abandoned all stealth. His rifle was trained on the back door. He was grinning. David realized that he could never bring his rifle to bear in time, nor could he dive for cover before the bullet struck. This was it. The end of the road. In

David's mind, he could see the finger pull the trigger, see the round burst from the barrel as it came for him.

A shadow passed over the sniper. His grin disappeared as he dropped the rifle and emitted a howl that competed with the roaring Apaches overhead. He brought his hands up. Gloved fingers pointed in all the wrong directions. It seemed as though Samantha was watching over them despite her own troubles. David ended the assassin's torment with a round from his appropriated sniper rifle and rushed into the cottage, pushing the kitchen table away and kneeling to inspect his wounded assistant.

Her complexion was waxy alabaster, her body still as a corpse. Blood soaked the hardwood planks under his boots. He found a flashlight in the pantry drawer and thumbed open her eyes one at a time, passing the light beam in front of her pupils. They dilated and contracted as they should. Her pulse was thready, but she wasn't dying. Not yet. David sat back and breathed a heavy sigh of relief. Maybe after all of this he and Marissa could share a hospital room and discuss the idiocy of superpowers and megalomaniacs. If they lived, of course.

Climbing onto the roof was a risky move considering his injuries, but the rickety ladder held his weight. His vision danced as he pulled himself over the eave, forcing him to catch his breath before scrambling to the cover of the stone chimney. He unslung the Steyr and wound his forearm through the strap for stability. A round slid into the chamber as he brought the scope to his eye.

"Good," he whispered.

Samantha had moved the battle several hundred yards away from the safe house. It wasn't much of a battle, really. Braithwaite was a seasoned warrior, and kept her on her heels with rockets and cannon fire. She wasn't on the offensive, and for good reason. Just as Braithwaite had planned. David knew Braithwaite was trying wear her down, exhaust her into surrendering. But she was still fighting, and now David was about to turn the tables.

He lowered himself to the shingles and unwound his arm from the strap, then rested the Steyr on the apex of the roof for stability. He raised his face to the sky to get a feel for the wind and adjusted the scope before looking through it. It was his first look at Braithwaite since their meeting in Sharp's conference room. He was shouting orders into his headset from inside the cockpit.

"Hello, Sunshine," David said.

His finger curled around the trigger. The Apache disappeared. David raised his head to find it listing to the side just before it righted itself and entered evasive maneuvers. Samantha was pushing back. The helicopter would be a twisted hunk of metal if she desired it so. It was a warning shot across the bow. David tore himself away from the scene and lowered his eye back to the scope.

The Apache's cannons churned out round after round at its target. Each one stopped just short of her, but interrupted her concentration and drove her backwards. The other Apache would hit her from another angle as soon as she centered herself. David zoomed the scope into the cockpit of the other chopper and found the pilot. He braced for recoil and squeezed the trigger. The glass cracked right in front of the surprised pilot, but didn't shatter. David cursed and reloaded the chamber. These were armored attack helicopters, after all. He would have to wait until the Apache circled back around to get another clean shot. With any luck he would be able to pierce the broken glass with a second round.

In the meantime, David put Samantha in his sights. Golden hair was plastered to her face and neck in sweaty strands. Her face was red and her chest was heaving from exertion. For all of her miraculous abilities, she was still a human being. She would tire.

Samantha flew out of his viewfinder. David raised his eyes above the rifle to see her rising high above the Apaches. She hovered there, waiting for something. Maybe she was buying time, making them come to her. The Apaches regrouped and ascended in tight formation. David looked down the scope and followed their pattern. He eased the Steyr to match, carefully plotting the trajectory of the one he had hit. David heard the Hydra rockets whistle from their silos, impacting their target with precision. He wanted to see if Samantha had withstood the onslaught, but was unwilling to give up his shot.

"Come on," he mouthed silently, "show me that sweet spot."

The Apache swiveled on its axis to turn its cannon toward Samantha. David depressed the trigger as the cracked windshield oscillated past his viewfinder. This time the bullet penetrated the windshield. The pilot jerked backwards in his seat. David reloaded as he poked his head up to see the result. The Apache pitched to the side, its rotors now perpendicular to the horizon line as it spun out of control. David held his breath, hoping against all odds that he didn't just kill Samantha's father or brother. But the co-pilot reined in the aerial beast and righted it just before it hit the ground. It swooped low and recovered, climbing into the air with frightening swiftness. Trees bent and swayed at the mercy of its downdraft, several outlying branches severed by the blades. David wiped the sweat from his forehead and turned his attention to Samantha, but his eyes were drawn away from her as Braithwaite's Apache banked toward the cottage.

"Uh oh."

The radio shouted static in his pocket. He pulled it out and listened as Braithwaite's voice crackled to life in his hand.

"*How do you like that Steyr?*"

David scrambled from the peak of the roof to conceal himself.

"I'd like it better with some armor-piercing rounds," David said. "How about you land that bird and I'll show it to you?"

The Apache stopped short of the cottage and wheeled around, hovering at Samantha's altitude.

"*I'd love to,*" came the reply, "*but I have something to show you first.*"

David climbed back up the roof just in time to see the twin Stingers ignite on Braithwaite's Apache. Samantha was being pelted by 30-

millimeter rounds from the other helicopter. She'd never hear the missiles coming.

"Samantha!"

David's warning was drowned out by whirring blades and pounding gunfire. He stood up and waved his arms. His own shouts deafened him. The Stinger missiles cut through air with alarming speed and precision. David fell silent, his hands gripping his skull in disbelief as he watched the missiles approach the unwitting Samantha. Even if she detected them at the last second and somehow managed to move, it would make no difference. The targeting technology was cutting edge. There would be no escape.

The missiles smashed into her at the same time, exploding in terrible fireballs. The shockwave hit the Apache closest to her. It went sideways as though a giant hand had swatted it aside like a pesky wasp. David was horrified as it disappeared into the trees below. That helicopter carried Samantha's brother. She was unaware of the tragedy, however, and lay unmoving at the end of a long stretch of ripped earth.

The short wave radio vibrated in his hand as Braithwaite's voice came through.

"*Fuck yeah! That's what I'm talking about!*"

David dropped the radio in disgust and shouldered the sniper rifle. He didn't know how many rounds he had left.

It didn't really matter anymore.

Chapter Twenty-Four

THE GLITTERING STAR WAS HER FAVORITE. The crescent moon and the multi-hued, ringed planets got in the way sometimes, but the star would always make its way back to her. Sometimes the shapes would just stop, filling her with anxiety and anger. She'd make them go around again.

Twinkle twinkle little star

How I wonder what you are

Mechanical notes played in time with the words. She reached out when the star entered her field of vision.

My hands are so small.

There were other shapes, but they weren't circling above her like the moon, planets and star. They came and went, cooing and singing to her. Samantha couldn't make out what they were, but she knew them. They made her feel loved.

I think I have grass in my mouth.

The heavenly objects shrank and multiplied. They twisted and coalesced into clear orbs that shimmied as they floated past her. An engine hummed, sending vibrations through the seat beneath her. She dipped the stick back into the bottle and blew. One of the bubbles found its way into Mommy's hair and popped. Mommy's hair was the color of blood for some reason.

Get up, Samantha.

I know you. You spoke to me when I was a prisoner. You spoke in my head.

In went the ringed stick and out came the bubbles. Daddy reprimanded her over his shoulder, but she didn't listen. She popped each bubble by looking at it and imagining she was squeezing it with her fingers.

Get up, Samantha.

Just a little bit longer. I hurt so much.

It was difficult to keep the plastic ring steady in front of her lips as the car jostled her, but she managed. Another batch of perfect, shining bubbles sprang to life on the other side of the stick. Samantha popped every one. Almost. This time there was a runner. It escaped through the open window. Samantha lurched after it, reaching for the bubble with all of her might. Daddy cursed and twisted the steering wheel in desperation. Mommy sucked in her breath.

Get up!

First came the scream of ripping steel, then the roar of the motor overcompensating when its wheels left the road. The thunderous impact provided a coda to the nightmare song. There were more bubbles than she knew what to do with. How could she possibly pop them all when she couldn't breathe? It wasn't until the last bubble left her darkening vision that strong hands clutched at her and pulled her from the car. The twisted heap of metal disappeared into the shimmering green depths below.

GET! UP!

Samantha's inhale was violent. She rose to her hands and knees and expelled grass and pebbles from her mouth in a series of hacking coughs. A faint, steady whistle was growing louder. Samantha willed herself into the air a split second before the space she had just occupied erupted in a cloud of fire and dust. The shockwave slammed into her, turning her world upside down. Something smashed into her back with a loud crack and she heard leaves rustling. A tree fell beside her, the trunk slamming into the earth as she rolled to a stop. The whir of helicopter's blades was close now, and the cannon fired its deadly rounds into the boles that surrounded her. She took to the air amid chunks of flying debris and weaved among the trunks, hoping they would provide adequate cover.

Every use of her power came at a cost now. She was more exhausted after each aerial maneuver, after each defensive construct she conjured to absorb or redirect the relentless attacks. They were wearing her down and they knew it. Her focus was slipping.

What can I do? They have Daddy and Cole strapped to those things.

She landed under a canopy of oaks and knelt on one knee to rest. Whatever had hit her had taken a serious toll. One second she was deflecting gunfire from the attack helicopter that carried Cole, and the next second she was eating turf. Her ears still rang from the explosion. Her entire right side burned. She smelled singed hair. Samantha understood that she couldn't beat them with brute force. Her powers were useless when Braithwaite was shielding himself with the two people she loved most in the entire world. The situation became more hopeless with every passing minute. She couldn't keep this up forever. Surrender was the only way to rescue her father and Cole. She would save them by working with Braithwaite.

No! Figure it out.

She tried to concentrate. The chopper was close now. This was it. There wouldn't be another chance. There wouldn't be another freakish power outage when Braithwaite had her back where he wanted her.

What would Evan tell me to do?

Her thoughts drifted to the salvage yard where he had pushed her to try harder. The Mercury. The magnet.

The crane.

She crouched and gathered herself, inhaling and exhaling with three deep, slow breaths. The pain and fatigue didn't fade, but they took a backseat to determination.

You can do this.

She shot skywards with such force that the oaks shied away from her passing. The chopper would spot her right away, but she wasn't hiding anymore.

Samantha wanted them to see her.

She extended her arms before her with hands in tight fists and willed herself into a direct collision course with the armored helicopter. As she drew near, she erected a barrier of force to fend off the expected cannon fire. Braithwaite didn't disappoint. A barrage of rockets accompanied the artillery. Samantha came full on, enduring the pounding as she played chicken with the helicopter, then banked away at the last possible moment. She got a good look at the man who had killed Evan, who had kidnapped her loved ones and tormented her. His eyes were narrow and tenacious, not at all worried that a human cannonball was about to smash through the cockpit.

Her bank took her into a wide arc. She tightened her trajectory and dove as the helicopter swiveled around to bring its armory in line with her.

Only gonna get one shot at this.

She darted beneath the vehicle at the speed of thought. Samantha didn't know much about military-grade choppers—or any choppers, for that matter—but she suspected their weapons had some way of pinpointing her location. She hoped the unexpected maneuver would buy her a few seconds to concentrate. Samantha pictured the piloting controls she had glimpsed during her all-too-brief flyby. She extended her will to every dial, flipped every switch, pressed every single button. She even yanked on the flight stick for good measure. Her father hung unconscious above her in the nylon restraints. She mouthed a promise to him as the helicopter went berserk.

"You're going to be okay."

It pitched and rolled on every conceivable axis, firing off missiles and bullets with wild abandon. The rear rotors sputtered and stopped, then started and stammered again. Samantha held her breath, trying her best to match the movements of the flailing underbelly and stay close to her imprisoned father. It took everything she had to mirror convulsing aircraft. It occurred to her in that frightening moment that she had done this before. Or, to be more precise, a less stressful facsimile of this.

Her father became a ball of ivory spinning in discord with a red and black wheel at incredible speeds. The difference in this scenario was that she would shatter the marble if she acted at the wrong moment.

You can do it. You can do it. You can do it. You can do it.

Samantha closed her eyes and summoned an image of the restraints snapping apart. She let out an explosive exhale and opened her eyes to find her father falling to his death. Her eyes were so clouded with tears that she almost missed him when she dropped to scoop him up. Relief turned to vengeful anger when she got a closer look at her father. He was bloody and bruised. His left eye was swollen shut and several teeth were missing.

Motherfuckers.

Samantha erected a protective bubble around them as she spirited her father back to the safety the cottage. She wanted nothing more than to stay with him, to make sure he was okay, but her brother was still up there. And now Braithwaite had no hostage to protect his chopper. Samantha let rage fuel her drained body and mind and launched into the air with renewed vigor. Braithwaite's helicopter still faltered not so far away, but the second helicopter was nowhere in sight.

"Samantha!"

She saw a familiar figure exit the trees far below. He carried a rifle in one hand and was pointing at Braithwaite's helicopter with the other.

David!

"Take him out! Now!"

Nothing in her life up to that point was more satisfying than when she pressed herself, arms outspread, against the armored windshield of the helicopter and put on the most sinister grin she could muster. Both Braithwaite and the pilot scrambled at the controls to try and throw her. Samantha rode the Apache like a champion bull rider, her eyes never leaving Braithwaite's. A low growl vibrated from her chest.

She flexed her arms inward, imploding the cockpit. Armored glass shattered and sprayed into the sky. The reinforced steel chassis crumpled in her fists like aluminum foil. Sparks flew as she pounded the control panels into an unrecognizable mass of metal, plastic and silicon. She ignored the bullets from Braithwaite's sidearm as she yanked the flight stick from its housing and tossed it over her shoulder. Satisfied, Samantha released the wounded chopper and allowed it to die. It disappeared into the trees and hit the ground with a jarring crunch. A plume of smoke rose from the canopy.

Samantha turned to find David rushing into the foliage several hundred yards away. A similar column of smoke wafted from the leafy roof near his entry point.

No...Cole...

David was standing in front of a ruined helicopter when she arrived. His hands covered his face. The helicopter was on its side, belly facing them. Cole was still strapped to the landing struts. His bottom half was all wrong, his top half raw and bleeding. His gentle face was now a blackened, burnt husk.

Samantha's voice was a high-pitched wail.

"Cole?"

She wanted to go to him, but was paralyzed.

"*Cole*?"

He wasn't moving. She couldn't tell if he was breathing. Denial took hold and she forced her unresponsive limbs into action.

"I'm going to get you out of there! Hold on, Cole! Hold on!"

Then David was there, wrapping her up in his arms and holding fast. "Samantha, there's nothing you..."

His voice trailed off as she easily shrugged away his embrace and ran to her brother. She fell to her knees before him, afraid to release the straps lest he die before she could speak to him one last time.

"Sammy," Cole said.

His burnt lips curled into something resembling a smile.

Only you and Daddy can call me Sammy.

"I tried, Cole...I tried so hard..."

Her voice choked up and she could say no more. Cole's arm reached for her. The skin was cracked and sloughing from the limb. She took his hand and pressed it to her wet cheek.

"You are..." he started, but blood erupted from his mouth.

She pressed her forehead to his hand. Her body was wracked with sobs.

"I'm sorry, Cole. Don't go. Don't leave me."

"You are...a miracle..."

Samantha's breath caught in her throat.

"Dad..." he tried to swallow, but instead coughed up more blood and bile. He finished his thought with extreme effort. "He...didn't think...I...knew..."

"Cole?"

The light in his eyes faded, his focus shifting from his despondent sister to points beyond.

"*COLE*!"

Samantha pivoted away and screamed. Tree trunks shattered and earth tore into the air in an arc of destruction before her. She exploded into the air and felt the reverberations of her next cry rip through the air around her. She spotted the wreckage of Braithwaite's helicopter through clouded, burning eyes.

Please be alive. I want to do it slowly.

David had left her alone with her brother and was now inspecting the ground near Braithwaite's ruined vehicle. His hand cradled his ribs. Samantha spied the co-pilot slumped over the console. She pushed him back into his seat with a telekinetic shove. His face and neck had slammed against the broken glass upon impact, killing him instantly. Braithwaite was nowhere to be found. David stood up and turned to her with sympathy written across his strong features.

Samantha didn't want sympathy. She wanted Braithwaite.

"Where is he?" she demanded.

David took a step back, his expression turning to alarm.

"I'm so, so sorry," he said. "I'm sure your brother was a good man."

"Where *is* he?"

She was unaware of her fists clenching as she advanced on him. David's eyes narrowed dangerously. He didn't retreat.

"You need to take second, Samantha."

She barreled past him and looked for signs of Braithwaite around the crash site. David's voice followed her.

"These Apaches are built for punishment. They have armored hulls and crash-resistant frames. Braithwaite survived, and he's long gone by now. The man is over-confident, not stupid. He won't take you on unless the odds are in his favor. We're safe."

"I don't want to be safe!"

Samantha took a step toward the woods and lifted into the air, but his next words gave her pause.

"He's trained to evade capture in enemy territory, Samantha. Hell, he trained me. We won't find him. *You* won't find him."

She halted her ascent and hovered motionless, unwilling to let David see the despair in her eyes.

"Samantha," David said, "we need you. I need you. Marissa is bleeding to death. Your father needs medical attention. I do too. We have to get out of here before the authorities arrive and bring everything from the local Sheriff to the Air Force. They're probably already on their way."

No, damn it. No!

"You can either level these woods and hope that you find him before you pass out from exhaustion, or you can spend whatever energy you have left helping the people who care about you. But if Marissa dies, you've let him take another life. He wins. Again."

With that, he turned and stalked away in the direction of the safe house.

"Make your choice, Samantha," he said over his shoulder. "Who are you going to be?"

She watched him disappear into the trees, then spun back to the woods beyond the fallen Apache.

Who am I going to be?

Chapter Twenty-Five

THE MYLAR BALLOON DRIFTED into Samantha's face for the third time, but she didn't have the heart to knock it away. The little girl in the patent leather shoes was asking her mother if daddy was going to be okay. The mother's eyes were reddened and sunken, her hair oily and unkempt. The little girl looked up at Samantha when her mother didn't answer.

"Is your daddy sick too?"

Samantha smiled down at her. "Yes, but he's here in the hospital where they fix people."

The mother was silent as she watched the floor numbers change. They exited on the third floor, the *tip-tap* of the girl's hard-soled shoes growing fainter as the elevator doors began to close. Samantha spotted a sign on the opposite wall before the doors met.

Floor 3

Oncology

Shit. Learn to zip it, Sammy.

Her All Stars squeaked on the waxed linoleum as she made her way through the maze of corridors. Nurses and orderlies clad in blue scrubs walked by with their noses in charts. Families gathered around the beds of their loved ones in the rooms that she passed. A familiar name adorned the placard outside of room 408.

Her father was on the phone, as usual. The television mounted on the wall played some sort of advertisement for medication. The disclaimers rattled on without pause.

"Send Thompson, then," he was saying as he waved her in. "Well I'm certainly not going. Figure it out."

He hung up the phone and returned Samantha's warm embrace. She sat on the edge of the bed and stole a piece of buttered toast from the food tray in front of him, brushing away the crumbs that fell to the bedspread when she bit into it with a crunch. He pointed his finger at her and called out to a passing nurse.

"Food thief! She's stealing my breakfast! Call my insurance company!"

"You're a rat," she said, grabbing at his finger.

Most of his bruises were now a brownish-yellow in their final stage of healing. The white gauze over his left eye was the only bandage left on his face. Her eyes drifted to the half-eaten piece of toast when his smile revealed the missing teeth.

"Don't worry about me, Sammy. Doctor Hill is going to fix me up. Give me all new choppers," he said. "Sorry, poor choice of words."

"Doctor Hill, as in *Centerville* Doctor Hill?"

Alan nodded and covered her hand with his. His features grew somber.

"I thought we'd spend some time at the old house," he said. "Gather some things for the funeral. Just take a break and be together."

Samantha was reminded of Cole's story about their father smoking in the backyard. She and her brother had grown up in that house, and she had followed her father to D.C. when Cole left for San Francisco. They still had family in the Midwest, and it was nice have a place nearby for holidays and gatherings.

"That sounds good, Daddy," she said, squeezing his hand.

I could use a break.

"What did you tell the police?" he said.

Samantha looked to the door and lowered her voice before answering. "What we all agreed on."

She put the piece of toast back on the plate and cleared her throat. "Daddy, I just want to—"

He held up a hand to stop her. "Not here."

She started to protest, but her father looked up at the television screen and picked up the remote to raise the volume. The news anchor's voice filled the hospital room.

"*...our crew was allowed nowhere near the area as it was being cordoned off by authorities on the scene...*"

An attractive broadcaster gave her report from behind a police blockade.

"*...there is still no confirmation as to who was piloting the crop duster or the helicopter, but sources tell us that the crop duster was illegally carrying hazardous materials and that the area will be under quarantine until the CDC and the FBI clears...*"

Samantha and her father exchanged glances.

That son of a bitch is covering it up.

David had told Samantha that Braithwaite had connections, but to pull this off meant he was in with the highest levels of government—or had dirt on them.

"*The Special Agent in Charge told Channel 9 Action News that he could not comment on an ongoing investigation, but that terrorism was not being ruled out at this time. We know that the helicopter was owned by a local flight school, but no one from the school has returned our calls as of this broadcast. However, we were able to contact an eyewitness. Mr. Tooms, how far away were you from the collision and what did you see?*"

The camera panned to an aging man wearing a straw sunhat.

"*Well it weren't no crop duster, that's for sure. I've flown plenty of crop dusters in my time. I was a couple of miles away, but I know the difference between a single engine and an attack chopper. We didn't have birds like that back in 'Nam, but I know the like."*

Samantha was enthralled as the man's story unfolded.

"*And you mentioned something else during our pre-interview. Could you share that with our viewers?"*

The microphone reappeared in front of his mouth.

"*These two choppers was attacking a flying girl. I think it was the same flying girl that saved all them people over in D.C. during the storm. I don't know of no other flying girls!"*

His laughter disintegrated into a wet, hacking cough. He spat.

"*How can you be sure it was a woman from so far away?"*

"*She went up real high and let out a holler that would put my wife to shame."*

The camera panned from Mr. Tooms back to the field reporter, who turned to address the camera.

"*Was the mysterious woman foiling a possible terrorist attack or was she involved somehow? We'll bring you the answers as the story unfolds in our continuing coverage of this disaster in Montgomery County. Back to you, Connor."*

The image shifted to a man with perfect hair sitting behind the anchor desk. Next to him was a blurry photo of Samantha hovering above the decimated Washington Monument. Below the image a caption read:

#HurricAngel Resurfaces?

Her father let the remote drop to the bed as the television went dark. Samantha could feel his eyes on her. She suddenly found her cuticles very interesting.

Samantha hadn't been on an airliner in ages. It was a direct flight from Reagan International to Dayton, a short hop that would have taken many hours on the road. She spent the majority of the journey staring through the window at the clouds rolling by.

I should be out there with them.

The feeling took her by surprise. She wanted to feel the winds buffeting her, roaring through her helmet. She could almost smell the fresh air that was no doubt quite chilly at this altitude. She didn't know how to ride a motorcycle, but Cole had said there was nothing like being a part of the elements when traveling—the sights, sounds, and smells were immersive. Now she understood.

"Drink, ma'am?"

The attendant was handing her father a plastic cup of red wine. Samantha hadn't even heard him order.

"Thank you, no," she said, returning to the window.

The drive from Dayton International Airport to Centerville was just as reserved. Her father had refused to let her lift her own bags into the rental car.

Does he know I can lift the entire rental car, bags and all?

After Cole's cryptic last words, she just wasn't sure. Her father's mood had shifted since the news report in the hospital room. He kept his eyes on the road and didn't say much, and when he did speak it was with great effort. Perhaps grief was setting in as things returned to normal. Or maybe it was the aftershocks of the trauma. Both reasons made perfect sense, and she couldn't fault him for either. Then again, maybe it was something more.

Their brief conversations centered around Cole's funeral arrangements. He had arranged to have Cole's body flown to Ohio for burial, but it wouldn't arrive until a full autopsy had been completed. When Samantha had left them outside the hospital emergency room that horrible morning, it had been David's idea to suggest that he had found Cole and Alan at the scene of a hit-and-run car accident. David had tried to calm the delirious father who, in his inconsolable grief, lashed out at David, breaking his ribs and lacerating his shoulder with a tire iron. Marissa's injury was explained away by a misfire of her conceal-carry weapon. The holes in these stories were large enough to drive a truck through, but her father was an accomplished diplomat and had a knack for persuasion. So far, the authorities weren't asking further questions. Samantha wondered if David had something to do with that.

We are so damn lucky.

The irony of her thought hit like a sledgehammer. She had been there when her father had first awakened. She recalled wishing that she could take on a hundred Apaches rather than tell him that his son, her brother, had died. She would never forget the look on his face. So no, they weren't so lucky. After the initial wave of hugging and crying had passed, she had learned that he and Cole had been trying to get a hold of her during and after the storm. He told her that she hadn't replied at first, but then came her text message begging them to get to Washington as soon as possible. Braithwaite was waiting for them when they arrived in the capital.

"Blame me," David had said. "We met on the train and I got you mixed up in some cloak and dagger bullshit with the government. Tell your father that I used you as a cover for an operation that went wrong, and they took it out on your family. Say that I never gave you the details of my mission in order to keep you safe. I failed."

"What if he was awake at the beginning of the fight with the Apaches? What if he saw me? There was no time to put on my helmet."

"Not likely. He was banged up pretty good, Samantha. And even if he was conscious there was no way he got a good look at you. Those things move too fast. You do too."

She hated lying, but it was to protect her father—as well as her alter ego as the super-powered savior of D.C. David's deceit was in their best interests.

"We'll be home soon," her father said. "Stop off at DLM first? Not likely to be anything in the pantry at home."

Samantha shrugged. She wasn't hungry, and hadn't been since Cole had died. Food was flavorless mush in her mouth.

The McAllister house had the typical musty smell of a dwelling that was unoccupied the majority of the year. Samantha entered the kitchen and set the grocery bags onto a layer of dust that had settled across the room's surfaces.

"Well, I know what I'm doing today," she said, swiping the countertop with her index finger. "What time is your dentist appointment?"

She poked her head into the dining room and living room. The furniture had been draped in white sheets. The curtains were pulled tight. Her father was inspecting the refrigerator when she returned to the kitchen. He withdrew a carton of milk and put it to his nose. His nostrils flared and he moved to the sink. "Whew! We've got to remember to throw out perishables when we leave."

"Dad, your appointment. What time?"

"Sorry," he said, looking at his watch. "One-thirty. We made it in plenty of time. I can drive myself. You don't need a car anyway, right?"

What does that mean?

He shut off the water and deposited the empty carton into the garbage can.

"No, actually I don't," she said.

You're imagining things, Sam.

"I'm going to get this place opened up while you're gone. It will be spotless when you get back."

"That's my girl," he said.

Samantha flipped on the hallway light as she ascended the stairs. Her bedroom had been converted into a guest room along with the others after her family had moved out. She ran her fingertips along the walls as she walked to the window, feeling the memories in the uneven surfaces where nail holes had once been.

This is where my 'N Sync poster hung.

She opened the window drapes and sat on the bed.

And here is where I kissed Paul Harrowman after Homecoming. I wonder what happened to him.

Other memories came flooding back, but she rose and left them in the room. There would be time to reminisce later.

She steadied herself before opening the door to Cole's bedroom. Even though it had been redecorated too, Samantha half-expected to see his music accolades on the walls and the dirty clothes covering the floor.

"I'm going to get cleaned up before my appointment. Wouldn't want to stink out old Dr. Hill. When you get a chance—"

Her father was lugging their bags up the stairs. When he saw Samantha standing in the bedroom doorway, he set them down and joined her there. His arm draped her shoulder and he pulled her to him. They stood in silence for a long while.

Cleaning a large, split-level home from top to bottom was a breeze when you didn't have to do any actual cleaning. Samantha made sure the sheers were closed over the windows before she began, then laid out the cleaning supplies and pulled the vacuum cleaner from the utility closet. It occurred to her as she set the tools into motion how far she had come in such a short time.

This is still kinda scary. Even after battling top-of-the-line military helicopters. I remember when I could barely lift my underwear from the ceiling fan. I'm stronger now. I can feel it. I just wish I knew why.

She would have pursued this train of thought, but simultaneously moving a feather duster, sponge, mop, vacuum cleaner and toilet brush required her full attention. The last order of business was carrying bags of trash out to the dumpster can, a task she completed with her own hands. No need for the neighbors to become privy to her secret.

Why, little Samantha McAllister has returned home. She sure has changed...

Samantha closed the garage door behind her and pulled the bandana from her head. She swiped the countertop again, inspected her finger, then summoned a bottle of beer from the refrigerator to congratulate herself on a job well done. The cap lifted off with a satisfying *twish!* as the bottle floated into her hand. She leaned against the sink and took a long draught. In less than an hour, she had made the entire house spotless. Just as she had promised.

Her father still wasn't home after a short nap on the newly-Febrezed sofa, so Samantha lounged on the backyard deck and sipped another beer. She tapped out a message on her new smartphone while she bathed in the afternoon sunshine. Fortunately for her, the wireless store had been able to retrieve the contacts from her purloined phone. She had been sure to add David and Marissa to the list.

David, Marissa

3:04 p.m.

Are you two doing okay? Mal's not causing any problems, I hope.

Samantha watched the phone for a few seconds after sending the text, but there was no reply. She scooped up her beer bottle and went back into the house. She was tempted to flip on the local news to find out what was going on around her hometown but decided against it. She had a feeling that the coverage would shift to the so-called helicopter accident, footage of her over downtown D.C. or, even worse, international news about terrorism. Samantha had seen enough of that for three lifetimes. She decided to pick up where she had left off with the reminiscing.

The folding ladder's springs groaned as it dropped to the floor of the upstairs hall, and the captured summer heat washed over her as she floated past the ladder and into the attic. The light bulb in the ceiling was still alive when she pulled the string. Her father or Cole must have changed it over the holidays.

Holy crap. Where do I start?

Boxes upon boxes of keepsakes littered the attic floor. A massive dollhouse Aunt Lizzie had given Samantha as a child was now draped in cobwebs. She remembered her parents being upset that they would have nowhere to put it. Her old crib was broken down and stacked against a wall. A card table near the entryway was loaded with collectibles and photo albums. Samantha picked up a random album and flipped it open to scan the photos, each one a moment frozen forever in time.

A seven-year-old girl wearing a gap-toothed smile and teddy bear barrettes the color of bubble gum. A boy in a Cincinnati Reds cap and a matching, toddler-sized jersey standing in front of the stadium, eyes squinted against the sun. A dark-haired young woman in a bathing suit holding a very young Samantha wearing a floppy sun hat and overly-large sunglasses.

I look nothing like her.

She closed the album and returned it to the cardboard box. Her toe brushed a container below the card table and she knelt to retrieve the cache of mementos. Three mechanical notes rang out from inside, as though she had disturbed an old jewelry box.

The color drained from her face.

She levitated the object from the box and held it to the light. Glitter sparkled from the heavenly bodies that hung below the bowed frame. There was the soft grinding of tiny gears as she located the key and commanded it to turn. *Twinkle, Twinkle, Little Star* resonated throughout the attic in gentle tones as the tiny comb made its journey across the studded drum inside the device. They were the notes she had heard while hallucinating from cold and starvation as she hung in the chains. It was the song that had played in her mind while she lay burnt and stunned in the dirt after the Apache's missile strike. She leaned against the card table, hands together in prayer formation over her lips. Her eyelids fluttered and closed.

"You used to wind that up every night, you know."

Her father stepped from the ladder into the attic. She hadn't heard him come in. "We'd hear it all night long through the baby monitor. Long before you were big enough to reach it."

What?

Samantha let the mobile drop into her grasp. The lullaby slowed in its final moments, then stopped. "You...you know."

It wasn't a question. He lifted it from her hands, his face shedding the years as his eyes fell over it.

"Your mother bought it for you when you were born."

Samantha watched him crank the key. He held it up before her and let it rotate as the song played again. The glittering star caught the light of the incandescent bulb overhead. Neither of them spoke until the song was over. He dropped his arm and perused the multitude of memories housed in the humid attic as he replaced the mobile in its container.

"Yes, Sammy," he said. "I know."

Oh my god...

She swooned and had to grip the edge of the table to steady herself. The sudden jumble of emotions created a confusing sensation; fear, guilt, sadness, happiness and, most of all, relief.

"I knew long before you could wipe your own ass," he said with a chuckle.

"Dad, what I was going to say earlier, at the hospital..."

She fell silent when the words wouldn't come. Her lips simply trembled, frozen against her will.

I'm so sorry. Cole died because of me. A lot of people have died because of me.

"At first, it was just that mobile," her father said, brushing by her unspoken confession. "Then, when you learned to walk, we couldn't keep a damned diaper on you. It was like we had a giggling, pink, two-legged pet that wasn't housebroken. You learned to do the airplane thing with your baby food all by yourself. But unlike your mom and I, you didn't have to use your hands. It was the damnedest thing."

He pulled something from one of the boxes and stood looking at it. She couldn't see what it was as his back was to her. He turned to face her as he continued. "It's strange, now that I think about it."

He reconsidered his words with a wave of his hand and nodded his head at her. "Well, strange beyond the obvious reasons, I mean," he said. "Your mother was never scared like I was. She delighted in your 'awakening' as she called it. She was...odd that way. I wanted to have you looked at, take you to the best neurological scientists I could find, but she forbade it. She made me swear on my life that if something ever happened to her and I had to raise you on my own, that I would never, ever tell anyone about you. I agreed, but our marriage became...strained after that. "

Samantha rubbed her eyes and stared at him in disbelief.

"Why didn't you tell me? Why didn't I know about these...these abilities until just a few months ago? How did this—?"

Her questions died on her lips as he held out the object he had retrieved from the box. It was a folded up newspaper clipping. She took it with trembling fingers and unfolded the brittle, yellowing newsprint.

FAMILY PLUNGES INTO LAKE
Woman Missing, Feared Dead

Samantha's world imploded.

The dreams during the discovery of her abilities and the visions during her torture coalesced into an epiphany that struck her like a freight train. Her mother had been in the car that day. The day of the wreck.

She sank to the dusty floor. Her body became rigid. Her mouth hung open and her eyes were wide with shock. It was too much. Evan. Cole. And now this.

Her father was there, gathering her up and holding her close.

"I didn't show you that to hurt you, Sammy," he said, "but you needed to know. It is a parent's duty to protect his child, but also to prepare her to live in the world after he is gone. A world that grows more dangerous with every generation. You have gifts I will never understand. After the crash, after your mother was lost, your gifts went away. They just disappeared, and I didn't know if they would ever resurface. To be honest, I hoped they would stay hidden forever."

He gripped her shoulders and pulled back so that she could see his face.

"You are special, Samantha. You are different, yes, but you are my daughter. *My* daughter. And I know you will do the right thing. Please know that none of this is your fault. Accept it. You didn't ask for it, I know. A tiger doesn't give itself its stripes, or a leopard its spots. But you were born with these powers just like you were born with that sharp mind and that pretty smile. Eventually, you will be an example to the world of what they could be and should be. Just like you were when you saved all of those lives during the worst hurricane in history. Just like you were when you took on those military killing machines to save your family. They say the true measure of a man is how he treats those who can do nothing for him and nothing to him. Well, Sammy, they have you on video over the Washington Monument showing your true measure."

Samantha heard her father's words, but couldn't process them. Not yet.

"Cole died, Daddy! I tried to save him! I can do all of these things, but I couldn't save Cole!"

She was shaking uncontrollably. He held her tight. "I know, honey. I know."

"He should be here, not me! If only I'd been smarter! Stronger!"

He pressed her face to his shoulder let her get it out, stroking her hair and rocking her until the heavy sobs trailed off into quiet sniffles. They still sat on attic floor sometime later.

"Daddy?"

"Yes?"

"Did Cole have a different mother?"

Her father stood and offered his hand.

"Let's get out of this hot box and discuss it over a cold beer. What do you say?"

Samantha's father handed her a bottle and sat down on the sofa next to her, pushing his salt-and-pepper hair from his forehead and taking a breath before he began.

"I met your mother about a year before you were born. It was an instant connection, really. She could complete my sentences for me. That sort of thing. Do you know what I mean?"

I hope to one day.

Samantha nodded, urging him to continue.

"After the wreck, after she was lost, I despaired. I became so depressed that I almost lost my job, and I had this precious little angel to take care of. 'Our Little Star,' your mom used to say."

His finger nipped at her chin as he rose to stand in front of the front window sipping at his beer. A long pause followed.

"Your grandparents and Aunt Lizzie were life savers during that time. Then, one day, Julia Hassledorf came back to town. We were sweethearts in high school, but college took us in different directions. We got married and, soon enough, here came sweet, stubborn Cole into the world. Julia died of Hodgkin's two years later. You were still very young. Too young to remember her."

Samantha took it all in. If she could have absorbed the pain etched across her father's face, made it her own, she would have.

But I don't have that superpower.

"I'm sorry, Dad."

"I got off topic," he said. "Your mother was a vision of beauty. Wise beyond her years. You could see it in her eyes. They were greener than the clearest emerald, like yours. They went on forever."

Green eyes...

Samantha leaned forward. "Her hair was red, right?"

"A very deep red, yes. Not quite auburn, more of a pure red, like—"

"Like blood?"

His face dropped. "Not the analogy I would use, but yeah. I guess you could say that."

Bad choice of words, Sammy.

"I'm sorry. I didn't mean...I wasn't..."

Again, there was silence. Samantha decided to break it.

"I wish I had known my mother. My last memory of her was of a bubble popping in her hair just before we went off the bridge. But I never knew if that was just a dream or what."

"You were obsessed with those godforsaken bubbles, Sammy." His smile faded. His eyes were far away, lost in a memory. He glanced at her as though he wanted to say something important, but held her eyes for a moment and decided against it.

"I'm alive today because you pulled me from that sinking car and took me to safety. I would have drowned if you hadn't risked your life to save me," said Samantha.

Her father's face twisted in confusion.

"Samantha, I was thrown from the car on impact. Right through the windshield. I never went into the river with you."

Her vision tunneled. Her palms erupted in a cold sweat.

What...what is he saying? If he didn't save me, then who did?

Her ringing phone startled her.

She sat motionless, trying to wrap her head around this new information. Her phone was insistent as it vibrated across the coffee table with each ring.

"Are you going to get that?"

She answered her phone with robotic movements, not bothering to look at the caller ID.

"Hello?"

"*Samantha? Oh, thank god,*" Marissa's voice was frantic. "*I just booked a flight to Mexico.*"

"Wait," Samantha leapt to her feet and turned away from her father, patting the air with her free hand. "Slow down. You did what?"

"*David asked me to book him a flight to Mexico. He said he needed to take some time for himself. But he doesn't do that. I think David found him, Samantha. I'm scared.*"

Samantha lowered the phone and turned to look at her father, who mirrored her concerned glance. She pushed her hair over the side of her head and raised the phone back to her ear. Her heart pounded in her chest.

"Tell me where."

Chapter Twenty-Six

"¿AMERICANO?"

David followed the boy's pointing finger to the disheveled hovel at the edge of town.

"Taberna," said the boy.

David pressed a ten-dollar bill into the boy's dirty hand and made his way down the dusty street. The bar didn't have a clever or inventive name. It didn't have a name at all as far as David could tell. It was straight out of a Sergio Leone western, but with a sheet of plywood standing in for the swinging saloon doors. The plywood burst open as a man stumbled out and threw up on the nearest wall he could find.

David was pretty sure he had the right place.

The cantina smelled of stale sweat and sour whiskey. Cigarette smoke drifted through the room in lazy tendrils. A filthy window near the front door admitted the only light except for the glow of a television mounted in the corner. The bar was a warped, stained mess consisting of several long planks laid out on a row of barrels with a couple of ratty and torn Mexican flags draped over the front in a weak attempt to cover the barrels. A trio of villagers played cards at one of the two lopsided, rotting tables. Their game paused as he walked past them to the bar, where he pulled out a rickety stool next to the only other patron sitting there. Several weeks worth of facial hair covered the man's face in a fine pelt. He wore a black bandana on his head with a matching tank top that revealed sleeves of tattoos over hardened muscle.

"Lieutenant Commander Daniels reporting for duty," David said.

He raised a hand to a mustachioed barkeep who emerged from a back room. "Dos tequilas, por favor."

Braithwaite finished his drink and accepted the offered tequila without looking at David. "'Lieutenant Commander Daniels', huh? Those were the days, D."

"Do you remember Karachi?" David said. "When that E.C. jumped out of nowhere during recon and tried to blow the hell out of us?"

"Hell yeah I do. The little fuck didn't have the balls to do it. I remember him standing there sweating and shaking. I think he shit himself. Could have fucked us all, though."

"Man," David said, "I've never seen Wally move so fast. He had that vest neutralized before half of the boys even knew they were in danger."

"That's why I always put you on point." Braithwaite pointed to his eyes with two fingers spread into a V. "Sharp eyes. Could assess the situation with speed and accuracy. So what's your assessment right now?"

They sat facing forward, glasses in hand. David counted three makeshift weapons within arm's reach should it go down right then, not including the shot glass in his hand. He held the glass high.

"I assess that Walter 'Boom-Boom' Pritchett was a good man who saved our asses many times over. To Wally."

The tequila went down smooth. Braithwaite held up two fingers to the bartender.

"I also assess that Wally didn't need to die for money," David continued. "We're better than that."

Braithwaite nodded. "We are. Unfortunately, the United States military didn't agree. Or have you forgotten?"

The barkeep set down two more tequilas.

"Forgotten that our entire squad got booted under your command? No, I haven't forgotten," David said.

David's former commanding officer faced him for the first time since entering the cantina. "I took the fall for my men. You were all honorably discharged. I wasn't so lucky."

"I still lost my job because you lost your focus, Glenn."

"Do you really believe that?"

David met Braithwaite's stare. "I believe that they were women and children."

"They were fucking terrorists, David. Informants. Spineless sneaks that dogged our every move that entire month."

David shook his head and poured the liquor down his throat. "I guess we'll never know who they were for sure, since none of them made it through the interrogation. Tell me, did the ten year-old give up any information before he drowned? Did the wives provide any strategic intel while you and Hopewell raped them?"

"We were at war."

"That's no excuse. They were human beings."

Braithwaite ignored the comment. "We are *still* at war. Those boys are over there with their hands tied behind their backs. Every move they make to protect American lives is being run through so much goddamn red tape it's a miracle they are even allowed to carry weapons."

David conceded the point and changed tactics. "And that's what it's about for you, isn't it? He with the biggest weapon wins."

"Hiroshima. Nagasaki," Braithwaite said.

"Saigon. Mogadishu," David countered.

The next two tequilas went down in silence.

"The asset can change everything, Daniels," Braithwaite said. "All I want is to end those monsters and bring our boys home."

"I know you do," David said. "So do I. But not this way. And her name is Samantha. You and Sharp knew who she was all along. You could have picked her up anytime."

"No. We wanted to know what she was capable of. Know her weaknesses to make sure we could hold her. Shape her. That was Sharp's idea. And Douglas's, I might add."

Braithwaite ordered two more tequilas.

"Who gave me up?"

"I have friends too, Braithwaite."

"Give me a name, D."

David stood up and slapped down several bills, then turned to face his former commanding officer. His body hid his other hand, which stuffed a bar rag into his front pocket.

"You want a name? Cole. That was her brother's name. The brother you killed."

Glenn Braithwaite wordlessly scooted his stool away from the bar. They exited the cantina together.

The bright afternoon gave David his first good look at Braithwaite. A gruesome laceration ran from Braithwaite's top lip to just below his right ear. It was still healing, and the light beard didn't hide the poor stitch work. He would never be rid of the scar that would form there, pulling his mouth into a rictus snarl.

"That Apache glass is a bitch, huh?" David said.

Braithwaite withdrew a shallow can from his pocket. He smacked his finger on the lid several times before removing it. The heavy pinch of tobacco slid between his lip and gum. His eyes never left David as he pushed the can back into his pocket.

Braithwaite ran his finger down the length of his facial wound. "Let's make it a set. What do you say?"

A long, serrated combat knife flashed in the sun. David wrapped the bar towel around his left hand.

"You didn't bring a gun? I thought I trained you better than that."

"Customs just wouldn't cooperate. Besides, Glenn, I want to make you bleed." David's toe dug into the dirt as he raised his fists.

"How many did you have before I got here, Glenn? You feeling up to this?"

He feinted a jab at Braithwaite's face, then flicked his boot out of the dirt when Braithwaite slipped the jab. Dust sprayed into his opponent's eyes. Braithwaite retreated to clear his vision but David pressed the attack, striking the closest target to him— Braithwaite's right knee. The knife flicked out in a low, defensive sweep, much faster than David anticipated. David's advantage was short lived as he hopped away with a gash on his shin. He cursed himself for taking the bait.

Braithwaite wiped his eyes with his free hand and blinked the rest of the dust away. Now on even footing, the combatants squared off and began to circle.

"Always that kicking bullshit with you," Braithwaite said. "Are you going to slap me, too?"

Braithwaite's lunge met empty air as David pivoted away. The follow-up backhand cut was redirected by David's toweled left hand. His heel smashed into Braithwaite's knee before they disengaged. For the hell of it, he backhanded his opponent across the face before darting away from the counter attacks. It was a glancing, superfluous blow, but the smacking sound was rewarding.

"How was that?" David grinned.

The next exchange was brutal. There were no more quips or taunts, no more attempts to gain the psychological edge. They both favored their wounded legs and were ready to end the dance. David knew that if he lost, Braithwaite would have an open path to Samantha. David wouldn't be there to guide her, to keep her centered. And if he won, Samantha could become who she wanted to be. Who she was meant to be. The stakes couldn't have been higher. David knew this fight wasn't about him.

Braithwaite's relentless attack styles switched from Filipino to Burmese to Indonesian. David had a difficult time parrying, and would have lost several digits if not for his towel-wrapped hand. He was bleeding in a dozen places. Every time he closed to grapple and disarm, Braithwaite would dart away with a retreating slash then come right back in with a series of thrusts. The man was a master of the blade. It was an extension of his hand, as if he had grown some horribly wicked claw.

David soon understood that he was outmatched, but there would be no concession. He attempted to lure Braithwaite's knife arm into a trap or a lock, but it was like trying to hold on to water. Braithwaite was too practiced, too well trained. David's non-lethal elbows and knees only slowed Braithwaite down.

David regretted not taking the time to find a firearm once he was in country. He could have planted a bullet in Braithwaite's twisted brain while the murderer sipped his cheap tequila. But he had been fortunate to find Braithwaite so quickly. He'd had no way of knowing how long Braithwaite would stay in the small desert town before moving on. There had been no time to acquire a gun, and now that he had found his quarry he was about to be gutted like a pig.

David over-committed to a feint with Braithwaite's knife hand. A glob of tobacco juice spewed from Braithwaite's mouth into his face, blinding him. The hammer fist follow up attack found ribs that had never fully healed from the battle at the safe house. David winced as the tender bones cracked again. He tried to retreat, but Braithwaite's ankle had slipped behind his. Braithwaite followed him to the ground with an overhand killing blow. The descending blade pierced David's defending forearm, catching between the radius and ulna with a meaty, wet thunk. The razor point drew a painful line down David's left cheek, missing his eye by a less than a centimeter.

David blinked in surprise when he realized that he finally had the knife trapped.

His vision swam as he wrenched his wounded arm to the side, forcing Braithwaite's knife—and the hand holding it—out wide. His knee slammed into Braithwaite's groin, eliciting a howl of pain. A sharp elbow connected with Braithwaite's jaw. The resulting crunch was satisfying. David completed the motion by twisting his body to the side, heaving Braithwaite into the dirt. This gave David time to wrench the combat knife free of his forearm—which also peeled it from Braithwaite's grasp. He fought for consciousness as the pain took hold.

The combatants rolled away from each other and staggered to their feet. David wiped the vile juice from his eyes. Braithwaite's smile was painted red with blood as he pulled a backup blade from his boot. It was a push dagger—a small, double-edged blade with a crescent pommel that nestled into the wielder's palm for more powerful thrusts.

"Well, you gave it your best shot," Braithwaite said.

David's ruined arm hung at his side. He brandished the stolen combat knife to keep Braithwaite at bay. "Yeah. So did you."

Braithwaite closed the distance between them with a head fake and a wide, sweeping overhead cut. There was no style now, only brutality. David managed to sidestep, but knew it would be over soon. He managed a couple of blocks with his wounded limb, but every impact jarred him. David's nervous system screamed at him to protect the limb. He ignored the protests.

David saw the killing blow coming from a mile away, but was helpless to prevent it. Braithwaite had him tied up limb over limb, close enough for David to smell the tequila and tobacco on his breath. The deathblow would find his heart through his floating ribs, then it would be over. David had led a good life. He had protected his country beyond his military service. Now he would die in combat. There was no higher honor for a warrior.

Something passed in front of the sun, casting a shadow over the allies-turned-enemies. In that split second before his death, David idly wondered why the shadow was shaped like a person instead of a bird or an airplane.

The final strike never came. Braithwaite cursed, staring in disbelief at his knife. David seized the moment and sank his blade into Braithwaite's thigh, then used his body weight to shove the man away.

Braithwaite hit the ground, his push dagger skittering away in a cloud of dust.

"Femoral artery. Well done, Lieutenant." Braithwaite said after a quick diagnosis of his latest wound. His lifeblood fed the arid soil beneath him with every beat of his heart.

David found the strength to salute the dying man. "It was an honor to serve with you, sir. For the most part."

He raised face to the sky and shielded his eyes against the sun. Only an empty, azure expanse greeted him.

"How does it feel to know your girlfriend saved your ass, David?"

David stood over Braithwaite. "Consider yourself lucky, Glenn. She told me she was going to pull you apart slowly, starting with your nuts."

Braithwaite's laugh was frail. "Please finish it. Just let me go in peace."

David considered his request for a moment, then eased himself to a knee beside his former commanding officer.

"I have more names for you. Latif Mattar. Makai Hameed. Tarana Sayed. Remember those names as you die a slow, lonely death. Remember the people you ordered me to...to..." He dropped the combat knife into the dirt and left Glenn Braithwaite to his well-earned fate.

Three blocks away, David found the boy who had directed him to the cantina. He held up another ten-dollar bill. "¿Médico?"

The boy pushed the money into his pocket and beckoned David forward with a wave of his hand. "Sígueme," he said. "This way."

David took one last look into the heavens and followed the boy deeper into the village.

Chapter Twenty-Seven

THE LAST BOX was full of books.

One of the movers pulled Samantha aside to suggest more efficient methods of packing when it took three of his movers to carry the heavy box into the townhouse. She listened with polite attention, then handed him a wad of cash and thanked him for his professionalism. She waited for the moving van to pull away from the curb before carrying the box into her den with little effort. It wasn't that she couldn't feel the weight of it per se, it was more that the weight just didn't seem to matter. She had gotten used to the strange sensation months ago. It was what kept her from ripping off doorknobs or breaking bones with a handshake.

Bethesda had been her father's suggestion. He owned a humble, two-bedroom house in the community, and thought it would be nice to have her close after what they had been through. She had agreed, convinced that her tiny third-floor walk up in Clarendon had become a crime scene during her captivity. She had declined the invitation to live in his house, and he had in turn understood that she needed her own space. The compromise had been a rental townhouse a couple of miles away.

She walked through the rooms and surveyed the clusters of bags, bins, and boxes, trying to remember what she had packed in each one. This was going to take a while. She peeked out of the front door to make sure that a neighbor wasn't strolling up her walk with a pie and a promise of ever-lasting friendship. Not that those were bad things—she was a fan of pie—but they wouldn't serve her purpose at the moment. She closed and locked the front door, then drew the curtains over the windows before moving to the middle of the living room and shaking her arms to loosen them.

"Okay," she said to no one in particular.

How does that old Chemistry Carl song go? A beaker of... A beaker of neaker... Yeah that's it. A beaker of neaker a vial of style and shakity shakity poof!

Box lids opened and bags untied themselves.

Chemistry is magic I will show you...

In the kitchen, dishes lifted into the air and dropped into neat stacks before drifting past the cupboard doors that opened for them. Silverware separated and grouped into utensil types before finding their designated drawers. The junk box simply upended into the junk drawer. Mal sprang out of nowhere to assassinate a pot holder that looked suspiciously like a bird.

...shakity shakity poof!

In the den, books lifted from the unwieldy cardboard box and arranged themselves first by author, then alphabetically by title as they slid onto the shelves of her new bookcase.

A tube and a tong a flask and a song and shakity shakity poof!
The lab is magic wait and see
shakity shakity poof!

Baskets and bins flitted up the staircase and emptied into closets, drawers and bathroom cabinets. Sheets unfolded and floated like ghosts onto her bed, pillowcases engulfed pillows that fluffed three times before settling over the sheets.

Spatula scoopula blippery boopula and shakity shakity poof!

These are what we use to make the

shakity shakity poof!

Furniture lifted and moved around her, settling into the layout she had pictured while signing the lease agreement. Lamps, photo frames, and other knick knacks found their places on the end tables.

A beaker of neaker a vial of style and shakity shakity poof!

Chemistry is magic I will show you...

Empty boxes broke themselves down and piled neatly atop one another. Bags were stowed away and empty baskets stacked into each other upstairs. The final touch was her favorite photo. In her mind's eye, it lowered gently to the nightstand beside her bed.

"...shakity shakity bunseny burnery shakity shakity poof!"

My god, I'm such a dork.

Samantha had just opened the curtains and plunked herself down on the sofa when the theme from *Mission: Impossible* erupted from the kitchen counter. She summoned the phone to her.

"Hey Daddy."

"*Hi Sammy. How's my little girl?*"

"Good. Just unpacked and I'm getting settled in. Did you know there is a crab shack just a block away?"

"*Of course there is,*" her father said. "*You're in Maryland now.*"

True.

"Where are you?"

She knew he couldn't tell her. It was a little joke they shared. She would ask and he would always reply the same way.

"*Classified. But I can tell you it's after midnight here.*"

"I think you just gave away State secrets, Daddy. Speaking of which..."

She let it hang in the air. Her father took the cue.

"*Yeah, that,*" he said. "*Some friends tell me there was a big shakeup in the intelligence community. Word is, there will be a closed hearing on the use of specialized defense contractors.*"

"As in mercenaries?"

"*Yep. Specifically their use in covert missions at home and abroad. Ever since 9/11, things have gotten out of hand. Too many, shall we say, 'unofficial' operations going on. You know, big money corporations running their own military operations overseas while being funded by our government.*"

"Good."

There was a lull in the conversation. Her father's voice took on a tone she recognized well.

"*Sammy, you're a grown woman now so you probably don't need me to tell you this, but you'll understand one day when you have kids. You need to be careful. You stepped into the light the moment you decided to risk your life to help those people downtown. You know what I'm talking about.*"

"I know, Daddy."

"*People will want answers, and they won't stop until they get them. Just please, please take a minute to consider your next steps with all caution. I know the kind of person you are. You won't let people suffer. Know that whatever choice you make, I'll be there for you and that I'm very proud of you.*"

Samantha lowered the phone from her ear and took a moment before replying.

"Thank you. I love you."

"*I love you, too,*" he said. "*Are you still going to your appointments?*"

"They aren't easy, but I'm going. She's a skilled grief counselor."

"*Good. Doctor Rothstein came highly recommended. And do you talk about the other thing?*"

"That's more difficult. Daddy, I can't tell her what I really went through. She knows that I was kidnapped and assaulted. I'm pretty sure she thinks it was rape, but I can't elaborate on the details without giving too much away. She wants to analyze everything in fine detail, and I can't...I mean, I don't want to relive that."

"She shouldn't need the details just yet, Sammy. You can be as vague or as specific as you want. But it will help to talk it through with her. It's part of the healing process. And you know that what you say to her is confidential, right?"

"I know, but I think this calls for maximum discretion. Don't you think? Anyone can be bought."

"That's my girl. Always thinking."

Samantha thought he was going to reiterate how important it was that she stay in therapy, but he changed the subject.

"Have you heard from David?"

"Yep, I'm meeting him in a little while. I'm not sure if it's a date or a job interview. He said he has a proposition for me."

Laughter erupted on the other end of the phone. Samantha had decided not to lie to him about the events at the cottage. Her father wouldn't be asking about David if she had misled him. The fiction David had concocted to let him take the blame wasn't fair to anyone, and lying to her father would only make matters worse. Their familial bond of trust meant she could tell him anything. So she had told him everything.

"If he used the word 'proposition', let's hope it's a job interview. The last thing you need right now is a little one running around harassing that cat you adopted. Especially if she takes after her mother!"

"Dad! Seriously?"

"Believe me, I know. I didn't sleep for three years."

"That's quite enough of that, Daddy." She couldn't mask the smile in her voice. "I'd better go get ready to be propositioned."

Samantha set the phone down and shook her head. For some reason, she couldn't get the image of flying babies out of her mind.

A crisp autumn breeze passed over the outdoor patio of the Occidental, caressing clothes, skin and hair with a promise of winter. Samantha spotted David at a corner table talking to a server while pointing out an item on the small menu.

Wine. Okay, that's a good sign.

David wore a suede blazer over a starched, white shirt and khakis that were a shade darker than the tan jacket.

Okay, is that business casual or date semi-formal?

She adjusted the low-cut neckline of her tight, V-neck sweater and tucked a stray lock of hair behind her ear. David had recommended that they keep their distance until the media frenzy died down. Sure enough, after a couple of months the media coverage of the flying woman and the quarantined area in Montgomery County had given way to reality television stars and the coming election. He had finally contacted her. But as she approached him, despite all they had experienced together in that short but intense timeframe, Samantha's thoughts were on that unrequited moment on the cottage porch. The warmth of his hands on her hips. His scent.

He stood up and pulled out a chair for her as she reached the table.

"Hi there," he said, taking her in from head to toe.

"Hey!"

Her palms were slick.

Do I hug him? Is he a hugger?

The answer came when he embraced her and pressed his lips to her cheek. Samantha returned the hug with pleasant surprise. Without thinking, she reached up and traced the thin pink line that descended down his left cheek. He didn't seem to mind.

I kind of like it.

"Good to see you," he said, motioning to her chair. "It really is."

Samantha let him push in her chair and set her valise next to a neatly folded napkin. David returned to his seat and interlaced his fingers on the table.

"Me too," she said. "I mean, you too. It's nice to see you too."

Shakity shakity poof! Dork.

His smile matched the pristine, white tablecloth. "After everything we've been through, you don't have to be nervous around me, Samantha. Ever."

The candid statement caught her off guard. She considered a defensive, sarcastic reply, but instead changed the subject.

"How's Marissa?"

"Marissa's well," he said, leaning back and tugging on his jacket. "She's been back to work for a while and just finished school. Honestly, I thought she would have moved the hell away from here to start a new life. I wouldn't blame her if she had. My letter of recommendation would have included something about her willingness to take a bullet for her employer."

Samantha's laugh was musical. She felt herself relaxing when he joined her.

"Are you all moved in?" he asked as their mirth ran its course.

"I am, but I have to confess that I'm going to miss our little game on the Orange Line."

"The Red Line has its cast of characters too, I'm sure."

"Is that what you are, a 'character'?"

"Some might say so. The dangerous, brooding type."

"More like the brave and selfless type."

She adjusted the placement of her handbag in the silence that followed. When she turned her eyes back to him she caught his gaze flickering from the neckline of her sweater back to her face.

Busted.

The server appeared with a bottle of wine just as David drew in a breath to speak. His face reddened. Samantha suppressed a smile.

"I ordered a Bordeaux. Is that okay?"

Samantha nodded and pushed her wine glass toward the server. David held his glass high once they were filled and the server had moved away. Samantha followed suit.

"To us," he said.

Whoa! Did he just say that?

Babies flitted about an imaginary nursery like wingless cherubs.

"Or should I say, 'Here's to hoping that you'll accept my offer.'"

The rich wine bolstered her against the chill in the air.

"That depends on the size of your package," she said.

David was mid-sip when he erupted into a cough. He dabbed at his chin with the linen napkin.

She continued as if nothing was amiss. "What compensation package comes with your offer?"

You're a bad girl, Sammy.

"Well," David gathered himself, though his face grew a deeper shade of red. "For one, I can help you with your money problem."

She cocked her head, eyebrow raised.

"I assume you still have the, uh, winnings you told me about?"

She nodded for him to continue.

"Okay. I can help legitimize that." His voice lowered as he leaned forward. "You'd be on my payroll. We'd channel those funds bit by bit into the fees I charge the federal government for my investigation work. You'd be surprised at how creative Marissa can be with invoices when she puts her mind to it. I'd acquire your services for an exorbitant amount, then use your own money to pay you. No one would notice if we did it over time and in small enough increments. And if you decided to hit Sin City again, we'd just follow the same protocol."

"But this is the federal government we're talking about," she said. "How can you hide it from them?"

"Because it would be hidden in plain sight. The very best hiding spot," he said. "Besides, we're talking about people who spend twenty grand on a box of pencils."

That could work.

Samantha lifted her wine glass and watched the red liquid swirl around inside of it. A sudden shout from the street startled her.

"Look! It's HurricAngel!"

Samantha's heart stopped. She couldn't resist turning her head. A tourist group rolled by on Segways wearing matching T-shirts and bike helmets. One of the teenagers pointed to the sky while the others guffawed at his cleverness. Samantha drained her glass and reached for the wine bottle to refill it. David was locked in a mortal struggle against the laughter that threatened to burst from his gut.

"Don't you dare," she said, reaching across the table to top off his glass.

He cleared his throat. For a moment, he appeared to be winning the battle, but then he cracked up. She was compelled to join in.

"So what are you thinking?" she said when they had regained their composure. "How would I earn my ridiculously inflated paycheck?"

"I'm glad you asked. I wouldn't require that much of your time, but every once in a while I might need some, shall we say, creative problem solving. Your special set of skills would come in very handy."

"You make me sound like Liam Neeson," she said. "What do you mean? Like bashing heads? You don't need me for that."

"No, not exactly, although you would be quite useful in that department. I'm talking about saving lives. Recon. Rescue. Infiltration. Information gathering. And yes, you'd run defense if necessary. I hope you're okay with that."

"I'm okay with that."

"Samantha, there is something else. Your case is the first one where—and please don't take this the wrong way—the supernatural, paranormal element was real."

Not the best choice of words, but alright....

"You think there could be others out there like me, is that what you're saying?"

"Exactly. Except with my luck I'd run across someone who isn't a genuine, good person who pulls off leather motorcycle pants like no woman I've ever seen."

"You had me at 'money laundering'," she said, feeling a heat rise in her cheeks that wasn't from the wine alone. "I guess I can find another bartender gig to pass the time when I'm not on a case with you."

David searched her eyes. "Samantha, you already have a job."

"But you said you wouldn't require much of my time."

He took a long sip, then said, "I need you to open your mind to another possibility."

Samantha's forehead wrinkled in confusion. He set down the wine glass and spun it around by the crystal stem.

"There is a philosophical argument concerning good and evil," he said. "There are a lot of them, actually, but this one applies to you so please bear with me. This argument posits that God must be inherently good in order for Him to exist. An evil God couldn't have created this beautiful world and all of the good within it, within people. An evil God wouldn't possess the raw material required to create the feelings of falling in love or meeting your child for the first time. It just doesn't add up. Now, let's say that man sitting over there in the green jacket is walking home one night and gets attacked by someone with a baseball bat."

Samantha glanced over her left shoulder and spotted the man he was referring to.

"The woman in the sun hat at the table next to him is walking the other way and sees this happening. She is carrying a firearm and is an expert marksman. She doesn't know the man in the green jacket, but can see that he is going to die a horrible death. She keeps walking. The man in the green jacket begs for her for help but gets beaten to bloody pulp. She had the power to stop it, but decided not to. Would you consider that to be an act of good? No. So if it is true that in order for God to exist He must be inherently good, yet He refuses to stop genocide and war and famine and murder and on and on...then God is not good, and by definition cannot exist."

Samantha tugged on her earlobe, eyes downcast.

Evan didn't put it quite so eloquently.

"I'm not God, David," she said.

"No, you're not God, but you are the closest thing I've ever seen. I watched you pull that minivan from the Potomac to save that family. I saw you descend from the stormy heavens to pluck those rescue workers from certain doom and give them a second chance at life. What else did you do during the hurricane? Who else did you save that I don't even know about? You are the definition of a good person. Not a god, a person. Forget the guilt you're carrying and get to work."

He paused to allow her to respond, but she stared into her wine glass.

"There are floods along the gulf coast. There are wildfires out in California right now. And that's just in our backyard. Girls and boys half your age are being trafficked all over the world. There are droughts in—"

"Okay, just stop. Stop."

He's right. You knew he was right before you ever met him.

Samantha put her head in her hands.

You've always known.

"Don't be afraid, Samantha."

Her head snapped up at those words. He held her gaze.

"I'll be here to help you help them," he said.

Samantha's hand covered her mouth. Her eyes found the man in the green jacket. He had just paid his bill and smiled at the woman in the sun hat as he got up to leave. The woman rolled her eyes and turned back to her conversation.

"No capes," said Samantha.

"What?"

"No capes."

The corners of David's mouth curled into a grin. He reached inside his blazer and pulled something from the pocket, then extended his closed hand to her. She blinked in surprise when a shiny, white marble rolled into her palm.

"For luck," he said.

"How did you—"

Sirens pierced the air as a trio of police cruisers raced down 15th street. A thunderous tremor shook their table, sending flatware skittering across the surface. A second jolt knocked over Samantha's wine glass. Gunshots rang out in the distance. A surge of pedestrians emerged from the south, flooding the sidewalks and darting into traffic as they fled...something.

David's chair toppled over as he stood. Their eyes met with purpose. He gave Samantha a reassuring nod that said "*I believe in you*" and turned to the startled people on the patio. His voice rose above the tumult.

"Oh my god! Everybody down!"

It was the perfect distraction. Samantha snatched a napkin from the table and burst into the air faster than the eye could follow. Her gaze traveled to the National Mall where police were evacuating tourists and spectators. There was motion near the Washington Monument—no, *on* the Monument.

She thought her eyes were playing tricks on her.

A monstrous, ape-like behemoth made of stone perched atop the broken obelisk, breaking off chunks of marble and hurling them to the ground with earth-shattering force. A lone figure stood at the base of the structure, ignoring the police who beckoned him to safety. The stone beast spotted the man and leaned over the edge, preparing to jump. The man didn't have a chance.

Here we go.

Samantha tied the napkin over her face.

ACKNOWLEDGEMENTS

I'D LIKE TO FILE THIS THOUGHT under Lessons Learned: writing a book is not for the faint of heart, and certainly not a weight to be lifted alone—even if you lift with your legs and not your back.

I have some lifelong friends who read the same books I do, and who years ago listened patiently as I detailed my plans for a fantasy novel replete with elves, dwarves, swords, and sorcery. Obviously that is not the story you just read, and for good reason. It sucked.

My threats to write a book loomed large in the twenty-plus years since that ill-fated fantasy idea, and it wasn't until last year that one of these friends said, "What are you waiting for?"

He had a point.

Maybe it was the surge of superhero movies on the big screen, or perhaps it was a resurgence of my fondness of comic books, but my love of fantasy took a back seat to origin tale set in the modern world of an every(wo)man who reluctantly becomes a virtual demi-god. The questions that arose from the idea were tantalizing. What would I do if that happened to me? What would you do? What would anyone do?

The story took on a life of its own, but it was still a heavy, heavy lift. I needed help.

When I thought I had polished the story enough to share, I gave it to my friends and braced for impact. Weeks went by and I heard nothing. Self-doubt snuck up on me like a ninja poised to strike. Did they hate it? Are they trying to spare my feelings, trying to figure out how to word it in a way that wouldn't imperil our friendship?

"Very unique, Jason. Very...um, unique."

"Well, it's certainly one of a kind."

"Now that's not something you read every day."

And so on.

Weeks turned into months, and still nothing. I trudged onward, working on the website and social media presence, and spending a lot of time trying to put a cover together. I forgot about the book for a while.

That was when the Emails started to come in.

Craig worded his constructive criticism with admirable diplomacy at first, as if testing the waters. But as he got further into the story—and after reassurances from me that he should just let me have it—more direct and forthright observations started filling my inbox. They were invaluable. He had lived in Florida for many years, so knew what being in a hurricane was really like. He had trouble keeping track of characters. (Who the hell is "Douglas" again?) Dialogue attribution, pacing, story flow, style—his feedback helped tremendously when I was so far into the forest that I couldn't see the trees, and my later drafts were better for it.

So thank you, Craig.

I found it a strange a coincidence, however, that Craig finished the book at approximately the same time as Jared.

Jared took a different tact. He ambushed me.

We had just wrapped up a conversation about work, family, religion, and video games over steaks and beers. Our checks had come and we were signing the receipts, preparing to part ways until the next time, when he said, "Oh, I read your book."

I didn't even know that he had opened the PDF file.

The next couple of hours (and more than a couple of beers) were spent in a rapid-fire interrogation of my old friend as I launched question after question at him. Overall impressions, clarity of story, character appeal... Thinking back, I probably should have given him some breathing room. But I was too excited and didn't want to forget all of the story points I wanted his opinion on. I blame Miller Lite.

He had read the entire book before discussing it with me, which was different than the progressive discussion I'd had with Craig, but Jared's observations were just as valuable. He concentrated on the parts of the story that stood out to him (which happened to be those that I had the most fun writing), asked for explanations about story points that were unclear, and was very frank about what characters he liked and didn't like. He came through for me when I was struggling with the title. The credit for Kinetic Star goes to him. (He assured me I could have it free and clear.)

But my thanks to Jared wouldn't be complete without a special mention of his daughter.

As I mentioned, video games are a typical discussion topic. Wireless headsets provide a window into the life of those you are playing video games with. He hears my dogs going crazy through my headset microphone while we speed through the streets of Los Santos in Grand Theft Auto, and I hear his toddler twins playing and singing and negotiating bedtimes. His daughter's renditions of Twinkle, Twinkle Little Star resonating through my gaming headphones must have taken root somewhere in my subconscious.

So thank you as well, little R.

I'd also like to extend my gratitude to my brother Brian, who schooled me in the finer points of riding a Harley-Davidson Fatboy in the wind and rain, and my friend Antwan, whose martial arts demonstrations from years ago are still etched in my mind and informed David's fight scenes. Thank you to my father as well, who sat through incessant book-writing updates even when he didn't ask for them.

And thanks to you, the reader, for experiencing Samantha's first steps with me.

I'll see you next time.

ABOUT THE AUTHOR

Jason Andrews is a mild-mannered website editor by day and vigilante writer by night. His passion for a good story can be traced back to the spinning comics rack in the local drug store, where he discovered modern mythological heroes in four-color newsprint.

Jason received his Bachelor's degree in English and began his career as a technical writer for a computer company. His interests have led him into drawing, music, and filmmaking over the years, but he always finds his way back to the keyboard.

His novel Kinetic Star is the first in a series that explores a unique take on the superhero genre. He lives in the Midwest with his two dogs, Banner and Freya.

CONNECT

Website
www.jasonandrewsauthor.com

Facebook
www.facebook.com/JasonAndrewsAuthor

Twitter
@writerandrews

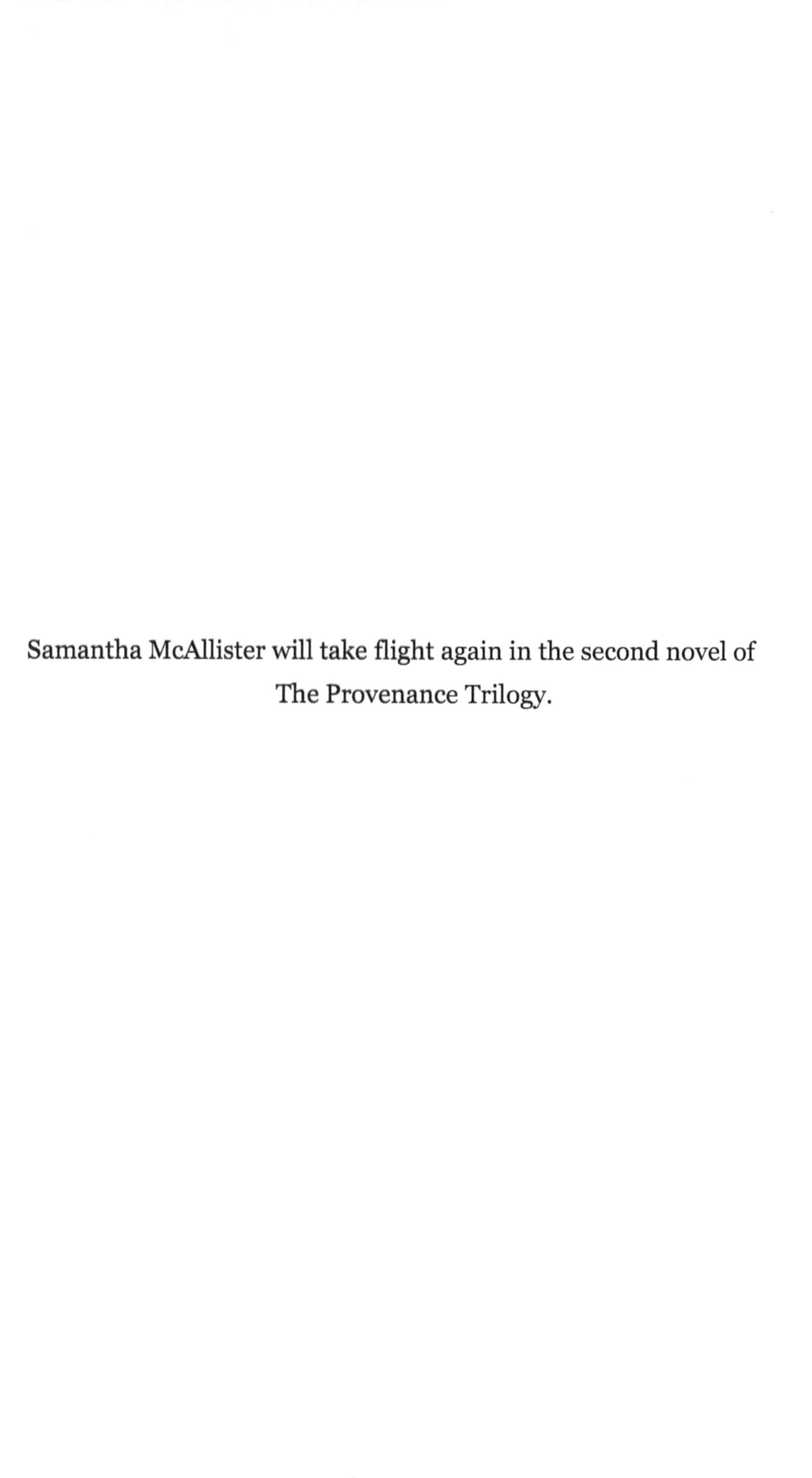

Samantha McAllister will take flight again in the second novel of
The Provenance Trilogy.

www.ingramcontent.com/pod-product-compliance
Lightning Source LLC
Chambersburg PA
CBHW030821310726
48980CB00006B/585/J

* 9 7 8 1 7 3 2 1 2 1 4 0 9 *